Jane Blanchard is .... sion
(Westcountry). Bor .... reer
in London as a mus .... such
as Status Quo and .... journalist with Mirror Group Newspapers. She worked as a
reporter and columnist for regional and national newspapers and magazines, before joining the news desk at
Television South West. Since then she's worked exten-
sively as a writer/producer/director on news, current
affairs, outside broadcasts and documentaries on subjects
as diverse as ballet, football and barbershop singing. Her
Consumer File series was the highest rating programme in
TSW's history. At Westcountry TV, she was a finalist at the
New York Film and Television Festival for her programme
about the plight of Romanian orphans. Recent successes
at Carlton TV have included a documentary series on the
history of ITV in the south-west.

Jane lives in Devon with her son Mark and her partner
Iain Blair (alias best-selling romantic novelist Emma
Blair). For more information on her books, please visit
her website at: www.janeblanchard.com

Also by Jane Blanchard

In Cahoots!

Nailing Harry

JANE BLANCHARD

A *Time Warner* Paperback

First published in Great Britain as a paperback original
by Time Warner Paperbacks in 2002

A CIP catalogue record for this book
is available from the British Library.

ISBN 0 7515 3212 6

Typeset in Berkeley by M Rules
Printed and bound in Great Britain by Clays Ltd, St Ives plc

Time Warner Paperbacks
An imprint of
Time Warner Books UK
Brettenham House
Lancaster Place
London WC2E 7EN

www.TimeWarnerBooks.co.uk
www.janeblanchard.com

To Iain
With all my love

acknowledgements

If you don't know me personally, please feel free to skip this bit. It's that small but very important section where I get to say a sincere thank you to those who matter.

OK, so they didn't sit down in my office and type the story, fret over the characters, and drink enough coffee to turn Brazil into a world money-player.

They were simply – there. They said all the right things at the right time: my partner Iain Blair, who spelled out the pitfalls of the 'second book syndrome', my son Mark, who persuades all his mates to buy my books for their mums, my agent Pat White, whose down-to-earth New York humour and advice I so value.

Then there are the fab folk at Time Warner Books – Barbara Boote, Joanne Coen, Tamsin Barrack and Alison Lindsay, who dispense cheerful encouragement and support just when you need it.

Wonderful friends including Rene, Jane, Elayne, Sally, Kathy, Cathy, Janet, Judith and of course the Curry Night Girls. Also colleagues at Carlton past and present who wanted to share in my excitement at being published the first time. Thank you all for being so supportive.

And finally to all the Harrys of this world. Please read this book and then feel free to eat my words!

chapter one

It was an all-too-familiar sight. Val Hampton had begun the evening, her usual scene-stealing self. But as the minutes ticked into hours, she turned into a time bomb. Her speech began to slur, cigarettes were lit and stubbed out almost immediately and her voice started to rise above those of the rest of the diners in the restaurant.

Val was a very striking woman, her thick blonde hair swept up in a chignon, and tonight wearing a fuchsia-pink suede suit, with long nails and spiky heels to match. At thirty-two, she was whippet-thin and well able to carry off the outfit. But it was always the same. Once the drink took hold, she somehow managed to transform herself from supermodel into supermonster.

From hovering attentively, providing a light for her frenzied stream of cigarettes, and constantly refilling her glass with aplomb, the waiters began to hold back, wondering if their overeagerness with the wine bottle was now perhaps the cause of the mayhem. Having taken in the Rolex, the expensive jewellery and perhaps caught a glimpse of Val's new shiny red top-of-the-range Toyota MR2 flashing into the restaurant car park, they thought they were in line for the Big Tip. But now their prey for the night was on the verge of losing them tips from just about everyone else in the restaurant. For Val was well into what the girls referred to as her 'pointing mode'. It always signalled the transition from her general irritation with life to restaurant rage.

'You see, Janet,' she boomed, pointing a dark pink talon in her direction, 'you'll never get another man if you don't make a bit more of yourself. I mean, you're actually looking quite nice tonight. That green is almost your colour. Not quite, but almost. Mind you,' she paused, taking another huge slurp of wine, 'you're no spring chicken, let's face it. How old are you now? Forty-eight? Forty-nine?'

'Forty-two actually,' replied Janet, a mixture of appalled and amused because she'd heard it all before.

'I'm sure you'd find someone if you did something about your hair,' continued Val unabashed. 'I'll give you the name of my stylist in London. Trained by Nicky Clarke, of course, so he's absolutely marvellous but not nearly as expensive. He'd sort it for under two hundred. That's what you need. A really good cut.'

And what you need is a really good smack, thought Janet. She rose from the table.

'Well, thanks for the tip, Val, but I must take myself and my overdraft off to the loo.'

Now far too pissed to take in the irony of what had been said, Val turned to the rest of the table and lowered her voice a couple of decibels. At least only the waiters would now be able to hear, instead of the entire kitchen staff.

'Of course, that's why Janet's husband left her,' she announced, taking another slug of wine. 'You can't expect to keep a man if you let it all go. You remember what Jerry Hall said, that thing about being a lady in the bedroom, a maid in the drawing room and kitchen.'

The others smiled, trying not to laugh.

'I think it was slightly the other way round ventured Nina, trying to suppress her giggling. 'I think the tart's supposed to be in the bedroom, not the kitchen.'

Val, now in a complete alcoholic haze and only picking up key words, continued: 'You see, Nina, that's exactly your trouble. Tart. Too much pastry. If you could cut down on your carbohydrates, you'd lose weight and live happily ever after.'

Nina, who, at twenty-eight, was fourteen years younger than Janet and much more sensitive to Val's bitchings, found herself coughing to cover up the sob she wanted to utter after hearing that remark.

'Back in a mo,' she muttered, also heading for the loo.

'Such a pity,' drawled Val, turning away from watching Nina's departing backside. Now there was only Liz left at the table. 'Such a pity she's got such a big bum. I'm sure it's down to binge eating. Detox, that's what she needs. Look at Carol Vorderman. Completely reinvented herself. All it takes is will-power and determination.'

Like your drinking, Liz thought desperately. Rescue came in the form of Janet returning from the loo.

'Funnily enough, I was reading a piece in the *Daily Mail* the other day and realized exactly what my problem is,' Janet announced with a twinkle in her eye.

'Yeah, like what?' drawled Val, inspecting her perfect pink nails.

'Anorexia,' declared Janet, trying not to laugh. 'I'm convinced I've got anorexia.'

'Don't be ridiculous,' shrieked Val. 'You're a good two stone overweight. Look, I know about these things. When s modelling, lots of the girls in the agency had anorexia or bulimia. Or both if they were really lucky. That's how they stayed slim.'

'Exactly,' Janet replied with a half smile. 'I've got the classic symptoms. When you've got anorexia, you look in the mirror and think you are enormous. I look in my mirror and think "omigod I'm fat" so therefore I must have anorexia.'

'But you ARE fat,' shouted Val, shoving back her chair and jabbing another nail in Janet's direction to emphasize the point. 'And you should do something about it. Do you really want to spend the rest of your life sneaking into Evans Outsize shops? You should eat less and exercise more. It's all a question of balance.'

Fuelled by far too much wine and too few lettuce leaves to register on any sort of calorie count, Val ignored her own advice and lost her balance completely, falling backwards into a pink suede mound on the floor. Conversations instantly hushed as waiters ran from all directions to help her up as fast and as inconspicuously as they could. It was not the sort of place to be falling down drunk. Sickeningly, Val still managed to look stylish, even when sprawled in a heap.

'Yes, balance, Val. You're so right,' said Janet, winking at the others. 'Anyway, let's not spoil a good meal by bringing up bulimia or any other eating disorders for that matter. Here comes Nina so I'll have a quiet word with her and see if she's a fellow anorexic. Then I suggest we order some coffee – sugar-free sugar and no-fat milk – and call it a night.'

Val, helped by a waiter, hobbled off to the loo to repair her make-up and check for bruises. Safely out of earshot, the other three breathed a sigh of relief.

'What a bloody nightmare,' said Liz. 'The minute any of us goes to the loo, we get slagged off. I have to say, I could see which way it was going tonight, and I've been sitting here crossing my legs. I didn't know I was capable of so much bladder control. I'm actually in pain right now, but if I disappear to the loo, God knows what she'd come out with about me.'

'I wouldn't worry too much,' said Janet. 'Whatever she says, none of us will believe it. It's very easy for Val to sit there, ex-model, wonderful wardrobe, loads of money, and finishing-school fingernails. And then pontificate when she's pissed, on everything from botox from detox.'

'Detox?' queried Nina. 'Is that what she calls her wine-only diet?'

'Wouldn't put it past her,' replied Janet wryly. 'What hacks me off is that we'll all have to be up and at work tomorrow. Val can lie in bed all day and savour her hangover. Different ballgame.'

'I don't know why we put ourselves through these evenings,' sighed Liz.

'Yes, you do,' answered Nina. 'We do it because we've done it for years.'

'We feel sorry for her despite the money and the looks,' said Janet. 'She's lonely and she's run out of friends. We're the only bunch left and let's face it, we're not exactly running her fan club.'

'Not surprising really,' said Liz. 'Especially given the way she slags us off behind our backs.'

'Oh come on,' said Janet. 'We all know why we really feel sorry for her. Because she's married to Harry.'

Janet, Liz and Nina sat huddled around a table in the tiny staff canteen, mulling over the previous night. They all worked in various capacities for Hartford Optimum Television, known locally as HOT. The company specialized in corporate television production, public relations, marketing and advertising. Selling Starts Here was the company's mission statement. Great things begin with a little ssh . . . was the office joke.

'Bit epic last night, wasn't it?' said Liz. 'What a waste of a great restaurant. I'll say that for Val, she does insist on taking us to some fantastic places. The bill she picked up would have paid my mortgage this month with change left for a few winning lottery tickets.'

'Yeah. I thought that monkfish thingy was fantastic,' said Nina. 'I wish I could cook properly. That might tip the balance with Sam.'

Sam in Accounts was the love of Nina's life, except that he didn't know it yet. She worshipped him from afar, convinced that one day, once she'd shed a stone, found the perfect outfit and learned to cook something wonderful that didn't come out of a box or a packet or involve a microwave, he would fall madly in love with her and transport her into eternal paradise. She had taken to flipping through bridal magazines at the hairdresser's, fantasizing about a long cream satin dress with medieval sleeves, a bouquet of blood-red roses and a trail of little bridesmaids all carrying hoops of flowers and behaving impeccably. The fantasy had moved on to her being the Bride of the Year, with Sam adoringly at her side and looking absolutely devastating in a morning suit, kissing her passionately at the altar before whisking her off on a never-ending honeymoon to Barbados. They would then, of course, live happily ever after in a beautiful thatched cob cottage, probably tucked away somewhere romantic in Devon, where they would raise beautiful and perfectly behaved high-achieving children, fed on candlelit gourmet meals. It was all up for grabs, if only she could stick with the Weight Watchers quick-start programme.

Nina was snapped out of her reverie by another woman joining the table.

'You missed a great night, Sue,' said Liz. 'The compliments flowed almost as much as the wine – straight down Val's throat.'

Sue was one of the gang of four usually invited to Val's restaurant evenings. Happily married with two young children, Sue worked as the head receptionist at HOT. She had not been able to get a babysitter and besides, one of the kids had been extra tearful, obviously going down with a cold.

'What happened? Don't tell me. The usual, I suppose,' said Sue, sipping her coffee. 'Let me guess. Val got drunk, starting pointing and shouting. Got rude and fell over.'

'More or less in that order,' replied Janet. 'Apparently my ex left me 'cos I'd let myself go. The mere idea that I asked Crippen to leave because of his horrendous temper had nothing to do with it. Oh, and by the way, I'm suffering from chronic anorexia. But that was my idea, not hers. Ha ha.'

'What about you, Liz? What's your current fatal flaw?' enquired Sue.

'Surprisingly, I got off very lightly this time,' replied Liz. 'I've come up with a new concept of crossing my legs, not going to the loo all evening and therefore sparing myself a whole load of grief. At the rate I'm going, I'll never need to do pelvic-floor exercises if I get pregnant. I was doing them all last night in the restaurant.'

Liz, newly turned thirty, and the clock ticking noisily on the nursery wall, was desperate to become a mother.

The search for a suitable father was on the verge of taking second place to just getting herself pregnant. Every man she met was vetted for possible fatherhood, and in her job as a researcher she certainly met loads of men. Trouble was, most were unsuitable. She'd just finished working on a series of advice videos for pensioners, so there hadn't been much pulling potential there. Her previous project had been on men's medical problems – mostly the 'down belows', as she put it – so that didn't exactly drum up any totty either. Just lorryloads of old men with prostate trouble. Every time Liz had sex, she did a pregnancy test afterwards. And even if there wasn't a boyfriend on the horizon, she sometimes did a test anyway. Just in case. She'd become quite adept at fiddling with spatulas and peeing into small containers.

'The trouble is,' said Janet, 'there are times when I feel really guilty about Val. I know she's rude and embarrassing, and says terrible things behind our backs. In a way, we're guilty of doing the same now. And she's the one who picks up the tab when we go out.'

'But then it's always her idea to go to expensive restaurants,' said Nina. 'I know what you're saying, but I am pretty sick of jibes about my bum. It's all very easy when you can sit there, stick thin and thirty-two, with bugger-all else to do every day except paint your nails, sit under a sun bed and spend money. I'm not surprised she doesn't have any friends any more. I should think she has difficulty keeping a cleaner.'

'Look, Val's got a major drink problem, let's face it,' said Janet. 'I'm certain she's on the pop through the day. She talks blithely about eating disorders. Well, she *is* an eating disorder. She eats nothing. You saw last night what she actually had; it was just a few bits of low-calorie lollo rosso and a fat-free cherry tomato. The rest was solid Chablis. When we meet her in a restaurant, unlike the rest of us, I suspect she's been on the wine all day, so she's just topping up. That's why she gets so pissed so quickly.'

'So what do we do about it?' asked Nina.

'Well, we can hardly tell Harry,' said Janet. 'He'd go ballistic. I'm pretty sure they have the most monumental rows a lot of the time. He's a big enough shit as it is. I'd love to know what state their marriage is in. She never ever talks about it. All I know is that Val is one very unhappy lady. It comes off her in waves. I don't how she puts up with him.'

'I don't know how we do either,' said Nina grimly.

Harry was their boss.

chapter two

The sun had been up for several hours before Val finally surfaced. Harry had long gone to work. The empty bed and the trail of dressing gown, slippers and yesterday's socks were testament to that. She dragged herself into the bathroom and groaned at the sight in the mirror. Her mascara had crept right down her cheeks, her skin was blotchy and angry-looking. She scowled at her reflection and stepped grudgingly into the shower. The hot jets reminded her that she had a real head-banger of a headache. She massaged the shampoo into her scalp, hoping it might deaden the pain. It didn't.

Downstairs she made a cup of tea and swallowed two paracetamol. There she took in another of Harry's trails. He'd made tea and toast, read the *Daily Mail*, smoked two cigarettes and opened the post. She cursed him aloud, resenting the fact that she had to clear up after him.

'Bastard,' she harrumphed at the kitchen mirror. 'That's what he is, a bastard. Oh dear, and you're not looking too terrific, yourself,' she told her reflection.

There were three things in life that Val Hampton would never accept. Firstly that she had a drink problem. That only happened to old blokes in doorways, fading matinée idols and stressed-out stock market traders, not women of thirty-two. Anyway, she dismissed, everyone drank the same amount that she did. Those silly units of alcohol thingies that doctors bleated on about were only for alcoholics, not people like her. Secondly that she ran the risk of being breathalysed. Again Val considered that driving around drunk was what everyone else did. The police were out looking for real villains, not people like her. And those who did get caught had it coming because they drove naff Ford Cortinas with furry dice and go-faster stripes. Lastly Val did not want to make the connection between thumping headache, roller-coaster stomach and several bottles of Chardonnay. To her, wine was an instant pick-me-up and if you drank enough it killed your appetite, thus keeping your ex-model figure eternally slim. Same deal with cigarettes. Handy appetite suppressants, never mind that they clogged up your lungs and arteries and put you at risk of heart disease. Again that sort of thing only happened to the old guys in the doorways, stressed stockbrokers and has-been actors in government health ads.

In fact, anything nasty only happened to other people as far as Val was concerned. Totally spoiled from the day she was conceived, Val had been educated at the best schools, where she, along with the other young gels, was told she was special. She only had to snap her fingers for a pony and there it was, as if by magic, bounding around a paddock. Her every wish was granted, her every whim attended to. She had inherited her model figure and looks from her mother, but again she'd made no effort. She didn't need to spend hours in a gym honing a perfect body. Even when she did a spot of modelling, it wasn't the ambitious, cut-throat sort of modelling, but more a touch of an 'It' girl of the day doing a sashay down the catwalk in aid of some jolly good cause. It wasn't for the money either, because Val didn't need any. Daddy had loads of it in Coutts.

Such an easy passage into adulthood did not do Val any favours. She could not understand the concepts of failure, being short of cash, doing without, or sharing. Val thought the idea of people doing their own cleaning and gardening rather quaint and archaic. The fact that they had no choice in the matter hadn't really occurred to her.

Some of the blame lay with Val's mother Sheila, who, despite just nudging sixty, was still a real beauty. Sheila had grown up in an ordinary middle-class existence where people did their own dusting, bought their cars on HP and saved up all year for a fortnight in Fuengirola. But she'd been catapulted up a couple of rungs by marriage. Keith Mortimer, a self-made millionaire several times over had been captivated by her, pursued her for a year and bombarded her daily with flowers, and in the end Sheila had agreed to marry him. Keith wasn't exactly the most devastating-looking man on the planet. He was short, stocky and bearded, with a rather inane grin. But Sheila saw a lifestyle she aspired to and grabbed the chance. From this rather doomed start, the marriage had surprisingly become a success. Keith couldn't quite believe his luck at what he'd landed and set about making Sheila's life as wonderful as possible. They lived in a beautiful Georgian mansion in the quiet Hampshire countryside, stuffed with antique furniture and fine paintings. It was also a far cry from the nature of Keith's business. He'd made his fortune from waste disposal, which they both felt privately did not go with their image.

Naturally the locals all knew about it and, behind their backs, referred to Sheila and Keith as Lord and Lady Muck. To their circle of friends, mainly drawn from other big houses in the area, they were Beauty and the Beast.

One of the factors that clinched the surprising success of the marriage was sex. Perhaps because Keith had not had much success with women before his marriage, he'd grabbed every opportunity for a legover as if it were his last, and had learned how properly to please a woman. As a result, despite the fact that they were approaching an age when most people would have packed it in and taken to tutting when sex scenes came up on the telly, Sheila and Keith were still at it like rabbits.

The marriage had been blessed early on with the arrival of Val, who proved to be the only child. The proud parents were even more delighted when they realized that Val had inherited her mother's looks, and so they idolized her and spoiled her. But in doing so Sheila conveniently forgot her own roots, and what life had been like before her marriage. So Val grew up not knowing what it was like to struggle. Keith, meanwhile, was pinching himself. He not only had a beautiful wife, but an equally gorgeous-looking daughter, now following in her mother's pretty footsteps and doing a bit of modelling.

Whereas Sheila had married Keith at twenty-five and had immediately been ensconced as lady of the manor, Val hadn't met and married Harry until she was twenty-eight. By then, most of her boarding-school friends had long since trotted up the aisle and into maternity wards, though not necessarily in that order. She suddenly found she had nothing in common with them. It was all baby talk, and in some cases, already divorce talk. Val's pampered existence had become boring. Even shopping, manicures, hairdressers, shiatsu massage, sessions in flotation tanks had become boring. What she needed was people, a job, a purpose. Except that she couldn't see that. Instead Val found a new friend, a friend who was always there, who never answered back or bore a grudge. Her new friend was wine. And as the friendship was forged, their meetings became scheduled earlier and earlier in the day, until a glass after breakfast became the norm. Granted, breakfast for Val was when most people were having lunch, so of course, it didn't count.

When Val met Harry, she had reached rock bottom with boredom. Boyfriends had come and gone, unable to satisfy her demands, embarrassed by her behaviour and her vacuous outlook on life. But when Harry set eyes on Val, it was almost like a repeat of her parents meeting. Harry was captivated, and although he was twelve years older than Val, and divorced, he pursued her relentlessly, just like her father had done her mother. So the circle was complete . . .

Except that Harry and Keith were like chalk and cheese. Where Keith had missed the boat where height and looks were concerned, Harry had fared better. He was tall and well built, though the muscles built up by an earlier rugby career were rapidly turning to fat, and too much claret had left him rather red-faced. Harry, however, thought he still looked gorgeous and that all women fancied him. Val married Harry because she was bored and a bit desperate, and because she wanted to be part of the glamorous world of television. She also assumed, wrongly, that Harry would be able to provide her with the kind of lifestyle that her father had done for her mother. Sure, there was a gleaming Mercedes that came with the job, the very respectable six-figure salary, private health care, share options and loads of first-class foreign travel. But Harry was not a multi-millionaire.

There was one other big difference between Val's marriage and that of her parents. Sex. Val had grown up knowing her parents were always busy in bed. From an early age she'd heard them humping away behind a firmly closed door and thought this was normal. So when she married Harry, she fully expected a similar amount of rumpy-pumpy. But Harry saw Val as a ticket to social cachet, and most of all as a possession. A very beautiful one, but a possession nevertheless. There was no onus on him to make any effort in bed. She was lucky to be there, that was his view. The fact that he was a fairly rotten and selfish lover would never have even crossed his arrogant mind.

With the ink barely dry on the marriage certificate, Harry discovered that Val was going to be a disappointing wife. The chances of his new bride turning into a domestic goddess were about as likely as spotting the Queen buying a lottery scratchcard. So the magic had soon worn off, the babies had not arrived and now, four years on, thanks to a well-stocked wine cellar, Val was not good news to come home to.

There was one silver lining to Harry's job. It had brought Val some new friends. She'd latched on to Janet, Sue, Liz and Nina at the first HOT Christmas party she'd been to. So desperate was she to meet up with them and fill some of the hours in her tedious life, she had taken their phone numbers, rung them up and insisted on taking them out for a meal. The phones had been hot that night, with everyone comparing notes and deciding that they had no choice but to accept an invitation from the boss's wife. And so the pattern had been set and was destined to be repeated several times a year. Val saw it as giving them a treat, doing them all a favour in granting them a glimpse of a lifestyle they couldn't afford. It never occurred to her that they might have been doing her the favour by turning up and putting up with her drunken rages and insults in public places.

Val bent down a little too quickly to reach for a coffee cup and saucer. All of a sudden, her head reminded her that it was hurting. With a brief lurch of conscience, she recalled the previous night and how she'd fallen over. Had she been over the top generally? She knew she'd delivered a few home truths to the girls, but was there a faint chance she'd embarrassed them? She picked up the phone to dial Janet's direct number, just to test the water. It started to ring. She changed her mind and slammed the receiver down again after four rings. Don't be ridiculous, she told the kitchen mirror. The girls thrived on her advice, looked forward to it. And her falling over was due not to too much wine, but to not enough practice on a new pair of Jimmy Choo heels.

'Get me the file on the Hartford tourism project,' shouted Harry Hampton from his office. Geraldine Taylor, his personal assistant, jumped to attention. The file almost at her fingertips, she was straight into Harry's inner sanctum quick as a flash.

'Good. Excellent. Coffee as well, Geraldine,' he bellowed, as he almost snatched the file from her hands. Geraldine scuttled off in the direction of the small kitchen down the corridor. She was used to Harry's manner and accepted it as par for the course. Geraldine had been brought up in a naval family where if anyone commanded

'Jump!' Geraldine's only query would have been 'From which window?' Well, at least that was the production office joke.

Harry sat back in his chair and flipped through the file. This would be an easy killing. Hartford Council's previous video was so old that everyone was in shoulder pads and practically humming the theme from *Dallas*. No wonder all the hotels, B and Bs and theatres were having such a hard time of it. HOT could create a really classy campaign that would put bums on seats, bodies in hotel beds and cash in the HOT coffers. But it was the same old question. How much would the council be prepared to pay? There was an old saying at HOT: What's the difference between a thirty-thousand-pound campaign and a sixty-grand one? Answer, nothing.

He reached across his desk to phone Janet. As he did so, he noticed that his shirt was a mass of tiny creases and cursed Val for the hundredth time that day. Considering the lazy cow did bugger-all, day in and day out, she could at least attempt a bit of ironing. Harry hadn't forgotten his northern roots where men were men and went out to work, while women stayed home, kept house and had babies. He allowed Val a gardener once a week and a cleaner twice a week but he expected her to do the rest. Sod the fact that she came from a wealthy background; she was his wife and should be doing all that stuff.

And as for babies, well, nothing seemed to be happening on that score. Perhaps it was just as well. He couldn't honestly see Val up through the night changing nappies. It would wreck her nails and she'd need an even longer lie-in than usual. Still, he couldn't deny, Val on a good day looked terrific on his arm. It had not done his position at HOT any harm at all.

17

'Janet? Two minutes in my office. Now.' He banged down the phone imperiously. He liked to keep them on their toes. Treat 'em mean, tell 'em nothing, that was his motto. Gave him the upper hand every time.

'I've been summoned to the bollocking room,' said Janet grimly to Liz. 'You'd better get the tumbrels ready. I wonder what the sod wants this time.'

Janet made her way out of the production office, down a short corridor and into the executive suite where Harry's office was situated. As she walked, she concentrated on deep breathing to help her relax, reflecting on how those telephone calls always instilled fear in her, even after all these years. It annoyed her that Harry could still make her quake. He rarely hinted at what any meeting was about. You never knew whether it was going to be a punch-up or a pay rise. And statistically it tended to be the first, rather than the second.

'Ah, Bancroft, take a seat,' he bellowed, not even glancing up from the open file on his desk.

'If I must,' Janet muttered under her breath. The visitors' seats in Harry's office were pitched a good few inches lower than his chair, all designed of course to give him a psychological advantage. Janet usually preferred to stand, giving her the temporary height advantage, but she'd learned over the years that if he shouted 'Sit!' it was probably in her best interests to do just that.

'Right, your name's on this one,' he barked. 'Hartford Council want a new tourism campaign. Their previous one's state-of-the-ark. I want something zappy, good script, and really grabby pictures.'

'What's the budget?' asked Janet, sensing a poisoned chalice.

'Cheap,' sneered Harry, 'and none of your business. But it's got to *look* expensive. That's why I pay you to run that production office. So get going. I want a draft script and a running order by close of play today. That's it. Scram.'

Without replying, because she knew well enough that Harry did not expect or encourage a response, Janet rose from the low chair, turned on her heel and walked out of the door. She half smiled to herself as she returned to her office.

'"Your name's on this one" my arse,' she muttered to herself. She had long got over the frustration of writing, producing and directing videos and programmes only to find Harry insisting his name be the only one on the end credits. Pays the mortgage, she endlessly reasoned with herself. Why make your life a misery, it's only a name on a caption roller, it's only rock and roll, not brain surgery.

But of course it mattered, it mattered a lot. Janet had learned that if you wanted to survive under Hampton's despotic regime, you kept your head down and just heaved a sigh of relief when the money arrived in the bank at the end of the month. Television was a shrinking market, and at the age of forty-two, as Val constantly reminded her, she was no spring chicken.

chapter three

The day was rapidly going from bad to worse. HOT had made the shortlist for the contract to produce a huge campaign for an insurance company, but they'd been pipped at the post by a rival. Nearly half a million pounds' worth of business had been lost. Harry stomped around his office, incandescent at the news.

'Get Simon and Joe in here immediately,' he shrieked at Geraldine, who, realizing that some blame-storming was about to take place, tactfully left her desk and went down the corridor to warn them. Although fiercely loyal to Harry, she did occasionally feel sorry for those who suffered at his hands.

Geraldine herself was one of the great HOT mysteries. No one could really work her out, or what went on inside her henna-bobbed head. She kept herself very much to herself behind the severe gold-rimmed glasses. She never gossiped, never commented or let slip the slightest whisper about her private life. She could have been anything from a lapsed nun to an ex-lap dancer, for all anyone knew. She seemed completely ageless and sexless. Life hadn't been all that kind either when the female bits and pieces were being given out. Geraldine was a sort of thin cylinder shape and didn't help the cause much by wearing no make-up and incredibly dreary clothes.

Geraldine also had no idea how much mirth she caused around the company. Her problem was language. She mixed her metaphors, got her words confused and would have given Mrs Malaprop a jolly good run for her money. Her daily pronouncements were known as the G-spots and were widely circulated on e-mail. Thanks to the computer world of grammar and spell-checkers, Geraldine had no problem in producing immaculate letters, reports and memos for Harry. It was just in the rare moments when she actually spoke that she opened her mouth and put her foot in it. It had all started when someone had joked about a new blonde secretary being the company's latest 'It' girl, and Geraldine had remarked that she seemed awfully young to be running the computer department.

Now Geraldine put her head round the production department door. Obviously some huge joke was in progress because everyone was creased up laughing. As, one by one, they clocked Geraldine, the laughter died away, except for Ray, the young office runner, who was still oblivious and in mid-flight on his joke.

'And then he said "A hard-on doesn't count as personal growth," so she said . . .' Ray faltered, suddenly aware that the laughter had stopped. 'Oh, shit.'

The silence was awful. Nobody trusted Geraldine, because she was so quiet and nondescript and because they assumed she was Harry's answer to MI6.

'Ehm, Joe and Simon, Harry wants to see you,' she announced in strident tones. 'I thought I'd better warn you, he's not best pleased. In fact, he's in a state of high dungeon.'

A gale of silent laughter whipped around the room,

with people desperately trying not to burst. As a result, most sat shaking silently at their desks.

Joe and Simon left the office, looking like prisoners going to the gallows.

'Wonder what the hell they've done,' said Ray, still smarting with embarrassment. 'It'll be me next, hauled over the coals by Harry for lowering the tone.'

'At least we got a good G-spot out of it,' said Fiona, one of the production secretaries. 'Must get that one out on e-mail.'

'Yeah,' agreed Ray. 'Good old Geraldine, she comes up with some corkers, doesn't she?'

'Just hope Joe and Simon aren't getting it in the neck,' said Fiona, looking extremely worried.

The row in Harry's office could have been heard in five counties. Despite the door being closed, the raised voices and swearing went on for what seemed like hours. A couple of producers took it in turns to wander down the executive corridor on various excuses just to monitor the situation. In desperation, they then pretended they were having a whip-round for someone's leaving present and got horribly embarrassed when various secretaries actually dipped into their purses to contribute. The racket from Harry's office was becoming very ominous. Faces got longer and longer when Joe and Simon did not return to their desks. What on earth was going on?

It was only hours later, when everyone in the production office gave up and plodded out through the main doors to go home, that Sue on reception quietly told them that Joe and Simon had left the building much earlier that afternoon.

'Sacked,' she whispered. 'Not allowed to return to their desks. I think you'll find them in the GX.'

The GX was HOT's local pub. Overlooking Hartford's historic waterfront, it had been a grain store for centuries, but a decade ago it had been bought by a brewery chain who'd converted it into a popular watering hole. Its real name was the Grain Exchange, but from day one it had been renamed the Groin Exchange, or the GX for short. During the day and straight after work, most of the HOT staff went in there for comfort, sustenance or a jolly good gossip. But from about nine in the evening it had earned a reputation as a pick-up joint for the truly desperate.

Joe and Simon were huddled in a corner, four pints and a few vodka chasers into a rest-of-the-day session. They had already moved down the agenda from shock mode to anger.

'What took you so long?' Joe looked up from his fresh pint.

'We've only just heard,' said Ray. 'The others are getting the drinks in. What'll you have?'

'A screwdriver would be great,' said Simon bitterly. 'Then I could stab the bastard.'

Ray and the others finally sat down with Joe and Simon, waiting expectantly.

'We were sacked,' said Joe bitterly. 'We were sacked because Hartford bloody Optimum bloody Television didn't get that big insurance project. The company got to the shortlist but the Fat Controller got a call to say the job had gone elsewhere. So the big bucks flew straight out of the window. I suppose this affects Harry's bonus and his legendary ability to creep to the board. I must say I'm gutted for him.'

'So why did you take the rap?' asked Fiona.

'Quite simple really,' continued Joe. 'A case of wrong

place, wrong time. Simon and I were involved in some discussions about the pitch for the insurance job. We threw in a few ideas, but uncharacteristically Harry insisted on writing the actual document. Makes a change, because he usually gets us poor sods to do all the work and then passes it off as his own. Well, this time, just for once, he wrote it, we never even saw it and it didn't get the deal. So guess who gets the blame – us.'

'But he can't just sack you,' said Fiona. 'There are supposed to be procedures, rules . . .'

'Since when has Harry played by any rules?' Simon interrupted. 'No, this is Harry's Game. Our contracts were up for renewal in a few weeks' time, so he'd have got rid of us then anyway. He told us we were incompetent and therefore in breach of our contracts so we were out. He also threatened to rubbish us around the entire industry if we didn't shut up and go quietly. In the end we decided it wasn't worth putting that to the test. So we said our bit and left.'

A shudder went around the table, followed by mutterings of sympathy. This wasn't the first time people had left the company too hastily for a leaving present.

'He had it all sewn up,' Joe continued. 'He paid us up to the end of the month on condition we left the building without returning to our desks, and put a gagging order on us. No cosy chats with the local media. We'd done enough damage to the company's reputation, he said.'

'Also helps to keep his slate clean with all the suits on the board,' replied Fiona.

'Oh yeah, it's brilliant. He's squeaky clean and is seen as a tough manager because he shovels all the shit on our heads. Easy life!'

*

'Janet? It's Sue. Sorry to ring you so late. Have you heard the news?'

'No, what? I've been out filming most of the day.'

'Harry's been at it again. Sacked Simon and Joe to cover up for the fact that we didn't get some big insurance job.'

'What? I can't believe it. They're brilliant, those two. The most creative people we've hired in ages. A lot of people had high hopes for them. God, he's a bastard.' Janet shivered involuntarily. Morale always dipped for weeks after something like this.

Sue continued: 'Also, Val rang up during the row and insisted on Geraldine putting her through. Said it was life and death.'

'And was it?'

'Was it heck. You know what a drama queen Val is. She'd broken one of her nails on the oven door and was demanding Harry bring home another one.'

'What, a nail or an oven?'

'Come on, you know what Val's like. Which is more expensive? Actually, I'm surprised she knew where the oven was in the first place. Anyway, do you know, he interrupted all the shouting and got Geraldine on the case. It's being delivered tomorrow. I know, because I got caught up in the calls to arrange it.'

Janet was still absorbing all the news. 'It's strange, isn't it? Harry's the biggest bastard that ever walked the televisual earth and yet when Val shouts, he jumps. What does this woman have that we don't?'

'A complete inability to keep anything shut, I should imagine,' said Sue wryly.

Janet was right. Morale next day took a nosedive as the news of Joe and Simon's demise went swiftly round the building. HOT employed around sixty people, some of whom – mainly in Accounts, Marketing and Development – were on the permanent payroll. In production areas, however, they hired as and when required, so the majority of Janet's team, for example, were on short-term contracts. The climate was such that people did come and go on a regular basis, but not usually in the manner of Joe and Simon.

Harry swept in with a real smirk on his face. He positively relished the effect sackings had on the staff. Being the archetypal bully, it gave him even more of the upper hand. Also, last night, he'd been granted a legover with Val and had given her a good seeing-to. It never occurred to him that Val, having been on the pop all day, and delighted that her demands for a new oven had been met so swiftly, had decided to give in. It was Harry's usual self-centred, brief performance, followed by snoring. Val was then left wondering why she'd put up with all that just for a sodding oven.

His self-satisfaction increased later that morning when the company chairman, Sir James Patterson Cripps, called him in to say that the Hartford tourism video was in the bag, thanks to the old-boy network. He expressed brief concern at losing the insurance job, but praised Harry's tough stance with the staff.

'Well done, Hampton,' said Sir James, pausing to puff on a huge cigar. 'Lead by example. Glad to see you remember the company mission statement. Selling Starts Here.'

Back in his office, confidence now brimming over, Harry summoned Janet to tell her the good news about the tourism campaign.

'They liked my treatment, then,' said Janet firmly.

26

'Nonsense, woman. They didn't have to bother to read it. It was my reputation that clinched it. When will you women ever learn: at my level it's all about contacts, contacts, contacts. In fact, most decent business these days is conducted on the golf course and in the boys' room.'

'Well, that lets me out,' said Janet sarcastically. 'And talking of letting people out, why on earth did you sack Joe and Simon? They were two of my best producers in ages. Those two had real promise, good ideas and knew how to implement them.'

Harry shot Janet a rather world-weary look to hide his sudden unease. She was trouble, this one, a bit too long in the tooth to be fobbed off. She was also brilliant at her job, managing the day-to-day production at HOT. He knew he couldn't do without her but he'd never admit that to her.

'Quite simple. It was a big job, they wrote the pitch, they got it wrong and we lost a good half-million pounds' worth of business. Not to mention losing the chance to expand our client list. So they were out.'

'But they didn't write the pitch,' said Janet, trying to keep the wobble out of her voice. 'They would have discussed it with me.'

'Oh, they wrote it all right. On my express instructions, they kept it confidential. That's the nature of this business, Janet. I'm sure I don't have to remind you. Too many prying eyes and ears in this place. Anyway, you might rate them, but unfortunately our potential client didn't, so tough shit. We can't afford to employ no-hopers.'

Janet knew when she was beaten. She was well aware of the true state of affairs, because she had spoken to Joe

27

late last night, but she also knew when to keep her head down. It was a case of survival.

'Okay, back to the tourism video. So do I go ahead, on the basis of the treatment I gave you?'

'Absolutely. Now get out.'

chapter four

Janet made her way back to her office, fed up to her back teeth and muttering under her breath. She was so angry that she almost collided with Geraldine, who was taking Harry's mid-morning caffeine in on a tray.

'If only I had a handy cyanide pill to pop in that coffee pot,' Janet remarked bitterly, forgetting momentarily that her comments might just go straight back to Harry.

'Come, come,' tutted Geraldine, unamused. 'These things happen. We must accept them. It takes two to tangle, you know.'

'Or even to tango. But your existence here doesn't depend on your marks in the Latin American section, nor on you getting every single spelling right one hundred per cent of the time,' said Janet crisply. Nor on your attempts at saying the company chairman's name, she thought. Sir James Patterson Cripps had, in Geraldine-speak, been transformed into Sir Pitterson Crapps on more than one occasion, amid silent hysteria.

'No, of course not,' said Geraldine huffily, 'but I hope those two young men aren't making out that they're escape goats over that insurance project.'

At the mention of escape goats, Janet completely lost it

and fled up the corridor, tears of laughter rolling down her face as she hotfooted it back to her office to tell her team the latest G-spots. That might cheer them up. She then had the unpleasant task of sorting out Joe and Simon's personal stuff and sending it on to them.

'Right, Liz, I want you to get started on the tourism job,' she said. 'I know we live here, but visitors don't. What we want is not just "this is the museum and oh look, that's the harbour". I want anecdotes, stories that bring the history to life. We have to persuade people watching the video to want to come here because it looks fascinating, even if it's raining cats and dogs. Which it is now.' Janet glanced out at the rain hammering against the windows.

'What's the time scale and budget on this?' enquired Liz.

'To echo the words of our führer, quick and cheap. The short answer is he won't say, so you can bet your Jimmy Choos – or probably Val's – there's loads of money washing around but we don't get to spend it. I would reckon on five filming days tops to do a reasonable job. Then we'll try and squeeze the system and spend a bit on post-production to make it look nice.'

'Shall I go and get a budget code then?' asked Nina, hoping for an excuse to visit the accounts department.

'Yeah, if it makes you happy,' laughed Janet. 'Go and see your beloved Sam. Don't pick up the phone, like the rest of us.'

Nina smiled her thanks, picked up her handbag and headed for the loo. She wanted a last-minute powder, touch of lippy and spray of perfume before going to see the object of her desire. Thank God she was wearing a black suit with a long-line jacket which minimized her bum.

Janet was just returning to the task of emptying Joe and Simon's desks when Ray the office runner came bursting through the door.

'You're unaccountably energetic this morning,' she said sarcastically, 'considering you were the life and soul of the GX last night.' Ray was known for his legendary hangovers.

'Sorry, Janet,' he said. 'I'm trying to get lashed only at weekends. Although I must say I got off quite lightly after that sesh with Joe and Simon. Anyway, guess what, I've just heard from the dreaded Geraldine that Fattie Hampton's having an office refurb.'

'What sort of refurb?' Janet was always nervous when HOT spent money on anything unnecessary or frivolous.

'Very swanky new desk and chair. Must have cost squillions,' replied Ray. 'Leather-top desk, looked like mahogany. And a big black leather chair.'

Make Harry even loftier, thought Janet bitterly. What a charmed life he led.

'This I must see,' she said, and made her way up to the executive corridor. She had long since dropped any pretence of defending Harry to her team. There was no point. She had to manage a roomful of intelligent people. They'd all worked him out and would have thought her daft if she'd stuck up for him. Everyone knew he was short on talent and big on getting bungs and bonuses. But it was Harry's reign of fear that they couldn't crack. Most got angry with themselves that he scared them so much. Janet was the only one who went some of the distance, but even she had to admit defeat most of the time when the going got tough.

'I've come to see the new furniture,' she said, sweeping past an open-mouthed about-to-protest Geraldine and into

Harry's office. 'Hmm, very nice, Harry,' she said, trying not to laugh. The chair was straight out of *Mastermind*. She could just imagine Magnus Magnusson's voice intoning: "Harry Hampton, controller of production. Your specialist subject is bollocking and your time starts now."

'What did you do to deserve this?' she asked him.

'Goes with the job,' he smirked. 'Sir James felt it was my due, so here it is. The paintings are arriving later on. Looks good, eh?'

Janet sat down in one of the new visitors' seats, which were even lower than the previous ones. The new desk was certainly a beautiful piece of workmanship. It was long and lean and very minimal. But there was one problem. Janet found herself sitting at direct eye level with Harry's crotch. Was this a new deliberate intimidation tack, or was Harry advertising something?

'I thought,' she paused, wondering whether to avert her gaze, 'you might like to view the catering college series today before it's dubbed. Would you like me to pop in the tapes now? Or would you prefer me to come back after the men from the Tate?'

'Sarcasm doesn't suit you, Janet. You must remember, I entertain important clients in here. We have to impress them and show them that we are a prestigious company with a big track record.'

And then you rook them rotten by charging them the earth for a poxy campaign we could put together for a quarter of the price, thought Janet.

'Bring those tapes in,' he barked. 'I'll look at them now.'

Watching the catering college videos from the comfort of his new chair, Harry reflected once again on the fact that Val did not live up to his job description for a wife. Why couldn't she cook, like other women? Or like the students in the videos, for that matter? Keep house like other women? Again because of his northern upbringing, he'd refused point blank to let Val have an allowance from her parents, reasoning that she'd just spend it on domestic help, leaving her to become even more dippy with nothing to do. The real reason, though he would never admit it, was that keeping her a bit short gave him the upper hand.

As the brief end credits rolled on catering college episode one, Harry thumped his new desk in temper.

'Get that Bancroft woman in here immediately,' he barked at Geraldine. Geraldine didn't accord Janet the favour she'd done to Simon and Joe by tipping her off. She didn't like Janet much, in truth, because she was one of the few who stood up to Harry, and Geraldine saw that as insubordination. She just dialled Janet's number and briskly told her to come in.

'Oh heck, I'm off to the bollocking room again,' said Janet. She left to the rest of her team humming the theme music from *Mastermind*.

'So how was Magnus?' they all chorused when she returned white-faced exactly two minutes later.

'I started but I didn't get to finish,' she half joked. She was secretly livid and trying not to show it. Morale was still too low after Joe and Simon's demise for her to have a real public go about Harry.

'Just a discussion about the end credits,' she whispered to Liz, who was her number-one confidante. 'The usual routine, off with my name as producer/director, on with his instead. I've got to get the graphics redone now so we can deliver. By order of the Third Reich.'

'The bastard,' said Liz. 'I doubt he even knows where the catering college is, let alone how to boil an egg.'

'That'll be why he and Val have a lot in common, then,' said Janet. 'I feel lunch at the Groin Exchange coming on. Fancy the idea?'

Over steak-and-ale pies and heaps of naughty chips, Liz and Janet surveyed the scene in the GX. There were solicitors out between adjournments, relaxing in the sure knowledge of receiving their fees, while in other corners, their clients sweated it out. City types who'd already made their money that day and might just not bother to return to the office, given a couple of large gin and tonics and a bit of gentle persuasion.

'Not much talent here,' observed Janet drily. 'They're either too young or too old.'

'Or too infertile,' said Liz too involuntarily for Janet's liking.

'What do you mean by that?' queried Janet.

'Well, look around,' said Liz. 'Those around the thirty mark. They're all drinking too much, smoking too much, overweight and unfit. It's bound to affect their fertility rate.'

'Do you have to view all blokes as baby-making machines?' asked Janet, fascinated. 'Are you always running open auditions for sperm banks?'

'Not exactly,' said Liz, lowering her head sheepishly. 'I just desperately, desperately want a baby. I can't seem to meet anyone. I've almost given up on that. They're either too young, too old, or too pretty. So I'm beginning to think I'd be better off sticking with the idea of having just the baby.'

'Aren't you cutting out the middle man a bit here?' asked Janet. 'I mean, wouldn't it be nice at least to start conventionally?'

'I'm not sure any more. I spent five years with Steve, we

34

talked about marriage, and then after all that he announced he didn't want babies. End of story. I mean, what's the point of having sex? That was what it was designed for.'

'Don't you think you're a bit young to be thinking this way? After all, you just picked the wrong guy with Steve.'

'Yeah, but every time I meet a new man – which let's face it is getting rarer and rarer, because they're so thin on the ground – I can hardly issue a questionnaire on attitudes to smacking, pocket money and feeding on demand.'

'Don't be daft,' replied Janet, trying not to laugh, because she knew Liz was in deadly earnest. 'All I'm saying is don't give up on the conventional route yet.'

'Well, you don't have kids; don't you ever regret it?' asked Liz.

'No, I can honestly say I don't. They never happened and with hindsight it was just as well. I was never one to coo into prams or kiss babies. So that ruled out a career in politics. No, in the circumstances, the choice was relatively easy. Anyway, Crippen wasn't into babies. He was more into having an Olympic-sized temper and other women's knickers.'

Janet never referred to her ex as anything other than Crippen so that she wouldn't have to utter his name. Clearly her marriage had had the most devastating effect on her, because she'd not been known to have a relationship since. Even Liz, who'd come to be good friends with her, sensed not to ask. She got the distinct impression that Janet had walked out with just the clothes she stood up in.

'Now, changing the subject,' as Janet always did when her marriage came up in conversation, 'the Hartford tourism job. I think it's time we raised your profile. You've been an ace researcher here for a couple of years and I think you're perfectly capable of putting it together yourself.'

'Whaddya mean?' Liz was stunned.

'What I mean is that I think you should take at least an assistant director role. I'll be in the background for any help you need, but I know you'll do a great job.'

'Bloody hell, Janet, are you sure?' Liz stuttered.

'Absolutely. Good, you're agreed,' grinned Janet, rubbing her hands together in delight. 'All I need to do now is formalize it. I'll pick a good moment with the Fat Controller. He'll probably want to have you in for a brief chat to pretend he had the idea himself, and then . . . Liz, are you all right?'

Liz had gone white, and slumped over her drink.

'No, I can't. I can't do that,' she pleaded. 'Please don't ask me because I won't do it.'

'What, go and see Harry? Look, we all know he's the World's Biggest Bully, but he really rates your work. Honestly, you're absolutely on home ground on this one.'

'No, I can't do it.' Liz's eyes filled with tears. 'And please don't ask any questions.' She fled to the loo, leaving Janet wondering what on earth was wrong.

Janet didn't raise the subject again. They returned to the office to find Nina checking into the Inn of the Sixty-Sixth Happiness. She was still reeling from the thrill of spending five minutes talking to Sam in Accounts about the budget code. And she'd nipped home at lunchtime and weighed herself. She'd lost a pound since breakfast.

If only the rest of it was that easy, sighed Janet to herself.

chapter five

'They were on my desk last night, honest, Harry,' pleaded a shaking Nina, close to tears.

'Well, if they were, they've grown legs and walked off into the bloody sunset,' roared Harry, thumping his new desk at the same time. 'You realize that if we . . . no, let me rephrase that . . . if YOU don't find them, that's four days' worth of editing down the fucking pan.' He paused, stabbing at the nearby calculator. 'That's not far short of four grand and that's just for the edit suite. That's before I pay for some poor mug to sit there and put it all together again.'

'I'm sorry, Harry, they were on my desk, ready to box up, and . . .'

'SORRY isn't good enough. SORRY is a STUPID word. You are STUPID,' he roared again. 'Well, I tell you this, if those tapes don't turn up by lunchtime, the cost of re-editing will be coming straight out of your salary.'

Nina went white. That was about three months' money after tax on her salary as a production secretary. She opened her mouth but no sound came out.

'Now get yourself and your fat arse out of this office and start looking.'

Tears now streaming down her face, Nina fled out of the room, colliding with Geraldine, who'd been eavesdropping outside. The files Geraldine had been carrying took flight and landed in a mess on the floor.

'Oh, you stupid girl,' wailed Geraldine from beneath her hennaed bob. 'You should watch where you're going. You'll have to help me clear this up and sort it out. Sir Pitterson Crapps is expected any minute.'

'Well, tough shit then,' replied Nina, as she carried on running down the corridor, heading for the ladies' loo for a good cry.

The office jungle drums were working overtime as usual. The row over the missing catering college tapes soon reached Janet's ears and she tracked down a distraught Nina barricaded in one of the cubicles and crying her eyes out.

'He said I had a fat bum and that I'd have to pay for it,' she mumbled through racking sobs.

'You what?' said Janet, wondering for one bizarre moment whether HOT were suddenly offering their staff free liposuction. 'Come on, hon, let's go and have a quiet coffee and you can tell me about it.'

Janet coaxed Nina out of the loo and into the tiny staff canteen, which was mercifully empty. They chose the most obscure corner and Janet gently persuaded Nina to go through what Harry had said.

'Now, I can assure you there's no way you'd be paying for re-editing. That's complete nonsense. He has absolutely no right to say that. We'll find the tapes, I promise you, even if we have to call in the cavalry. I'll get everyone on the case, even Interpol if I have to. The tapes exist. They're there somewhere. So don't worry about that.'

The other subject was a more difficult issue. It would be a complete sham for Janet to pretend Nina didn't have a big bum. She'd have to have been registered blind to be unaware of it, and besides, Nina discussed it constantly. She was always on different diets, different exercise regimes in an attempt to reduce it. It was one of those hereditary features over which she probably had no control. The sad thing was that Nina was an extraordinarily pretty girl, with lively blue eyes and a personality to match. She had her pale blonde hair cut in a short, sharp style that really suited her. From the waist upwards she was a size 12. But from the waist down she was a 16 and counting. Because she was a cockney, the chaps in the production office had nicknamed her the London Derrière. When Janet found out, she made them swear on pain of death not to let her know. Nina would have been devastated.

'If I find any one of you so much as whistling the Londonderry Air or anything else for that matter, I'll have your guts for garters,' she'd warned them. 'You'll think Harry's a real soft touch after I've finished with you.'

Nina had begun to calm down now as Janet spelled out a plan of action to find the missing tapes.

'As for Harry's remarks about your bum, just remember that his isn't as pert as it used to be. Ray told me the gossip is that the company had to buy him that new chair because he'd got too heavy for the old one and they couldn't get the parts to repair it.'

Back in the production office, Janet told the team what had happened and announced a full-scale search.

'Down tools, folks, just answer the phones, but please go through every drawer, filing cabinet, folder, nook and cranny until you find them.'

This was no mean feat for thirty creative people who weren't the tidiest on the planet. Janet began on her own filing cabinet. She pulled out the top drawer and looked in. Was she imagining something or was it not quite as she'd left it? The next drawer looked normal, but there was something about the bottom drawer that made her wonder.

Ray, the office runner and oracle of all gossip, came over in 'have you heard' mode.

'It might be nothing,' he said conspiratorially, 'but several people have said they think their stuff's been got at. Not quite as they'd left it, things moved around, that sort of thing. One or two who leave their computers on all the time have found some of their e-mails have been opened.'

'Hmm,' said Janet, half to herself. 'I wonder, I just wonder.' She looked back at Ray. 'We could all be getting paranoid. Well, even more than usual. Anyway, Ray, let's just find those tapes and worry about this other stuff later.'

Her phone rang, bringing their conversation to a convenient end. Janet did not want to go any further down that particular road. It was the dreaded Geraldine, tutting down the phone.

'I've been trying to ring you for ages,' she said. 'I wish to lodge a complaint against one of your team.'

'I'm very sorry, Geraldine, but we have a crisis on here at the moment. We have some tapes which have gone walkabout and we have to find them,' said Janet sharply. 'That's much further up the urgent list than sitting at my desk awaiting your call. Anyway, briefly, what's your problem?'

'I think it is more *your* problem. Nina Blake came out of Harry's office at great speed, ran straight into me and all my files went all over the floor. That was bad enough, but we were expecting Sir Pitterson Crapps at any time. It would have looked terrible. And she was extremely rude.'

'I'm sure even Sir Crapperson Pitts would have totally understood,' retorted Janet, taking a leaf out of Geraldine's book and scoring another hit for the G-spotters. Predictably it passed straight over Geraldine's head. 'Anyway, I know Nina would not have done it on purpose,' she continued. 'What exactly did she say to you?'

'"Tough shit",' said Geraldine. 'That's what she said, "tough shit".'

'Sounds a fair assessment to me,' retorted Janet and slammed down the phone. Serve the stupid cow right.

A cry of triumph went up. The tapes had been found in the bottom drawer of Joe's now empty filing cabinet. Janet smiled grimly to herself. She'd personally cleared out his cabinet completely the previous day. The tapes had been planted. Ray was right. There was something up.

Janet drove home that night with a heavy heart. Something was going on but she couldn't pinpoint what it was or make much sense of it.

As she put the key in the front door of her modest little terraced house, she made a decision to treat herself to a takeaway. Sod cooking tonight, she thought. I'm too mentally exhausted.

She phoned through an order of chicken biryani and a couple of poppadoms and opened a bottle of Beaujolais while she waited for the delivery boy. The events of the past few days were rattling around in her head. She could at least understand Harry's twisted motives for sacking Joe and Simon. They'd just been treated like cannon fodder to protect his skin. But why was Liz so terrified at the thought of talking to Harry? Was it that she was afraid to be on her own with him? Something must have happened to make her feel like that. And why had the tapes gone missing and then been planted in an empty cabinet, a cabinet she'd been the last to use? Was there someone in the department trying to undermine her? It definitely wasn't Nina or Liz, which narrowed it down to a possible fifty-odd others to choose from. A hopeless task. Or was it Harry on yet another of his control-freak kicks? Could he be capable of sneaking into the production office after they'd all gone home, running the risk of being spotted moving tapes from one place to another or having a rummage through her desk? For the life of her Janet couldn't imagine why he'd go to all that bother.

She glanced at her watch. Eight o'clock. Sue might just be home by now. She'd been working the late shift this week. Janet picked up the phone and dialled.

'Sue, it's Janet. Am I interrupting meals and stories?' She could hear small voices in the background.

'No, it's all right, Jon always sees to the kids when I'm on lates. What's up?'

'Oh, fairly shitty day, that's all. Lost tapes, lost tempers. That sort of stuff. Also a couple of mysteries I'm trying to unravel. Can I pick your brains for a minute?'

'Of course. Fire away.'

'What time did Harry leave the building last night? Can you remember?'

'Oh, that's an easy one,' said Sue brightly, 'because it was unusual. He went way after you lot. In fact it was just minutes before I left at seven thirty. I remarked on it as he went through reception. He muttered something about being overworked. He's normally out on the dot of six. You can almost set your watch by it.'

'Interesting,' said Janet. 'And one other thing that puzzles me. Liz seems absolutely terrified of him. I only really discovered that today.'

'I think we're all terrified of him in one way or another,' replied Sue.

'No, this was different. Real paranoia. Can you think of any reason why?'

'No, I can't, not at all.' Sue was usually the soul of discretion. 'You know I tend to keep my mouth shut. It's better in my sort of job, but in this instance, if I knew anything I would tell you. Liz has never said anything to me. I did hear on the jungle drums that there had been some kind of mega row today.'

'Oh, that was the saga of Nina and the missing tapes. Harry also told her she had a big bum. Nice one, eh?'

'I'm afraid I heard about that too. Mind you, he can't talk. Have you seen him squeezing himself into that Mercedes these days? Shoe horn wouldn't come amiss.'

'Oh, must look out for that! Thanks, Sue. See you tomorrow.'

Over the solitary takeaway and the Beaujolais, Janet pondered some more. Was Harry searching the office, planting tapes? Was he trying to undermine her?

She was just dozing through a rather dreary Hollywood thriller when the phone rang. It was Sue.

'Want the good news or the bad?' she said.

'Go on, whatever.'

'Val's just called. Booked us all in for dinner in a couple of weeks time.'

'Oh, shit,' said Janet. 'It only seems like a couple of lifetimes ago that we had the last fiasco. I wish she'd stop this.'

'Me too. With that amount of notice, I'll not be able to

use the "let-down-by-the-babysitter" excuse like last time. Nina and Liz have agreed to go. But then, you say yes to anything when there's a pistol planted against your temple.'

'Let's hope it's a more mundane evening than the last one.'

chapter six

'Smirk alert, smirk alert,' warned Ray as Janet sat down to wade through the morning post and her e-mails.

'What is it this time?' she queried, only half listening.

'Harry's been reported looking very pleased with himself,' said Ray conspiratorially.

'And to what do we owe this underwhelming pleasure?' said Janet vaguely, gazing at her computer screen and deleting all the junk mail with one definitive click.

'Well, strictly *entre nous*, it sounded like some sort of holiday freebie,' said Ray.

'How come I'm head of this department, have been here for years and yet know nothing? And you're the office runner, been here five minutes and you know everyone's blood group?' said Janet, now giving him her full attention.

'Thought it was in my job spec,' grinned Ray. 'I was in really early this morning to deliver the post. Harry's office door was a couple of inches ajar and I caught a few key words.

'Like what?'

'Like "Algarve", "five star", "first-class seats", that kind of thing.'

'Maybe he was just booking a holiday,' said Janet.

'Nah,' said Ray. 'It just didn't sound like that. Not at eight o'clock in the morning It seemed a bit too clandestine to be legit. More like a favour being called in.'

'And you have a very fertile imagination,' Janet sighed. Except he was probably right. Harry had a terrible reputation for being King of the Freebies. She'd stumbled on it herself first hand when HOT had won a contract to make a video series about old family-run boat yards. An old sea dog at one of the yards had let slip that the big white yacht down the end was being built for a 'Mr Hampton'.

'Now put your overly busy mind on the back burner and tell all those here that I want to hold a short meeting in about five minutes.'

'Sure thing,' replied Ray, saluting. Good lad, she thought, bright, hard-working and worth giving a break if she could create one.

Janet sipped a coffee and pondered again on the missing tapes episode. It couldn't really be Harry. Okay, he'd worked unusually late, but what would he gain by searching the office and moving tapes about? He had absolutely no motive whatsoever. Granted, he was a control freak, but this was just damned stupid. No, it must be someone else; perhaps there was some petty jealousy going on that she hadn't clocked.

'Okay, folks, this won't take long.' She addressed the troops, perching on the end of her desk in the style of a Channel 5 newsreader. 'I wanted to thank you all for helping to make a thorough search for the tapes yesterday. Much appreciated, especially by Nina, and we got the result we'd hoped for.'

There was a small round of mock applause.

'But it does throw up some serious issues. First of all, yesterday's search reminded me what a messy load of idiots we are. Tapes, files, notebooks, just general stuff strewn everywhere. Empty coffee cups, plates, yoghurt pots, plastic spoons, pizza boxes. I can't believe you all go home at night and make stuff off *Blue Peter*. So the message is, stop collecting the bits to make Tracy Island, clear up your mess and keep your desks tidier, then if something goes AWOL again we've a fighting chance of finding it. And I won't have to call in the Thunderbirds.'

'Now the second thing is more sinister. A number of you reported to me that you thought your stuff had been moved about a bit, desks rearranged or filing cabinets searched. Not quite as you'd left it, was the phrase. There were too many reports for it to be a coincidence. It saddens me to think that someone here is intent on mischief-making, and I must warn you that if it happens again and I find the culprit, then it'll be the loyal order of the boot. Make no mistake, we cannot and will not tolerate someone hell-bent on a sabotage mission. They will be sacked.'

A shudder, followed by low-voiced reaction, went around the room.

'So I urge you to keep a closer eye on your belongings. Anyone with information is welcome to talk to me or e-mail me in confidence. But I have to say, I think it's a very sad day that I have to stand here and say this. Okay, folks, back to your looms.'

As the morning wore on, Janet received ten jokey e-mails all citing Geraldine as the culprit, with motives ranging from 'her desperate ambition to be a contestant on *Whose Tape Is It Anyway?*' to 'her subconscious desire to write a book entitled *Pronunciation is the thief of time*'.

'Starting a business called Say It With Flour' was another cruel suggestion, with a footnote adding that it should be wholemeal flour to match her dreary outfits.

By lunchtime, Janet was convinced it was not an inside job. Someone would have squealed, or at least dropped a hint. However, she still hadn't got to the bottom of Harry's unusual state of happiness. He was obviously up to some sort of mischief, but supersleuth Ray was now out on a shoot for the rest of the day, so that source of information had dried up. She arranged to meet Sue for lunch in the canteen. She'd know.

'Any idea why Harry's allegedly cock-a-hoop?' she asked.

'Yep,' said Sue, triumphantly. 'Free holiday. He's going on a jolly.'

'Where's he going?'

'The Algarve.'

'Look, it's only supposition. How did you get to hear?'

'Ray told me on the sly. Perhaps he's been chatting up Geraldine.'

'Doubt it. He can't stand her. But he always knows the gossip, that lad. He's not usually wrong either.'

'Anyway, trust Harry to get something for nothing, the jammy sod. Wherever it is, the food will be better than this muck.'

They were wading their way through a soggy vegetarian lasagne and some garlic bread in which the bread was very much the side order to the garlic.

'Blimey, they'll smell us coming,' said Janet. 'Good job I'm not planning to have sex tonight. I'd knock some poor sod out from a mile away with this breath.'

'Is there a man in tow? Is there something you've not told us?' asked Sue, straight on the case.

'No, don't be ridiculous. I was only joking. I gave up men years ago, or rather they gave me up. More trouble than they're worth.'

'I don't think you should generalize too much,' said Sue softly. 'I know it's easy for me to sit here knowing I've got Jon and the kids to go home to, but isn't it worth taking another risk, to find someone special?'

'Oh, I dunno any more,' said Janet, suddenly looking wistful. 'I dreamed of all that happily-ever-after stuff and where did it get me? Precisely nowhere. At least now I have my own home, car, hair and teeth and I can sleep easily in my bed, albeit alone. At least I can't kick myself out, or two-time myself. Okay, I'll admit I get lonely sometimes, but I've discovered there are times when chocolate really can solve all your problems.'

'Can't convince you then, can I?' said Sue, laughing.

'Nope. And by sheer coincidence there was one of those blindingly obvious surveys out last week. You know, the sort where they discover after years of painstaking research and squillions of spondulicks that in fact half the married population is female. Well, last week's little bombshell was that they've discovered that more women prefer chocolate to sex. Again obvious. We all knew that one. No fear of pregnancy, no grunting, no wet patch, no post-bonk snoring either. And you get the whole bed to yourself. Look on the positive side. With chocolate, you can take as long as you like or just have a quickie nibble and save a bit for later. It's much cheaper than condoms and there's no risk of cheating.'

'But there are down sides to chocolate,' retorted Sue. 'You get spotty, you get fat, so you need a new wardrobe of clothes, which requires you spending all your money. So suddenly a Cadbury's Flake or a Fry's Chocolate Cream is looking like a major investment. Talking of which, shall we go mad and have some of that chocolate cheesecake for pudding?'

'Might deaden the garlic,' agreed Janet. 'Anyway, you don't need chocolate. You could crawl all over Jon tonight if you felt like it.'

'Not after a day's shift here and two small children to read a bedtime story to. I doubt I'll be bodice-ripping material after all that.'

For the third night in a row, Janet drove home deeply disturbed by events at work. What a terrible week it had been, what with the sacking of Joe and Simon, followed by the catering college graphics row, the missing tapes mystery and now the office poltergeist. And on that one, she was becoming more and more convinced that the culprit was not from the production department at all. There were those who had their differences, didn't speak to each other or were ex-lovers. But not one single person had squealed or even come up with a possible suspect. She also wondered what Harry was up to. Normally he crowed to her about anything interesting he was doing, especially if it involved a little boasting. One of his favourite tricks was to collect an award in, say, New York, and then allow the person who'd actually done the work to meet him at the airport and have the thrill of driving him back to the office while he delivered a blow-by-blow account of the ceremony, the frantic networking and the glorious champagne piss-up afterwards. So why wasn't he boasting about the freebie week in the Algarve? On the other hand, with his six-figure salary Harry could afford to go to most places he fancied. So what was so special about this trip?

Janet shrugged to herself as she popped a pizza in the oven. While she waited for it to cook, she thought a little more about her chat with Sue on the subject of men and chocolate. She thought enviously of Sue and her cosy lifestyle. She'd be home now with Jon, tucking up the children, and then they'd be sitting down together in front of the television over some delicious snack. Sue was one of those domestic goddesses who effortlessly conjured up all sorts of delicious morsels out of nothing very much, whereas Janet's cooking had collapsed and promptly died in the seventies. She could rustle up a prawn cocktail, steak and chips and pass off a Black Forest gateau out of a box as her own. But she'd lost the cooking plot when she left Crippen and couldn't keep up with all the celebrity chefs mucking about with bits of lemon grass and ten different types of olive oil.

Perhaps that was why she hadn't met a man since. Perhaps Crippen had e-mailed the entire male population and warned them about her cooking. Perhaps there was something in the old adage that her grandmother had always trotted out, that the way to a man's heart was the way you braised his kidneys. She'd have liked to cook Crippen's kidneys all right, that at least she did know. But the rest of the time, cooking for one was no fun at all.

Thank God it's Friday, thought Janet, as she swung into the HOT car park. Morale might perk up after a decent weekend. The day's agenda included a meeting with Harry on the subject of the Hartford tourism project. She and Liz spent an hour going through the treatment, the budget and a draft script before making their way to the executive corridor, Liz as white as a sheet.

The ever-faithful Geraldine was sitting, expressionless, at her desk outside Harry's office, clicking away on her computer. What went on behind those severe glasses?

wondered Janet. Probably not a lot. There was definitely less to Geraldine than met the eye.

'Geraldine's looking a triumph of taupe today,' whispered Liz as they swept past. Geraldine's dress sense, or rather lack of it, was a constant source of amusement in the production office.

'Right, siddown,' barked Harry, indicating two chairs in front of his desk. Janet had warned Liz about the new seating arrangements and the eye-line view of Harry's undercarriage.

They outlined the way the video and the website would look, showed Harry some storyboards and went through a rough budget sheet.

'Right, leave this stuff with me. I'll get on to the council,' he snarled.

So you can get all the kudos with your important friends in Hartford, thought Janet.

'And you can save money on this budget by getting the bloody graphics right first time,' said Harry with his usual thump on the table. 'My name only as executive producer on the end credits. Company policy. No one buying this video will give a shit who shot it, lit it or made the tea. Geddit?'

If it's not that important, you pillock, why are you making such a fuss about it? thought Janet.

'Is it company policy to have only Harry's name on end credits?' asked Liz as they walked back to their office.

'Is it heck,' replied Janet. 'He just made that up. Anyway, did you like the new seating arrangements? All designed to distract us, I suppose. There didn't seem to be very much going on down there. The way Harry swaggers around, you'd think he was hung like a donkey. Looked more like a hamster from where I was sitting.'

Liz looked shocked. 'Sorry, Janet, I didn't dare look. I felt too embarrassed. I just hate going into his office at the best of times.'

Hmm, thought Janet. She really is frightened of him. I wonder if I'll ever get to the bottom of it.

'Still no mention of the freebie,' she continued. 'Unlike Harry not to take the opportunity to gloat. Very odd.'

'It could be quite simple,' said Liz. 'Perhaps he wants to give Val a surprise and thinks we might blow it. After all, he knows we see her socially from time to time. Or anti-socially, depending on how you look at it.'

'Perhaps he wants to kid her that he's paid for the trip. It could be just that. I'm beginning to think I'm reading too much into too little. I must chill out over the week-end. Are you doing anything exciting?'

'I'm going to stay with my sister,' said Liz.

'That sounds nice. But I hope you're not going to get all broody and miserable seeing her kids,' said Janet suspiciously. Liz's younger sister had twin daughters of eighteen months.

'No, no,' she replied. 'But I did read this week that one of those supermodels borrowed somebody's baby and held it for a day and then got herself pregnant.'

'Most people find sex is a bit more reliable. C'mon, Liz, it will happen to you. Probably when you're least expecting.'

'That's the trouble, I do want to be expecting,' said Liz wistfully. 'I'm frightened it will never happen to me.'

As they reached their office, Janet couldn't fail to notice the baby and parenting magazines sticking out of Liz's bag on the floor next to her desk.

chapter seven

The great thing about inviting people over to dinner, mused Janet, was that it forced you to get the vacuum cleaner out. She'd spent all Saturday morning at the supermarket and now she was on a dust-busting mission. The place now reeked so violently of bleach and polish that two spiders who'd quietly set up home in the bathroom decided it was time to move on.

It was a beautiful May morning and whilst the sunshine streaming through the windows was a welcoming sight, it did show up how badly everything needed a good scrub. At least it would be almost dark by the time her guests arrived.

Janet was now knee deep in cookery books, trying to knock up some potted shrimps to start, followed by a chicken chasseur-type casserole (the sauce by arrangement with a packet). She'd already burned her fingers twice on the oven door, so she put on some cheerful music to stop herself getting into a temper over it all. Unfortunately Dire Straits' 'Sultans of Swing' proved to be too uplifting when the pan with the cheat's chasseur sauce was accidentally thrown in the air. Oh to be Delia Smith, live in that wonderful conservatory and make millions writing cookery books. If I were Delia, Janet mused, I'd spend the proceeds on a resident chef. If I were Delia, I'd also employ someone to scrape the sauce off these cupboard doors.

With fifteen minutes to blast-off, Janet lit the candles and oil lamps placed around her sitting room cum dining room. She stood back to admire the effect. I might not be able to cook, she thought, but my God, I can light a candle. At least they made the table look good. She'd just poured herself a glass of Merlot as a reward for all her efforts when she heard the doorbell.

Joe and Simon stood on her doorstep, grinning and clutching carrier bags full of bottles and cans.

'Your local off-licence had a sale on,' said Simon. 'We couldn't resist. I wonder if they do reward cards there if you spend loads.'

'I should know,' replied Janet, kissing each of them lightly on the cheek.

'Hey, nice place, Janet,' said Joe. 'Something smells fantastic. Oh, it's me,' he added, sniffing his armpits. 'Only joking. We're starving, now that we're the newly impoverished. The nouveau pauvre as opposed to the nouveau riche. Or as Geraldine would put it, the niveau rouche.'

Janet poured them huge glasses of wine as they made a beeline for the table.

'Let's not do all that Bombay mix foreplay stuff, let's just get stuck in,' said Simon.

'Phew, I'm fresh out of Bombay,' grinned Janet as she disappeared into the kitchen.

'I know just how you feel, ducky,' said Simon.

'So how's your week been since Harry sent you on your way?' said Janet, returning with the potted shrimps and a basket of French bread.

'Well, we've tried mugging, ramraiding, joy-riding, begging and extortion. Only the tame stuff so far,' said Joe. 'No, seriously, I've got an interview upcountry with a small indie production house. Rubbish area but the money's good. And I'd be nearer my girlfriend. So double whammy.'

'And what about you, Simon?' asked Janet, already clearing away the first lot of plates and marvelling that the mountain of bread had almost completely disappeared.

'I've got a mate in London who's trying to fix me up in an ad agency. So fingers crossed.'

'I'm really pleased,' said Janet. 'And don't forget what I said about references. I'd be delighted to write glowing accounts about you both.'

'Well, that certainly wasn't on offer from Harry. All he threatened to do was rubbish us around the entire industry if we didn't leave quietly. More importantly, the HOT-heads would have started asking questions. This way Harry keeps a clean sheet and we're sent like lambs to the slaughter.'

'A case of Silence of the Lambs,' said Joe. They all laughed.

'Well, you'll get great references from me. Might be worth giving my home address and telephone number rather than work, though. I don't want anybody snooping. I keep thinking I'm imagining things, but there's something going on in that building. I can't put my finger on it.'

Over the chicken chasseur à la packet and plates of steamed vegetables which Simon and Joe pronounced 'mental', Janet outlined the mysterious goings-on since they'd left the company.

Joe and Simon looked at each other and started to laugh. They laughed until they almost doubled up, tears rolling down their cheeks. Janet found herself laughing too, but hadn't a clue why.

'I just wonder if the fat sod actually believed us,' said Simon, still spluttering.

'If it's true, then it was worth being sacked,' replied Joe, wiping his eyes with his napkin. 'Well, almost.'

'Put me out of my agony, for goodness' sake,' said Janet, now on the edge of her seat with curiosity. 'No pudding until you tell.'

'Right, right, of course we'll tell you,' said Simon, calming down immediately. 'It started during the big row. I suppose that was the moment when we knew we had nothing to lose.'

'What started?' urged Janet.

'Well, I guess we egged each other on,' continued Simon. 'It was really only a parting shot, but we implied that a secret file was being kept on Harry's activities and we told him we knew what he was up to.'

'We kind of pretended we knew he was involved in all sorts of stuff.' Joe took up the story. 'We muttered mysteriously about backhanders, sexual harassment, that sort of thing. We rounded it off by saying he was a lousy boss and that everyone had zilch respect for him, and that it was only a matter of time before the board heard about it and demanded the file.'

'And how did he react?' asked Janet.

'Well, he was shouting and thumping the desk, but that's the norm with Harry. But then he demanded that we named names; he wanted facts.'

'A bit odd if he's nothing to hide,' said Janet.

'Exactly,' said Joe. 'But it was as though we'd stumbled on something. By that time we knew we were out of a job anyway and we wanted our little bit of mischief before we left. Mind you, I'm sure Harry's capable of all that sort of stuff, but why on earth would he bother to get upset? Anyway, now we've told you, it's time for your part of the bargain. Where's that pudding?'

'Oh wow, retro food,' shrieked Simon in delight as a Black Forest gateau à la Sainsbury's freezer cabinet, customized with dollops of double cream, appeared on the table. 'Blimey, you're clever, Janet.'

She'd deliberately left the washing-up until the morning. Joe and Simon had offered but she'd turned them down. They'd been ridiculously brilliant guests, considering her cooking. She'd enjoyed their company enormously, but she'd enjoyed even more hearing how Harry had got a slight bit of comeuppance.

As she stacked the plates and filled the sink, she thought some more about what Joe and Simon had said. It did somehow make sense. Harry'd got the wind up about a file on him. That was why desks had been searched. Maybe the planting of the 'missing' tapes had been his revenge against the whole department. Or perhaps it was a simple case of him trying to justify the sackings. If anyone was going to keep a file, he would inevitably suspect the production department. They bore the brunt of his anger and his ego, day in and day out. In that office he had a whole marching army of enemies. Joe and Simon had hit the nail on the head when they said that no one had any respect for him. Harry also hated not being in control. The idea that someone might be keeping tabs on his affairs would have sent him into orbit. Was Janet the prime suspect? After all, she was one of the few who stood up to Harry. She'd better watch her step.

*

The staff at Hartford Optimum Television had finally declared it summer. The weekend sun had decided to stay on for Monday morning. Winter sweaters and dark jackets had been abandoned. Everyone seemed to have dug into their wardrobes and come out wearing last summer's sale disasters.

Ray came bouncing in to inform the general populace that Geraldine had finally become a fashion victim.

'You're not looking too clever yourself,' tutted Liz, trying to stick up for Geraldine, although she couldn't for the life of her think why. Ray was wearing a bright floral shirt in black, tan and yellow. She bent down to her handbag and fished out some dark glasses.

'Cor, that's better. You look like a walking migraine in that shirt,' she said.

'If you think that, then keep those glasses on when you see Geraldine,' said Ray. 'It's bye bye boring old beige and hello hot pink. She must have had a bunk-up at the weekend or undergone some kind of irreversible brain surgery. She's looking like a camouflaged blancmange.'

'This we must see,' said Liz. 'Perhaps boring old G-spot is becoming a fashion statement after all.'

'Don't worry,' said Janet, grim-faced. 'I'm on the case. I'm heading that way. The Fat Controller's just summoned me.' Everyone started humming the *Mastermind* theme.

Janet was just musing about what a rotten start to the week it was to have an audience with Harry and his crotch, when she was stopped in her tracks. Geraldine, sitting at her desk outside his office, truly did look like a camouflaged blancmange. The dress was a sort of voluminous purple and pink concoction, wild by anybody's standards, and completely off the Richter scale by Geraldine's.

Steeling herself not to say anything, Janet swept past and into Harry's office. Yet again, she found herself angry that her heart started pounding the minute she crossed the threshold.

'Good news, Bancroft,' Harry crowed, motioning her to sit down and leaning back in the *Mastermind* chair. 'Clinched a good deal. A series of video shorts with Hot Breaks For Heartaches, plus a really whizzy website. They do singles holidays for saddos. They want ten fifteen-minuters on various holidays, mostly the unusual ones that need more of a hard sell. Your team will love it, something to get their teeth into. Murder-mystery weekends, photography weekends, rambling, line dancing, that sort of stuff.'

Why is the bastard telling me all this? thought Janet, as she smiled sweetly at him. It was Janet who had initially gone to see the people at Hot Breaks For Heartaches and persuaded them that they badly needed some promotion work. She had made the contacts and written the pitch. Harry was now so bound up in his own lies, he'd forgotten what had happened and thought he was still talking to the board.

'Are we confining it to the breaks in this country, or are we including some of the foreign stuff, like the two-week watercolour course in Tuscany and the Provençal cookery weekend?' asked Janet sweetly. Not that I know anything about this company, she thought to herself. Like hell!

'Nope,' said Harry, completely missing the irony. 'Sorry, just the UK stuff. Beggars can't be choosers. Anyway, shove off and get your best people on to it.'

Janet rose, picked up the file Harry handed her and made to leave. At the doorway, she turned back with a mischievous look in her eye.

'Oh, by the way, did you know the catering videos turned up?' she said. 'Would you believe, they were *exactly* where we'd left them. Just some confusion along the line. Mind you, I have had a word with the troops about keeping the office tidier. Shouldn't happen again.'

And with that she swept out, colliding with the ever-eavesdropping Geraldine.

'All you people go round at such a rate of knocks,' she tutted.

'Wow, great frock, Geraldine,' Janet replied. 'That's quite a statement.'

She could have been mistaken, but she thought she saw Geraldine blush for the first time. Perhaps there was a pulse beating under there somewhere after all.

Sue and Janet picked a quiet corner of the GX and sat down. They were both starving, and waited impatiently for their broccoli and Stilton soup and fresh bread.

'I've got to tell you this out of the office and it's totally confidential,' said Janet. 'At least the ashtrays probably aren't bugged here.'

'Okay, understood,' said Sue.

Janet outlined Joe and Simon's visit at the weekend and their invention of a secret file on Harry's alleged activities. She then explained her theory that Harry had moved the tapes the night he'd stayed late.

'I hope I wrong-footed him this morning, because I told him the tapes had turned up in exactly the same place after all,' finished Janet.

'How did he react?' asked Sue.

'He shot me a rather strange look, but I was already on my way out and I didn't want to give the game away.'

'So what happens now?'

'Firstly, I want you to tell me that I am not totally paranoid and reading things into all this that don't exist. And secondly, if you say I'm not paranoid—'

'Which you're not. Your theory makes perfect sense to me.'

'Well then, secondly, it occurred to me that if Harry thinks there's a file on him, perhaps we should create one.'

chapter eight

Over the soup, Janet told Sue about Harry's latest trick, passing off the Hot Breaks For Heartaches triumph as his own.

'It's pretty sick-making, isn't it? I find a brand-new client, persuade them they need a campaign, suss out what they can spend, come up with a treatment and a reasonable budget—'

'And then Harry has an attack of instant Alzheimer's, thinks it was all his idea and gets the glory,' finished Sue.

'Yep,' said Janet. 'That's about the size of it. And then of course he has to have a jolly good crow to those poor souls who came up with the idea, about how it's done. It makes me furious.'

'I'll tell you what would make you even more furious,' said Sue.

'Wassat?'

'Maybe this is the source of the holiday freebie rumour. What Ray told me was all based on what he'd overheard when he was delivering the post early morning down the executive corridor. Harry was on the phone with the door slightly open, and he caught a few cryptic words.'

'Cor, Val's in for a treat then,' said Janet. 'Although it's a bit wasted on her. I suppose one sunkissed holiday beach is the same as another if you're blind drunk.'

'Don't forget we're having another blind-drunk evening with her ladyship later this week. We could mention it then.'

'Or not. Maybe Harry's gone all romantic and he's keeping it as a surprise for her,' said Janet. 'If it is a freebie from this holiday company, then he's not likely to sound off about it, is he?'

'Absolutely not.'

'I don't know why, but I have an overwhelming instinct that we should say nothing about this,' said Janet.

'I think you're right,' conceded Sue.

'Now, changing the subject, I thought I might put Liz on to the Hot Breaks project. They specialize in singles holidays, so maybe there's a chance she'd meet a new man. Do you think it's a bit unsubtle? I mean, do you think she'd automatically think that we're trying to sort out her love life?'

'In a word, yes,' said Sue cheerfully. 'Of course she knows damned well we want her to get married and live happily ever after in Mothercare. Subtlety doesn't come into it. And, come to think of it, we haven't been to a good wedding, or even a christening, in ages.'

When Janet got back from lunch, Nina was positively skipping around the office, much to the amusement of Ray.

'I've lost five pounds this weekend, and two inches off my bum,' she announced.

'Marvellous,' said an unimpressed Ray. 'Must be a weight off your behind, I mean, mind.'

'Don't be sarky,' answered Nina. 'Look, this skirt isn't tight any more. I did it all with a seaweed wrap.'

'Fabulous,' replied Ray, as Nina demonstrated her swirling skirt. 'Wouldn't be any good for me, though.'

'Why not?'

'I don't look good in green.'

'Oh gawd, don't be ridiculous, Ray. Now, be honest, does my bum look less big than it did on Friday?'

'Yes, absolutely. In fact I spotted it across the car park this morning,' said Ray, quite truthfully.

'What?' Nina was agitated. 'My bum or the fact that it's a bit smaller?'

'Oh, everything,' said Ray vaguely. Women, he'd never understand them; they were a constant mystery, apart from being expensive, moody and invariably late.

'Do you think Sam will notice?' pursued Nina.

'Bound to,' Ray lied, trying to redeem himself. 'If I can notice the difference from across the car park, Sam will definitely clock it.'

Nina happily skipped off up to Accounts on some bogus excuse to see the object of her desire.

'One day, Ray,' said Janet, 'you will understand why women are so obsessed with their appearance. We're all convinced that one day we'll be the perfect shape, find the perfect outfit that'll make us look like Audrey Hepburn, and then life will be sublime.'

'Who's Audrey Hepburn?' he asked.

'Before your time,' tutted Janet. 'She was an actress, very beautiful, very elegant and very gamine.'

'Gamine for anything?' asked Ray, suddenly interested.

'No, not where you're concerned. She had more class. For a start, she wouldn't have even allowed you to collect her milk bottles dressed in that shirt.'

Ray glanced down at his multicoloured floral number and grinned.

'Does my head look big in this?' he joked, pretending to model in a mirror.

'Yes, and it will become even more swollen by the time I've beaten you senseless with my handbag,' laughed Janet. 'Now bugger off and do some work.'

Janet went off to view a rough cut of the Hartford tourism video Liz had been working on. They sat in the darkened edit suite waiting for the tape to be spooled back to the right time code.

'Will Harry want to view at this stage?' said Liz, trying to keep the wobble out of her voice.

'No, doubt it,' said Janet. 'Look, I know it's none of my business, but you really mustn't get so scared about Harry. God knows, I shake in my shoes sometimes, but he's just a shit, basically. And not even a talented shit at that.'

'Hmm,' said Liz, more than a tad meaningfully. One day, thought Janet, I'll find out what's happened there. One day.

'Now, the good news,' she said out loud, 'is that we've won a contract to produce some short films about various types of holidays.'

'Oh, brilliant,' said Liz, immediately fantasizing about locations from Florence to Florida.

'Sadly, not all that exotic, I'm afraid,' replied Janet. 'What's your line dancing like?'

'Fat Controller calling, Fat Controller calling,' said Janet in mock station announcer voice. 'Don't worry, Liz. He just wants to thank you for the Hartford tourism video. No hidden agenda, just savour the moment. He likes what you did. Most of the time he thinks we're all pond life. This is our rare chance to surface.'

'I can't go in there,' Liz mumbled, close to tears. Ashen

66

and shaking, she fumbled for her handbag under the desk.

'Look, I'll come with you if you like,' soothed Janet. 'He's only a great big fat chauvinist bully. Nothing more than that.'

'I don't care what you say, I won't go in there. Anyway, I've got a splitting headache, I must go home.' And with that, Liz picked up her bags and made for the door.

Janet steeled herself to go up to Harry's office.

'Where's Liz?' barked Harry, hardly looking up from the report he was reading.

'Gone home with a splitting headache,' said Janet. Was she imagining it, or was he not the least bit surprised? Perhaps she was reading more into this than met the eye.

'Women's problems, I suppose,' he growled. 'All you women are the same, you and your bloody PMT.'

'That's not very PC, Harry.'

'I don't give a bugger about being PC. The only PC I'm vaguely interested in comes in boxes from PC World. And that's a world away from you lot and your stupid girlie problems. You specialize in messing us all around by getting pregnant, and then it's full speed ahead for the Big Skive.'

'Big Skive? What on earth do you mean?' asked Janet, feeling herself beginning to boil.

'Relaxation classes, time off for a scan, oh I feel sick every day and I might just throw up over my desk, the baby could arrive at any time, and then I must have a nice big chunk of maternity leave while the rest of you do all the work.'

'Well, seeing as I've never had children, this sort of chat is wasted on me,' said Janet, wondering how on earth they had managed to reach such a thorny subject so quickly. She thought of all the women, like Liz and Nina, with so much to offer, who'd give up everything to become a mum if they got half a chance.

'Excuse me, but where do the chaps stand in all this?' she enquired. 'I seem to recall Loopy Liam taking absolutely yonks off because his girlfriend had left him.'

'Exactly my point,' said Harry, thumping the desk as he always did to emphasize a point. 'Liam had a breakdown, perfectly understandable.'

'Crystal clear to me,' Janet muttered, half under her breath. 'So your girlfriend pushing off ranks higher than the trauma of bringing a new life into the world.'

As she walked back to her office, she realized that Harry hadn't even mentioned the Hartford tourism video, let alone thanked her and Liz for all the work they'd put in.

Liz had meant what she said. She'd gone home for the day. Janet's chat with her about her role in the new Hot Breaks series would have to wait until tomorrow.

Janet went back to her desk, where the e-mails were piling up thick and fast. She was still wading through the morning's post when Sue called up from reception.

'Don't forget we're going out with Val on Friday,' said Sue. 'She's booked some new Mexican place down on the waterfront. It's had fantastic reviews.'

'In that case, let's enjoy it for the first and last time,' said Janet. 'Once they've seen Val in action, you can be certain there won't be a reprise.'

'Talking of which,' Sue lowered her voice conspiratorially, 'have you thought any more about keeping a file on Harry? I think you should, you know, just dates and times and short accounts of each horror story.'

'Oh, I dunno,' replied Janet. 'A bit of me knows that I should, but there's another bit of me that's ridiculously loyal to Val and therefore Harry. Crazy though it sounds, I don't like all that scurrying-behind-your-back stuff. I'd rather be upfront. If I'm going to be unpleasant to Harry, then I'd rather do it to his face.'

'I'd like to do something to his face,' said Sue ruefully.

It was eleven o'clock and Val was still in bed, contemplating the empty hours ahead. A fashion preview at Ginette, an exclusive boutique in Hartford, was proving very tempting. Val liked to be ahead of the game in the fashion stakes. Her wardrobe bore the battle scars of that particular illness. Pashminas in every colour, quilted Chanel bags, Fendi baguettes and bowling bags, Jimmy Choo spiky heels; anything that had a waiting list was on Val's wanted list. She had to have that cachet of leading where others followed. And that included ruthlessly marching it all down to the charity shop the moment it was copied on the high street. Val thought of it as merely recycling. No wonder the boutiques always invited her to their previews; she was such a good customer. Val didn't do sales, and couldn't understand why anyone would want to. 'End of the season', 'reduced', 'special purchase', these were alien concepts.

She picked up the phone and rang an old school friend, Charlotte.

'Is Mummy there?' she asked the small voice who answered the phone. After a long pause, a very harassed Charlotte came to the phone.

'Hi, Charlie, it's Val. Listen, I'm going to a preview at Ginette today. Fancy coming out to play?'

'I'd adore to but I've got Henry down with chicken pox, the nanny's just given in her notice and a man's coming to repair the tumble dryer.'

'Oh, bugger,' said Val, wincing at the screams of small children in the background. 'I really felt like a girlies' day out. Never mind, I'll give Susie a call.'

Susie was another old school chum. She'd recently married a chap who did something whizzy in the City and so far was a kids-free zone. She might be available.

Susie's answering machine immediately diverted to her mobile.

'Hi, it's Val. Where are you?'

'Working, darling.'

'Working?'

'Yes, working, sweetie. You know, that thing where you do stuff and they pay you. I'm in this really, really boring office answering the phone and causing chaos.'

'I thought George had promised to love, honour and keep you in Vivienne Westwood?'

'Yeah, so did I,' said Susie. 'Didn't last long, did it? It's not going so well for George at the moment. He didn't get the bonus he'd hoped for. So I've got to work. Dreary, isn't it?' She paused, and Val could hear the click of a lighter and then Susie taking the first big drag.

'Shame, darling. I'd hoped you'd come to a preview at Ginette. We could have had such fun—'

'Oh, for fuck's sake, what kind of place is this!' Susie had suddenly turned her attention away from the phone and was now talking to someone in the office. Voices were raised. 'I didn't realize I'd boarded the ark. No-smoking policy? How can anyone manage that? How totally bloody ridiculous. Oh, Val, are you still there? Did you hear that? Ridiculous, I have to go outside for a fag. Anyway, hon, can't come to the preview. Joined the working bloody classes. Might as well go and put a flat cap on and join them for a fag break.'

Val tried two more old school friends without success. One was away in Italy, according to her housekeeper, and the other was apparently being induced with her third child.

She felt a familiar wave of loneliness sweep over her. Why couldn't she rustle anyone up to go to the preview? What a sad person she'd become. She went downstairs to the kitchen and opened the fridge. A glass of chilled white wine, just to cheer me up, because I deserve it, she thought. And then perhaps another.

Most of the bottle and a packet of cigarettes later, she climbed into her MR2 and drove to Ginette for the preview.

'I know you can do this,' Janet was telling Liz. 'You're long overdue to take more control on a project, and I think this is the perfect one. Especially as you're on a roll after the HOT tourism video. It was a great piece of work.'

Liz sat at her desk, stony-faced.

'Hey, listen, this is a promotion,' pursued Janet. 'You're supposed to be leaping about in excitement. I might be able to get you a decent pay rise after this.'

Still Liz said nothing.

'It's Harry, isn't it?' said Janet. 'Well, whether we like it or not, he's part of the deal here. We go to interesting places, meet interesting people and flog ourselves making interesting videos. The offices aren't bad, the crews know some good jokes, and even the canteen's pasta is sometimes al dente. The only down side is Harry. Every silver lining has a cloud, you know, and ours is the Fat Führer.'

'Look,' said Liz at long last, her voice wavering. 'I'd like to produce the series. I really would. But I'd have to do it without him knowing, if you understand. I don't want any dealings, or any hassle, with him. So could I produce the series but we not tell him? Just pretend that you're doing it.'

'That's the oddest request I've ever heard,' replied Janet, completely flummoxed. 'But if it makes you happy, then fine. You make the programmes, I'll deal with Harry. But sooner or later he'll find out. Sooner or later you'll have to deal with him, unless by chance he leaves the company.'

'Huh! There's about as much chance of Harry leaving as a one-legged man winning an arse-kicking competition.'

'True, but it's a gorgeous thought, though,' Janet grinned. 'Also, if Harry left, we wouldn't have ordeals like Friday night to put up with either.'

'Friday?' asked Liz.

'Our night out with Val. Sue keeps reminding me. We're all booked in at the new Mexican place on the waterfront. It's supposed to be wonderful.'

'No evening's ever wonderful with Val,' said Liz, cheering up visibly as the conversation veered away from Harry. 'Merely eventful. Anyway, one last query. Did you put me on the holiday series in the faint hope I'd meet some new man?'

'Never crossed my mind,' said Janet, unconvincingly.

'Hmm, just as I thought,' replied Liz, laughing. 'I don't hold out much hope of meeting Mr Right at a line-dancing seminar or a patchwork sesh.'

'Keep an open mind. At least he'd be good on his feet or handy with his fingers.'

Another fashion mission safely accomplished, Val left the Ginette boutique laden down with carrier bags containing two shift dresses, a fantastic sparkly cocktail number and all the shoes and bags to match. She'd wear one of the dresses when she took the girls out the following night. Pity they weren't in the right pay league for Ginette's fabulous stuff.

Back home, Val threw open the front door and chucked her bags down in the huge polished oak hallway. Plenty of time to hide them away before Harry came back from work. He was away so much these days, or working late, he never noticed what she wore anyway, so why worry. If she'd answered the door naked he'd still have shouted about the importance of having his dinner on the table. The jolly effect of the champagne at Ginette had now worn off. Time for a top-up, she thought, heading for the kitchen to grab a glass of wine. Also, while the coast was clear, she could put some of the empties and the Ginette carrier bags into black bin liners.

Thursday blurred into Friday. Val awoke with a hangover, trying to focus on the alarm clock. Shit, it was past midday. Loads to do.

She crawled out of bed to run a bath. There was the gym, her reflexologist, a manicure and then the hairdresser's, and she had to get them all done by six o'clock. Good job I can organize myself, she mused, unlike the silly HOT girls, who never made the best of themselves.

Damn her old school friends for being too busy to turn out for the fashion show. Damn the HOT girls for being too poor to turn out for the fashion show. And damn everyone for her having to go alone. It wasn't quite such fun on your own. Nobody to swank to.

Still, she'd give the girls a treat tonight at the new Mexican restaurant. They'd probably been looking forward to it all week, whereas for her it was just another meal she didn't have the bother of cooking. Better have a glance through the papers to find out what was happening in the world, so she could at least follow what they'd all inevitably be rabbiting on about.

Val couldn't admit, even to herself, that the girls from HOT were now increasingly the only company she had.

'How much longer do we have to endure this?' said Nina to the assembled group in the canteen. 'When will it dawn on her that we only go because she asks us and because she pays and because she's the boss's wife?'

'If it was going to dawn on her, it would have done so quite a few mornings ago,' said Liz. 'I personally hate these evenings so much I wish I could wriggle out of them, but I feel I'd be letting you lot down if I didn't go.'

'God, we are all a pathetic lot,' said Janet. 'Let's call this thing what it really is. It's not guilt, pity or sticking up for each other; it's job preservation. And there's nothing wrong with that. Or put it another way, an evening out in a decent restaurant, leaving aside the spectacle and the insults, is another way of making up our salaries. And keeping our jobs.'

'You're right,' chipped in Sue, bringing a tray of coffee over to their table. 'But I think it's time we started to make subtle changes to the way we behave towards her. Instead of taking all the drunken insults on the chin, or listening to fictitious accounts of each other's love lives every time someone goes to the loo, I think we should bite back a little. Just give as good as you get. If she insults you, then lob one back.'

'Bit difficult when you're two stone overweight with a big bum and no prospect of reducing it, and she's an ex-model with a stick-insect figure plus a monthly clothes allowance that's probably five times my mortgage,' said Nina bitterly.

'She can be Claudia Schiffer, Elizabeth Taylor and Mata Hari all rolled into one for all I care,' said Janet. 'The woman's bloody rude and that ain't pretty.'

'It's time we put up a fight,' said Sue. 'She'd be a better person for it in the long run. If she starts up her nonsense tonight, bite back. See what happens.'

Over coffee, the four women fell into the usual discussion about how long it would take for Val to get drunk, insult the waiters and fall over. Modest bets were placed.

chapter nine

Que Pasa?, the new Mexican restaurant, was heaving. It was so packed with animated diners making huge dents in their pay packets that the relentless salsa music was effectively reduced to a subliminal murmur. The restaurant was lit by a mass of different-coloured Tiffany lamps over the tables, reflected by huge mirrors on the walls. Waiters in long starched white aprons negotiated the tables, holding trays above their heads with dishes balanced precariously.

Val instantly hated it. She liked exclusive places where she could be the centre of attention. This was a mistake.

Janet, on the other hand, breathed a sigh of relief. In a place this busy, this noisy, Val and her antics would be a mere blip on the screen. She sipped a glass of mineral water, grateful that she was wearing a strappy summer dress, because with all those bodies and a rather thundery May night outside, it was steaming. She glanced around the table. Liz and Nina were looking as relieved as she was that there was so much distraction. Sue was politely having a conversation with Val, nodding in all the right places but clearly bored out of her skull. She kept firing 'please rescue me' arrows at the others, but they took no notice and just smiled sweetly back.

'Unusual for you to be showing a bit of cleavage,' said Val, glancing disdainfully at Janet as she lit a cigarette. 'You should think about investing in a minimizer bra. Makes such a difference if you're a bit top-heavy.' Val, of course, being an ex-model and still catwalk-thin, had virtually no boobs at all.

'Actually, I think Janet looks terrific,' interrupted Sue. 'Sorry, Val, but you're a bit off the mark on that one. Cleavage is cool this summer. I read in the *Mail* only today that breasts are being worn big this year. So it must be true.'

'Absolutely,' said Liz. 'If you've got it, flaunt it. I only wish I had it.' Liz, tall and willowy, could eat anything and never put on a pound, much to the mock disgust of the others.

But Val wasn't listening to any of this. Unbeknown to them, she was now well into her second bottle of wine, having already drunk one at home just to get herself in the mood for the evening.

'Of course you really should think about your colour before you display that amount of flesh, Janet,' she ploughed on. 'You should give serious thought to some regular sun-bed sessions. Get rid of that pale skin.'

Janet bristled. Liz and Nina bristled. Sue smiled across at Janet and winked as if to say 'go for it'.

'Absolutely *not* on the agenda,' announced Janet.

Val looked startled. No one ever questioned her advice on clothes, hair or make-up. Ever.

'Don't tell me you're hoping to be pale and interesting,' sighed Val as she began rifling through a very small crocodile clutch bag. 'I must fish out a card from my beauty salon for you. They're not the cheapest in town, but you get what you pay for. A few sessions would really make a difference.'

She handed over a card and snapped the bag shut again.

'On the contrary,' said Janet, taking the card without glancing at it, 'far too risky. I wouldn't touch one of those sun beds with a disinfected barge pole. And apart from the danger of skin cancer, a tan is definitely out. It's really dated. Pale is the new brown.'

It took Val a few seconds to assimilate all this. Suddenly her beauty empire's foundations were beginning to feel decidedly rocky.

'Absolutely right, Janet,' chipped in Nina. 'I love the new look, I'm going for it myself. You can wear so many marvellous colours if you're pale. Also, you don't have to walk around slapping grease on all the time to stop your skin flaking. And of course you don't end up with a hide like an old crocodile handbag.'

'Well, sweetie, this one's hardly old, and it cost more than you probably earn in a month,' hissed Val, tapping her bag. 'Anyway, are you still trying to get it together with that ghastly bloke in Accounts? What's his name, Sam?' The wine was really beginning to hit the spot. She took another enormous gulp.

'Only a question of time,' said Janet promptly, before Nina could reply. 'Sam's mad for Nina. He's just plucking up the courage to ask her out.'

'I very much doubt it,' continued Val, now really riled. 'Nobody'd want to go out with the London Derrière, would they?'

Despite the noise, the music and the frantic bustle of the restaurant, an immediate and dreadful silence descended around the table. Nina, initially puzzled at the nickname, looked quickly around at the others. Their downcast looks made her realize they knew exactly who

Val was referring to. As if the comments about Sam weren't bad enough, to find that her bum was the butt of office jokes was just too much. Tears welling up, she picked up her handbag and fled to the loo.

Val, even in her alcoholic daze, sensed she'd gone too far. She called imperiously to the waiters for dessert menus.

'Hate this place,' she proclaimed in just about everybody's earshot. 'Full of plebs and people who don't wash under their armpits. I expect they all enjoy snooker and Stella Artois. We'll go somewhere decent next time. Get out your diaries, girls.'

Without responding, Sue got up and left the table in search of Nina, while Janet and Liz had an attack of convenient deafness and pretended to be completely preoccupied with the dessert menus. Val was left high and dry, having issued an invitation that had been ignored by all.

'More wine,' she shrieked to a passing waiter. 'And take these ghastly plates away.' The waiter gathered up the plates, aware that a tip was now about as likely as him winning a lottery rollover.

Oh no, here we go again, thought Janet; cue insults about Sue and Nina.

'Of course, Sue's aged,' paused Val, 'so well. Amazing for her age, especially after having those ghastly kids. It's only a question of time, though.'

'Time, though, what?' asked Janet.

'Till she finds out,' said Val, viciously.

'Finds out what?'

'Oh come on, Janet, till she finds out her husband's bored and is having an affair.'

'Don't be ridiculous. Sue's one of the most happily married people I know. And so's her husband. The entire world's dog population would have to stray before it would even cross Jon's mind. Look, Val, it may come as a shock, but some people value what they have and are prepared to work at it.' She just stopped herself from adding 'unlike you' to the end of the sentence.

Val shot her a mutinous look and took another huge slug of wine.

'Well, you mark my words,' she snarled, lighting a cigarette.

'Rubbish, Val. If you haven't anything good to say, shut up.' Janet pulled herself up short. She could be talking herself into getting the sack at this rate if she wasn't careful. She deliberately changed the subject.

'Anyway, Val, have you booked anywhere nice for a holiday this year?' She smiled sweetly. God, she sounded like her own hairdresser.

'No,' said Val, rather abruptly. 'In fact, that subject's a bit of a sore point. Harry has to go away soon to some conference, and I bet it's somewhere interesting. The bastard won't take me. I've got to hang on until September when we go the Maldives again.'

'That'll be nice,' said Janet enviously. 'It'll soon be September. Not long to wait.'

'It bloody is,' said Val, in a rage again. 'And anyway, I'm fed up with the Maldives. I get so bored kicking around at home. And Harry's always bloody working. How many hours do they expect? He's rarely home before nine. Perhaps it's my cooking.'

'I didn't think you did any cooking,' said Janet, mentally starting to take notes.

'Well, I can open packets and use a microwave, just like the next person, but it's not really my thing. Mummy always had a cook, so I never saw the need.'

'You could learn, take classes.'

'Don't be ridiculous,' said Val, tossing her head defiantly. 'Harry married glamour, not a galley slave.'

'Anyway, what's this conference Harry's going to?' Janet probed gently.

'No idea, not interested, but it's coming up soon. I thought I might move back home with Mummy and Daddy for the week. Live in a decent house for a change, with proper staff. Anyway, here comes Nina now. I think I might put her in touch with my personal trainer. Get some exercises sorted to shift that derrière. Do you think she'd be offended?'

'Yes,' said Janet. 'Definitely.'

'Good,' said Val, not listening. 'I'll dig out his phone number for her tomorrow.'

Sue and Nina reached the table through the throng and sat down again.

'No desserts,' bellowed Val at them all. 'Too many calories. Just coffee.' With that, she waved again to a passing waiter. But the wine had taken control. Her flailing arm caught an almost full bottle of red wine, which promptly toppled, spilling its contents all over the table. The wine began trickling into their laps. Val, already on her feet to avoid the drips, stalked off to the loo, leaving the others to mop up as best they could before a posse of waiters bearing towels converged on their table.

'I am *not* doing this again,' said Janet, quietly, white with rage. 'So help me, I am not doing it again. I don't care any more that she's the boss's wife. She's a monster. I give you notice that I will invent excuses, I will enter a convent, I will even appear on *Supermarket Sweep*. But I will not do this again.'

'Agreed,' replied Sue, relieved that an end was in sight. 'Let's meet next week, just the four of us, and work out how to knock this ridiculous scenario on the head.'

'Good idea,' said Nina, her eyes smeared black from sobbing in the loo. Waterproof mascara had claimed another victim. When you want to remove it, you need a chisel. When you don't, it smears everywhere.

Janet fished in her handbag for a pen and paper. As usual, this ended up involving a systematic turnout of kit. Janet, being a practical soul, never went anywhere without her filofax, camera, spare film, sewing kit, super-glue and two bunches of keys, most of which she hadn't used for years. Then there was make-up, purse and a plethora of pens, receipts and business cards.

'I swear this handbag's haunted,' she muttered, turfing the contents out on the table. 'I'm sure it's my mother at work.'

'I thought your mum was dead,' said Sue, puzzled.

'She is, but she comes back to haunt me. My mother adored handbags. She'd have happily taken root in the bag department at John Lewis. I'm sure she rearranges things in my bags so I can't find them. I know she's watch-ing over me, because when I can't find something, I think of her. She was exactly the same. Buy my ma one of those organizer bags with lots of handy little pockets, and she'd lose everything. Sadly, this is now my inheritance.'

'Quick, put that away,' said Sue urgently, nodding in the direction of Janet's filofax. Val had emerged from the loo and was heading back to the table, a little unsteady on her feet. Waiters hovered, unsure of what she might do next.

Janet hastily stuffed the filofax back into her bag. She still hadn't found a pen.

'Let's meet this time next week,' whispered Sue. 'And definitely no Val on the agenda.'

'Lovely evening,' slurred Val expansively, flopping back on to her seat. 'I'm sure you must all look forward to our little get-togethers.'

Before any awkward silence could follow, Val conveniently filled in the gap herself, losing her balance on the seat and falling backwards on to the next table, clutching the cloth as she went. Diners ducked for cover as chairs, bottles, glasses and dinner plates went flying, scattering their contents like machine-gun fire in all directions.

For the second time that evening, Janet, Nina, Sue and Liz were mopped down by apologetic waiters, along with the next-door-table diners, who were none too amused to discover that their outfits were now spattered with refried beans and jalapeño peppers.

As usual, Val managed to emerge unscathed. Her new lilac Ginette shift dress did not catch a single drop of the low-flying goo. She tutted loudly as everyone else was sponged down, and then made a huge performance about insisting on picking up the bill for the neighbouring table's dinner. The salsa music was suddenly cranked up several notches to distract attention from the ongoing drama.

'A challenge for Stain Devils then,' said Liz, trying to control her anger. 'This lot'll never come out.' She was wearing a cream linen dress and jacket to match that she'd planned to wear to a wedding later that month. Now patterned with red wine and the remains of someone's nachos, it would have made the perfect outfit for the grand opening of an abattoir.

Janet, Sue, Nina and Liz made their way towards the exit, feeling very conspicuous and very stupid. Val, as usual, strutted along like a peacock, looking as immaculate as ever. However, as she reached the small cloakroom by the exit, she started swaying precariously, before completely losing her balance, only managing to stay upright by pulling down a coat stand, complete with a dozen or so jackets and brollies. Once more, waiters rushed in her direction, now mightily fed up with all the problems she was causing. There hadn't been so much food flying since Hartford Players' last Christmas panto.

chapter ten

Harry was sitting smugly at his desk. He'd had a good weekend, all in all. Val had been compliant for once, and he'd spent Sunday morning giving her a serious shagging. She'd also not hit the roof when he'd again mentioned a conference he might be going to. That was unlike Val, he mused; she normally went berserk if he went anywhere interesting and didn't take her. Instead, she seemed to be relishing the idea of a few days in Hampshire with her parents.

'Geraldine,' he bellowed, 'coffee and the Hot Breaks file. Now.'

Geraldine, now firmly back in beige because it was raining, scuttled in with the file and then out again to fetch the coffee.

Harry leaned back in his seat and lit a cigar. He flipped through the file and had a think. This was a big project and he was determined to get it right.

'Get that Bancroft woman in here,' he demanded, as Geraldine reappeared with a cafetière, cup and saucer.

'Harry, I hope you don't mind me saying, but you're not supposed to smoke,' said Geraldine nervously.

'Yeah,' said Harry, still preoccupied with the file.

'It might set off the smoke detectives,' said Geraldine.

'That should give the girls a thrill!' He roared with laughter.

Mystified at his remark, Geraldine went round the office, opened a window and scuttled out again. Harry smiled to himself. Even he had heard the jokes about Geraldine's famous G-spots. But on the plus side, she was fiercely loyal and kept her mouth firmly shut. That, to Harry, was worth its weight in gold. He was also aware that she wasn't exactly the most popular person within the company, keeping herself very much to herself. He liked that too, because as he saw it, it enhanced his power base.

'Ah, Janet, come in, sit down,' he shouted, stubbing out his cigar with venom. Janet reluctantly took up her usual vantage point opposite Harry's crotch.

'I've been thinking about the Hot Breaks project,' he said. 'Might bring in a big shot on this one. I know your lot have their hearts set on it, but you've got to keep that department running with all the other ongoing jobs. Decided I'm going to put a heavyweight on this one.'

'You mean a bloke,' said Janet, trying to keep the bitterness out of her voice.

'Yep. Had a chat with Steven Byfield last week. He recommended a real hotshot with an impressive track record. Might get him down for a chat.'

Steven Byfield was Janet's predecessor. He'd left HOT to go up north to a plum job back in his home town. He'd gone by the time Janet had joined the company, but she'd got the impression that he was well liked. Since then, staff turnover in the production department had been so great that no one from Steven's era remained.

Harry was relishing this. He loved undermining Janet, and this was a perfect opportunity.

'Steven was a great operator here, well respected, good motivator, great loss to the company. So if he says this guy's good, then he probably is.'

'When are you interviewing him?' said Janet, trying not to sound disappointed.

'I'm meeting him for lunch,' smirked Harry. 'Once I've talked through the project with him and sorted out a contract, I'll introduce you.'

'Sounds like it's done and dusted then,' said Janet.

'Yep, more or less. I've heard what this chap's worked on and it's serious stuff. Give your lot a kick up the backside, won't it?'

'Well, they won't exactly be ecstatic when they hear,' said Janet resignedly. 'More underwhelmed, I'd say. There was a lot of competition over who'd get to work on this one. But we'll give this chap a warm welcome and of course I'll put my best researchers on to it.'

'Good, good.' Harry leered at her. 'Now bugger off and get some work done.'

He sat back in amusement as he watched her leave the office. Yes, it was all going well. His thoughts went back to the weekend and his Sunday-morning session with Val. She'd even managed to cook something half decent, even though he had found the Marks and Spencer cartons in the bin afterwards. Might buy the silly cow some flowers on the way home tonight.

What Harry didn't know, of course, was that Val had had a rare attack of remorse about Friday night's scenario in the Mexican restaurant. She'd woken on Saturday morning with a whopping hangover and realized for once that she had behaved badly. She vaguely recalled colliding with a table and food showering everywhere. Eventually she'd ferreted in her bag and found a Visa receipt for over seven hundred pounds. That confirmed that she'd paid not only for the girls, but also for the table next door. Oh well, an evening to remember, she shrugged. But there was still a nagging doubt, as she stared at the bleary face in the bathroom mirror, that she'd somehow upset someone. So she tried to make it up by being nice to Harry.

While Harry was sitting in his office, relishing the wheeling and dealing he was planning, for Val the week ahead stretched out like an interminable sea of boredom. She'd eventually got up and had a coffee over daytime telly, but now what? She could ring a girlfriend and meet for lunch, but she was still stung by all the rejections last week. Even if any of them were free, the talk was all babies these days. Val didn't know the price of Pampers and had no intention of finding out.

She poured herself a glass of wine and flipped through her address book, trying to find an old school friend who was child-free. Page after page indicated familiar names with new ones scribbled next to them, changes of surname on marriage plus children's names as they arrived. One or two already had husbands' names crossed out. They were the least fun because their sole topic of conversation was custody battles and the cost of their lawyers. It all boiled down to Susie again, the friend whose husband's City job hadn't quite lived up to expectations.

'She's on a fag break, love,' said a cockney voice. 'She'll ring you back.'

At least she hasn't been fired, thought Val, recalling their last conversation. She poured another glass of wine and painted her nails as she waited for the call.

'Val, it's Susie. Brilliant of you to ring, sweetie. Let's meet for lunch. One o'clock. Somewhere nearby. I only get an hour.' She rang off abruptly.

Thank God I don't have to put up with that shit, mused Val as she got ready to go out. She put on one of her new shift dresses from Ginette. Pale blue, with a soft cashmere cardie and suede spiky heels to match.

An hour later she was nursing a large glass of wine in a little French brasserie just round the corner from Susie's office. Susie came in, shaking the rain off her trenchcoat and umbrella.

'You look wonderful as always,' she said, taking in Val's outfit. 'Can tell you don't work, sweetie.'

'How's that?' queried Val, lighting a cigarette.

'You wouldn't be able to walk from the nearest car park to my office in those heels,' she laughed. 'Listen, darling, I've joined the Dark Ages. It's bloody archaic. People ring up, they get stroppy, you have to be nice to them, it's ghastly.'

'What do you do there?' said Val, taking menus from a waiter.

'Market research, you know, that stuff where women in sensible shoes hang around on street corners and pounce on you with questions about custard powder.'

'You don't have to do that, do you?' Val was appalled.

'No, thank God. I just answer the phone and help collate the reports. Anyway, let's order quickly, because I have to be back on the dot of two. Pasta's fine for me,' she added, glancing quickly at the menu.

'God, it sounds like school again,' said Val.

'Not far off. I wish now I'd paid more attention to maths and typing. I was more keen on learning how to arrange flowers and how to get in and out of a sports car. Didn't think I'd ever need all that other stuff.'

'How long are you going to do this for?' asked Val. 'What's happened to George's job?'

'Well, basically he missed out on a big promotion, and then they cut his bonus because he buggered up some deal, so it effectively halved his salary. And we'd just taken out a huge mortgage.'

'So what does that mean?'

'It means, sweetie, that we have to sell the house.'

'But don't your earnings help a bit?'

'Hey, Val, get real. I earn diddly-squat, but it might at least help to pay for the solicitor.'

'Solicitor? For the house sale?'

'No, sweetie, for the divorce.'

Before they could continue, two waiters arrived bearing a huge steaming bowl of pasta, which they proceeded to ladle out with great aplomb. This was followed by a bit of show-biz with a huge phallic pepper mill. They then hovered, topping up wine glasses and hoping to pick up the threads of what sounded like an interesting conversation.

Val had to wave them firmly away before Susie could continue.

'Divorce. Yes, the D-word. Isn't it frightfully grown-up?'

'No, it's awful. I'm really sorry. It only seems last week I was in Jasper Conran, drinking champagne at your wedding.'

'Last summer, actually. After George cocked up at work, I went off him in a big way. We ended up not speaking, just shagging.'

'Bit like me and Harry.'

'Don't tell me yours is on the rocks too. I've got this marvellous solicitor, I'll find you his card.' Susie started to fish in her handbag.

'No, it's not got to that. In fact, I've never even thought about it. No, Harry and me, we're all right really. Probably because he's not there much. In fact, he's off to some conference at the end of the month and I'm quite looking forward to having the place to myself.'

'I've always thought he was a bit of a bully,' said Susie, offering Val a cigarette, then taking one herself and lighting them both. 'But there again, perhaps it's just the age gap. What's the difference between you two?'

'Twelve years.'

'At least he's in a good job. And you're not losing your house.'

The waiters were back, scooping up the hardly touched plates and bringing cappuccinos.

'I'm really sorry it's got to this,' said Val. 'But you don't seem all that upset.'

'No, I'm not, am I?' said Susie, cheerfully. 'I'm having an affair with my boss.'

'Bad news,' said Janet to Liz as they sat down to a coffee in the staff canteen. 'Harry's hiring in some whizz-kid to produce the Hot Breaks series,' she said apologetically. 'I feel awful now because I had hoped you could have had a big role in that. I know you wanted to keep it a bit low-key but you were really ready for this. There will be a next time, I promise, if I have anything to do with it.'

'Honestly, Janet, I'm rather relieved. You know my thoughts on the subject. I just didn't want to be in Harry's firing line. I'd much rather take a more secondary role.'

Janet stirred her coffee thoughtfully. 'I think you'll be the only person on the planet who will look at it that way. Lots of people in the department wanted to have a crack at that. Let's see what this new chap is like. Harry's insistent that I put the best people on to the series under him. So you're still in the frame as associate producer if you don't mind, plus I thought I'd give Bob and Nick a go.'

'Good idea,' said Liz. Bob and Nick were two fairly new researchers who were already making their mark as budding workaholics.

'That's settled then,' said Janet, getting up to go. 'Let the excrement hit the ventilation.'

Janet was right. There was uproar about Harry hiring in a producer on what everyone saw as a prestige project. The whingeing went on all week until she had to call an impromptu meeting and put a stop to it.

'Whether we like it or not,' she announced, 'Harry's the boss and what he says goes. I know we all think it's unfair, but moaning and groaning won't make any difference. I too would like to have played a more key role, but Harry's keeping this one close to his chest. So just accept it and get on with your work. Paul Burns is the new producer/director Harry's hired and he arrives on Monday. So I don't want any rubbish from any of you. We will make him welcome, we will be helpful, we will be cheerful. If he's as good as I'm led to believe, then we will all learn from him. A lot. He has a very impressive CV.

'Now, Liz will be associate producer on this project, and Nick and Bob will be the researchers. Wish them luck and shut up. This isn't *Stars in Their Eyes*, this is real life.'

chapter eleven

Friday night at Janet's was to be the council of war on Val. It was a week on from the disastrous Mexican evening, and the clothes worn that night were still going back and forth to the dry cleaner's in an attempt to shift the stains.

'Come scruffy,' Janet had insisted. 'I'll light candles so you'll all look marvellous if you're too tired to tart up. I'm warning you now, I can't be bothered to cook, so it'll be an Indian takeaway and a pudding out of a box.'

They all sat comfortably around the table, scooping up the last of the lamb korma with chapattis, swished down with cans of Bud.

'We have to find a way of stopping this restaurant lark without inciting anything,' said Sue, opening the bidding. 'We could fob Val off by each of us not being available on different dates, so she could never sort out an evening.'

'But that's only a temporary measure,' said Nina. 'I think we've got to be more brutal than that. I think someone should just tell her to her face.'

'What?' said Janet. 'Something like "We all hate you, Val, your stupid evenings and you falling down drunk." I'm sure she'd appreciate that.'

'Well, I don't appreciate what she called me,' said Nina,

still deeply upset at the discovery of her nickname. 'I've felt a complete berk all week. I think everyone's staring at my bum and laughing. I've lost all confidence and I blame Val.'

'She didn't make it up, though,' pointed out Janet.

'No, but at least I wouldn't have found out about it if she'd kept her stupid gob shut.'

Nina was close to tears again. Sue moved the conversation on swiftly.

'I think we should look at the root of the problem,' she said. 'Now, we could say it's Val's drink problem, we could say it's because she's lonely, and we could say it's because she's spoiled. But I think we have to go further back than that to the real root of the problem. And that's Harry. Harry's the reason she's lonely. He's never there. Harry's the reason she drinks. If he treats her like he treats people at work, then she has every reason to get pissed.'

'But she doesn't have every reason to be rude and insulting to us,' chipped in Nina.

'Well, that's drink talking, but also she's been very protected,' said Sue. 'She's come from a privileged background. Mum and Dad have pots of money, she's been to a posh school, she's done a bit of modelling so she's used to turning heads. But now she's married to Harry and she's met an even bigger ego on a stick.'

The others nodded in agreement. More beer was produced. Several slurps on, Sue continued.

'What we need to do is tackle Harry, and that's difficult, because he's not just her husband, he's our boss.'

'Our problems would be solved overnight if Harry left the company,' said Janet thoughtfully. 'If Harry jumped or was pushed, our lives would be sublime. Well, almost.'

Sue took a deep breath and surveyed the others.

'I don't know whether I should tell you this.' She looked suddenly troubled. 'It's more than my job's worth, but there again my job's not worth much as far as Harry's concerned.'

'Well, go on.' Three pairs of eyes bored into her.

Sue realized there was no turning back. She coughed and fiddled with her beer can, hoping the spotlight would be turned off. The three pairs of eyes continued to bore.

'Okay, I'll tell you. It's only a theory, it's just a suspicion, a gut feeling, but you get a real sense of people's characters when you sit at that reception desk and take their phone calls or pass on their messages. Watch them go in and out of the building.'

'Yes, go on,' the three pairs of eyes urged.

'Well, things don't quite match up,' said Sue, choosing her words carefully. 'Harry's up to something. He leaves the office bang on six, but he doesn't always go straight home. If I work a late shift, I occasionally get a call from Val, usually a bit pissed, surprise, surprise, asking where Harry is. Say nine o'clock. So what does he do in those three hours?'

'He might be going out for dinner with a client,' said Janet. 'That's perfectly feasible.'

'No, wrong body language,' said Sue. 'When you sit at that desk long enough, you spot it. Someone leaving the building *after* work moves in a very different way to someone leaving the building to do *more* work.'

'My God, you could give Desmond Morris a run for his money,' said Liz in awe.

'If he's out late, why doesn't Val just ring him on his mobile?' asked Nina.

'Good question,' said Sue. 'When Val rings the office in the evening, she's already tried him on his mobile and it's

95

switched off. Always. That's why she rings. Now, during the day, Harry's a mobile phone-aholic. He's got the damn thing permanently clamped to his ear. Two rings max and he answers. But not during this mysterious three hours between six and nine. It is always switched off. Out of curiosity I even tried it myself the last time Val rang. I thought she might just be too pissed to get the number punched in, but she was right. It was switched off.'

'So, a secret woman,' mused Janet. 'I must say, I never suspected that. Not with a head-turner like Val in tow.'

'I haven't said that,' grinned Sue, who was now beginning to enjoy the limelight. 'But here's another thing. If his and Geraldine's direct lines are busy or they're both away from their desks, their calls get diverted to the switchboard. And just occasionally a woman phones for Harry. Distinctive voice, slight Italian accent. Again, when you do my job, you tend to pick up on voices.'

'What happens when she rings him?' asked Janet.

'If I can't put her through, she never leaves a message, nor a number to call. Never.'

'So what else do you sense?' asked Janet. 'Come on, Sue, you're on a roll here. Trot it all out.'

'Well, this rumour about the freebie holiday.'

'Yes?' they all chorused, the room now electric with anticipation.

'It's true,' Sue announced.

'For definite?' asked Janet.

'Abso-defo-lutely,' said Sue triumphantly. 'And how do I know? Because his tickets and hotel voucher arrived today, delivered by courier.'

'How do you know that's what they were?' asked Liz, incredulous.

'Quite simple,' said Sue, laughing. 'You don't have to be

Miss Marple to work that one out. It said "Tickets" on the envelope.'

'That could be anything, though,' said Janet. 'Theatre tickets, train tickets, parking tickets. We can't jump to conclusions.'

'Oh yes we can,' said Sue. 'I called through to Harry to say that some tickets were in reception for him. All I got were the usual unpleasant grunts. Then a guy from Hot Breaks For Heartaches rang just to make sure that the courier had delivered the air tickets and hotel voucher for Mr Hampton. In view of Harry's earlier reaction, I didn't bother to pass the message on. There was no need, you see, because he already knew they'd been delivered.'

'Well, well, well,' mused Janet as she eased a coffee and walnut gateau out of a supermarket box and cut it up into slices. 'Slaved for hours over this, so you'd better enjoy it,' she threatened.

They had a short coffee and gateau intermission. Everyone fell silent for a few seconds, as they took a mouthful.

'I think I thawed it out rather beautifully,' said Janet, trying to take some credit. 'Now, back to the plot. It does all tie in with what Ray overheard that morning. At the time I thought he was gossiping, just for a laugh, but I did question him about it quietly and he swears it's what he heard.'

'How Harry thinks he's going to pull that one off, I don't know,' said Sue. 'Unless we've got this very wrong, he's actually taking Val as a surprise and it's totally legit. Well, more or less, as freebies go.'

'I doubt it,' said Janet. 'I've known Harry for too long. If he's up to something, he's usually up to his armpits in it.

Everything Harry does is for one purpose and one purpose only. It's called personal gain.'

'This still doesn't solve the problem of Val,' said Nina. 'I don't want to be in the same room as that woman any longer. She may be the boss's wife, she may look like a supermodel, but she's a superbitch as far as I'm concerned.'

'Agreed, but if we're to solve Val, we probably have to solve Harry as well,' said Sue.

Suddenly Janet thumped the table in triumph. Coffee cups jumped and candles flickered precariously.

'I've got it,' said Janet. 'What makes Harry twitchier than anything? Answer: when he's not in control. When he doesn't have all the trump cards. Or when someone's got something on him.'

'I'd like to get something on him,' said Nina. 'Some of the canteen's disgusting lumpy custard for a start.'

'No, seriously, do you remember when Joe and Simon hinted that there was a secret file being kept on him? Of course it was a hoax, but at the time I thought it was an interesting idea. Well, suppose we take that one stage further. Sue and I half joked about keeping a file on him, dates and times of incidents, that sort of stuff, but let's delve a little deeper. Let's find out what happens between six and nine, for a start. Let's find out about this freebie holiday. Let's find out what he's really up to. It could be much worse than we thought.'

'You mean, snoop?' queried Liz, who'd been remarkably quiet throughout the evening.

'Yep, snoop,' said Janet. 'But let's not risk getting caught. We'll log all incidents, dates, times, et cetera, and put the information in a designated pot in the computer system.'

'Bit risky,' said Sue. 'Harry's been snooping around the offices, hasn't he? And nothing's safe in any part of the computer. Better to write things up and store them somewhere off the premises.'

'I'll take notes,' exclaimed Janet, 'then I'll pop them in my handbag and put them into my computer here at home. Then we run no risk of being found out.'

'Hang on a minute, though,' said Sue. 'I thought your handbag was supposed to be haunted.'

'Yep, it is, but my mother will be watching over it.'

They began to plot. Sue would monitor calls as best she could, noting when Harry left work and the dates and times that Val rang in wondering where he was. Plus she would try to get some sort of handle on the woman with the Italian accent by noting the number she rang in on. Liz, since she was working closely with the people from Hot Breaks, would try to suss out whether Harry had indeed landed a freebie. Nina, as production secretary, would keep an eye on the office. She would make notes of instances where files or belongings had been moved, and monitor any relevant gossip. All notes would be handed to Janet personally and the whole thing would be codenamed Operation Haunted Handbag.

The war council meeting over, Janet got up to make more coffee. The evening had begun on a note of low morale and had ended with a battle plan and a triumphant air. They agreed to reconvene in a fortnight at Sue's house.

'It's kind of weirdly exciting,' said Sue to Nina as they walked back down Janet's path to their respective cars.

'Well, if it shuts that silly cow up, then it's all worth it,' said Nina, who was still seething about Val's remarks. 'So long as it brings the pair of them down, it suits me.'

chapter twelve

The first Monday of June, and the only thing flaming about it was a row breaking out in the production office between the tropical team and the shivery radiator huggers over the temperature of the air-conditioning. In the midst of this, Janet had to go off and meet the new whizz-kid producer, Paul Burns.

Harry sat crowing in his *Mastermind* chair as Janet was introduced to a man in the loudest pinstripe suit she had ever seen. Al Capone would have killed for the pattern alone. Along with the wide lapels, trousers with huge turn-ups, red silk tie and matching handkerchief, Paul Burns had a tan that would have done George Hamilton proud. He looked more like a spiv from *Bugsy Malone* than a programme producer. Suddenly Janet felt too casually dressed in her black and white spotted dress and long black cardigan.

Harry did the honours and then summoned the perennially beige Geraldine in with the coffee. He gave Paul a brief rundown about the company and the proposed campaign for Hot Breaks. The conversation took twenty minutes, punctuated constantly by mobile phones going off. Harry took four calls and Paul Burns five. Bit excessive for your first morning at work, thought Janet. Clearly it didn't bother Harry, who nodded appreciatively at everything Paul said.

To her shame, Janet found herself listening more intently to Harry's calls for clues, following Friday night's war council, rather than to all the discussion about the company and the project. It all seemed harmless enough, except that she found herself wondering why people would ring his mobile when he was more likely to be at his desk during business hours. She was musing on this when she suddenly became aware that Harry had asked her a question and she had no idea what it was. She feigned a coughing fit.

'When my production head has recovered her health, I'll get her to introduce you to the team you'll be working with,' glowered Harry. 'See you for lunch, Paul. I've booked a table at Shiraz.'

Shiraz? I've never been taken out for lunch at Shiraz, thought Janet bitterly. Typical blokes, bond together instantly like Loctite and off they go to spend huge dollops of company cash. If I whacked in a bill for pie and chips with Liz at the GX, I'd get a lecture on saving money. Mustn't get bitter, though, she thought, leading Paul out of Harry's office and down the corridor to her department.

Introductions to Liz, Nick and Bob over, Janet installed Paul at Simon's empty desk and showed him how to use the phone and boot up the computer. She then handed him the Hot Breaks file and left him to it.

She'd hardly settled at her desk to whizz through another fifty e-mails when she was summoned back to Harry's office.

'Burns is top-notch,' he bellowed at her. 'Make sure

your people get their act together. This has got to be good, or else.'

'How much do you want me to get involved?' asked Janet.

'I'm taking personal charge of this one. Just recognize that Paul's a good operator and leave him to it,' said Harry. 'Listen and learn, this chap's dynamite.'

Dynamite or not, Paul Burns spent the morning peering at the Hot Breaks file and then disappeared off without a word for lunch with Harry. Neither returned for work that day.

'Janet? It's Liz. I'm back in the office at lunchtime. Can we meet for lunch? The Groin Exchange? Great.'

Janet replaced the phone in its cradle. Liz sounded really fed up. She'd been on the road for three days, doing a recce and setting up filming for the Hot Breaks series. Perhaps the enforced jollity of line dancing and murder mystery weekends was getting to her.

Janet went back to her current project – a video series and website for a chain of estate agencies. Not quite in the league of Hot Breaks, but a chance to snoop around other people's houses and film them. It was going to be a big money-spinner for HOT, with the bonus that it would be an ongoing earner for at least a year because of the need for constant updates. The properties were being divided up into millionaire bracket, waterside and seaview properties, equestrian, farms, flats, urban, and first-time buyers.

There was keen competition, particularly among the girls in the office, to work on the series.

'Glorified window-shopping,' said Ray, scornfully. 'You girls are only ever a whisper away from a chance to spend money.'

'Not at these prices,' replied Janet. 'Some of them are so wicked, even if the entire office clubbed together we couldn't afford them.'

'Might be cosy, though,' said Ray. 'Bags I bunk up with Veronica.'

Veronica was the current office fantasy girl. Tall and blonde, with endless legs and rumoured-to-be-enhanced boobs, she had just joined the company and was working alongside Nina as a production secretary. Nina lived in fear that Sam might take a pop at Veronica and blow her chances for ever. Despite looking as though she'd stepped from the pages of *FHM*, Veronica was never destined to fit in with the general lunacy and terrible jokes in the department. She kept herself aloof and the blokes soon realized that although she looked like a dead ringer for Caprice, she wasn't much fun. So Nina, for all her angst, was still the most popular production secretary because she told a good joke, could drink a pint and was once spotted in the car park changing the air filter on her car.

Janet made her way to the GX, ordered a spritzer and sat in a corner waiting for Liz. Her mobile went off. Probably Liz, to say she was delayed. She rummaged through her handbag to find her phone. It never mattered which zip pocket she put it in, it was never there when she wanted it. By the time she'd found it, the caller had rung off. The display told her it was HOT reception desk. She pressed last-number redial.

'Don't tell me.' Sue answered immediately. 'You couldn't find the phone in that bloody bag of yours.'

'Yeah, sorry,' replied Janet, bootfaced.

'Well, here's one for Operation Haunted Handbag,' said Sue, triumphantly. 'Two calls yesterday for the Fat Controller from the Italian job, and Val phoned up at nine forty-five last night wondering where Harry was. He'd left at six on the dot, as he's done every night this week.'

'And?'

'And yes, his mobile was switched off. As soon as I'd got rid of Val, I tried his number.' She mimicked the recorded message: '"The number you have dialled has been switched off. Please try later." Have you ever known Harry's mobile to be switched off?'

'Nope,' said Janet. 'Harry has no shame about answering his phone wherever he is. I've even seen him take a call in the middle of one of our press presentations. How was Val, by the way? Did she invite us out again?'

'No, mercifully not. But there again, she sounded rather pissed. Having said that, how would we know? I'm not sure what she'd sound like sober. Is it possible for Val to go out and not fall into other people's dinners?'

'No idea,' replied Janet. 'Anyway, gotta go, Liz is heading this way for a pow-wow. Keep up the good work.'

Liz sat down, distress written large on her face. She might as well have carried a placard.

'Gin and tonic, please,' she said.

'Blimey, you are fed up,' said Janet, scuttling off to the bar to fetch Liz's drink and order a couple of prawn sandwiches.

'Cheers, it's a double,' she said, plonking the glass down in front of Liz who immediately took a huge slug.

'Paul Burns is total crap,' Liz announced. 'Apart from his appalling dress sense, he hasn't a clue what he's doing. He just sits there with his Gucci briefcase full of gizmos, and in between the endless calls and e-mails on his laptop and twiddling with his vast collection of electronic organizers, he comes up with gems like "Oh, you know what you're doing," "I'll just leave you to get on with it" or my personal favourite, "Yeah, whatever." It's almost as if he doesn't know how to do the job.'

'What exactly *has* he done so far?'

'Bugger all,' she spluttered, taking another slug of gin and tonic. 'I've been out on the road, setting up and doing a little bit of pre-filming for the first two videos, but I don't really know what he wants. I assumed that as he was hired to direct the series, that's what he would do, but he seems hell bent on staying out of the fray. I get the distinct impression that I'm going to end up directing them as well. And then I can predict it all: I'll come back with the thing shot one way and he'll say, "No, no, no, I wanted it done another way." I just know that I'll end up taking the blame.'

'Hm, this is serious,' said Janet. 'Tell you what, if he's in the office this afternoon, I'll have a word with him. And if I don't get any joy, I'll go and have a moan to Harry. It would be great to shoot down his new wunderkind.'

'No, don't do that. Don't go to Harry, I mean,' said Liz, that anxious look back in her eyes.

Janet looked at Liz for a moment, taking in the ashen face and frightened gaze.

'What's up with you about Harry? Look, we all know he's a big fat bully, but for you it's something else, isn't it?'

'Yes, well, um . . .' faltered Liz. 'I did have a problem with him a while ago, but it's quite a long time ago and I really can't talk about it.'

'Are you sure that's wise? Whatever it is, it keeps coming back to haunt you. Wouldn't it be better to get it out of your system?'

Tears started to trickle down Liz's face. She took another determined slug of gin and tonic, followed by a deep and purposeful breath.

'Yes, you're right. I should tell someone, and that some-one should be you, because I trust you, Janet. I don't want anyone else to know because . . .'

The tears were rapidly turning from a trickle into a deluge.

'Go on, spit it out. It will make you feel better.'

'This has to be in total secrecy. I don't want anybody to know except you. Understand?' she said, wiping her eyes frantically with a tissue.

Janet nodded.

'It was just after I'd joined the company, about two years ago. I'd only been there about three weeks when Harry turned up on my doorstep late one night.'

'Whaaaat?' Janet wished she'd ordered a large gin too.

'He . . . he . . . foisted himself on me. He'd brought a bottle of something with him. God knows what was in it, but it knocked me almost unconscious.'

Liz stopped to take in the shock on Janet's face. She took another slug and continued: 'It was only a few weeks after my mother died, and I'd been drinking that night because I was so upset. I'd sat in front of the telly, had a good cry and drunk a bottle of wine. So I was very vul-nerable. When he turned up on my doorstep, I couldn't quite take in what was happening.'

'Did he say why he was there?' Janet asked.

'I recall some crap about him fancying me the minute I'd arrived at HOT. Thought I was very special and that he could really help me with my career. That was why he was there, to push my corner, get me up a rung or two, that sort of thing. But – and here's the clever bit – we had to keep it a secret because the others would suspect he was favouring me. Of course, I look back now and it's all bollocks, but at the time I believed what he said. Why shouldn't I? Except that he made me cement our new "relationship" with a drink from this mystery bottle, and next thing I found myself in bed, not a stitch on, with Harry putting on his clothes to leave.'

'Bloody Nora,' said Janet. 'And why on earth did he think you'd keep your mouth shut?'

'Well, the next day I went in to confront him about what he'd done. He accused me point blank of being a liar and said that I must be imagining it. Worse still, he warned me that what I'd said amounted to slander and that if he caught me telling anyone else I'd not only get the sack, but he'd take legal action and refuse to give me a reference.'

'Phew, very clever. But it couldn't have just been a nightmare, could it?' said Janet, her mind racing. 'On your own admission, you were upset about your mum.'

'No,' said Liz, smiling bitterly. 'I knew he'd had sex with me. Apart from the tell-tale signs, I eventually decided to do a pregnancy test just to be sure.'

'And?'

'It was positive.'

chapter thirteen

They ate their prawn sandwiches in silence. Janet went to fetch more drinks from the bar. For once, she was totally speechless. Liz gathered strength from her second gin and continued the tale.

'I'd only just got the job. It was like a dream come true; I felt it was a whole new lease of life that would help me through my grief over Mum. I'd always wanted to get into telly or film and I couldn't believe my luck. Next thing I knew, I was having an abortion.' She started to cry again.

'Liz, I had no idea,' comforted Janet. 'What a truly horrible thing to happen. Forgive me for asking the obvious, but are you sure it was Harry's?'

'Absolutely. I hadn't had sex for months. Mum got ill, I'd been commuting to the hospital to see her. Didn't have time for a boyfriend. So it wouldn't have needed a DNA test.'

'Did you tell Harry?'

'God, no. He'd already threatened me with legal action and the sack. No, I couldn't cope with any more from him, so I went and got sorted out. The trouble is,' she started to break down again, 'now I so desperately want a baby, and maybe that was my only chance. There's always a risk you can't have one, after you've had an abortion.'

'Liz, I'm sure you'll meet someone smashing, have lots of gorgeous babies and live happily ever after,' soothed Janet. 'But I don't think you'd have liked a mini Harry, would you? Besides, to be briefly practical, you'd have had an uphill struggle to get him to recognize the baby as his, let alone stump up some maintenance. No, perhaps it was the best thing to do.'

Liz took another huge slug of gin. 'It's a bit ironic,' she continued with a half-smile through her tears, 'that of all people, Val should pick on me to join her little social outings. That's why this must remain a secret. In a funny way, I feel slightly sorry for her, forking out for all those expensive meals. Buying dinner for a woman who got pregnant by her husband.'

'Well, let's hope we can stop that soon. I think even Val might have recognized that she blew it last time,' said Janet. 'Normally by now she's on the blower arranging another of her ghastly soirées. Anyway, at least I now understand exactly why you so hate going into Harry's office.'

'I've never gone in there on my own, only with one of you lot, and even then I've managed to avoid it where possible,' said Liz, still sniffing. 'But do you know, after we had that meeting about Harry and Val at your place last week, my mind went back to that dreadful night and I remembered some more about what happened.'

'Oh, what in particular?' Janet was trying not to sound too curious.

'Two things. Firstly, I had the distinct impression that he didn't expect me to refuse him. He was arrogant enough to think I must fancy him rotten. And secondly, the stuff about me being so talented and him "helping me" with my career sounded like a very well-worn path.'

'I think it probably is,' sighed Janet.

Back in the production office, a Friday-afternoon atmosphere was in full swing. With the weekend in their sights, everyone was behaving badly. Ray was winding Nina up, claiming Sam had been headhunted by a big multinational. Nick, one of the researchers on the Hot Breaks project, was very publicly chatting up the haughty Veronica, who was wearing a face like fizz, but definitely not of the champagne variety. And there was general outrage because someone had started a rumour that from Monday every member of staff would be charged for coffee.

Against this furore, nobody noticed Liz's recently tear-stained face and swollen eyelids. She sank down behind her desk, grateful to be on home territory. Paul Burns was nowhere to be seen.

'Anyone seen Paul?' enquired Janet.

'Paul who?' came back the general response.

'I hope he Burns in hell,' joked Ray. 'Along with Harry. They seem to be new best friends.'

Janet sat down at her desk and whipped through the e-mails that had arrived since lunchtime. Fifty-three! How did anyone get any work done any more? She decided to devote the rest of the afternoon to the new property series, but the same dilemma kept coming back into her head. Should she go and have a word with Harry about Paul? Should she leave him to dig his own hole and fall into it? Or would Liz, as she predicted, get the blame if Janet didn't say anything? She picked up her phone and dialled the dreaded Geraldine.

'Harry Hampton's office,' came the imperious voice.

'Is he there?' asked Janet.

'No, he's having lunch with Paul and the boss of Hot Breaks.'

Janet looked at her watch. It was 4.30.

'Just a quick snack then,' she said, jokingly. Humour was, of course, always lost on Geraldine.

'I think you ought to know, it's a very important project,' Geraldine replied huffily. Janet immediately read the implication in her voice, namely: it's out of your league, luv.

'Pity, I did want to have a chat with him about that very project before it gets too far down the road,' said Janet, trying to sound unruffled.

'I really don't think you should be bothering Harry about it,' bounced back Geraldine, who couldn't resist putting the boot in. 'Remember, he's used to handling top-level projects like this. Been doing it for years. It's all mist to the grill for him.'

Janet paused to unravel what she'd just heard. 'Absolutely, Geraldine,' she agreed. Then she replaced the phone and burst into fits of laughter.

'I claim the best G-spot of the week,' she proclaimed to all those in earshot. They all screamed and applauded, all except Veronica, who everyone was now convinced had had a humour bypass.

Janet was just immersing herself once again in the property file when Sue rang from reception.

'Got time for a quick coffee?' she asked. 'I've another contribution to Operation Haunted Handbag.'

They met in their usual corner. Sue was looking triumphant once again, absolutely bursting to impart some gossip.

'Get a load of this,' she said, eyes gleaming. 'I've only got cover on reception for five minutes so I'll have to tell you quickly.'

Janet nodded, indicating for her to go on.

'Val rang up this afternoon to speak to Harry. Pissed as usual, bit slurry down the phone. I put her through to Geraldine, who must have told her that he was out to lunch with Paul and someone else. Then she rang back to say she'd tried his mobile and it was switched off. Now, we know what that means. It means he might be somewhere or with someone he shouldn't. So I did a bit of detective work.'

'What did you do?'

'I got Geraldine to tell me where they were lunching. Hold on to your hat here, it was at the Grand.'

The Grand in Hartford was so unbelievably grand that even Val didn't take the girls there. Michelin-starred, with the London Met Bar atmosphere and prices to match, it featured in all the 'great restaurants of the galaxy' lists. Lunch for three – Harry, Paul and the Hot Breaks supremo – would come to something in the region of three hundred pounds. And the rest, especially if they went through the vintage wine list and the best port.

Sue continued her tale: 'So I rang the Grand and said I had an urgent message for Mr Hampton, who was with a party having lunch. They put me through to the maître d' and I said that a bit of discretion was required. I had a call from the gentleman's wife, which might be a bit awk-ward, bearing in mind the company. I sort of hoped that he might just tell me who was at the table. And sure enough, he did! There were four people, not three. Three men and a woman. I asked him if he might help me out

112

by describing the woman. In his words, she was young and dark-haired. Italian-looking? I queried. Yes, he said. We left it that he would discreetly tell Harry to call his wife when he had a moment.'

'Amazing, well done,' replied Janet. 'I hope this isn't going to rebound on you.'

'No, I thought about that,' said Sue. 'My fallback position to Harry is that Val was sounding a little strange, i.e. pissed, on the phone and I felt I had to get a message to him as a matter of urgency. The maître d' sounded delightfully camp and was obviously used to having a restaurant full of people who were with people they shouldn't have been.'

'Interesting,' mused Janet. 'Obviously it could just be a coincidence. She might be the wife of the Hot Breaks guy, or even Paul Burns. Although I can't believe there's a woman in *his* life, not with that ghastly wardrobe. But the clue is the mobile being switched off. It seems that whenever Harry's mobile is off, he's up to something.'

Janet went back to her desk, hand-wrote some notes about their conversation and stuffed the piece of paper in her handbag. Another contribution to the home computer. She also looked up a certain Manchester phone number and resolved to give it a try when she got home.

She'd intended to call a short meeting about the property series but it was now too late. Everyone was packing up, intent on a couple of swift ones in the GX before heading home for the weekend. Normally she'd have gone too, but she was suddenly troubled by the events of the day. What on earth was going on?

She headed home in her battered old Citroën. A supper of easy-cook pasta, a couple of glasses of rouge and the rest of the day's papers suddenly seemed like the best thing in the world. She put her key in the door and opened it with that familiar pang of regret. A whole weekend ahead of her and no one to share it with. Janet knew she'd missed out on relationships. Occasionally, she'd look misty-eyed at couples choosing furniture, pushing supermarket trolleys or going out for a pub meal together. Then the horror of her own marriage would return and she'd always come to her senses. Yes, she was better off single; she knew where she was, how much she had in the bank, and there'd be nobody to moan if she bought a pile of clothes she didn't need.

She put on a pan of water for the pasta and poured the first glass of wine. Val would probably be well into her second or third bottle by now, and giving Harry a hard time. She glanced at the phone. No, she'd make that call after supper. Just unwind from the day before ringing. She put on a favourite pair of jogging bottoms – not that she'd ever jogged in them – took off her make-up and then put the chain on the door.

In the end, curiosity overcame her. She turned off the gas under the pan and dialled. The phone seemed to ring endlessly. Just five more rings and then I'll put it down, she thought. Oh, all right, just another five. Then someone answered.

'Hi. This is Janet Bancroft from Hartford Optimum Television. I don't suppose Steven Byfield is still on this number, is he?'

'Yeah, I'll get him for you.'

Silence, broken by the sound of clip-clopping up and down uncarpeted stairs. It seemed an eternity.

'Hi, Janet, it's Steven Byfield. You took over my job, if I remember.'

'Yes, got it in one. I'm sorry to bother you, especially as

we've never met, but I wonder if you could do me a favour.'

'Well, I'll try. Ask away.'

'Look, I know it's a lot to ask, but could this conversation be in complete confidence? It's about Harry Hampton. I'm taking a risk here, because you could be his all-time best friend for all I know.'

There was a pause and then Steven started laughing, a real belly laugh.

'Harry? My best friend? Do me a favour. Biggest shit that ever walked the earth.'

Janet heaved a sigh of relief. He really did sound genuine.

'Could I ask why you think that?' she probed gently.

'No secret. I caught him out trying a spot of wheeling and dealing. At first he tried to get me on board, I suppose in the hope that I'd shut up. And then when I refused, he made life very difficult for me.'

'Like how?'

'Oh, all the usual bullying stuff. Not putting me in the picture on things and then giving me grief. Insisting on putting his name on credits when he'd had bugger-all to do with it. I once did a huge motoring project, wrote the pitch, got the job, produced and directed it. And then Harry insisted on putting his name on it, claimed credit, sucked up to the board and got another big fat pay rise. Sound familiar?'

'Absolutely. Carbon copy.'

'Well, leopards don't change their spots. And bastards, just like nuns, don't change their habits. So what's he up to this time?'

'More of the same, actually. But that's not quite why I'm ringing.'

Janet went on to outline the hiring of Paul Burns, how impressed Harry was with his CV and how they were now new best mates, disappearing off for expensive lunches and leaving all the work to everyone else. When she'd finished, Steven burst out laughing again.

'Sorry for all the hilarity,' said Steven, trying to control himself. 'And I'm sorry Burns is giving you all so much grief, but you can blame it all on me.'

'How on earth . . .?'

'I'd always wanted to pay Harry back for what he did to me, but he's a clever sod. I left in the end when a good job came up. I didn't want him messing it up for me with one of his revenge references. Anyway, I recently saw my way to a payback situation. We had Burnsie here on a short-term contract. It was like having another Harry on board, bit of a slippery character, with his nasty suits and bogus CV; short on talent, long on bullshit. Couldn't direct the traffic, let alone a programme. Also, as we discovered after he'd left, prone to fiddling, and I'm not hearing violins in this particular instance. So one day I rang Harry up and recommended Burns to him. I figured they'd be kindred spirits. I was very matey down the phone, asked after everyone and muttered all the right phrases. Harry must have swallowed it. Burns is very plausible and the CV's amazing. It's complete fiction. So you see, this is magic news, Janet. It was a long shot but worth it. You come up to Manchester, petal, and I'll buy you the best dinner in town.'

chapter fourteen

Liz was halfway through watching *When Harry Met Sally* for the umpteenth time. It was her favourite film, except that she wished Billy Crystal's character had been called anything but Harry. She'd just reached the fake orgasm scene in the diner when the phone rang. For one delicious moment she thought, 'Sod it,' then she felt trapped by its urgency. Who could it be this late? What if it was some terrible emergency?

She reached out over the back of her settee for the phone, contemplated it for a few seconds and clicked the green button.

'Hello,' she whispered.

'Liz, it's Janet. You all right? You sound as though you're being stalked.'

'Might as well be, after the sort of day I've had,' she replied.

'Yes, yes, yes,' screamed the television.

'Strewth, Liz, what the hell am I interrupting?'

'Nothing,' said Liz, rather detached.

'Yes, yes, yes,' screamed Meg Ryan, in mock ecstasy.

'What on earth's going on? Are you all right? And for God's sake, don't say, yes, yes, yes.'

'Yes, yes, yes.' Meg was at it again.

'Sorry, Janet, it's that crazy scene in the diner from *When Harry Met Sally*. You know the one.'

'Hm, can't remember back that far. Anyway, I'm surprised you're watching that, with its unfortunate title,' mused Janet. 'Let me tell you the tale of When Harry Met Paul Who'd Met Steven.'

'You just lost me,' yawned Liz, reluctantly turning the sound down on the film. But once Janet had related her chat with Steven Byfield, suddenly Liz was up off her settee and jumping around her tiny flat in delight.

'Fantastic. Best news I've heard all week. Trouble is, it doesn't solve my problem with Paul Burns. I've still got to carry him. Knowing my luck, I'm probably carrying him all the way to the bank too. I bet he earns squillions more than me.'

'Yes, undoubtedly,' said Janet, knowing that Harry liked to reward those who were loyal to him. She'd always suspected that Geraldine was on a fat screw. 'But somehow we've got to let Harry know how ineffectual Paul Burns is.'

'How the hell are we going to that?' asked Liz.

'Easy. We'll pick a day next week, better still two days. And these will be days when you are scheduled to direct sequences he should have been doing himself. You pick the most difficult ones, and let me know in advance.'

'Then what?' asked Liz, tiredness creeping back.

'I will make sure that absolutely everyone in the department is out on a shoot, or up to their armpits in editing, or in meetings that can't be cancelled. I might book leave so I'm out of the frame or there again, I might stay around for the sport.'

'What sport?'

'You're going to phone in sick and leave Burns in the

118

lurch. That should flush something out. He's either talented and lazy, in which case we'll all finally get to admire his handiwork. Or he's completely useless and lazy and our suspicions will be confirmed. And I must say, that last scenario gets my vote.'

'We're supposed to be shooting the line-dancing Hot Break on Friday and Saturday,' said Liz, flipping through her diary for the next week. She was surprised at her own instant acceptance of the plan. 'That would be perfect because it'll be a bit complicated to shoot and he'll have to juggle with music too. I already know that at least two women on the course don't want to be filmed, so we'll have to make sure we avoid them in all the shots. Also, the woman running the tuition side is unbelievably difficult. A right old diva. Thinks she knows everything about telly because about twenty years ago she was interviewed in the street by Esther Rantzen.'

'Sounds perfect then,' said Janet. 'Don't forget, you must drop out at the very last minute so he can't just cancel the shoot.'

'Yes, yes, yes,' said Liz ecstatically.

By midweek, Janet was so fed up of complaints and whingeing about Paul Burns, she felt like going sick herself. All the moans and groans were the same: his unfortunate manner, his downright rudeness, he didn't seem to know what he was talking about, he expected everything to be done for him. In other words, rude, thick and lazy. The only things that everyone admired were his epic lunch hours, ability to take nonstop mobile phone calls, and endless wardrobe of deeply vulgar flashy pinstripe suits, all double-breasted with wide lapels and turn-ups. He looked more like City Boy than Telly Man.

Liz had been tearing her hair out, producing research and recce notes that just sat unread in ever-growing piles on his desk. Burns just wouldn't or couldn't make a decision. He'd avoid it by suddenly disappearing for one of his mega cigar breaks. When the going got tough, the tough went smoking. Which was most of the time. This meant Liz couldn't firm up any filming because she didn't know exactly what he wanted.

'It's all very well going for a fag break,' observed Ray. 'Most people have a few puffs and come straight back in. But Burns' cigar breaks are something else. He's out there watching the rain drying followed by the grass growing. He's out there so long he could do with another shave. Thanks to all that cigar smoking, he'll end up being the healthiest bloke in this building.'

'How come?' asked Janet.

'Outside in the fresh air all the time, while the rest of us idiots answer his calls, take messages and generally do his dirty work.'

Film crews had begun reporting that they were forever seeing Paul Burns outside the office, cigar in one hand, mobile in the other. It was fast becoming an office joke.

'I've told him about those two women on the line-dancing break who don't want to be filmed,' said Liz. 'He's just not taking this on board at all. I've had to go ahead and book three cameras, extra lights and a steadicam for this shoot. If I waited for a decision, I'd be drawing my pension. And possibly my own teeth.'

'Difficult for me, because Harry's insisting it's Paul's baby,' said Janet. 'I've been told to keep out of it. Sorry, I can't really help you.'

They were having their conversation a couple of decibels up for the benefit of the rest of the office.

120

Bob, one of the researchers, was listening intently.

'Does seem daft,' he said, 'that you're out of this one, Janet. After all, you're head of the department.'

'Boss's orders,' said Janet with a half-smile. 'Not worth crossing Harry. You know what he's like when he's made his mind up. Paul is in charge on this one, and that's that.'

'Well I think that's crap,' retorted Bob. 'The man's a complete super-tosser. I'm trying to set up the murder-mystery weekend break, and the way it's looking, it's still a complete bloody mystery to me. Whatever I ask him, he just says, "Do what you think," or "Up to you." And that's only when I can catch him between calls on his mobile. He's permanently out to lunch.'

Janet smiled to herself. Burns wouldn't be out to lunch any longer if everything went according to plan later in the week.

Harry was busy congratulating himself on hiring Paul Burns. He sat back, gently swivelling in his huge chair as he contemplated his office. Burns' arrival had really shaken up the production department, especially Janet. Although he grudgingly admitted to himself that she did a good job, he'd never dream of telling her so. It was absolutely a non-starter to tell a woman she was good at anything. She'd get far too big for her boots. No, it served Janet right to have the rug pulled from under her from time to time. Nothing like keeping all of them on their toes. Staying in control, that was the name of the game.

Also, Burns was far more likely to keep his mouth shut on the little deal they'd hatched over lunch at the Grand last week. Yes, men were much better at wheeling and dealing than women, who tended to be obsessed with all that moral rubbish about right and wrong.

As Harry flipped through some trade papers, the now familiar niggle began to infiltrate. It was the conversation he'd had with Simon and Joe the day he'd fired them. That secret file they'd mentioned. Some of their accusations had hit home. Did they know something? It was still bothering him. He'd have to have another snoop around the office one evening, check a few drawers, look in some computer files, especially if some of the idiots in there had left their computers on. Or maybe he'd rope in Geraldine to do that. Brilliant idea. She'd do his dirty work and no questions asked. Now that was the sort of woman who got his vote.

'Geraldine,' he barked, 'coffee, in here, now, chop chop.'

Geraldine, looking spectacularly drab in a grey and white striped dress and very mumsy sandals, scuttled in the direction of the coffee machine.

As she reappeared with the coffee, Harry was sitting back in his chair smoking a huge cigar.

'Shut that door and siddown,' he bellowed. 'There's something really important I want you to do . . .'

Zero tolerance of Paul Burns and his behaviour was beginning to creep in. Even Liz, slightly buoyed up by the revelation of how he'd been hired, was beginning to stand up to him. She'd been up to her armpits sorting out locations and interviewees for the next two programmes, while Burns, mobile permanently clamped to his ear, was giving her huge lists of things to do.

'Sorry, Paul, I just can't leave my desk right now. I've got about ten calls out to all sorts of people. If I start rushing around the tape library pulling out rushes, I'll miss the calls and have to start all over again. Sorry, can't do miracles.'

'This place is ridiculous. I'm amazed anything gets done at all,' Burns grumped, looking around the office trying to catch some poor sod's attention to do his dirty work for him. Everyone deliberately avoided his gaze and looked very intently at their screens. Angrily, Burns stalked out of the office in the direction of the tape library. A few minutes later he was back, empty-handed and fuming.

Janet, having observed all this, surreptitiously dialled an internal extension. 'Well, what happened there then?' she whispered quietly to Bill, who ran the library.

'In time-honoured tradition, the peasants are revolting,' he said, chuckling. 'I told him to look up the tape numbers on the computer, just like everyone else. Well, that's not exactly true, of course, because we always help people we like. But this chap's such a pain in the arse, he can paddle his own canoe as far as we're all concerned.'

'How did he react?'

'Put it like this,' said Bill. 'We had a . . . let's call it an exchange. He was so pompous and rude that he must have had one-to-one tuition from the Hampton charm school. So in the end I pointed out that sarcasm was just one of the many services we offered.'

'Ooops, he'll go straight to Harry,' warned Janet.

'He can go straight to hell as far as we're all concerned down here,' replied Bill succinctly. 'And we'll help him with the packing.'

'Funny, a lot of people have chosen that destination for him.'

Janet replaced the receiver, smiling to herself. The peasants really were revolting. In all the years she'd worked at HOT, she'd never known such an unprecedented wave of hatred about someone after such a short time. It was an awesome achievement.

The phone rang immediately. Janet steeled herself, fully expecting it to be Harry ranting about something. But it was Colin, their most popular cameraman, asking for a quiet word with her in the canteen. She left her desk, following a glowering Paul Burns, who was obviously heading for another all-boys-together pow-wow with Harry.

Colin was sitting in the furthermost corner, two coffees already on the table.

'Let me guess, a Burning issue?'

'Got it in one,' said Colin. 'In all my years in this game, I have never come across quite such a pillock. We've done some shooting which, frankly, would have been a fiasco if Liz hadn't been there. The guy has no idea what he's doing. I'd asked him about how he wanted the interviewees framed, what filters he wanted, how he wanted the whole thing to look. And he just kept saying, "Whatever" or "Do what you want." He completely exasperated Ron, the sound recordist, who's the most placid bloke on the planet. In the end, Liz and I had a quick confab during one of his endless phone calls and salvaged what we could. But even after that he managed to walk through several shots, and we lost some more because he wouldn't switch off that bloody phone.'

'You're booked for the line-dancing next weekend, aren't you?' said Janet.

'Yeah, much against my better judgement. Why on earth aren't you involved in this series?'

'Good question. I'd rather not go into that. Can we have an off-the-record discussion? I think there are some things you ought to know.'

'Of course,' Colin assured her. 'We go back a long way, Janet.'

She briefly outlined how Paul Burns had come to be hired and how Harry had deliberately kept her off the series. She also told him of the likelihood that Liz would not be on the line-dancing shoot. She didn't want to compromise Colin when the balloon went up.

'I would just ask you one thing. If it all goes wrong at that shoot, don't bail him out. Just get straight on the phone to Harry. At home if necessary. And if you feel that strongly about it, then make your comments known to anyone from the Hot Breaks company.'

'Janet, I'd be delighted. And if anything does go wrong, I'll call you too, if you don't mind.'

'I insist,' she said.

chapter fifteen

'Janet, it's Val. How are you?'

That last bit nearly sent Janet reeling off her chair. It also sent two files of notes to the floor, scattering their contents. Scrabbling around to pick them up bought Janet a bit of time before she had to reply. Val never, ever asked how anyone was. She always knew exactly how they were and put them right on it in no uncertain terms. There was a brief flashback to the fiasco in the Mexican restaurant: Val falling into a table, refried beans scattering like a turbo muck-spreader; Val bringing down a coat stand; and of course Val managing to leave her usual immaculate and expensively dressed self, while the rest of them looked like extras from *The Godfather IV*.

'Fine, thanks,' she lied. 'How are you?'

'Oh, *comme ci, comme ça.* Bit bored really. Just been shopping, bought some nice clothes, nothing much, just a few cheapies from Ghost, and nowhere to wear them to.'

She's run out of people to do the swank to, thought Janet. I don't feel the need to ring someone up when I've just snapped up a cardie from BHS.

'So I thought I'd phone a friend,' pursued Val.

Why don't you ask the bloody audience instead,

thought Janet. This was a novel approach from Val; she sounded different somehow. Perhaps she was sober for once. Also, being referred to as a 'friend' was slightly unhinging. What was occurring?

'Are you free for lunch today?'

'Sorry, Val, up to my eyes.'

'How about tomorrow then?'

'No good either, I'm afraid,' said Janet, glancing at her wall chart. Not that she needed reminding. Tomorrow was Friday and the first day of the line-dancing shoot. It was also the day Liz was going to phone in sick and leave Burns to get on with things himself. Janet wanted to be there to mind the shop. On the other hand, Val witnessing some of the action might just work to their advantage.

'Tell you what,' she said. 'Let me juggle a few things around and see if I can get out for an hour tomorrow. I'll call you back.'

Janet noted down Val's mobile number and pondered for a few seconds. She called Sue in reception. Five minutes later they were huddled over cappuccinos in the canteen, with Janet outlining the game plan for the next day.

Liz would be ringing in at eight o'clock to say she was sick. Throwing up and diarrhoea had been chosen as suitable-house confining conditions, coupled with 'I could try and struggle in but I might be a bit of a liability.'

'I've made sure that absolutely everyone is either out of the office, editing or doing something unmissable tomorrow so that there is absolutely no back-up. That way Paul Burns has to show us all what a little whizz-kid he really is. Colin's on camera tomorrow, and he's had such a gutful of this pillock that he will not be doing any missionary work to save the shoot. He's furious with him, so I suspect the second call you'll get will be him to speak to Harry.'

'I should imagine you'll get a panic call pretty soon after that from Paul,' said Sue. 'It's brilliant that I'm on early shift tomorrow because I'll get to witness all the action. By the way, the security guys are thinking of reporting him.'

'Oh, why?'

'Apart from the fact that he treats them like dirt, he keeps parking in the visitors' bay because it's nearer and he can't be bothered to walk from the staff spaces. And he's been caught smoking those stupid cigars in the building.'

'He's really picking up Harry's habits then,' said Janet.

'Absolutely.' Sue nodded. 'He positively refuses to dial his own numbers when he's using a land line, so he gets us to look up the number, ring and then have the bother of putting them through to him. Makes him sound important to the people at the other end. He called me a silly cow the other day because he wanted Directory Inquiries and it had the temerity to be engaged.'

'Are you going to complain?'

'We all thought about it,' continued Sue, 'but you know how useless it is going to someone like Harry. No, we'll deal with it in our own way.'

'Now, my final problem is Val. She's rung just now. And don't faint, she asked me how I was.'

'Good grief. Do you think she's given up the drink?'

'Dunno, but she did sound a bit different. Chastened somehow. Anyway, she wants to meet me for lunch.'

'New and dangerous territory, I'd say.'

'Well, she got quite persistent,' continued Janet, 'and in

the end I thought tomorrow could be a good day. She might just get to witness some of the Paul Burns drama first hand. Whaddya think?'

'I'll make sure you get a few crisis calls on your mobile while you're out,' promised Sue with a grin.

Janet went back to her desk, tapped in Val's mobile number and got the answering service. She left a brief message saying that tomorrow for lunch was fine.

Friday dawned, sunny with a cloudless blue sky. 'Expect the unexpected,' said Janet's horoscope. Now there was a clairvoyant's cop-out. 'Be prepared for the twists and turns of a roller-coaster. It might give you high cheek bones temporarily, but by tonight you'll be back to face the music.'

Perhaps we've got this horribly wrong, she thought in panic. Supposing Steven Byfield had been lying about Paul Burns' abilities? What if he really was a hot-shot director, one of those very-creative-but-deeply-unpleasant-with-it characters? What if Harry found out about the plot that was about to unfold? Would this mean her job was on the line?

She picked up the paper again to read her alternative horoscope. Janet had been born on the cusp of Aquarius and Pisces. Although she was really Pisces, if the prediction was depressing she then read Aquarius on the basis of a balance of probabilities. Today Aquarius was no better. 'Ever had that feeling that no matter what you do, it all goes wrong. This is the day, so remember and appreciate the times when it all goes right. Why not write off the day and go back to bed with a large gin?'

If only, if only, she thought, shuddering for a moment

at the prospect of being sacked by Harry, never working again because he'd rubbish her around the industry, and then being condemned to a life of total penury. It was tempting to take her morning tea and toast back up to bed and hide under the duvet for ever.

She opened her kitchen curtains. Lazing in her tiny garden was certainly another tempting option. It was a blaze of colour, with terracotta pots spilling over with blood-red geraniums, blue trailing lobelia and snow-white alyssum. If she phoned in sick too, not only would she distance herself from the drama of the day, but she'd also avoid lunch with Val.

Nope, she said aloud to the kitchen mirror, I promised I'd be there to observe. I can't back out now. Also, she knew deep down that she was far too intrigued to stay at home. No, it had to be done. She marched upstairs purposefully for a shower.

'Liz has just rung in.' Sue spoke with a straight face, as one of the security guards was sitting next to her at the reception desk. 'She sounds terrible.'

'What's the problem?' asked Janet, looking instantly a picture of concern. At this rate she'd get into RADA.

'Been up all night with the trots. She thinks it might be food poisoning. She's been violently sick too. She sounds ghastly.'

'Okay, thanks, Sue, I'll pass that on. What a pity, it's the line-dancing shoot starting today. We were all hoping for a few laughs about that one.'

Janet went into the production department and sat down at her desk to deal with piles of post and e-mails. She looked deliberately at the roster. Yes, everyone was really, really busy today. Apart from Nina and Veronica, she wouldn't be seeing much of anyone else. Perfect, she thought as she dialled Paul Burns' mobile to deliver the terrible news. Predictably, it was busy.

Nina bustled in with a pot of coffee and cups.

'Never known it so empty in here,' she said. 'It's like the blinkin' Rue Morgue. Everyone's out today by the look of it except you, me and her.'

She indicated with a flick of her head the beautiful but snooty Veronica, who, as usual, was trying to type with impossibly long nail extensions.

'Liz has phoned in sick,' said Janet. She'd thought it best to tell only essential people about the plan. 'Eaten a dodgy curry or something.'

'Cor, that'll give Paul Burns the shits then, won't it?' said Nina. 'He'll have to do some work for a change, ha ha. Serves him right. Shall I give her a ring, see if we can do anything?'

'No, she's had a rotten night. I think we should leave her in peace. I'll try Paul again, although I don't know why I'm bothering because his bloody mobile's permanently engaged. I want to be able to tell him myself and then measure the shock waves down the phone line.'

Paul was still engaged. Did he ever get off that phone? How come his brain hadn't fried? Or perhaps it already had. How could anyone tell? Oh well, on with the estate agents' video series, which was shaping up quite nicely.

Half an hour later she finally got through. Paul Burns was clearly beside himself at the news. He shouted so loudly he almost didn't need a phone. Janet had to hold the receiver a good six inches away from her ear.

'I've travelled all this way just to find out that Liz is ill!

Bloody women, so bloody unpredictable. And thanks a bunch for letting me know. I've never worked with such a load of amateurs in all my life.'

'Well, thank you for that, Paul,' said Janet smoothly. 'I'll pass on that sentiment to the rest of the team. And I'll give your best wishes to Liz. I'm sure you'll be sending her flowers. I have been trying to ring you for the past half an hour but your phone has been constantly engaged. You really ought to invest in a second mobile, you know.'

'Look, I'm here in the backside of nowhere and I've no idea what's been set up. I'm going to look very stupid.'

No change there then, thought Janet. 'Nonsense, Paul,' she continued briskly. 'Liz left copious notes on everything that needed to be done. Obviously you have your copy, so I know you'll be completely au fait with everything she's set up.'

'I . . . I . . . think I must have left them in the office. Anyway, send one of your people up here immediately so we can get on with things. I demand an assistant director on this shoot and I want one now.'

'Let me look at the roster,' said Janet, pausing to create the effect of searching through a long list of names. 'Oh dear, I haven't got a spare bod at all today. Would you believe it, just about everyone's out of the office on various things. And of course I have to turn around an estate agents' project fairly urgently. Nope, sorry, can't help.'

'Then stuff the estate agents,' shouted Paul. 'I don't care what you or anyone else on the planet's doing, I want an assistant director.'

'I think I heard you the second time. Sorry, but Harry told me very firmly that I was definitely hands-off on this

132

one. He knows a whizz-kid when he sees one. And even I'm aware that you're a very experienced director. It's on everyone's lips. No need to be modest,' she added gushingly. 'Tell you what, just in case you've lost Liz's notes, I'll fax you over a copy at your location. I've got the number here. She's so efficient, that girl. You're lucky to have her on the series. She's one of my best.'

'She's no fucking good if she isn't here,' he shouted.

'Sorry, Paul. Don't get paid enough to hear that sort of language. I'll fax over the notes. Have a good shoot.' As she replaced the receiver, she could still hear him ranting.

'Yeeeeeessssss,' she shrieked in triumph to the phone. Nina scuttled over to her desk.

'This is a set-up, isn't it?' she whispered, suspicious all of a sudden.

'Yep,' replied Janet, grinning. 'Liz isn't sick at all, but we thought it best to keep it quiet so that people would react naturally. Sue knows and so does Colin. I've asked him not to rescue the shoot but just to do what Burns asks him. He's sick to death of him too.'

'Brilliant,' said Nina, clapping her hands in delight. 'And there's nobody free to rush up there either.'

'All part of the plan. Also, I'm having lunch with Val today – God knows why – but I thought I might give her a taster of what goes on here. With a bit of luck I'll get a few more abusive calls from Burns while we're in the wine bar. And I've just had another brilliant idea . . .'

Val arrived on time, immaculate in black Jasper Conran with a pair of her trademark spiky heels. Unfortunately, her earlier mood of conciliation had evaporated, along with the first bottle of wine of the day. Cigarette dangling from red-painted lips and fuming because Sue wouldn't let her stand and smoke in reception, she was waiting in the visitors' bay next to her MR2.

When Janet appeared, in cream chinos and a loose white cotton shirt, a look of undisguised disdain passed across Val's face. They climbed into the car and zoomed off at an alarming rate down to the local wine bar, Plonkers.

'Dreadful name. God, it's ghastly,' shuddered Val, taking in the plain wooden seating and spit-and-sawdust atmosphere.

'Well, we all like it and it's handy when you don't have much time,' said Janet, surreptitiously checking her mobile to make sure there was a good signal. They read the chalkboard menu, Val glancing round to make sure that all the clientele had noticed her.

'This place really is full of Plonkers,' she said, a little too loudly. 'I didn't realize men still wore white sports socks with loafers. Eugh.'

'Each to their own,' said Janet, handing her a menu. 'Don't want to hustle you, Val, but I don't have much time. It's proving a difficult day.'

Val was already too pissed to be listening and didn't pick up on Janet's last remark.

'We'll have a bottle of the Sancerre,' she announced pompously to the waiter. 'I'll have the salade niçoise, and for you, Janet?'

'I think I'll go for the steak-and-ale pie.'

'Far too fattening. You'll never get a man if you don't stop all this junk eating,' said Val, pointing a Rouge Noir-painted talon in Janet's direction. 'Pick something healthier.'

Even the waiter looked appalled. Janet was just about to reply when the shrill of the mobile phone came from the depths of her handbag. She scrabbled to find it.

'Oh God, the haunted handbag strikes again,' she muttered, scattering pieces of paper, her notes from this morning's exchange with Paul Burns. She hastily stuffed them back. They were to be typed up when she got home later that day.

'Haunted, why's it haunted?' said Val sarcastically. She'd picked up on that one all right.

'Oh, things in it vanish and then reappear,' said Janet, still delving for the phone.

'You really shouldn't carry around so much junk. Look,' Val said, producing her small Prada clutch bag. 'Just enough room for my lippy, powder, credit cards, car keys and mobile phone. What else would anyone need?'

'Bit different when you work,' muttered Janet bitterly. 'Oh, bugger, I've missed the call now.'

She dialled 121 to retrieve the message. 'You have one new message,' soothed the voice mail. 'Where the fuck are you?' screamed Harry so loudly that even Val heard.

She dialled his direct line, keeping the phone just a fraction away from her ear so that Val could hear the tone of the conversation. Predictably, he launched straight into a torrent of abuse. It was all Janet's fault, Burns shouldn't have been left in the lurch without Liz, this was an important client, one of HOT's biggest contracts for ages, Janet herself should have left immediately to be on location . . . Janet just let him rant until he ran out of steam. Then she launched calmly into a reply.

'Harry, you hired a top-notch director, you showed me his CV, and you told me very firmly to stay off the case. You brought in a big shot to do this project in order to give my lot, and I quote, "a kick up the backside". I'm sure Paul Burns can do this shoot with his hands tied behind his back. Meanwhile, I am having lunch with your wife.'

As she cut him off, a salade niçoise arrived in front of her. She noticed that Val had already got through most of the Sancerre.

chapter sixteen

'Sorry about that,' said Janet, putting away her mobile. 'Slight problem, nothing to worry about.'

'Does he always shout like that?' said Val.

'Oh, you know Harry! But I never take it personally,' Janet lied, amazed at the calm that had come over her. She must get Val involved next time there was a major cock-up. Normally she'd be shaking like a leaf after that onslaught. She managed a couple of mouthfuls of the salade niçoise before the mobile went off again.

'So sorry, Val,' she apologized, fishing out the phone once more. This time it was Paul Burns, ranting because he'd discovered that two women on the line-dancing break had refused to be filmed and were now giving him grief.

'It was all in Liz's research notes, Paul,' Janet said smoothly. 'Even I knew that and I'm nothing to do with this project. I was told strictly hands-off by Harry. With your experience, I'm sure you'll sort it. Have fun and we'll look forward to you teaching us some of the steps on Monday,' she added triumphantly.

She returned to her salad and the now empty bottle of Sancerre. Val had polished off the rest while she was on the phone.

'More wine,' Val demanded of the hovering waiter.

'Not for me, Val. Afternoon's work ahead of me. Don't you think it's a bit risky driving if you have any more?'

Val was about to launch into one of her tirades, punctuated by the painted-talon-stabbing routine, when she was stopped in her tracks. Into the wine bar came a smiling Nina, followed by Sam from Accounts. Nina half waved to them in acknowledgement before they were guided by a waiter to a table at the far end of the room.

'Good God, the London Derrière out with a man. He must think he's watching the world on widescreen.'

'On the contrary,' said Janet. 'That's Sam from Accounts. He finally plucked up the courage and asked her out. They're very much an item now, despite what you said.'

Val lit a cigarette and took another slug of wine. She loathed being proved wrong.

'Well, it won't last,' she almost spat. 'No man would want to be seen out with a butt that size.'

'Sam clearly doesn't see it as a problem. Anyway, Nina's a popular girl. I gather there's quite a waiting list, but he's the only one for her.' At this rate, thought Janet, not only will I have waltzed through RADA, but I could be straight into the National Theatre.

Sue was hovering at the reception desk, dying to find out what had happened.

'I managed to bat all the calls from Harry and Paul on to your mobile,' she grinned. 'How did it go?'

Janet regaled her with what had happened over lunch.

'Apart from accusing me of wearing junk, eating junk and carrying junk around in my handbag, Val was better behaved than usual. By that, I mean that she didn't fall over, scatter food over people or terrorize waiters, so I guess that was a bonus. However, she sank so much wine that she drove up the middle of the road all the way back from Plonkers. It was so scary that I made a virtual will. I've left you my collection of Russ Conway records, by the way.'

'Oh, thanks heaps,' replied Sue. 'So long as it includes "Side Saddle". I'm just amazed she hasn't been done for drinking and driving before now. But that's Val. She gets away with it all the time, lucky sod. If we did it once, it would be a case of instant fine and ban. It's not fair.'

'My other little bit of mischief has paid off, though,' said Janet. 'I told Nina to set up a lunchtime meeting with Sam to discuss the budgets for the property project and how they were going to code them. I told her to book a table at Plonkers and put the bill on her expenses. I'm hoping it might get them together, but it also gave me the satisfaction of getting back at Val over her bitchy remarks.'

'Did it work?'

'I think something registered, but it might have been merely the Sancerre.'

Nina came back from lunch, flushed and obviously happy. To Janet's delight, and Veronica's scowling, she announced that not only had they sorted out all the budget codes, but Sam had asked her out to dinner on Saturday night. After she'd done a celebratory skip around the office, she went off to make some tea.

'Any calls?' Janet asked Veronica.

'Yeah, plenty,' she replied sullenly. 'Harry, Paul, Harry,

Paul, then Harry, then Paul, oh, and one from Colin but he'll ring you again later.'

'Right, I'll just go and see Harry then,' Janet said, with determination in her voice. I will *not* quiver in my shoes, she told herself as she entered the soft grey hessianed walls of the executive corridor. But the bespectacled Geraldine, clacking away on her keyboard, was minding empty offices. The management, including Harry, had obviously gone home early.

'Harry's having a late lunch,' Geraldine announced imperiously, 'and I don't blame him after all that hassle this morning.'

'What hassle?' beamed Janet innocently.

'Oh, the woman running that dancing course thingy is threatening legal action.'

'Really?' Janet fought an inner battle to keep a broad grin off her face. This was the ghastly woman with the ego problem Liz had mentioned. No doubt Burns had rubbed her up the wrong way. He certainly managed to do it with just about everyone else.

'I'm sure the talented Mr Burns will sort it all out,' she continued. 'After all, that's exactly why Harry brought him in. I must say, he's been an inspiration to us all.'

Geraldine glanced up from beneath her hennaed bob and gave Janet a slightly puzzled look. Watch this space – between my ears – it seemed to say. Then she clicked back into blind loyalty mode.

'Harry only hires the best,' she pronounced, with a look that suggested he might have made a bit of a cock-up in Janet's case.

'Oh well, I'll leave you to it. Have a nice weekend. Doing anything special?' It suddenly occurred to Janet that she'd never before asked Geraldine that type of question.

Geraldine was equally stunned to be asked and at a loss to answer.

'I, er, we, er that is, a friend and I are going to see *Carmina Piranha*.'

'Oh, marvellous,' said Janet, mentally adding the latest G-spot to the already bulging file.

Val arrived home in a temper. She'd been looking for fun, sophisticated chat, a laugh. But instead she'd been dragged to that appalling wine bar, sidelined the entire time by a mobile phone and then given a lecture on drinking and driving. How dare Janet? Who did she think she was? From Val's point of view, Janet's only saving grace was that she always looked like a sack of potatoes, which had the effect of making Val look even more glamorous.

Val went into the kitchen, opened a bottle of white wine and poured herself a large glass. Then she picked up her address book and had another flurry through it. Page after page of friends from school and modelling days, now all unavailable, bogged down by kids and boring husbands. Perhaps if she and Harry had a baby it might improve her social life. She could at least then join in all the nappy chat, it would please her parents, who were now dropping huge hints about being grandparents, and it might make Harry get home a bit earlier.

She flopped on to one of the big cream leather sofas in their sitting room, lit a cigarette and flicked on the television. Channel after channel offered her nothing of interest: reruns of old game shows, vintage episodes of soaps, endless makeovers of people and their ghastly houses and gardens. God, they were all at it. Soon they'd be running out of people and places to be made over. She refilled her glass and lit another cigarette. Life was boring and it was all Harry's fault. Then she remembered that he was going away at the end of the month. Even more boring. The room began to sway, the television lost focus, and soon Val was sound asleep.

By the time Janet left the HOT offices, she was completely drained. All she could think about as she pointed her car in the direction of home was a scented bath, a warm dressing gown, a little microwave something or other to make up for the lunchtime salad she'd hardly touched, and then bed. The strain of the day had suddenly caught up with her.

She walked wearily through the front door, flicked on a couple of lamps, put on some soothing classical guitar music and double-checked that her answering machine was on. Peace and quiet, that was what she needed. She flopped down on her old sofa and gazed around the place. Could do with an overhaul, but at least it was cosy and warm. She wondered for a minute how Geraldine was getting on with *Carmina Piranha*. Perhaps the opera had been re-scored with a snappier beat.

The ping of the microwave coincided with the sound of the phone. There was no contest; the Chinese chicken and cashew won hands down. Except that she heard Colin's voice leaving her a message. He wanted a chat about what had happened during the day. She gobbled down the chicken as fast as she could and pressed the call-back button.

'Well?' she said expectantly.

'Where do I begin?' said Colin. There was no mistaking the exasperation in his voice. 'That man is a complete buffoon. He's done about as much filming as

I've undertaken keyhole surgery. Didn't have a clue about what he wanted, walked through shots, refused to switch off his phone, insulted the interviewees. You name it, he did it. He upset the woman running the course big-time. Mind you, that wasn't difficult. She was a complete road accident. Big fat cow with a voice to match.'

'I heard from the dreaded Geraldine that she was making some sort of complaint. I hope it's not against you.'

'No, sweet, of course not. There were two women on the course who didn't want to be filmed. Now that's always a nuisance from my point of view, but it's not insurmountable. But it was all too much for that idiot. He kept on insisting that I film wide shots which included them. Well, they would have been unusable and a complete waste of time. So in the end we had a stand-off. Then the women complained, quite rightly, to Mrs Bossy Boots and war was declared. Tomorrow's shoot's been cancelled because of it.'

'Did you ring Harry to report?'

'Tried during the day but he was busy. The way that weirdo Geraldine protects him, you'd think he was running the bloody Kremlin or planning the next world summit. Mind you, Burns got through on his perennial mobile, of course. God knows what was said but I expect I've been rubbished behind my back. Fortunately I have Ron as my witness. He was equally pissed off. We took one or two other little precautions to cover ourselves.'

'Like what?'

'Oh, you'll find out. I'll keep it up my sleeve for now.'

'Good day all round then,' said Janet. 'I enjoyed a certain

amount of abuse from Paul and Harry. All topped off by lunch with Val.'

'Must have been a bit of a belter, then,' said Colin. 'I've just tried Harry at home to register a formal complaint. Val answered, and to be frank, she sounded blind drunk. What did you girls get up to?'

'Not me, matey. I think Val had had a few before she arrived. I had so many calls on the mobile during lunch that she polished off the best part of two bottles of Sancerre. Then I had a white-knuckle ride back to the office in her car.'

'Well, it sounds as though she carried on, because when I rang this evening, she was well and truly vino collapso.'

'Harry not there?' asked Janet.

'No, apparently not.'

'Interesting. Did you try his mobile?'

'Switched off.'

'Hmm, even more interesting.' She reached for paper and pencil.

Saturday dawned bright and sunny. Even the flowers seemed to be looking skywards to say thank you. A pale pink clematis vied with a deep scarlet rambling rose for prime position on the small garden wall in front of Liz's flat. Janet put down her Sainsbury's carrier bags on the front step and rang the doorbell.

'Supplies for the patient,' she grinned when Liz opened the door. 'Can't have you staggering around a supermarket in your state of health.'

In Liz's tiny galley kitchen they unpacked bags of mixed salad, sirloin steaks, french bread, white wine, plus all the usual basics. Soon the steaks were sizzling under the grill, the salad was dressed and the bread cut up and ready to serve.

'I thought we'd eat in the garden as it's such a lovely day,' said Liz. 'Don't worry, we won't be spotted. For a town flat, it's really secluded.'

'Everyone at the office hopes you'll get better soon,' said Janet sarcastically, taking in Liz's Bermuda shorts and strappy tee-shirt.

'Do you think anyone twigged?' Liz asked anxiously.

'The only people who officially know are Colin, Sue and Nina. I thought it safest to keep the number of people in on it to a minimum.'

Over the steak and salad, washed down by copious amounts of chilled Chardonnay, Janet recounted events at the line-dancing weekend. Liz laughed uproariously when she got to the bit about the woman who ran the course.

'I knew she was trouble, that one, when I was setting it up. Maybe I've had a lucky escape. I do hope she makes a complaint to Harry.'

'Oh it's worse than that. Today's shoot has been cancelled, with everyone citing irreconcilable differences. I wouldn't imagine the people from Hot Breaks For Heartaches are going to be all that bowled over. If I were you, I'd stay off on Monday. Keep out of it.'

'I hope I'm not going to be blamed for what's happened. Harry's bound to be looking for a scapegoat,' said Liz, the old familiar fear creeping across her face.

'No, you won't be blamed. I have a copy of your notes, detailing all the potential problems. Colin and Ron are on your side. They were there, don't forget. They witnessed the whole thing. And Colin hinted that he'd taken a few precautions himself. I think I can guess what.'

'Puts Harry's mystery freebie in jeopardy, doesn't it?' said Liz. 'But mark my words, Harry will wriggle out of this one as usual. Someone else will cop the blame.'

'Not this time. I have a feeling . . .'

chapter seventeen

It was Black Monday in every sense. The weekend sunshine had evaporated and now it was hot and humid, with storm clouds threatening to deposit their contents all over Hartford.

News of the events of the previous week had obviously spread like wildfire. All the production office staff seemed to know about what had happened, even though the vast majority had been out of the office on Friday. Clearly phones had been hot over the weekend. People were openly laughing about tales of Paul Burns' incompetence. Like all good gossip, the tales had grown like Topsy. Now the fat woman had taken on legendary status, apparently kicking Burns into Casualty with her cowboy boots. One joke doing the rounds was that Burns had won the Queen's Award for Industry for single-handedly causing his mobile phone company's shares to rocket. Another joke was that *OK!* magazine were going to cover him unveiling a new phone mast which was to be named after him.

Janet sat at her desk, regretting bitterly that she couldn't join in the revelry. Any minute now the phone would ring and it would be Geraldine summoning her to

Harry's office for one of his legendary blame-storming sessions. At least she knew him well enough not to be wrong-footed.

When the inevitable call came, she picked up a file and made her way slowly and deliberately to Harry's office.

'Siddown,' he bellowed, engrossed in the paperwork on his desk.

Janet sank down into her usual chair. Harry didn't look up for a few seconds, during which time Janet became transfixed by the sight confronting her. She was reminded why some of the girls in the office referred to him as 'No Balls Hampton'. The thought made her grin.

'I don't know why you're smiling,' he barked. 'This is no laughing matter.' He thumped what was obviously the Hot Breaks file on his desk. 'I warn you, Janet, heads will roll.'

'Any particular ones in mind?' She couldn't believe how calm she felt. It must be the under-the-desk discovery.

'Don't be fucking flippant with me. Or yours will be the first,' he hissed at her. 'Let me make myself clear. This is an important project, it's worth a lot of money and it was totally fucked up on Friday.'

'Why are you telling me this?'

'You're head of the bloody production department. The buck stops with you. It's your fault.'

'Sorry, Harry, you can't have it both ways. You hired in Paul Burns; you told me in no uncertain terms that he was the man for the job, and that I was to keep out of it. Which I did.'

But Harry wasn't listening. 'I've had a madwoman on the phone ranting to me about the behaviour of our crew on Friday. As a result, the shoot's been cancelled. Hot

Breaks have probably lost customers, we've lost the item and we'll have to reshoot at our own expense. And this company has been made to look incompetent.'

'So who are you going to blame?'

'Well, for a start that stupid cow shouldn't have gone sick.'

'By stupid cow, I gather you mean Liz,' said Janet, still amazed at her own calm.

'Yes, I bloody do. She shouldn't have been ill, she was probably skiving. Anyway, she should have warned Paul about this stupid cow running the course.'

'There seems to be a whole herd of stupid cows in this story, Harry.' She smiled sweetly at him. 'But there's one complete dolt-brain, who stands head and shoulders above the rest, and that's Paul Burns. Liz couldn't help being sick. But Paul Burns could certainly do himself a favour by learning to read. All the pitfalls of this shoot were clearly outlined in Liz's notes.' She patted the file on her lap and then selected a piece of paper from it.

'Let me read you an extract,' she continued. "Confidential Warning", it's headed. Then Liz writes: "I anticipate problems with Mrs Saunders. I have briefed her very thoroughly about the complexities of the filming and how we may ask her to do some things twice or possibly three times for different camera angles. She's very dismissive and pompous, a classic know-it-all. I have undertaken that we will not include in the edited product the two people on the course who did not give their consent. We will endeavour to exclude them during the filming to put their minds at rest." I think that's perfectly clear. Unfortunately, it wasn't for Paul Burns because he obviously didn't bother to read the notes before he went off to the shoot. And before you start disagreeing, Harry,' she pointed a finger at him, Val-fashion, 'Paul phoned me on Friday spitting teeth because of course he hadn't a clue what he was doing.'

Harry sat back, his face contorted with rage. Janet noted with secret amusement that he was wearing one of those incredibly naff shirts, blue and white stripes with a plain white collar. The type spivvy politicians wore with pinstriped suits and clashing ties.

'Where's Paul today anyway?' she continued. 'It's only fair he should be part of this discussion.'

'He phoned in sick this morning,' barked Harry.

'Oh, not skiving then,' said Janet, getting up from her chair. The irony of her remark was wasted on Harry. 'Why don't we have another chat when Paul comes back? After all, if there are another seven of these pieces to shoot, he might as well get it right next time. Perhaps we should give him another chance.'

Janet returned to her office, shaking like a leaf. She'd been so calm and controlled, but now it was over she was suffering delayed shock. She'd given Harry a real shock too, and he knew it. After making a quick call to Colin, she replaced the receiver and smiled. 'Gotcha', she muttered, wishing she could down a really large gin and tonic and then feeling ashamed because it was only 9.20 a.m.

Harry paced around the office, white-faced with anger. That cow would have to go sooner or later. She was getting too smart for her own good. He hated losing control of situations. Clearly Paul Burns had been set up by the pair of them, Janet and Liz. Too miffed to cope when real talent was brought in over their heads. He'd have to speak to the Hot Breaks people and do some damage limitation.

He sipped his coffee, lit a cigar, sat back in his chair

150

and spent a few minutes mentally preparing his speech. Then he shouted at Geraldine to get Hot Breaks on the line.

'David Rawlins? Harry Hampton here. How are you, mate? Good. Good. Spot of bother on Friday but it's been dealt with. As you know, I put a real hot-shot director on to this project and of course he's used to dealing with more able people. One or two of our girls haven't shaped up to the standards he requires. So rest assured, heads will be rolling. We'll obviously reshoot at our expense. And of course the first thing I did this morning was to send flowers and a note of apology to Mrs Saunders. Yes, yes. Absolutely. Now, how about dinner on Friday? Good, I'll get Geraldine to book. Okay, matey, see you then.'

He slammed the phone down and breathed a sigh of relief. Salvaged that one. He glanced around at the paintings on his office wall. Yes, originals certainly did have a certain cachet. And the little deal he'd done with the gallery ensured that quite a few more would be winging their way to his home, all of course paid for by the company.

'Geraldine,' he barked through the open door. 'Get fifty quid's worth of flowers off to that madwoman who phoned this morning. Oh, and book a table for four at Shiraz for Friday night.'

Nobody had ever seen Nina work so hard. She whipped through a pile of electronic filing like a whirling dervish, she jumped up and cheerfully made coffee for up to twenty people at a time and generally skipped around the office with a grin stretching from ear to ear.

'If you didn't get it at the weekend,' said Ray, 'I'd like to know what you did get to make you this bloody happy. Whatever it is, where can I find some?'

Ray, usually the fount of all good gossip, obviously didn't know about Nina's date at the weekend with Sam.

'Mind your own blinkin' business,' smiled Nina, delighted to get one over on him. 'What did you do at the weekend?'

'Don't even ask. I can't believe I'm telling you this, but I got dragged along to see *The Sound of Music*.'

Several people overheard this confession and started to laugh. Choruses of 'Do Re Mi' started up, with the emphasis on the Ray.

'Well, it wasn't quite what it seemed,' said Ray, now horribly aware that everyone was listening. 'It was billed as the ultimate karaoke event. They had all the words of the songs burned into the film so everyone could join in. And loads of people came dressed as nuns, or Nazis, or goatherds, or dressed in curtains. It was quite a scream, actually, because you could boo the Baroness and hiss at the Nazis and cheer during the flaky bits. God, I can't believe I'm confessing this to you lot. I'll never live it down.'

'The funny thing was, though,' Ray lowered his voice to talk to Nina, 'when I saw all those people in costume, I had this weird fantasy of Geraldine dressed up as a nun, complete with wimple.'

'Oh, don't be daft,' Nina laughed, skipping off towards Janet's desk at the other end of the office.

'Can we meet for lunch?' she whispered to Janet. 'I think I may have a contribution to the Haunted Handbag.'

An hour later they were in a favourite corner of the GX, tinkering with penne and arrabiata sauce as Nina gave Janet a blow-by-blow account of her date on

Saturday night. Apparently it had gone well, and she and Sam had now swapped home phone numbers, with another date planned for Wednesday evening.

'Good job you're not seeing him tonight,' said Janet. 'This sauce is loaded with garlic. The GX should open franchises in China. It would sort out their population problem overnight. I'm going to have to keep my distance from everyone this afternoon after this lot, and I don't even have any red-hot bonking on my agenda.'

'Well, it's about time you did,' said Nina, desperate not to monopolize the conversation with her new-found happiness. 'Bleugh. You're right about the garlic. Maybe I'll keep away from Accounts this afternoon.'

'Anyway,' said Janet, scooping up the last of the sauce with some ciabatta, 'what's the latest offering for Operation Haunted Handbag?'

'As Head of Office Snooping,' said Nina, lowering her voice conspiratorially, 'I have to report that the office has been got at again.'

'Whaddya mean? Bugged?'

'Well, I wouldn't put it past them. No, things have been walking again. At least two secretaries told me some of their e-mail had been read when they checked this morning. A couple of the researchers remarked that their stuff had been moved and put it down to the cleaners. But I just know that my desk has been shuffled about a bit.'

'How can you tell?' asked Janet sweetly. Nina was renowned for having the most untidy desk in the building.

'I'll ignore that remark,' Nina grinned. 'My filing trays were all over the place and my drawers had been gone through.'

Janet laughed. 'I occasionally lie in bed and fantasize about someone going through my drawers.'

'Then you would have to cut out the garlic,' said Nina. 'No, seriously, it was just like last time, when the catering college tapes went missing and I copped the blame for it.'

'So Harry's been on the prowl again,' said Janet thoughtfully. 'Perhaps it was Friday night, after the line-dancing fiasco. I was summoned to the bollocking room first thing this morning over that one. All my fault, apparently. Oh, and Liz's for having the temerity to be ill!'

'Oh, shit. That must have been terrible.'

'Oddly enough, after all these years of dealing with Harry, shaking in my boots and dreading those sorts of show-downs, for the first time ever I really did stand my ground. The funny thing is, it was actually easy. For a start, it was very firm ground that I was on. Burns is such a plonker and I had Liz's notes about the shoot. But there were a couple of other things that struck me as I sat there.'

'Like what?'

'Well, Harry was wearing a particularly nasty shirt – you know that stripy sort with the contrasting collar. Always look as though they ran out of material. And there was something else.'

'Like what?'

'No balls. I had to sit in that ridiculous visitor's chair with the eye-level view of his crotch. And there was one other thing.'

Nina raised her eyebrows quizzically.

'I found myself emulating Val with her famous finger-pointing routine. There was a moment when I wagged a finger at him, and do you know, he really flinched.'

'Obviously gets a lot of it at home,' said Nina.

They paid up and went back to the office. Paul Burns' Mercedes was parked in a visitor's space, right in front of the main entrance. So he'd returned to face the music.

'Geraldine? Janet here. As Paul's back now, I'd like to set up a meeting with him and Harry at three. Is Harry free then?' Janet kept her voice loud enough for Paul to hear from his desk. She wasn't going to consult him on the matter. 'Yes, urgent need to discuss the next Hot Breaks programmes. Good, we'll come in at three.'

Paul Burns went momentarily white. It wasn't a colour that went with his outfit today. Sporting a green, red and yellow striped blazer and wide cream trousers with turn-ups, he looked as if he'd have been more at home sipping Pimm's at Henley. And after the weekend fiasco, that was where he'd probably have preferred to be. Suddenly his mobile phone went off. The old confidence instantly returned. He was once again on familiar ground, talking to one of his many callers, who all seemed to go by the name of Nigel. There always seemed to be deals going on.

Janet quietly opened one of her desk drawers. There at the back was what she was looking for. She shut the drawer firmly and watched the clock tick round until three.

chapter eighteen

Harry did all the talking. He ranted, he raved, he shouted, he seethed. It was all directed at Janet. Liz was off the series, she could walk the plank as far as he was concerned. Paul Burns needed and deserved better support; this was a big project for HOT. It could lead to many, many more very prestigious and lucrative contracts, but not if there were any more cock-ups. Harry strode about the office, thumping his desk every time he passed it.

Janet sat impassively as the torrent was unleashed. Beside her, Paul Burns lent silent support to Harry, nodding sagely at appropriate moments.

'I will not have my . . . I mean . . . our reputation fucked up by some stupid fat woman running a linedance class of all things. That bloody woman has caused so much trouble. She's complained to Hot Breaks, the people in the class have complained. This is jeopardizing the whole project, and future projects to come.'

Not to mention your freebie holiday, thought Janet. Wait until he's finished. Keep calm, say nothing.

Eventually even Harry ran out of steam. Then Paul Burns took up the reins.

'I've never worked with such incompetents in all my

career,' he proclaimed. 'I was promised your best researchers and what do I get? Absolute crap. It just beggars belief. And as for the crew, downright rude, bolshy, uncooperative, didn't seem to know what they were doing. I can't believe I was expected to work with people like that. I really don't know how you run a department with such a lack of talent.'

Janet finally stood up. She shot them a look of utter contempt, then she calmly produced a VHS tape from a file she'd been holding and strolled over to the bank of machines on a wall of Harry's office.

'Guys, I'd like to show you something that you might find quite riveting,' she said, picking up the remote control from Harry's desk. She aimed it at the machine and pressed 'play'. Paul smiled contemptuously; Harry sneered. That was all about to change, she was certain.

It was rather like the fascination of watching security videos on *Crimestoppers*. The line-dancing session was in full swing, with the enormous Mrs Saunders, resplendent in stetson, cowboy boots, a Union Jack-patterned flippy short skirt and suede-fringed top, demonstrating some of the steps. Ludicrous would have been too kind a word, and a decent sports bra wouldn't have gone amiss. Suddenly Paul Burns barged into the shot, stopped the demonstration and demanded that she do it again. Grudgingly she obliged. The demonstration started again, only to be interrupted by Paul off camera obviously taking a very noisy call on his mobile. Mrs Saunders visibly bristled but soldiered on. Several more noisy calls followed, all picked up on the sound track, including one to the ubiquitous Nigel, one to book theatre tickets and another to check a stock price on the Nasdaq. Her patience now in tatters, Mrs

Saunders could be seen striding heavily across the room towards Burns, who was still behind the camera, to demand that he switch off the phone. An argument ensued along the lines of 'We're here to film your silly little line-dancing session and this is a Hollywood director you're talking to. And no, I won't switch off my phone. I'm important.'

The next section included a discussion between Colin, the cameraman, and Ron, the sound recordist, on the shooting of a particular sequence. Colin could be clearly heard having to spell out to Paul that if he continually got into shot and didn't switch off his phone, the film would all be unusable. 'If we shoot it from here, it will be completely uneditable,' Colin was pointing out. 'If we move to the position near the window, it just won't cut. It'll cross the line from here. The lighting's all wrong for a start. The shots won't match.'

By now, both Harry and Paul were surreptitiously looking around for the remote control, which Janet still held firmly in her now rather sweaty hand.

The grand finale was a spectacular row: Paul Burns versus the two women who had asked not to be filmed. Paul's attitude could have been best summed up as 'tough shit'. He pompously told them he knew nothing of this request and thought it was the most ridiculous thing he'd ever heard in his entire and very extensive career. Colin then made a rare appearance in front of his own camera, waving Liz's research notes in front of Paul. 'Well, we knew about it several days ago. It's all in there, mate,' he said. 'It's all in our film briefs too.' He then proceeded to apologize to the two women for Paul's behaviour in the most charming way.

Janet stopped the tape. There was a pause.

'A picture paints a thousand words, as I think you'll both agree,' she declared, unsmiling.

'How dare he film all that,' spluttered Paul, crimson with anger. 'That's outrageous.'

'No, just out in the open. A couple of tips about filming, Paul, that I'm very happy to pass on,' said Janet smoothly. 'Firstly, if that little red light's on at the front of the camera, then he's rolling. And secondly, if you want your cameraman to stop filming, just say, "Cut." I'll leave you two gentlemen to enjoy the rest of the tape.'

She walked out of the office without even glancing at Harry. Standing right outside the door and therefore caught by surprise, was Geraldine, who immediately pretended to be scrabbling around her desk for a pen.

'Why not try a glass up to the wall next time?' said Janet as she swept past. 'Much better sound quality.'

'Hmm, the *Hartford Echo* is starting a campaign about mobile phones,' said Ray, feet up on his desk because Janet was out of the office.

'What about them?' asked Bob, one of the researchers, who was taking a call on his and at the same time trying to have a fag by hanging out of an open window because he couldn't be bothered to go outside to the smokers' hut.

'They want to ban them in public places, bars, restaurants, that sort of thing,' said Ray, skimming the article. 'Good idea, if you ask me. I get really sick of people on trains, answering their phones by shouting, "I'm on the train," to which the rest of the carriage choruses, "So are we".'

'Well, it won't stop Burns, will it?' said Bob, rolling his eyes. 'His phone's actually welded to his ear. I should know, I have the misfortune of working with him on Hot Breaks.'

Janet slipped back into her desk at the other end of the office. For the second time that day, she'd have killed for a large gin and tonic. Perhaps she should keep a minibar in her filing cabinet. Her head was now filled with questions. What would happen now? Would Harry carry on defending Paul, or would he find some reason to get rid of him? The one thing she was sure of was that Harry, as always, would come out of it squeaky clean. She was just starting to think about a treatment for another of the property bulletins when Paul Burns came into the office. Without a word, without a glance, he started to clear his desk. It didn't take long. He'd never spent much time there anyway. Then he picked up his briefcase – Gucci, of course – and walked out without a backward glance.

'Bloody hell, that was a whole five minutes without a call on the old mobile,' remarked Bob. 'Hey, get me the *Guinness Book of Records* on the phone immediately.'

'He looked a bit stroppy,' said Ray. 'Perhaps he's upset that he didn't finish that line-dancing course. I really could see him in a ten-gallon hat, prancing around doing all that yee-haw stuff.'

'God knows what he'll do with the murder-mystery weekend I'm setting up,' said Bob. 'I'm dealing with actors, and you know how stroppy they can be.'

'Maybe you could make him the murder victim.'

'Brilliant idea. Trouble is, everyone would have a motive.'

Janet replaced her phone and walked down to where Bob and Ray were sitting.

'Hanging out of the window smoking doesn't count in a no-smoking office,' she said, trying to keep a straight face.

'Er, I was trying to get a signal on my mobile,' muttered Bob.

'Don't be ridiculous. Paul Burns doesn't have that problem,' said Janet sternly. Then her face broke out in a huge grin.

'Or rather, should I say, Paul Burns *didn't* have that problem. I've just heard that he's left the building for good. Gone, kaput, finito.'

'That's fantastic,' they both chorused, not quite believing their luck. 'Drinks all round in the GX after work!'

Janet went back to her desk and quietly dialled a number.

'Thank you, Colin. That was utterly magnificent. It was far more than you promised . . . Yes, yes, it did the trick . . . Yes, he's gone. Won't be darkening our doorstep again . . . No, I didn't get a chance to view it beforehand, so I took a huge flyer on it . . . No, the office was too busy and also, remember, Burns was here. I had to trust what you said and just shove it in the machine . . . You bet I was shaking. The beauty of it was that everything he denied, all the lies, it was all there on the tape. It was a wonderful moment. I will always savour it . . . The rest of the series? I'm hoping Liz will direct. Just have to sort it with the Fat Controller . . . After today? A pushover, I hope. A huge drink next time I see you . . . Yes, it's a promise.'

She replaced the receiver. The phone rang again immediately.

'Elvis has now left the building,' said Sue. 'Is this what I hope it is?'

'Yep,' said Janet in triumph. 'Did you not detect the smell of burning martyr when he left?'

'I think I probably did,' said Sue. 'This is fantastic news, and I insist on a blow-by-blow account. We must have a Haunted Handbag meeting soon. I've something interesting to report.'

'So has Nina. Stuff's been moving again. How about my place on Friday night?'

'Brilliant. I'll tell Liz and Nina.'

Harry sat back in his *Mastermind* chair and contemplated the fiasco he'd just witnessed. Janet had certainly played a blinder, he had to grudgingly give her that one. As for Burns, he'd had the rug pulled from under his feet.

He went across to the VHS machine and ejected the tape. Then he flipped up the back of the plastic cover with a pen and pulled out yard after yard of tape. Satisfied that it was wrecked beyond repair, he dropped both tape and box in the bin.

Harry did not like being made a fool of. And Janet, being a typical female gasbag, would not keep her mouth shut. Everyone in that production office would know about it by teatime.

'Get me Steven Byfield,' he shouted to Geraldine, who was deliberately keeping a low profile but romping home ahead of the field in the Curiosity Stakes.

'Steven, it's Harry Hampton at Hartford Optimum TV. How are you doing, matey? How's it all going?' Harry had never been particularly friendly with Steven, even before his untimely departure. Steven was too smart and too nosy for his own good. But Harry was never averse to a bit of creeping, especially when it involved personal gain.

'Fine, fine,' replied Steven. 'Just finished a series on after-dinner speakers called *Accustomed As I Am*. Network snapped it up, so watch out for it soon. And you?'

'Oh, ducking and diving, the usual.'

'So, what can I do for you?' said Steven, trying to hide the suspicion in his voice. Any call from Harry was always bad news.

'Paul Burns.' Harry's voice was suddenly cold.

'Oh, Paul Burns. Did you hire him in the end?' said Steven innocently.

'I did.'

'And how's he doing? Has he won you any awards yet? Only a question of time, you know. A unique talent.'

'Unique talent, my arse,' Harry hissed. 'That's precisely why I'm ringing. Had to let him go. I sacked him this afternoon. He was total fucking crap.'

'Let's see. Paul Burns?' pondered Steven theatrically. 'Bullshitter extraordinaire, CV with more holes in it than a colander, inventive references and qualifications. Ability to upset people without even trying. Rude, pompous, lazy. Inability to put a sentence together. Perennially clamped to his mobile phone. Still the same?'

'That's him. So why the fuck did you recommend him?' Harry was now incandescent with anger and thumping his desk so loudly that Geraldine was wondering whether she'd burst an eardrum if she followed Janet's advice and put a glass to the wall.

'I recommended him to return a – well, let's call it a favour. It goes like this, Harry. I work at HOT in charge of the production office. I make wonderful programmes, come up with fabulous ideas, create amazing campaigns, work my butt off. You take the credit. I discover you doing a major fiddle with backhanders all over the place. Bungs to the left of you, bonuses to the right.'

'This has got absolutely nothing to do with Paul Burns,' spluttered Harry.

'Oh yes it has,' contradicted Steven, enjoying himself

163

hugely. 'Paul Burns was one of the most incompetent oppos I have ever come across. Up here, we endured the over-the–top zoot suits, the wall-to-wall mobile phone calls, the ducking out of doing anything because he couldn't actually do it. And I felt that you deserved this most talented man, plus his unusual wardrobe. Which is why I recommended him to you.'

'You total bastard,' barked Harry, now white-faced and livid.

'So, Harry,' continued Steven, 'it was a bit of a long shot really. You didn't have to hire him. But you did, so I guess that makes us fifteen-all.'

chapter nineteen

Val couldn't understand why Harry was in such a filthy mood. He'd wrong-footed her by coming home early, barging into the house just after five o'clock in a monumental fury. At least it wasn't her fault. He was so angry that he hadn't even shouted at her because he'd found her, feet up on the sofa, watching re-runs of *Dynasty*. He didn't even shout at her when she couldn't come up with any sort of suggestion for dinner.

He poured himself a huge gin and tonic and stomped off round the garden. Thank God he's off on this business trip at the weekend, she thought. Good bloody riddance. She'd go to Hampshire, see her parents and get together with some girlfriends. Then the same old pang hit her. The only girlfriends she seemed to catch up with these days were the four from HOT. Maybe they'd know why Harry was in such a strop. Maybe she'd invite them over to the house while Harry was away. Oh God, that meant cooking. No, she thought, she'd get in a chef. That would impress them. She began to plan.

Harry burst in through the French windows and headed straight for the gin bottle again.

'What's up with you?' she enquired casually. 'Bad day at work?'

''Course it bloody was. Why do you think I'm so angry, you stupid cow? Are you blind or something? Now get off your arse and get some dinner sorted. No, on second thoughts, I can't face another evening of your burnt bloody offerings. We'll go out. You'll have to drive. I'm over the limit now.'

Val went upstairs and changed, pathetically pleased that he wanted to spend a whole evening with her. And even more pleased that it didn't involve cooking. She put on another of the new sparkly cocktail numbers she'd bought from the Ginette fashion show. It was a deep plum-red shift dress with shoestring straps, and she'd managed to get some wonderful Italian patent-leather kitten heels in the same colour. She'd lie about the price, if he bothered to ask. Harry rarely noticed if she was wearing anything new. She swept her blonde hair up into a pleat, painted her nails to match the dress, and she was ready to go.

She came downstairs feeling particularly glamorous and hoping for some sort of compliment from Harry. But he was still in the blackest of moods.

'Oh, you ready? Right, let's go. I've booked Shiraz while you were upstairs tarting up. We'll go in the Merc. I can never get into your bloody stupid Toyota.'

That's because you're too fat, she thought. They set off for the restaurant, which was on the other side of Hartford. During the five-mile journey, Harry harangued her nonstop about her driving. By the time they arrived, they were both in even blacker moods.

'Your usual table, Mr Hampton?' enquired the camp maître d'.

'No, by the window, I think, this time.'

'Oh, you've been here before.' Val shot him an accusing look. She turned to the maître d', flashing a huge smile. 'My husband likes to keep me locked up in a cupboard. Never takes me anywhere.'

With Harry still glowering, they took their seats and were presented with menus.

'So where do you normally sit?' Val enquired. 'In some dark secretive corner, I suppose.'

'Oh, for God's sake, Val, let up. I bring clients here. They don't always want to be on view to all and sundry. Now shut up. I'm hungry and I want a drink.'

He turned to the hovering waiter. 'Large gin and tonic for me and mineral water for the lady. She's driving. Then we'll have the scallops to start, followed by the sea bass. Oh, and get a bottle of Pauillac opened, ready for later on.'

Val knew Harry well enough to know there was no arguing with him, either about the choice of meal or about anything else for that matter.

'So what's wrong, Harry?' She was dying to know.

'Oh, never you mind. I'd like to see that bloody Janet Bancroft swing from the rafters. But other than that, just a normal day.'

'Janet? What's she been up to?'

'None of your business. Don't want to discuss.'

'I bet you're looking forward to the conference, aren't you?' Val was hellbent on making some sort of conversation.

Harry looked blank.

'The conference thingy this weekend; you're going away on business, aren't you?'

'Oh yes, the conference. Yes, yes, of course. And a lot of meetings. For God's sake, Val, shut up. All right?'

They finished the meal in silence, Harry polishing off

all the wine with Val sipping her mineral water and looking enviously as the last glass disappeared down his
throat.

Liz was still reeling from the news. She caught sight of
herself in her hall mirror with a stupid grin plastered
from ear to ear. So Paul Burns had finally gone. The plan
had paid off. And even Harry had got his comeuppance.
Just for once she'd have given anything to be in his office,
to see their faces as the tape was played.

Then she shivered at the prospect of being in Harry's
office. She shivered some more at Janet's suggestion that
she take over the directing of the Hot Breaks series as
originally mooted. Janet had been very persuasive.

'I know why you ruled it out last time, and I do understand,' Janet had said, 'but the tables have now been
turned. Burns made such a monumental cock-up that the
only way is up. You can do this standing on your head.'

In the end Liz had reluctantly agreed, but on the basis
that she never went into Harry's office alone. Janet said
she would put the idea in principle to Harry.

Liz wandered back into her kitchen. The mention of
Harry's name always sent shivers down her spine, and
she thought back to that terrible night he'd turned up at
her flat. And the consequences. At least the Paul Burns
episode had gone a little way towards paying him back for
what he'd done.

Harry finally lost his temper big-time when they reached
the police station.

'It's utterly impossible, it's bloody ridiculous,' he
shouted, red-faced with anger. 'She can't possibly be over
the limit. She didn't have a drink all evening. The silly

cow drank water because she was driving. Your testing kit must be faulty. I demand it be checked. Immediately.'

'Sir, I suggest you calm down. Your wife was breathalysed at the roadside after the accident. She was found to be well over the limit there. Now she has agreed to be tested here, and I'm afraid the tests show she's two and a half times over the limit. Sorry, sir, it's standard procedure. She'll be summonsed to appear in court later this week.'

Harry thumped the inquiry desk, forgetting he wasn't in his own office.

'Do that again, Mr Hampton, and you might find yourself in trouble,' warned the duty sergeant. 'Have *you* been drinking, by any chance?'

'Yes, of course I have,' snapped Harry. 'But that's why I wasn't driving, you stupid—'

He stopped himself with an effort and his mind went back to his gleaming gold Mercedes, now sporting a completely stoved-in wing. Silly cow, he thought. Women, bloody awful drivers. But how could she have been over the limit?

Much, much later that night, Harry and Val went home in a taxi. The Mercedes was towed to a garage for repair estimates. Val fled upstairs to bed without a word. Harry went into the kitchen, rummaged in the flip-top bin and saw the evidence. Half a dozen empty wine bottles. He poured himself another huge gin and tonic, went into the sitting room and quietly seethed. Then he went upstairs to the spare room, and lay down hoping that Morpheus would sweep away the remnants of possibly the worst day of his life.

It made page three of the *Hartford Echo*: MEDIA BOSS'S WIFE MORE THAN TWICE THE LIMIT. The report carried pictures of Val

leaving the police station, dressed in one of her trademark short skirts and high heels, with her blonde hair
swept up and dark glasses hiding any facial expression.
There was a shot of the Mercedes smashed into a tree,
plus an official portrait of Harry, all smiling, cigar-
smoking corporate success. Obviously supplied with glee
by the PR agency that handled HOT affairs.

The story went round the office like wildfire. Ray photo-
copied the page and distributed it like hymn sheets.

'Bet Val never expected to be a page three girl,' said
Sue, ringing from the reception desk. 'Do you think one
of us should ring her, express sympathy, et cetera?'

'I will if you like,' offered Janet. 'I'm feeling a mite more
sympathetic to her at the moment, after my little victory
over Harry. Mind you, we can hardly be surprised at her
getting caught. I'm just amazed she's got away with it for
so long. We'll have quite a lot to discuss at our Operation
HH meeting on Friday. By the way, I'm planning a film
show, so make sure your video hasn't been booked out by
the kids.'

Janet sipped her coffee and dialled Val's number. Best
get it out of the way early. Also, Val might just be sober.

'Val? It's Janet. So sorry to hear what's happened.'

'Yeah, well. Got caught, didn't I? I'll probably get a
year's ban. Having to go around in bloody taxis now. Just
too ghastly. Harry was unspeakable. The whole evening
was a nightmare. I gather he'd had a bad day. He did a bit
of ranting about you too. Is there some sort of problem
going on at work?'

'Not now.' Janet smiled to herself. 'All sorted and taken
care of.'

'Look, Harry's away next week, so I wondered if you'd
all come over for dinner,' said Val. 'It would cheer me up.

170

I wouldn't cook, sod that. I'd get a chef in. How about Tuesday?'

'I'll ask the girls and let you know.' Janet replaced the phone. Now that would be like entering the lion's den, except that the lion would be playing away somewhere else.

To: Harry Hampton
From: Janet Bancroft
Re: Hot Breaks For Heartaches
In view of the recent difficulties on the above, I'd like to suggest that as it is such an important and prestigious project for the company, it is put into the safest hands. As Liz is now fully recovered from her illness, I'd like her to work on this project as director. She's already across all the subjects in the series so she's an obvious choice. I am very willing to be involved in this project now and will undertake to be project producer. As Liz will be out on the road for most of the time, I suggest that I will be the point of contact with you on day-to-day matters. Your thoughts, please.

To: Janet Bancroft
From: Harry Hampton
Re: Hot Breaks For Heartaches
Agreed.

The Gang of Four met at Sue's house on Friday evening. Sue's husband Jon had taken their children to the cinema to see the latest *Star Wars* film so they could have the house to themselves. The other three were secretly disappointed. Because none of them were parents, they all enjoyed the rough and tumble of Sue's kids, who were well behaved but also spirited. They'd each brought sweets or chocolate for them as well as the usual bottles of wine.

'Don't worry,' said Sue, knowingly, as she stuffed the multi packs of Mars bars, KitKats and Smarties in the fridge. 'They'll be mega-hyper when they come back after the film and a bucket of popcorn. Thanks, girls. Really kind of you. Supper won't take long. And if it's crap, we'll just get stuck into the chocolate.'

She went back to tending the pasta and delegated the wine-pouring to Nina. Soon four huge glasses of Mâcon were poured and three toasts declared.

'To Paul Burns. Good riddance!'

'To Val. Shame about the arrest, but you've had a jolly long run.'

'To Harry. Serves you right for being a complete bastard.'

Then they all sat down in Sue's tiny dining room. Sue emerged from the kitchen with steaming bowls of tagliatelle and a seafood sauce bursting with prawns, mussels, squid and hake and laced with tomatoes, herbs and garlic. Silence descended, punctuated only by exclamations of delight. A raspberry pavlova was greeted by another cheer. When that had been demolished, they went through to the sitting room, and Sue poured coffee while Janet made a brief announcement.

'It gives me great pleasure to show you how Mr Paul Burns met his Waterloo. Watch out for the glamorous Mrs Saunders – line-dancing's answer to Barbara Cartland. In other words, a large pink blancmange wearing ten tons of make-up.'

They all sat transfixed by the tape and burst into applause at the end.

'I have a sneaking feeling that Harry's copy ended up in the bin,' said Janet afterwards. 'Fortunately Colin made two copies, and this is mine to keep. I shall always treasure it as one of the happiest days of my life at HOT. The Day of the C Word.'

'What C word?' Liz asked suspiciously.

'No, not that one. C is for comeuppance,' retorted Janet. 'And not only that, I spoke to Steven Byfield today. Remember him, the chap who did my job before I arrived, and left in a mysterious haze?'

'Yes,' they all clamoured.

'Well, he took a call from Harry after the great Burns departure.'

'And . . .' Sue said impatiently.

'And then Steven called me.'

'Yes . . .' They were now all desperate. Janet paused, glanced round at them theatrically, took a slug of wine and then proceeded to relate Steven's account of the conversation, ending with his remark to Harry about the score being fifteen-all.

'Sorry, Janet, but that's not fifteen-all,' said Nina. 'That's game, set and match to Steven. What a brilliant long shot.'

'Yes, it was,' said Janet. 'And now we need to think about what we do next. I must say, our first strike was a great success, but don't underestimate Harry. He'll wriggle out of this one, just like he's done before. Also, his hackles will be severely up after the business with Val. Talking of which, our about-to-be-banned friend has invited us over to their house on Tuesday.'

'Well, count me out,' said Nina. 'It was bad enough spending evenings getting personal abuse from Val in restaurants without going to their home for a further onslaught from her rotten husband.'

'Ah, but remember, Harry won't be there,' said Sue. 'He's off on the mystery freebie early next week. This is a chance to snoop.'

'I'm not sure either,' said Liz, shooting Janet a knowing look. It was the last thing she needed, to be sitting at Harry's table, drinking Harry's wine. They all looked to Janet for a decision.

'Well, I say we go,' she said firmly. 'If we're going to crack this whole business, we ought to find out what really makes him tick. You know what it's like when you visit someone's home, you learn so much about them so quickly.'

'I hardly think Harry and Val are going to have pink crinoline lady crocheted toilet roll covers,' said Nina. 'Or garage glasses, moquette settees and bubble oil lamps.'

'It's up to you lot,' said Janet. 'But personally, I can't wait to have a good snoop.'

'I'll go,' said Sue, emphatically.

'Not me,' said Liz.

'Count me out,' added Nina.

chapter twenty

They decided to have pre-dinner drinks and a council of war at the GX before driving over to Val's house. Then it was agreed that they'd travel together in Janet's car on the basis that they could arrive and leave en bloc. Blatant curiosity, the chance for revenge, and a certain amount of cajoling had finally overcome the reluctance of Nina and Liz.

'If it's a truly hideous house, then at least we'll dine out on it for a while,' said Sue. 'If it's fantastic, then we'll be able to get even angrier with Harry. See, either way we win.'

'Don't forget, our job tonight is to find out what Val thinks Harry gets up to when he's not with her,' said Janet. 'Any observations, make mental notes and then we'll all compare.'

'We still don't know very much,' Sue reminded them. 'All we know so far is that Harry goes home late on Mondays and Thursdays on a regular basis. His mobile is switched off from six when he leaves the building until about ten o'clock when he gets home. We know an Italian-sounding woman makes fairly regular calls to him but never leaves a message. He's gone on some mystery conference and business trip but we don't know precisely where and his phone was switched off all day today.'

'How do you know?' asked Nina.

'Because I had a message for him. Nothing urgent, but it gave me the excuse to keep trying him rather than speak to the dreaded Geraldine. In the end, even Geraldine said she didn't know why his phone was off.'

'Well, well,' mused Janet. 'That's unusual.'

'The other thing is that Geraldine's been clocked doing a bit of snooping,' said Sue.

'Blimey, how did you know that?'

' 'S easy. I meant to tell you at our last HH meeting but I was overwhelmed by the brilliant video. Also, I've now had a chance to confirm it.'

'What sort of snooping?'

'Oh, spotted in the production office opening drawers, that kind of stuff. Anita told me.' Anita was another of HOT's receptionists, who'd been on late shift the previous week.

'I *told* you things had been moving,' said Nina triumphantly. 'Nice of Harry to get old G-spot doing his dirty work. Just typical.'

'Isn't it time we told Harry subtly that we know what he's up to?' said Janet. 'You know, leave a few messages lying around to show we've rumbled him. How about inventing a few files with provocative titles and see if he opens them? It could be quite fun!'

'Fun?' queried Nina sarcastically.

'Yeah. For example, I might leave my computer on and I might just have a file in there called Harry's Game, or Hassle With Harry, or something that would grab his attention.'

'What would you write in the file?' asked Liz quietly.

'Oh, either leave it blank or write something that looks irresistibly provocative, like "I've had the photos developed."'

'And of course he couldn't say anything because it would be tantamount to owning up,' finished Sue.

'By the way, one other snippet,' said Janet. 'Veronica's resigned. She won't say why but I just have the strangest feeling it's something to do with Harry. She handed in her notice yesterday and wants to leave this Friday. Let's see if we can find out the true story on that one.'

'Drink up, everyone,' said Sue, glancing at her watch. 'Time to visit Hampton Court!'

They rang the doorbell, using the delay to size the place up. They'd already noted with envy the carriage driveway, the leaded windows, the immaculate front gardens and lawns. It was one of those modern mini mansions that screamed, 'We've got loadsamoney!'

'Seeing as it's Hampton Court,' said Nina, grinning, 'do you think there's a maze?'

'Not much point in asking Val,' replied Liz. 'She's in a permanent one herself.'

'It's probably pseudo-*Hello!* magazine,' remarked Janet as they waited. 'Lots of very tidy rooms with large sofas and photogenic dogs.'

'Hmm, not that posh. Answers her own front door,' observed Nina, hearing Val click-clacking across the inevitable parquet flooring towards the front door. She greeted the four of them like long-lost friends and ushered them straight into an enormous sitting room. It was very Harry. Huge cream leather sofas, chrome and glass tables, enormous paintings, elaborate chandeliers and chrome table lights greeted them. Sue asked for the loo and was shown to a room nearly as big as the entire downstairs of her house. The walls were covered with awards and posters connected with HOT. Harry was certainly claiming credit for an awful lot of projects and wanted visitors to his loo to be left in no doubt as to how successful he was.

Val was a surprisingly good hostess. She seemed more relaxed on home ground, buzzing around with exquisite canapés and plying her guests with champagne. This gave her a chance to dot in and out of the kitchen, where she could refill her own glass secretly and take a few surreptitious swigs. She'd decided that after the court case, where she'd been banned from driving for a year, it wasn't good form to be seen drinking at all. At least by having to sneak out into the kitchen, it would ration her intake and she might manage to stay reasonably sober. Val was also smarting from a failure. She'd tried to give up drinking the previous day – and only managed to last for a morning. Given that she'd not got up until eleven o'clock, and had succumbed to a glass of vino by one, it wasn't too impressive an effort. Tonight she'd at least pretend she'd given up.

Twenty minutes in, no one had been insulted, criticized or stabbed in the back. And Val was still upright. Dressed in her favourite fuchsia pink, this time cropped linen trousers and a raw silk top, she seemed rather contrite about losing her licence. Perhaps there was a nicer person trying to get out after all, thought Janet, having a sudden tiny rush of guilt. It didn't last long.

'Hm, interesting outfit, Janet,' remarked Val, sweeping Janet's long black satin jacket to one side and exposing the less than perfect body it was intended to hide. 'You really ought to come to Ginette's next fashion show.'

That nicer person had obviously decided to go back in again, Janet decided. Leopards don't change their spots, she reminded herself, wincing as her flab was displayed for all to behold. She waited for a further onslaught of criticism about her weight, but was mildly surprised when none came.

They were ushered into a dark green dining room, where a mahogany table big enough to seat at least twenty was laid with gilt-edged white plates, gleaming silver cutlery and candelabra, crisp white napkins and bottles of Chablis chilling in ice buckets. Charlie, the chef Val had hired, turned out to be a cheerful cockney who could cook up a storm. He brought in plates of oysters nestling in beds of crushed ice. Nina's face fell immediately. She'd never eaten oysters before, mostly because she didn't like the look of them. Timidly she copied what everyone else did and shovelled one into her mouth.

'Blimey,' she said, making a face. 'Like swallowing snot. Sorry, Val, no offence.' She waited for a torrent of abuse and ridicule from Val, but there was none. Something had definitely changed for the better. Perhaps appearing in court had taken Val down a peg or two.

Over the main course of mixed fish kebabs, lemon couscous and the most delicious salad of rocket and frisee, Val was still very preoccupied. She badly wanted a lot more to drink and not being the centre of attention in some crowded and fashionable eaterie had taken the challenge out of the evening.

'Lovely house, Val,' said Sue appreciatively. 'I adore the paintings in this room. Which one of you's the collector?'

'Oh, not me,' said Val, dismissively. 'They're all Harry's choice. They just turned up one day recently.'

Oh, really? thought Janet, realizing suddenly that they looked suspiciously similar in style to the new paintings that had appeared above and behind the *Mastermind* chair. Probably another of his little freebies. God, he never stopped.

'How did Harry take the news about your driving ban?' enquired Janet, as casually as she could.

'He went berserk,' said Val, shoving her plate aside virtually untouched and lighting a cigarette. 'He hasn't really spoken to me since, which is totally unfair. The police test kit must have been faulty. I certainly wasn't over the limit. But anyway, he's been a total pig, and it's probably just as well that he's off at this telly conference thingy.'

'Where is it exactly?' asked Janet lightly.

'Manchester, I think,' said Val vaguely. 'All I know is he's away for a week. What they all find to talk about, God only knows. It sounds sooooo boring. I'm hoping he might have forgotten about the court case when he comes back. I'll just go and help Charlie bring in the pudding. Back in a mo.'

Val click-clacked off in the direction of the kitchen. She had no intention of helping Charlie do anything. She just wanted a decent-sized glass of wine, and she wanted it double quick.

'If Harry *is* in the Algarve, how's he going to pass off a week's worth of suntan when he's supposed to be in Manchester?' half whispered Janet with a grin.

'Oh, they'll have had a freak heatwave up there,' said Liz, who had finally relaxed a little. She still hated being in Harry's house. It made her flesh creep.

'Val doesn't seem to be drinking at all,' observed Nina.

'Hm, I'm not so sure,' said Janet. 'I think that's what these constant trips to the kitchen are all about. Having made all those excuses about the faulty testing kit, she can't be seen to be knocking it back. I think she's doing a Cleopatra on us.'

'Cleopatra?' they all whispered.

'Yeah, Cleopatra,' grinned Janet. 'Queen of Denial.'

They had to suppress their laughter as Charlie and Val emerged from the kitchen, each carrying a pudding. One was a coffee and walnut gateau decorated with chocolate coffee beans, the other a miraculous meringue affair with spun sugar, raspberries and cream. Silence descended for a while as they plunged into a dessert heaven. Val, of course, had her trademark mouthful, moved the rest around the plate with a fork and then lit a cigarette.

'So, what are you doing for the rest of the week? Going up to join Harry?' asked Janet, still trying to sound casual.

'Omigod, no,' replied Val. 'Far too ghastly. It rains in Manchester and they all wear flat caps and talk like *Coronation Street*. No, I'm going to stay with my parents in Hampshire. Get some serious shopping done. I don't even know where Harry's staying, which suits me fine, because then I have the perfect excuse not to call him.'

'Won't he expect you to ring him on the mobile?' Janet pressed gently.

'Oh, no. He's taken to switching it off a bit lately. At one time it was permanently on and frying his brain. Well, maybe now it's been roasted!' Val laughed uproariously at her own joke and swayed precariously on her chair. The surreptitious swigs in the kitchen had suddenly taken effect.

She now pointed a bright pink nail in Janet's direction. 'By the way, Janet, I hear you're in the doghouse.'

'Really?' said Janet. They all sat up, suddenly more attentive.

'Yeah, the night we went out for that stupid dinner, Harry was in a right old temper and mentioned something about stringing you up. Do tell. I've been dying to know.'

'Hm, last Monday, let me see. Just a normal happy day at the office as far as I can recall,' said Janet sarcastically, noting that her theory about why Val kept disappearing to the kitchen was beginning to stand up.

'Oh, wait a minute, let me think,' she continued, pausing for effect. 'It was Paul Burns' leaving day. That must have been it. Perhaps Harry was upset at him going so early on in the Hot Breaks project. I must say, we were all surprised.'

'No, not that,' said Val, now grappling with her fading memory and the effect of more than two bottles of Chablis in as many hours. 'He was definitely very cross with you.'

'Perhaps Harry knew I wouldn't be able to do half as good a job,' said Janet cynically.

'Yeah, that's probably it,' said Val, now not really listening. 'That chap, whassisname, was shit-hot apparently. Geraldine told me, and she ought to know.'

The others didn't make eye contact in case they laughed openly.

Val half stood up, noticed the room swaying and promptly sat down again. 'There's something really odd about that woman,' she announced, pointing a selection of pink nails around the table.

'Oh,' said everyone in chorus. 'Do tell.'

Val tried to stand again, and this time lurched to one side, dragging the starched white tablecloth with her. The others made a dive to stop the candles, plates, glasses and cutlery heading for the floor. But Val was now too pissed to notice.

'Geraldine has a *big* secret,' she persisted.

'Go on,' they urged.

'You'll never believe it.'

'Of course not,' they chorused, still gripping the table-cloth.

'Guess.'

'Don't know.'

Val lit a cigarette, pausing for effect. Although she was now well gone, she still had a sense of timing. Finally she put down her lighter, exhaled dramatically and propped her elbow on the edge of the table. In her haze, her elbow slipped and she shot forward, narrowly missing falling head first into the remains of her raspberry pudding.

'Geraldine's surname is Taylor, right?'

'Right.'

'Geraldine's middle name is Nancy.'

'Okay.'

'So that makes her initials GNT. G 'n' T, gin and tonic, geddit?'

They all feigned hysterical laughter.

'Bet she never thought of that when she married Mr Taylor,' said Val, stubbing out her hardly smoked cigarette.

'Mr Taylor?' said Sue in surprise. 'We didn't know there was a Mr Taylor.'

'Well, there *was* but he divorced her. Oh, absolutely yonks ago.'

'Poor Geraldine,' said Janet insincerely.

'No, poor Mr Taylor,' retorted Val, attempting another rise from the table. 'Let's leave this lot and chill out.'

They all trooped back into the sitting room and flopped back on to the cream sofas.

'Why poor Mr Taylor?' persisted Sue. 'Why did he divorce her?'

'Ha ha, Harry told me,' said Val, giggling softly. 'You'd never guess, looking at Geraldine. I mean, she's so bloody boring.'

'No we can't guess. We give in. Why was it?' said Sue.

'He divorced her,' Val's words were almost incomprehensible now, 'for too much hoovering and too many demands for sex.'

They all thought they were going to explode. Val, however, was out cold.

chapter twenty-one

The mobile phone campaign in the *Hartford Echo* was gathering momentum. Every week the paper carried more success stories, listing public places where mobiles had been banned.

'I'm surprised there's any mileage in this,' said Ray, feet up on a desk, 'now that our very own Olympic gold medallist in the individual phone event, Paul Burns, has left town. And the current world mobile champion is away on the Costa del Manchester. They'll be tearing down loads of redundant phone masts now that the network has been so freed up.'

Janet was only half listening. She was whipping through her e-mails as fast as she could. She was due to start filming the property project in a few days' time and there was still much to do in the fixing and scripting before she would be happy. There was always a period just before the start of an important project when Janet got really nervous. She'd come to realize this was a good sign, that the stress meant her brain was in gear.

'Sorry, Ray, what did you say?' she said absent-mindedly.

He tapped the paper. 'Just that Don't Fry Your Brain Campaign the *Echo*'s running.'

'Oh, that,' she said, disappointed. 'Thought for a minute you had some good gossip.'

'As a matter of fact I do,' said Ray, immediately lowering his voice and sticking his head between the computer screens for privacy.

'Do you know why snotty totty Veronica's leaving? The real reason?'

Janet shook her head and gave him her full attention. 'I thought it was just a personality thing.'

'I've been sworn to secrecy, but . . .'

'You're going to tell me anyway,' finished Janet. 'And no, I won't give you a reference for that job at MI6.'

'Harry made a pass at her.'

Janet's heart skipped a beat. She could feel herself fingering her handbag, perched on top of her filing cabinet. They adjourned swiftly to the canteen, where, over cappuccinos, Ray told her what he knew, namely that Harry had turned up at Veronica's flat armed with a bottle of champagne and tried to charm his way into her underwear, via the 'Babe, I could help you go places with this company' route.

'All the subtlety of a brick,' said Janet. 'So how did she react?'

'Offered him sex and travel,' grinned Ray. 'In other words, she told him to fuck off.'

'Would you do me a favour?' said Janet on the spur of the moment. 'There's something I'd really like you to do for me.'

Janet and Liz met up in the GX for lunch. Liz was anxious to talk through the next two Hot Breaks episodes as they were her first solo efforts. The worried look in her eyes had made Janet realize it would be a good idea to get her off site for an hour, so they'd decamped with all Liz's files of notes and treatments. They toyed with grilled chicken and Greek salad while they went through the final details of the portrait-painting weekend and the murder-mystery break.

'Talking of mysteries, I think I've discovered another one,' said Janet when they'd finished. She poured Liz the last of the wine they'd had with their meal, then carefully outlined the little she knew about Veronica's encounter with Harry.

'The interesting thing is that Harry got it badly wrong with Veronica,' she continued. 'With you it was totally different, because you were so vulnerable at the time. Veronica's a fairly snotty cow and her heart's not in this business. If Harry had made the threats he made to you, all that "You'll never lunch in this town again" nonsense, Veronica wouldn't have cared less. She's looking for a suitably rich husband, not a future in corporate television. And certainly not a quick hump with old Hampton. If Harry'd muttered about giving her a good reference, she'd probably assume it was something to do with the national grid and a large country estate with shooting rights.'

'He certainly fouled up there.' Liz, who'd been visibly shaken by Janet's revelation, was cheering up a little. 'No wonder he's been in such a vile temper recently, one way and another. And Val's starring role in court didn't help matters much.'

'Anyway, by the time he comes back from Manchester's Portuguese quarter, Veronica will have gone, problem solved,' said Janet. 'Except that I'm thinking of enlisting Ray's help in something. I think we'd better have another meeting of the Haunted Handbag committee later this week.'

Veronica's leaving do on Friday turned into an all-day affair. It was not a reflection of her popularity, more that the production office crowd were in desperate need of a party. There was plenty to celebrate: the departure of Paul Burns, plus the luxury of having had a whole Harry-free week.

It started with people drifting across to the GX for lunch. July had suddenly turned scorching, so an advance party was sent ahead to bag all the outside tables. On guaranteed hot sunny days, the GX staff fired up a big barbecue, and soon about thirty people from HOT were tucking into burgers, hot dogs and salads. There had been a whip-round and Nina had been dispatched to buy a present, but with only fifteen quid extracted from around forty people it was always going to be a challenge. She chose a framed print on the basis that it wouldn't betray how little they'd raised.

By early evening they were all back around the outside tables at the GX, with Veronica insisting on buying champagne for everyone. Egged on by the company, Ray decided to make a speech. Somewhat the worse for wear, he rose to his feet.

'Veronica,' he said, 'sorry you're leaving. I thought you were a stuck-up, snotty cow, but tonight I've realized you're not. Nice champagne, petal. Cheers.'

They all raised their glasses. Veronica, also somewhat the worse for wear, took absolutely no offence, and even began to think they weren't such a dreadful bunch after all and perhaps she shouldn't be leaving. Then she thought back to that slimeball Harry and promptly changed her mind again.

'Speech, speech,' they all cried.

'Thank you, one and all,' she said in her cut-glass accent, sweeping back her blonde mane with one hand and raising her glass with the other. 'And thank you, Ray, for that charming speech. I have to admit I've never been called "petal" before. I think I'll miss you after all. With the exception of one person.'

They all started humming the *Mastermind* theme.

'Here's to Harry, wherever he is tonight,' said Nigel, one of the researchers.

'Up yours, Harry!' the cry went up.

'Is that why you're leaving?' asked Nigel innocently. Veronica went purple with anger, put down her glass and stalked off to the loo.

Silence fell immediately.

'Shit, did I say something wrong? Has Harry humped and dumped her or something?' Nigel looked aghast.

'Nah,' said Ray nonchalantly, giving Janet a sideways wink. 'If anything, it should be the other way round. You know Harry fancies anything, with or without a pulse. Come on, mate, a girl looking like Veronica does, of course he'd want a bit of that. What Harry doesn't know is that she views us all, him included, as some sort of pond life.'

'Yeah, you're right, mate,' replied Nigel, draining his champagne. 'Still, she came up trumps tonight. She's probably like a lot of women, heaps more fun when she's pissed. Do you think he did try to give her one?'

'Don't know, and for God's sake, don't ask,' said Ray, nodding in Veronica's direction. She was heading back to the table. 'Whatever it was, she wasn't having it. Serves Harry right. Living up to his name.'

'How d'ya mean?' asked Nigel.

'Hampton. Hampton Wick,' grinned Ray. 'Cockney rhyming slang. Nuff said.'

Because Janet, Sue and Liz had each drunk a couple of glasses of champagne and Nina hadn't because she was on another of her bum-reducing diet regimes, they piled into Nina's car, heading once again for Sue's house. They'd agreed to have their Haunted Handbag meeting there, but only on condition that they picked up a takeaway to save Sue cooking.

They arrived on Sue's doorstep clutching carrier bags of Chinese food and were greeted by her two children jumping up and down in delight. Not at seeing them; just at the thought of Chinese, which was their favourite.

Half an hour later, with the three carrier bags now stacked up with empty containers, everyone flopped back in their seats, pleasantly full. Even Nina, who'd suffered a temporary loss of will power when she smelt the food.

'Thanks, girls,' said Sue. 'It was a real treat not to cook, especially on such a hot night, and also for the kids. They just love Chinese.'

'Yeah, we noticed,' said Nina. 'They were like locusts. Still, it's good news: the more they eat, the less I do. Got to get another inch off my bum. I've got loads of incentive now.'

Nina's relationship with Sam was going great guns. He'd recently hinted at taking her on holiday to Rhodes later in the summer, which had given Nina an attack of the wobbles.

'Has he booked it yet?' asked Liz.

'Yes, today,' said Nina. 'I'm so excited, but I'm also terrified.'

'Why?'

' 'Cos he'll see my bum. We'll have to go to the beach and all that stuff.'

'Well, that's the whole idea, isn't it?' said Janet, grinning. 'Anyway, you go to bed with the guy; he must know every inch of you by now.'

'He takes his glasses off and I insist on lighting the smallest of night lights because I tell him it turns me on.'

'Oh heck, Nina. You can't go on like that.'

'Well, I've managed so far.'

'But you can't live your whole life making him miss Vision Express appointments and saving the planet by using tea lights.'

'Oh, I'll find a way,' said Nina. 'Anyway, I'm meeting his parents next week.'

'Blimey, this *is* serious,' said Janet. 'Here, save some of that egg-fried rice, we might need it for your wedding.'

'Oh shut up,' said Nina sheepishly. 'But he is just totally scrummy.'

'And talking of sex, what about Geraldine, eh?' said Janet. 'I thought sex and shopping went together, but sex and hoovering. That's a new one. Or maybe it's all to do with being a sucker.'

'I haven't been able to look at her this week in case I laughed,' said Sue. 'With Harry away, my dealings with her have thankfully been minimal. I've managed to avoid any eye contact when she's come through reception.'

'I can't imagine Geraldine having torrid sex, let alone rushing around sensuously with a vacuum,' said Janet. 'Perhaps that's why she's so vacuous.'

'I must say, that's the first time Val's ever made me laugh,' remarked Liz. 'I really didn't want to go to Harry's house, but it was worth it. Anyway, what's this new plan you've got for Operation Haunted Handbag?'

Janet paused and collected her thoughts. The only way they were going to find out what Harry was up to, she explained to them, was to follow him on Monday and Thursday nights. Now, it was impossible for any of them to do it unless they put on some ridiculous disguise and borrowed a different car. But there was someone in the office who could, and who had already agreed to do it.

'Who?' they all chorused.

'Ray,' said Janet. 'This week, while Harry was away, Ray bought himself a motorbike. You know boys and their toys. Well, Ray's got the whole bit, leathers, helmet, et cetera; in other words a disguise and a different vehicle. Ray knows an awful lot of what Harry's up to. Don't forget, he found out about the freebie holiday ages ago, and he found out why Veronica was leaving. There's a budding investigative journalist in there. He's just as intrigued as we are, so I say we should let him have a go.'

'What if he's discovered?' asked Liz.

'I think Ray can wriggle out of that,' replied Janet. 'If for some reason Harry got suspicious, Ray would just abandon the chase. It's as simple as that.'

'Do you think Val suspects anything?' said Sue.

'Nah,' chipped in Nina. 'She's too pissed most of the time for it to cross her mind. And too full of herself.' Nina still hadn't forgotten, and had no intention of forgiving, the London Derrière jibe.

'I'm not so sure now,' mused Janet. 'I think Val's had a bit of a rethink since her presentation at court! She was certainly different at home. I know she passed out eventually, but she wasn't quite as obnoxious as usual and at least she didn't create a scene or fall over.'

'I wonder if she did go to Hampshire. It might be worth a casual call to see if she's heard from him,' said Sue.

'Good idea,' said Janet, reaching for her handbag and beginning the customary five-minute search for her filofax. By the time Sue had made a pot of coffee and brought it in, Janet was finally dialling Val's home number.

'It's diverting to her mobile,' she told them, with her hand over the receiver.

'Val? Hi, it's Janet. Just thought I'd ring to say thanks from all of us for the other night. Great fun . . . No, it was fine you falling asleep. You must have had a hard day . . . No, we all helped Charlie clear up . . . Anyway, just wondered how you are? . . . At your folks'? How lovely. Heard from Harry? . . . Right, right . . . Well, thanks again and have a good weekend, bye.'

Janet switched off the phone. They all looked at her expectantly.

'I can't believe I'm saying this, but she sounded relatively sober. Perhaps she can't get to the wine bottle so easily at her parents' house. Anyway, just the one call from Harry. The conference allegedly goes on over the weekend and he returns on Monday.'

'She doesn't sound remotely curious, by the sound of it,' said Sue.

'Nope,' agreed Janet. 'I think, all in all, she's pleased to see the back of him.'

'Me too,' said Liz.

At that moment, Sue's husband Jon put his head round the door.

'Hi, girls,' he greeted them. 'Cor, something smells nice. Monosodium glutamate! You've had Chinese. Any left?'

'No, sorry, darling,' said Sue grinning. 'How about some sex and hoovering instead?'

They all fell about laughing.

chapter twenty-two

She'd grown up with it, yet, strangely, it came as a shock. Val had been at her parents' house for a couple of days when, on Sunday afternoon, her mother, still glamorous at sixty, said casually, 'Your father and I are going upstairs for a while.'

She'd almost forgotten her parents were still at it like rabbits. It had been so much part of her childhood. When her mother mentioned going upstairs, that meant do not disturb. Unlike most children, for whom the thought of their parents having wild, abandoned sex induced vomiting noises into invisible airline paper bags, Val was used to her parents sloping off for a lovemaking session.

The shock for Val was more a reminder that she and Harry didn't do this. They never had. Harry was always far too busy wheeling and dealing, meeting important people, to be spending an afternoon in bed with her. Their sex life was a brief bump and grind at night if he was in the mood, or an occasional Sunday morning.

Although her parents' Georgian mansion was huge, vast enough to be able to keep well away from the sound of bedposts rocking or springs creaking, Val decided to go out. Because of the ban, she could hardly borrow a car and go shopping. Instead she opted for a walk around the grounds. The gardens always looked fantastic at this time of year.

But before she could go out, she'd need a decent drink. She found a bottle of Sancerre in the fridge and poured herself a glass, then sat down at the huge kitchen table to leaf through an old copy of *Hampshire County Magazine*. She noted two of her old school friends beaming from the social pages, presenting charity cheques and wearing inane grins and ridiculous hats. Very mother-of-the-bride, she thought; they'd managed to make themselves look a good ten years older. She shivered and poured another glass. A sudden feeling of loneliness overwhelmed her. Harry away, all her friends married with kids – or in Susie's case having an affair with her boss – even her parents upstairs shagging. Everyone seemed to be getting it except her. To stave off further misery, she gulped down the rest of the bottle and went out into the sunshine.

The gardens really were looking magnificent. The terrace at the rear of the house looked out over immaculately clipped lawns bordered by sculpted trees and shrubs. Over the stone balustrade from huge urns spilled hundreds of geraniums, petunias and trailing lobelia, in deep pinks, purples and blues. Beyond the gardens rolled the yellowing wheat fields owned by her parents and farmed by tenants. Keith and Sheila actually owned everything they could see from the house, and all thanks to her father's waste-disposal business. He'd worked hard, been incredibly successful but still found time for her mother. So why couldn't Harry be the same?

Val felt in need of another drink but forced herself to keep walking. The more she marvelled at the gardens, watching two swallows racing each other across a perfect blue sky, and noticing the flowers opening up as if in gratitude to the warmth of the sun, the more she realized how empty her life had become.

'I hate Harry,' she proclaimed aloud, and then put a hand to her mouth as if to indicate a slip of the tongue. But the words had been spoken, and spoken aloud. From that moment on, she knew she really did hate him. Suddenly she was stone-cold sober.

By the time she got back to the house, her mother was busily mixing gin and tonics for them all before dinner. Her parents both smiled at her, with that inner glow that comes from a shared intimacy. Lucky sods, thought Val. She smiled for a moment, remembering a woman describing having sex with a famous and very fat politician as being flattened by a huge wardrobe with the key sticking in the lock. It could have been Harry. She shuddered again, realizing she didn't want that any more. Did that mean her marriage was dead, or would the magic return? Had there been any magic in the first place? Should she have an affair? Would that solve things? Even top agony aunts would have their work cut out for them with a slippery bastard like Harry.

'I thought we'd eat in the dining room tonight, instead of the kitchen,' said her mother. 'Eve's cooking something rather special, so we'll do it properly.'

Eve, the housekeeper, was the most brilliant cook, so if she was doing something special then it certainly would be amazing. The dining room was one of the most magnificent places in the house, with French doors opening on to the terrace and a fantastic view of the garden.

'Sounds lovely. In that case I'll go and change.' Val ran up the huge sweeping staircase in the main hallway, two at a time, just like she had as a child. She had a quick shower, redid her make-up, pinned her hair up into a chignon and put on a midnight-blue chiffon shift dress that Harry absolutely hated.

'You look wonderful, darling,' said her father, greeting her with a kiss on the forehead. 'Doesn't she look beautiful?' he added proudly, turning to his wife. 'My goodness, you do take after your mother.'

They both beamed at her lovingly. Val was so overcome with emotion she felt her eyes sting with tears. Get a grip, she told herself, it's only because Harry's not like this.

The meal was well up to Eve's standards. Tiny scallops flash-fried to perfection, followed by John Dory cooked in butter and fresh herbs and served with mounds of baby asparagus, sweetcorn and crispy mangetout.

'Sorry the Sancerre wasn't quite chilled,' said her father deliberately. 'I'm sure I told Eve to put one in the fridge this morning.'

Val looked down hurriedly at her empty plate. They knew, she realized. But what else did they know?

'Mum,' she started, feeling her eyes well up, 'Dad, there's something I want to tell you, ask you. I'm just so confused. Oh, I don't know any more.' She burst into tears and hid her face in her napkin.

When she'd calmed down a little and wiped her eyes, she blinked, looking at them both.

'There's something I have to tell you, something I only realized this afternoon but I know it's true.'

'Yes, darling?' said her mother gently.

'I hate Harry. I loathe him and I don't want him near me any more.'

There were more tears, followed by racking sobs into the napkin. She felt a comforting hand touch her arm.

197

'We know, dear. We've known for a long time,' said her mother simply.

Janet had left her car in the HOT car park over the week-end, because of Veronica's all-day leaving bash. She'd quite enjoyed being carless for once. It made her walk to the corner shop, stroll to the off-licence, linger in the park. She savoured the fresh air and the prolonged hot spell.

Local news bulletins were already warning of bans on hosepipes, sprinklers and car washes, but Janet didn't care. She was enjoying the feeling of the sun beating down on her face and seeping into her bones. Everyone looked happier; people seemed to stroll rather than scuttle everywhere at top speed. The pubs of Hartford overflowed with customers spilling out on to pavements, clutching cooling pints of lager as the sun continued to beat down.

I wonder what the weather's like in Manchester, Janet thought idly. Scorching, said the *Daily Mail*. And probably that lucky sod Harry would get away with it again. A week in the Algarve with his mystery mistress, return bronzed and rested after a week of sun, sea and probably nonstop bonking, and then pass it off as a week slaving away at a conference. Unless, of course, that was exactly where he was. Perhaps they'd got it all wrong. Maybe they'd imagined all this and it had got seriously out of hand.

No, no, she reasoned with herself, he'd not discussed the conference or any business meetings with her; he hadn't even given Val the name of his hotel. Where was he after work for three or four hours on Mondays and Thursdays, and who was the mysterious Italian-sounding woman? If he was on the straight and narrow, why had he made a pass at Veronica? And why had he done the same to Liz?

'Sorry, Harry, you're a big, fat, randy, arrogant, rapidly-going-to-seed complete and utter shit,' she announced aloud to a row of terracotta pots containing purple fuchsias. She was sitting in her tiny garden enjoying the last of the Sunday-afternoon sun and waiting for Liz to arrive to give her a lift to the car park. This really was bliss: a glass of ice-cold fruit juice, the luxury of the Sunday papers and all the time in the world to read them. No computers, no e-mail, no pagers trilling or vibrating. Also, having ascertained that the neighbours were out, she'd even put on an ancient bikini and slapped on some factor 15. Getting burned would make the flab look ten times worse than it was already. A tan might make her look at least a bit thinner. She must have fallen asleep, because the next thing she knew, the doorbell was ringing.

'Christmas come early here?' remarked Liz, stepping over the doorstep. 'Look at your conk. You'll put Rudolf out of a job.'

'Shit,' said Janet, glancing in the hall mirror. 'Must have forgotten that bit when I slapped on the cream. Just what I need tomorrow. I've got a meeting with a pile of extremely posh estate agents. They're all fraightfully yah.'

'Oh, it'll have calmed down by tomorrow,' said Liz. 'If not, you'll have to tone it down with some slap. Anyway, you might be able to match Harry with his perma-tan all the way from Portu . . . I mean Manchester.'

'Do you know, I've decided I'm going to press him about this conference he supposedly went to,' said Janet. 'Six months ago my confidence, or lack of, would never have allowed me to. But I really am going to quiz him.'

'I'm several light years off that stage of life,' said Liz. 'I think I'll always avoid Harry whenever I can, for obvious reasons. I suppose I'm being far too hopeful, but do you think he'd ever leave HOT?'

'No, I don't.' Janet shook her head. 'I think he's on far too good a number. We've seen the house now; Harry's not exactly down to his last Mercedes, is he?'

'Also, that kind of power base takes a long time to build,' said Liz.

'Exactly,' replied Janet. 'Bullying, cheating, creeping, wheeling and dealing, it all takes years to perfect. No, Harry isn't going anywhere.'

'Not unless he's pushed.'

'Exactly.'

Sunday night's gathering humidity finally broke in the small hours of the morning. The heavens released their torrential load and the temperature dropped dramatically. By Monday morning, everything looked fresher from the downpour but the sun had declined to show up. Grey skies threatened more rain.

Harry stormed into the office in a mood to match the weather. He'd come home late last night to an empty house and an empty fridge. Val was still at her parents' and had left a brief message on the answering machine saying she was staying on in Hampshire for another day or two. Harry had flung down his suitcase full of dirty washing and cursed the fact that he'd dumped at Gatwick all the swimming trunks, shorts and tee-shirts he'd bought on holiday. If he'd known the silly cow wasn't going to be there, he'd have brought them home, run them through the washing machine and passed them off as old stuff. Val would never have noticed, or cared. But even she would have clocked swimming shorts covered in sand and still smelling of the Atlantic if they'd come straight out of his case.

On the other hand, it had suddenly struck him that he'd not a clue how to use the washing machine. No, chucking out the evidence had probably been a wise move.

Despite having had a week of nonstop nookie without a shred of guilt, he'd still found himself absurdly angry that Val wasn't at home. She should have been there, welcoming him with open arms. And legs, he added to himself. There'd be hell to pay when the stupid tart got back. He found himself almost savouring the prospect of a row.

He thought back to the week he'd had with Gina in the Algarve, staying in the finest hotel, in their best suite, with its paradise view over the sea and the spectacular rugged coastline. A week of wining and dining in Portugal's finest restaurants, a couple of rounds of golf on the Algarve's most exclusive courses. It had all been courtesy of the Hot Breaks company, in return for the spot of creative accounting he'd done to give them an apparently sizeable discount on the production costs. Except, of course, that he'd massaged the figures to make it look as though he was offering them a huge undercover saving when in fact he was actually quoting the going rate and more. If Hot Breaks thought they were getting a bargain in return for Harry's luxury trip, then they were happy. And Harry was happy too, because a perk such as this luxury trip was absolutely his due. He sat back and mentally totted up what it would have cost. Limo complete with champagne to and from Gatwick, first-class plane seats natch, a five-hundred-pound-a-night suite, meals, vintage wines and cocktails all signed for. Not much change from ten grand. Now that was what he called a freebie.

It had been fun, of course, especially having sex on tap provided by Gina. And yet, and yet . . . there'd been times when he had to admit he'd got bored. Bored with all the endless luxury, the immaculate service, the hand-picked staff whose brief was to provide for their guests' every whim. There was something missing, and Harry knew exactly what it was. Conflict. There were no rows, no arguments, no desk to thump, no deals to be struck, no one to shout at, no oneupmanship. He didn't even have to chase Gina around the bedroom. There was no sense of conquest; she was there for the taking whenever he fancied it. Instead of their twice-weekly evening quickie sessions, furtive lunches and the odd night in a hotel, they'd had a whole week together, and somehow it had taken the challenge out of it.

And there was another cause for alarm. He sensed Gina might want to change the ground rules after their week away. She might suddenly make demands on him that he couldn't fulfil. She might ask him to leave Val, or worse, she might phone Val and give her all the gory details.

Coming back to an empty house had strangely stimulated Harry. He knew he could have a really good shouting match with Val when she got back and he was already relishing the thought. It would redress the balance of power and put Val firmly in her place, plus it would wipe out any guilt he might have about Gina. Yes, he was looking forward to a good old row.

'So how was Manchester?' Janet's voice broke into his thoughts.

'Oh, fine,' said Harry, snarling at her for interrupting his fantasy.

'You look really, really tanned,' she continued, standing in the doorway of his office. 'If I didn't know you'd been up north, I'd have sworn you'd spent a week in some expensive little European hotspot.' She paused, willing him to answer. Or open mouth and insert foot.

His face never flickered. Harry was the consummate liar.

'Don't be ridiculous,' he snapped.

'Anyway, how's Val?' Janet never asked Harry how Val was. Harry flinched momentarily.

'Whaddya mean?' he snarled suspiciously. 'She's in Hampshire with her parents.'

'Oh, do pass on my best when you speak to her,' said Janet triumphantly, as she noted Harry now watching her with hooded eyes. 'I'm sure she told you, we had a fantastic evening round at your place. Brilliant food, a really good laugh. Best evening we've all had for ages.'

'I am pleased,' he snapped, glaring at her. So why can't the fucking cow be there with a meal on the table when *I* get home? he thought. God, there'd be a row when she came back. 'Now bugger off and do some work.'

'Welcome back then,' Janet added sarcastically. She turned tail and strode off to her office, smiling to herself and wondering with a slight shudder whether Harry's tan was an all-over job.

chapter twenty-three

The *Hartford Echo* had stepped up its anti mobile phone protest. The Don't Fry Your Brain campaign now included an offer to send a reporter/photographer along to any public place where readers thought mobile phones should be banned. The idea would be to confront the users and try to persuade them to take their calls elsewhere or switch off their phones.

'What a pity Paul Burns isn't here,' said Janet, putting her paper down as Ray brought her in a coffee.

'Are you feeling all right?' queried Ray. 'I thought we all loathed the bastard.'

'No, the *Echo* campaign,' she said, tapping the paper. 'They're whipping up opposition to people who use mobiles in stupid places, like cinemas, theatres and so on.'

'Yeah, if you remember, I told you about it when they started it.'

'Well, now they have upped the ante with this new naming and shaming idea,' continued Janet. 'You can nominate places where you don't want mobile phones used, and with the consent of the management, presumably, they'll send a reporter along to confront the suspects.'

'Paul Burns would have looked really good on the front of the *Echo* in one of his zoot suits,' said Ray, relishing the thought.

'Anyway,' said Janet, lowering her voice. 'How's our little arrangement going? Any luck yet?'

'Not so far. I've probably been a bit too careful in following him at a safe distance and then lost him in traffic. But it's Monday, so I'll be having another go tonight.'

'Better to be careful, though,' cautioned Janet. 'What would you say if he clocked you?'

'Oh, I'd say I'd just had my tarot cards read and they'd spookily described a particular pub, and so I was compelled to go there by a mystery force.'

Janet roared with laughter. Ray was certainly resourceful. He promised to ring her at home that evening if he had any luck. She gathered up her file ready for a meeting with the estate agents about the video news releases. She sensed it would be long and tedious.

Val gazed out at the Hampshire countryside from the train window. The chalk landscape of the Hampshire basin gave way to the softer rolling hills of Wiltshire and finally they were drawing into Hartford. She thought back to the conversation she'd had with her mother that morning. She'd never felt as close to Sheila as she had today. They'd had a long heart-to-heart about Harry, marriage and sex – in that order.

Val was simply staggered that her parents had known she was so unhappy, particularly as she had only realized it herself yesterday.

'We couldn't tell you, darling,' her mother had said calmly. 'If we'd told you we thought you were making a mistake, it would have made the flames of passion even more intense. Our only hope was to say nothing and pray you'd see Harry for what he was.'

'But you sat back and watched me marry the sod,' Val had said in amazement. 'Why on earth didn't you stop me?'

'What? A grown woman? And also, what if we were wrong? What if there had been qualities in Harry you'd seen but we hadn't? No, we couldn't interfere. We had to let you make your choice. Just as you are now. Are you really sure it's over?'

'You don't need to ask, do you?' said Val, miserably.

'No, I probably don't,' said her mother.

'God, I'm beginning to realize how much you both must have suffered,' said Val.

'Not as much as you,' replied her mother simply.

Sheila would never have dreamed of telling her daughter how much she'd changed since she'd met and married Harry. How she and Keith had quietly despaired, watching their daughter turn into a monster, demanding, self-centred, irrational, deeply unhappy and often drunk. They'd realized that Val was echoing Harry's nastier habits. They'd also suspected Harry was having affairs and almost hoped Val would do the same. Perhaps that way she'd escape the marriage, or at least meet someone else more worthwhile.

'How come you and Dad have lasted so long? What's your secret?' Val had asked in desperation.

'Hmm,' said Sheila, gazing down at her coffee cup demurely. 'Oh, all right, I'll tell you. Your dad and I made a pact when we got married. We agreed that sex was really important and that we didn't want that side of our marriage to slide. So,' she hesitated again, 'we promised each other we'd have sex every day. Obviously it's a bit of a tall order but that was our aim, and mostly we've stuck to it.'

'Bloody hell,' exclaimed Val, embarrassed because her mother had never before directly discussed her sex life. 'Is that normal? Harry does once a week if I'm lucky, and then only when there's a z in the month. I often wonder if he's playing away.'

The look on her mother's face said it all. Val found herself bursting into tears again. Despite saying it, she hadn't really believed it.

'Only you can decide what to do,' said her mother calmly. 'You'll know when it's the right time.'

'You said when, not if,' replied Val between sobs. She lit a cigarette to calm her nerves.

'My advice, for what it's worth,' said her mother, 'is to bide your time. Don't rush into anything. Take a long hard look at the situation before you do anything.'

And with that, Val had bidden her parents a tearful farewell and been dispatched on a train back to Hartford and Harry.

At the station, her mother had slipped a small parcel into Val's bag and told her to open it at a quiet moment on the journey. When she'd torn the brown wrapping off she'd discovered a thin paperback entitled *So You May Have a Drink Problem*.

'Shit', she said aloud, 'I do and they know.' It was that bloody bottle of Sancerre. She was drawn to a question-naire at the beginning of the book. A quick tot-up of her scores revealed she was well up the 'functional alcoholic' zone, as opposed to 'social drinker' below or the 'complete wino' above. I can't possibly be anything like a tramp swigging meths, she thought to herself, but the quiz certainly threw up the possibility that she was not that far away. Getting violently drunk, throwing up, memory loss, split nails, and drinking in the morning were all signs of impending doom. She must get a grip on this. Bit difficult, though, when you lived with a pig like Harry.

Janet stifled another yawn. Estate agents had their own jargon and their own special speech patterns. Talk about the weather or the state of the monarchy and they could pass for normal. But the minute she mentioned buzz words like 'ensuite' or 'inglenook', the two suits sitting in the HOT boardroom immediately lapsed into smoothy sales pitches. The words 'desirable', 'affordable', 'spacious' peppered every sentence. They forgot that they weren't actually selling properties to Janet. They were supposed to be having a discussion about video newsletters and an interactive website. Janet found herself being lulled into a confused stupor by their patter. One of them, a bumbling ex public school type called Hugh, who had clearly mod-elled himself on Hugh Grant playing a bumbling ex public school type, appeared to know only two other words. These were 'potential' and 'cool'.

Janet was trying to impress upon them the essence of speed when it came to video production.

'If we can shoot on a Monday, log and edit on Tuesday and transfer on Wednesday, by Thursday you'll have sev-eral hundred VHS tapes in your branches ready for the weekend onslaught and your website bang up to date,' she explained.

'Cool, cool,' said Hugh, coming to life again.

His colleague, Ralph, older and even more institution-alized, launched into a speech in clipped pre-war BBC tones speculating about what sort of reach the website would have. Janet had already made a presentation on that very subject, based on some up-to-the-minute research. In her frustration and boredom, she found herself trying to spot a sentence which didn't include Ralph's particular *mot du jour*, which was 'affordable'.

'Most property websites are getting a very respectable number of hits,' she put in. 'By far the most successful, if we believe the figures, are the sites that are easiest to use. People do seem to get put off if the website isn't punter-friendly. There's enormous potential for growth out there.'

'Potential, yeah,' contributed Hugh, reawakening to his favourite word.

'Affordable,' nodded Ralph in agreement.

'If we stick to this routine,' said Janet firmly, 'I can block-book the camera crew and edit suites and then we all know where we are.'

'Cool,' offered Hugh. She began to wonder how he ever managed to sell a hamster's cage, let alone a house.

'Right,' she said, meaningfully gathering up her files. 'I'll get you a final costing and then hopefully we're in business. Thank you for your time, gentlemen.'

'Cool.' Hugh proffered a slim and sweaty hand that was anything but. 'Great potential.'

She saw them out of the building and headed up to Harry's office. Outside, Geraldine sat on her customary guard duty, only today she was surreptitiously reading a magazine.

'Any good celebrity goss?' asked Janet, assuming it would be *Hello!* or *OK!*. Or even possibly *Sex and Hoovering* magazine.

Geraldine shot her a venomous look, mostly because she'd been caught out good and proper.

'Actually, it's *Classic FM* magazine,' she said, salvaging her dignity.

'Didn't know you were a Beethoven buff,' said Janet.

'Well, yes,' winced Geraldine, who hated having to reveal anything about herself to anyone. 'There's a free CD this month of Placebo Domingo. He's got such a lovely voice.'

'Placebo?' said Janet. 'Didn't know you were an opera fan. What's your favourite?'

'Oh, let me think,' said Geraldine, pausing in the hope that Janet would go away. 'Puccini, Mozart, that sort of thing. But I also like general classical music. My all-time favourite is Versace's *Four Seasons*.'

'Me too,' said Janet, trying to contain herself. 'That's the beauty of Versace. A total classic, such lasting appeal. I believe Liz Hurley's a fan.'

'Yes, well, I wouldn't put it past her,' said Geraldine tartly, regretting letting her mask slip and praying for the phone to ring. Harry's angry voice saved her from further conversation.

'Bancroft, in here, now,' came the familiar menacing tone, accompanied by thumping of the desk. 'I want a full update on the property project.'

'Cool, cool,' said Janet. This new confidence in Harry's presence was taking even her by surprise. As she briefly outlined the meeting she'd had with the estate agents, Harry sat back in his chair and lit a cigar.

'Harry,' she pointed out with a small smile, 'you're not supposed to smoke in the building. You'll have the fire brigade out in a minute. Mind you,' she paused for effect, 'that cigar does smell good. Very evocative, reminds me of hot countries and balmy nights.'

She stared blatantly at him for a second, wondering if he had gone the tiniest bit pink under the perma-tan. Thrown by her remark, he quickly stubbed out the cigar.

How very un-Harry-like, she thought. How stupid of me to light up a Portuguese cigar, thought Harry.

'Now, I've had an idea for a new pitch,' she continued. 'There's a chain of restaurants starting up, only half a dozen in the pipeline so far but the whisper is that they have some big investors and plans for lots more. The company's called 3F, which stands for Food From Films, and each restaurant is named after a big movie, with the food and decor to match.'

'Sounds interesting,' said Harry, eyes lighting up like the display on a cash register. 'Go on.'

'For example, Casablanca will serve Moroccan food and be done out like Rick's Bar, Apocalypse Now will be Vietnamese food with all the staff in flying suits, Shakespeare in Love will be all doublets and hose, and venison. And then there's Gigi, all French food and fin du siècle. I think it's a great idea, with loads of visual potential.'

God, she was beginning to sound like Hugh.

'I want it,' slammed Harry. He sat bolt upright in his chair and shouted at Geraldine through the office door: 'Get me everything on 3F. Janet will give you the details. Get moving on it, the pair of you. Now.'

He sat back again, watching Janet's departing back. She was bright, that one, and getting just a bit too bright for her own good, he thought. He mused about the project she'd mentioned. It certainly sounded very promising.

He dialled a number and waited impatiently. Pity about the cigar, he thought, glancing at the ashtray.

'Gina, darling,' he half whispered seductively. 'Can't make our usual tonight. Sorry, honey, too much work, it's all stacking up. They couldn't manage without me last week. I'll make it up to you on Thursday . . . Look, I'm sorry . . . Yes, we had the most brilliant week . . . Yes, yes, of course I love you . . . Bye.'

Trouble brewing there, he thought, scratching his chin. He didn't want a fight on his hands. No, tonight belonged to his row with Val; that was, if the silly tart deigned to turn up.

As Val sat in the taxi home from the station, her mother's words came back to her. Yes, she would bide her time and take some legal advice, and no, she wouldn't have a knee-jerk reaction and run away.

As the cab snaked up the lane to their house, she shuddered from the very depth of her being. Keep calm, she told herself repeatedly, stay calm and just keep a watching brief. A man is presumed innocent until he's found guilty. She'd need to know for sure about any affair he was having before she could do anything. She'd want proof. She suddenly felt very fearful about the future. If she left Harry, what would become of her? She'd be second-hand goods, a woman with a failed past, and now officially a 'functional alcoholic'.

Mercifully Harry wasn't back from work. A riot of summer colour greeted her as she stepped out of the cab and paid her fare. Banks of fuchsias and roses were just reaching their peak. Unlike me, she thought miserably. At thirty-two, it was downhill all the way from now on. Past her prime, she mused, just fitted in between Harry's various conquests. What a fool he'd made of her.

She went through the vast entrance hall, threw her bags down on a scarlet velvet sofa and strode purposefully into the kitchen, heading for the drinks fridge. She had too much on her plate to pack in alcohol just yet. She opened a bottle of chilled white wine and poured herself a huge glass. She needed all the help she could get in facing Harry. Practically downing it in one, she poured another. She felt the cold liquid seeping into her body, giving her an instant lift. She ferreted in her handbag and found her cigarettes and lighter. The first big drag had a calming effect. Curse non-smoking trains and taxis, she muttered to herself, but at least they made you appreciate the first cigarette after your journey.

She was just settling down in the sitting room, shoes kicked off and feet up on one of the settees, watching a travel programme on Spain, when Harry burst in through the door.

'So good of you to turn up,' he snarled.

'Great to see you too,' she retorted. 'You remind me of that bull.' She indicated the animal that had just appeared on the screen. 'The crowd like the aggressive ones best.'

'Stupid tart,' he muttered under his breath. 'Why weren't you here when I got back last night?'

'Because I was being thoroughly spoiled at my parents',' she replied. She knew Harry hated any reference to them. He didn't like to be reminded that they were richer than him. Before he could open his mouth to reply, she was at him again.

'That's a pretty amazing tan for Manchester,' she said accusingly, pointing a deep scarlet nail in his direction. 'I'm surprised you managed to get so brown, seeing as you were stuck in a conference all day long.'

For once, Harry was speechless, his mouth open like a vacant haddock. Val got up from the settee and lurched towards him, with the aim of examining the extent of the amazing tan.

But as usual, luck was on Harry's side. The best part of a bottle of white wine had gone to Val's head and she caught one of her beloved Manolos on the edge of a Persian rug and sprawled at his feet. Harry felt he'd been let off a murder charge.

The shock on both sides instantly defused the situation. Val sheepishly regained her balance and composure while Harry silently thanked his lucky stars for the reprieve.

'Look, let's celebrate my homecoming,' he said more affably. 'Why don't we have a special night out tomorrow?'

Val lit another cigarette and contemplated this new Harry. Her brain was too fuddled with the drink and the fall to make any sense of it. She nodded dumbly in agreement.

'We'll have an early dinner and I'll get tickets for the theatre.'

Harry? Theatre? These were not words that usually went together. Val was now totally confused. Quick flashbacks to the conversations she'd had with her mother now seemed unreal. Had she imagined it all? Either way, she felt threatened by Harry's sudden new tack. Was he on a big guilt trip, or was it to do with the fact that she was now a fully qualified functional alcoholic. Dizzy spells, memory loss, falling over. There'd been big ticks against all those. Had she ticked the box marked 'Husband possibly playing away'? Val couldn't remember.

chapter twenty-four

Geraldine stared at the phone and decided to bite the bullet. She disliked Janet, over what she considered her disloyalty to Harry, but she needed to get something right. She dialled Janet's number.

'Er, Janet, it's Geraldine. I need your help.'

Janet pulled a face at the receiver. Geraldine needing help? Was there a doctor in the house?

'Harry's asked me to book theatre tickets for tonight. Any idea what's on and reasonably good?'

Janet took a swig of coffee and thought quickly. Be nice to the silly cow, she thought. This might lead to some interesting information for Operation Haunted Handbag.

'Well, there's a production of *The Importance of Being Earnest* on at the moment,' she said. 'It's had quite good reviews. The only other thing is some Gilbert and Sullivan; Hartford Amateur Musical Society is doing *The Gondoliers*. It's probably crap, though. They're not known as the HAMS for nothing, you know. Anyway, I thought you'd have been a bit of a theatre buff, Geraldine.'

'No, no,' said Geraldine, retreating back into church-mouse-with-attitude mode. 'I'm not effluent enough to go to the theatre very often.'

Geraldine being effluent. What a waste! Janet struggled for some measure of composure. 'Let me know what Harry decides,' she said at last, 'and I'll fish out the reviews. By the way, who's he taking?'

There was a pause. A most interesting pause.

'Val, of course,' said Geraldine tartly.

'In that case, the Gondoliers might as well ditch their oars. I definitely don't think that would be Val's scene.' Oscar Wilde wouldn't be much better either, unless the costumes were by Jasper Conran and they served unlimited white wine throughout the performance.

Janet replaced the phone and immediately dialled Sue's extension. She related Harry's theatre plans and the latest G-spot.

When Sue finally stopped laughing, she asked how Ray had got on tailing Harry the previous night.

'No dice,' replied Janet. 'Harry changed his pattern and went straight home to Val.'

'Hmm, I can see this whole thing falling down around our ears,' said Sue. 'Without a routine, we can't just keep on following him. There'd be no point.'

'Let's give it another couple of weeks,' said Janet. 'Then we'll all look for other jobs.'

Janet returned to the now bulging estate agents' file, which she'd jokily marked 'Affordable Cool'. She'd better get on with this one, set the wheels in motion. And then at some point later on through the contract, she'd hand it over to one of her producers. Possibly Liz, when she'd finished the Hot Breaks project.

Nina, in a delicious daydream about her forthcoming Greek holiday with Sam, wafted across the office, mentally on the beach on Rhodes and slapping on the coconut oil.

'Sorry to break into your reverie, but any chance of a coffee?' said Janet. 'Also, could you hook out last Tuesday's copy of the *Hartford Echo*? I'm looking for a review of *The Importance of Being Earnest*. It's on for a few weeks. And guess who's going?'

'No idea.'

'Hold on to your hat: Val and Harry.'

'Good grief. Not Val's scene, is it? Nor Harry's, I would have thought. Do you think there's a touch of guilt trip about all this?'

'Yes, I certainly do,' said Janet. 'It sounds from this theatre trip as if Harry's got away with it despite that disgusting tan. Ray's been trailing him on his bike, but last night Harry went straight home.'

'Pity,' said Nina. 'I'll make your coffee extra strong then.'

An hour later, Janet had completed the first scripts for the Affordable Cool project. She relaxed for a few minutes and flipped through the copy of the *Hartford Echo* that Nina had brought her. The play had been given a reasonably good review, and she sauntered around to Harry's office to show it to Geraldine. She shuddered at the sight of Geraldine's choice of outfit: a putrid-green knitted tunic and long skirt, completed with some rather ghastly dung-coloured beads. Very effluent, she thought.

'Bancroft? You, in here, now,' shouted a familiar voice.

'Good morning, Harry.' Janet dropped a mock curtsey. 'I was just giving Geraldine a review of *The Importance of Being Earnest*. I gather you're going tonight. It certainly sounds like a good production.'

'Never you mind,' said Harry ungratefully. 'Siddown.'

Janet sank into her customary position in front of Harry's crotch.

'Now,' he leered, 'I've had a great idea. There's a company called 3F. They're opening a chain of themed restaurants based on famous films all around the country. We want that job. I've got Geraldine to hook out all the background. It could be a biggie for us. We could do their news releases on video, manage their website. Cover all the openings. This one's got legs.'

Janet smiled outwardly and seethed within. Here was Harry back to his usual trick of passing off her ideas as his own. And probably getting all the credit and the bonuses from the board as well. He threw a file across to her. A quick flip-through revealed a brief company profile and some phone numbers.

'If you recall, Harry, this was my idea,' she said drily. 'I told you about it yesterday.' But Harry wasn't listening. He was back into his wheeling, dealing and bleeding 'em dry mode.

'I'm having dinner with their managing director later this week,' he continued, unflinching, 'so I want some facts and figures and a treatment from you before then. And it had better be good.'

'Sounds like a job for Paul Burns then, rather than silly old me. After all, it was only my idea,' Janet snapped back. Instantly she regretted it. Harry had gone white with rage. He looked as though he might hurl something at her.

'You do as you're told, or you'll be taking an early bath here, make no mistake.'

Rather like a dying man watching his life pass before him, Janet saw her mortgage, council tax, car HP and all the other bills wafting before her eyes. Jobs like hers were very few and far between. That was why most people stuck it out at HOT, despite Harry.

'And don't think you'd get any sort of reference from this company,' he hissed at her. 'Do that treatment, do it well and do it in two hours, or you're dead in the water.'

Janet stood up, turned on her heel and walked out of his office without saying a word. She shook all the way back to her office. Sinking into her chair, she put her head in her hands in a mixture of despair and exhaustion. It was all a waste of time. Harry was just too powerful for the Haunted Handbag committee.

The phone trilled sharply.

'And another thing,' yelled Harry, 'any developments, any important snippets on this project, you ring me immediately. Day or night. My mobile will be permanently switched on. Geddit?' His conversation was accompanied by audible thumps on his desk.

'Okay,' said Janet wearily. 'I get it.'

She glanced at the file Harry had given her and put it on top of Affordable Cool. Suddenly the estate agents seemed a rather attractive, hassle-free option. She was just throwing away the copy of the *Echo* from which she'd cut the theatre review when she had an idea.

Over hot beef sandwiches and spritzers on the outside terrace of the GX, Janet outlined the morning's events to Sue and Nina. They were horrified to hear that Harry was back in bullying mode.

'I thought we were really getting somewhere,' said Nina. 'What with Val's drink-driving case, and him skipping off to that sun-drenched beach in Manchester, I thought he was losing his grip.'

'So did I,' said Sue. 'Obviously leopards don't change their spots. Or in Harry's case, big fat bastards don't bother to file their claws.'

'I shouldn't think Val's having much of a time,' said Nina. 'And perhaps it serves her right.'

'At least she can drink at home all day now that she can't drive her car,' observed Sue.

'She did that anyway,' replied Nina. 'I probably shouldn't say this, but I bet Harry had a better time on the Mancunian Algarve than he would have done at home. Perhaps that's why he's got all stroppy again now that he's back with Val.'

'Could be,' said Janet, 'but then the theatre stuff wouldn't fit into that scenario. I got the distinct impression he was angry that she was still staying at her parents' place when he got back.'

'It seems to me,' said Sue, 'that Harry not only wants it all, he wants to be boss of everything. Plus, of course, he enjoys a good row.'

They all nodded in agreement, sipping their spritzers.

'So what's this idea you had?' asked Nina, gazing sky-wards in an attempt to top up her tan with the last of the summer sun.

Over cappuccinos, Janet outlined her plan. Back at the office, she made one phone call. Everything was in place.

Val decided to go for it. She put on a pale pink beaded dress with shoestring straps plus a cashmere cardigan in a deeper pink. She slipped into a new pair of fiendishly expensive spiky heels she'd bought in Hampshire, picked up the matching clutch bag and went downstairs.

Harry was doing his best to hide his anger at being kept waiting. He'd left the office especially early for this and here she was still fiddling about upstairs. He strode up and down the hallway, cursing under his breath. When at last Val appeared, they climbed into the Mercedes without exchanging a word and sped off to the restaurant. It was a new French place that had opened on the other side of Hartford. Val had picked it because, being new, at least she hadn't fallen over in it. Also, being French, they allowed smoking. Always a plus factor with Val.

The meal was stunning. Val toyed with a warm salad of bacon and quails' eggs to start and then turbot for her main course. As usual she moved most of it around her plate and then lit a cigarette. Harry stopped himself from telling her off. It always provoked a conversation about money and comparisons between his admittedly comfortable salary and her parents' premier-league lifestyle. Harry wasn't tight but he hated waste. They both avoided mentioning the previous week. Harry did not want to discuss his conference in Manchester with her, nor did he want to hear about the week she'd spent at the family pile. Val didn't want to discuss anything at all with him either, so they lapsed into silence, punctuated by offering each other lights for his cigar and her cigarette.

'How's work?' she eventually asked.

'Busy. Some big projects on the go and one potential biggie in the pipeline,' said Harry. Val didn't pursue it, to Harry's relief. He liked to keep his business dealings to himself. He didn't want her prying into his affairs, in case they led to his affair with Gina. To keep her happy, he'd ordered a bottle of wine with the meal, but only had one glass himself. The publicity about Val's drink-drive charge had been quite enough.

Bill paid, they set off for the theatre, again without much to say. Val found herself lost in thought about the advice her mother had given her last week. She was now thoroughly confused about her feelings for Harry and the state of the marriage. But as her mother had said, there

221

was no rush. She needed to think some more. And get some proof.

They arrived at the theatre with five minutes to spare and were shown to their seats, front row of the dress circle. Geraldine had pulled strings to get the best tickets. The lights dimmed and the play began. The *Echo* reviewer was right, it was a good production and the actress playing the indomitable Lady Bracknell was just that. The audience became immediately caught up in the action, and even Val, who couldn't remember the last time she'd been to the theatre, found to her surprise that she was enjoying it.

The play was just reaching the big scene where Lady Bracknell demands to know about Jack Worthing's parentage. He explains that he was found in a handbag in the cloakroom at Victoria railway station. An air of expectation ran around the audience as they braced themselves for the big line.

'A handbag?' roared Lady Bracknell with sneering disdain.

There was a big theatrical pause while Lady Bracknell gathered herself up to full disgust. In the silence came the trilling of a mobile phone.

'A mobile?' offered a member of the audience in suitably Lady Bracknell-esque tones. Everyone started laughing.

Val looked down at the audience in the stalls below. They were all glaring her way as the mobile carried on its incessant trill. She looked quickly to the right and left of her. All eyes seemed to be on her. She shrank back in horror.

Next thing she knew, Harry was wrenching his phone from his inside pocket, sweat pouring from his brow.

'What?' he raged into it. 'Fuck off. Of course I can't talk. I'm in the theatre.'

People started to tut loudly in Harry's direction. Lady Bracknell assumed control.

'A mobile in a handbag?' she proclaimed imperiously, earning a huge round of applause and gales of laughter. The play carried on and the magic swiftly returned. But not for Harry and Val. They sat there trapped in their front-row circle seats, like prisoners awaiting sentence.

The second the curtain came down for the interval, Harry stood and pulled Val up by the arm.

'Out of here,' he fumed.

'Who was it?' said Val, stumbling in Harry's rush to get out. 'Harry, stop, I've lost my shoe.'

'Oh, shut up, you silly cow. Just let's get out of here.'

As they reached the foyer, Val gave up hobbling along on one four-inch heel and took the shoe off. At that moment, a flashbulb went off and a man rushed up to Harry.

'What the fuck do you want?' said Harry, red-faced with anger.

'I'm from the *Hartford Echo*,' the reporter started. 'We're running a campaign about mobile phones in public places . . .'

But Harry didn't stop. He frogmarched the now barefoot Val out of the building, down the steps and on in the direction of the car park.

chapter twenty-five

THE IMPORTANCE OF BEING HARRY, screamed the front-page headline of the following day's *Hartford Echo*:

Film supremo Harry Hampton found himself well and truly in the frame last night when his mobile phone went off during a performance at the Civic Theatre. The Hartford Optimum Television chief's phone started ringing just as actress Julia Sandringham was about to deliver the immortal line, 'A handbag?' during a performance of Oscar Wilde's *The Importance of Being Earnest*.

The *Echo's* Don't Fry Your Brain Campaign, dedicated to restricting the use of mobile phones, has been appealing to the public to help ban their use in designated areas. Mr Hampton ignored recent pleas from theatre staff for members of the audience to lodge mobile phones in the foyer before entering the auditorium. After being booed by the audience, he and his wife Valerie left the theatre during the interval and did not return to their seats. As he stormed out, Mr Hampton refused to comment. His wife, a former model, appeared to lose one of her shoes in their rush to leave the theatre. It's the second time in recent weeks that Mrs Hampton has hit the headlines. She recently pleaded guilty to driving while more than twice the legal alcohol limit.

After the play, members of the cast said they had heard the phone go off and claimed it had definitely distracted them. All said they completely supported the *Echo's* campaign. A spokesman for the theatre said that forty members of the audience demanded their money back, claiming their enjoyment of the performance was ruined by Mr Hampton's phone.

Meanwhile the *Echo's* campaign grows apace. In the past week, five top restaurants have announced a ban on mobiles. Diners are being invited to leave their phones with the cloakroom attendant . . .

Janet smiled as she reread the front-page article, then folded up the paper and dropped it in the bin. The rest of the production office were far more demonstrative. Several punched the air, and there was brief talk of having an Importance of Being Harry party at the end of the week.

'You could come as Lady Bracknell,' suggested Ray, bowing to Janet in mock deference. 'We could cast Geraldine as a maid. Just a walk-on part, no words to get in a twist. Or perhaps a non-speaking nun. Some of them take vows of silence.'

'With Geraldine's gift of the gab, she'd probably think she was in *The Impotence of Being Ernest*,' observed Janet.

'To appear in the local paper once, Mrs Hampton, may

be regarded as a misfortune,' continued Ray in Lady Bracknell-esque tones, 'but twice in a month looks like carelessness.'

Everyone screamed with laughter.

'I did the bloody play for A level,' said Ray. 'I just knew it would come in useful sometime.'

'Okay, a joke's a joke, now get back to your looms before Harry hears this lot and fires us,' Janet warned. 'Nina, do us a favour. Get in a round of strong coffees. The caffeine might give our brains a boost.' Nina disappeared to the small kitchen at the end of the production office.

'Worked a treat, didn't it?' said Sue, phoning from reception. 'Everyone's been chuckling on their way through here this morning.'

'Harry in?'

'Yeah, crack of dawn, face like thunder.'

'No change there then.'

'The Italian woman phoned just now. Harry must have already been on the phone, so her call got redirected to me.'

'How do you know it was her? What did she say?'

'Just drawing on aeons of experience in this job, darlin',' laughed Sue. 'It was her all right, accent is unmistakable. She never leaves a message but she wanted to know if Harry was in. I detected a very controlled anger in her voice.'

'Not surprising really, when you see the man you're having an affair with plastered all over the front pages with his wife all done up to the nines,' said Janet. 'I must say, to be fair, the photograph of Val was stunning. You can see exactly why she was a model.'

Janet was right. Val did look amazing. The pink

sparkly dress was a knockout, even in a black and white photograph. The fact that Val was barefoot, clutching a bag and one shoe, somehow contrived to look incredibly sexy. It would have done even Liz Hurley proud. No wonder the Italian hackles were up. Harry really did have trouble coming in all directions.

'Let's hope they put on *The Rivals* next week,' said Sue. 'Then Harry could take them both, they could slug it out in the stalls and the *Echo* would have another great photo scoop.'

They both hung up. Janet surveyed the scene in the office. Everyone was now engrossed in their work or on the phone. She'd make one quick call.

'Freddie? It's Janet. Nice picture. Got my timing right, didn't I?'

'Spot on, girl,' came the gravelly Essex voice. 'Couldn't have been better if I'd cued you in. Don't like the look of your boss. Deeply unpleasant specimen. Couldn't have happened to a nicer bloke. We'll do lunch next week.'

'Yeah, somewhere quiet, though.'

'Totally understand,' said Freddie. 'Don't want people putting two and two together.'

'Oh well, wish me luck. I might as well go and face the music now.'

'Good luck, love.'

Janet replaced the phone and marched off to Harry's office, knowing it would not be pleasant. She felt like a convicted prisoner crossing the Bridge of Sighs, allowing herself one lingering look across the Venetian lagoon before being banged up for ever.

Val stirred, vaguely aware that the phone was ringing. For a few seconds, she wasn't sure whether she was at her parents' house or back home in Hartford. Disappointed, she realized it was Hartford, but at least Harry had obviously gone off to work. As she grasped the receiver, she noted with shock that it was just past midday.

'Val? It's Susie. Just seen your picture. You look amazing.'

'What?' mumbled Val, still coming to. 'What are you on about?'

'You're on the front page of the *Echo*,' continued Susie. 'I must say, they're all impressed in this shit-hole that I know you. We must do lunch soon.'

'What's on the front page?' said Val, groping for her cigarettes and lighter.

'Sweetie, it's all about your amazing visit to the theatre. "The Importance of Being Harry",' read Susie. '"Film supremo Harry Hampton found himself well and truly in the frame last night when his mobile phone went off . . ." Sweetie, you could get sponsorship from Vodafone.'

'Stop, stop. Oh, shit,' said Val, becoming alarmingly awake. It all started to flood back, including the late-night silent drinking session she and Harry had embarked on when they'd got home from the theatre.

'Everyone here's dying to meet you,' said Susie, 'especially my boss, but you'd better keep your mitts off him.'

'You still having that affair?' asked Val, getting her brain into gear.

'Absolutely, and he's leaving his wife,' added Susie triumphantly. 'We must meet up soon. Got loads to tell you. Shan't be doing this pigging rotten job for much longer.'

'Okay, hon,' said Val, stubbing out one half-smoked cigarette and immediately lighting another. 'Sorry, I was fast asleep. Rather difficult evening.'

'Time you dumped that fat bastard,' said Susie brightly. 'Lunch next week, yah?'

Val staggered to the bathroom and stared at herself in the mirror. She looked anything but amazing. Last night's drinking and all the recent tensions were showing in her face. She bent down and threw up.

Deep breaths, keep calm, Janet told herself as she strode down the corridor in Harry's direction. She had avoided this all morning, until the *Echo* first edition came out, certain that she couldn't have pulled off feigned innocence about her phone call. That would have required too much acting. At least this way there would be two rows for the price of one: row one about the phone call, and then row two about the newspaper coverage about the phone call.

'Ah Harry,' she said, as evenly as her nerves would allow. 'Didn't realize my call last night would cause such a furore. Just seen the *Echo* piece. Sorry, but you did say I was to call any time, day or night, about the Food From Films deal.'

'You stupid fucking cow—'

'And there's really good news. In fact, I got it confirmed this morning.'

'Bloody idiot, I've a mind to have you sacked—'

'It's in the bag, Harry. Providing we get our costings right, it's a deal.'

'What?' At the sound of the magic word 'deal', Harry suddenly looked like a rabbit caught in car headlights.

'Well, after I suggested . . . er, we discussed it on Monday, I wrote a quick treatment and sent it plus a copy of my . . . er, our catering college videos by dispatch rider to their offices straightaway. Just thought it would show that we have a track record in the field, so to speak. I was working here really late last night on the estate agents' scripts, and by pure luck, I got a call from the company's marketing chap.'

She paused, noting Harry's utter astonishment and

hoping that her face wouldn't give away the fact that the call had happened much earlier in the day.

'He apparently went overboard on it and rang to say yes, you're on. So I called you to tell you the fantastic news. Having seen the *Echo* piece, I'm really sorry I picked such a bum moment—'

'Yes, you bloody well did—'

'But you did say to ring if there were any developments, so I just did as I was told. Anyway, we had another chat this morning and it's in the bag. I must say, I'm impressed at the speed of their decision-making. They're a young company and they want to expand quickly. It seems they're very keen on our input.'

'Well, I'm sure I'll clinch things properly when I have dinner with their MD later this week,' said Harry loftily, regaining his composure.

'I think that will be a formality.' Janet smiled at Harry's crotch. 'They've asked for a budget to be e-mailed today with a view to me starting filming next week. So it's Thunderbirds Are Go.'

Harry would have loved to have taken ten years off his age immediately by looking puzzled about the reference to *Thunderbirds* but he didn't trust himself. Anyway, Janet didn't wait for a reaction. She got up and left his office. She walked past Geraldine's desk trying to stop the huge grin on her face. She kept walking until she reached her office, where she picked up her bag and headed for lunch in the GX with a waiting Sue and Nina. The champagne was already on ice.

'To the Impotence of Being Harry,' they all toasted.

Having finally resurrected herself, Val went downstairs and flopped down in the sitting room. She didn't bother

230

to open the curtains because she still felt queasy and had a pounding headache. After Susie's call, the phone had gone again. One call was from an *Echo* reporter, hoping for a follow-up, and the other was the boss of a local modelling agency who'd clocked the photograph. She'd told them both to get lost.

She dialled Harry's direct line. It was engaged, so the call was diverted to Geraldine.

'What's all this *Hartford Echo* nonsense?' she demanded. Geraldine meekly explained.

'Well, I don't exactly feel like popping out to my local newsagent's and submitting myself to more embarrassment,' snapped Val. 'Nor can I just jump in a car these days.'

'I'll fax it to you,' offered Geraldine, anxious to appease her. 'Did you enjoy the play?'

'Of course I bloody didn't,' shouted Val, and then regretted it because it made her head hurt even more. She continued more calmly: 'Why on earth Harry wanted us to go in the first place, I don't know. One of his more stupid ideas. And then because of his bloody phone we had to leave at half-time. By the way, where did he stay in Manchester last week?'

Val caught even herself by surprise with the suddenness of the question.

Geraldine panicked. 'Oh, I can't remember,' she spluttered. 'Somewhere in the city centre.'

'You must know, you're his bloody secretary, having to send him faxes and all that sort of stuff you lot do,' said Val, growing more suspicious by the second.

'I've probably thrown away the booking form,' said Geraldine triumphantly. 'Sorry, had a big desk clear-out on Monday. Can't help, I'm afraid.'

She knows, thought Val. She knows what Harry's up to.

'Pity,' said Val acidly. 'I'd like to stay there sometime. It must have a fantastic solarium.'

She slammed down the phone, shaking with a mixture of anger and shock, then lit a cigarette and headed for the fridge. Her mother's book and all its good advice would have to wait for another day, or another decade at this stress rate. She knocked back two big glasses of wine and then thought about breakfast.

The phone rang again. She snatched it up and barked, 'Hello!' down the receiver. Silence. After a couple of seconds she slammed down the receiver and dialled 1471 to see who'd called.

'You were called today at thirteen forty-seven. The caller withheld their number.'

She abandoned breakfast and headed upstairs again for a shower. She'd just got shampoo all over her hair when the phone went again. She rushed out, blinking hard as the shampoo stung her eyes. Once again no one spoke. Once again the number had been withheld.

Val flung down the phone and seethed aloud. She sensed someone had been at the other end, waiting for her to speak. Next time I'll give them something to listen to, she vowed. Five minutes later the phone rang again.

'I don't know what sort of game you're playing, but you can fuck off and die!' Val shouted.

'I beg your pardon,' said a familiar voice. It was Janet, ringing after an attack of remorse about the newspaper set-up. She'd felt a tiny bit guilty that Val had copped it in the paper as well as Harry. Val had had her fair share of trouble lately.

'It's all right, Janet,' said Val. 'I suppose I ought to be

getting used to this lark by now, though I never got this sort of coverage even when I was a model.'

'Everyone thinks you look great in the photograph,' said Janet, trying to compensate.

'Everyone except Harry, I should think,' said Val bitterly. 'I didn't see him this morning but I should imagine he's in a pretty foul temper. Well, even more foul than usual.'

Janet apologized for the fact that it was she who had made the fateful call.

'Not your fault, sweetie,' said Val, warming a little. 'God knows why Harry insisted on us going in the first place. We never go to the theatre. I'd rather sit home and watch soaps, frankly. By the way, did you try to ring me just now?'

'No. Anything wrong?'

'No. Nothing really. I had two calls just now from someone, except that no one spoke and they withheld their number.'

'These things happen,' replied Janet. 'Perhaps it was just a wrong number. You know how dopey people are. You'd think they'd just say they'd got the wrong number.'

'No, I got the distinct impression someone was listening to see what I sounded like. By the way, was Harry really in Manchester last week?'

Janet was taken aback at the directness of the question.

'Well, I think so,' she started in reply.

'But can you prove it? Do you know for certain that's where he was last week?' Val was sounding very persistent.

'No, I can't prove anything. I had no reason to ring him, but if I had, I'd have rung his mobile. Sorry, that one's a bit of a moot point. Why? Do you doubt him?'

'Yes. Absolutely.'

chapter twenty-six

Harry sat reflecting in his *Mastermind* chair. He couldn't believe the trouble coming in from all sides. His power base was feeling decidedly threatened.

He'd just put down the phone on a screaming Gina. She'd gone into an Italian crescendo after seeing the picture of Val in the paper, and he knew that some nasty threats involving his marriage were possibly just around the corner. He pondered on how Val would react if she found out about Gina. He never understood quite why women got so worked up about fidelity. After all, the lazy cow was on a bloody good deal. She didn't have to work, she could just sit around all day painting her nails and she clearly did just that. She wasn't famed for her cooking. Gardening and housework were no-go areas because as Val constantly reminded him, she hadn't been brought up to do that. The only area in which she'd excelled recently was a magic act involving the contents of the drinks cabinet. Maybe if she filled her days usefully, she might keep off the pop.

She's just a spoiled cow really, thought Harry, blaming her parents once again. He couldn't, however, deny the frisson of pleasure he'd experienced at seeing the amazing picture of Val in the paper. That was his wife, looking like a supermodel. Desired by many and owned by him. Why couldn't the silly cow just learn to stuff the odd mushroom and stay out of trouble?

As for Janet, he'd have stuck pins in a voodoo doll if he'd had one handy. She'd dropped him in the shit twice in as many months. He was still sore about being outsmarted over the Paul Burns episode, and now the bitch was at it again. Ringing him at the theatre, making him look a fool. Trouble was, she'd also come up with yet another top-class project. At least he could use the Food From Films deal to fend off any hassle from the board about the Hot Breaks project.

He fleetingly considered sacking Janet, dumping Gina and divorcing Val. Now that would be a serious clear-out. Trouble was, he liked having a gorgeous-looking wife, lusted after by other men. Janet seemed to keep striking gold with the deals lately. And there was no greater aphrodisiac than a powerful job and a bit on the side. No, sod it, he'd stick with them. For the time being.

Janet was now on overload. She was working overtime to get the Food From Films treatments and rough scripts together, plus the final setting-up of Affordable Cool. She couldn't lean on Liz because she was still busy on the Hot Breaks series, so she resigned herself to working late every evening this week. Harry, of course, would yet again take all the credit, swanning into dinner with the boss of 3F at the end of the week waving Janet's file of work and passing the whole thing off as his own.

Nina, seeing Janet was under pressure, brought her a strong coffee.

'You all right?' she asked. 'Can I help?'

'Not really, Nina, but thanks,' said Janet wearily. 'It's all bearing down on me a bit. I could do with a holiday but I've too much to do. And it's all for the benefit of that fat sod down the corridor.'

'It's time we had another HH meeting,' said Nina. 'Or at the very least a girlies' get-together. You need a bit of cheering up. How about Friday night? Come to my place. I'll fix it with the rest of the girls.'

With that, Nina withdrew. Janet smiled a grateful thank-you and returned to the files. She had until the end of the week – just two days to get everything in place. At least Friday night with the Haunted Handbag committee would be fun.

Janet arrived late, last and full of apologies. They were all crammed into Nina's small but cheerful flat. She didn't have a dining table so they all sat either on the sofa or on the floor of her sitting room. Out of her tiny galley kitchen Nina had produced a huge platter of mozzarella, tomatoes, avocados, parma ham, melon, artichoke hearts and olives, all served up with warm ciabatta bread. They washed it down with copious amounts of Valpolicella.

'Very apt wine in the circumstances,' remarked Sue. 'Let's hear it for Val and the Valpolicella.'

'Good job Val's not here to fall over,' replied Nina. 'My sofa hasn't been Scotchguarded. It wouldn't half stain.'

'Food's apt too,' said Sue. 'Italian flavour to the evening. In honour of Fattie Hampton's mystery bit of Italian skirt.'

'Not quite such a mystery now,' said Janet, revived by a glass of wine and something to eat. She'd been dying to tell them but wanted to pick her moment.

'Go on,' urged Sue. 'You know something, don't you?'

Janet triumphantly described how Ray had at last been successful. Disguised in his motorbike leathers and helmet, he'd followed Harry the previous night as usual, but this time he hadn't lost him. The Mercedes had sped off out of Hartford to a village twelve miles away. There Harry had parked outside a small cottage with, according to Ray, the familiarity of someone who'd been there before. A dark-haired woman had briefly appeared at the door before he'd disappeared inside. Ray had then tried Harry's mobile which had been—

'Switched off,' they all chorused in triumph.

'Oh, and it gets better,' said Janet. 'I did a quick search on the electoral roll. Gina Scarparo. Sounds like our Italian telephonista, doesn't it!'

'What happens now?' asked Nina.

'I'm going to have a word with my friend Freddie from the *Echo*. He's got some very long lenses.'

'You sound a bit less defeatist than you did earlier in the week,' observed Nina.

'Yes, I've been having a rethink. Earlier this week we had the same old scenario of Harry yet again pinching my idea and passing it off as his own. Since then I've done eighteen-hour days to get yet another money-spinner for the company up and running. Tonight, as I was leaving to come here, absolutely on my knees with exhaustion, Harry was off to an expensive restaurant for dinner with the MD of the Food From Films company. Waving my file, my ideas and my efforts. Last night, while I was slogging over a computer, he was cavorting with Signorina Scarparo and probably planning their next foreign jolly.

'Well, I've decided, I've had enough. Either he goes or I do. I can't continue like this. It's wearing me down and

237

I can't take much more. So I think the fight is really back on.'

The others were clearly impressed at this new resolve as they stacked the plates ready for sticky toffee pudding and coffee.

'I think you should record your next big row with Harry,' said Liz suddenly. 'It's time we collected some of this sort of evidence. Just get it on tape, even if it's only stored for a rainy day.'

'Liz's right,' chipped in Sue. 'If this whole thing was to blow up in Harry's face, he'd wriggle his way out of it, just as he's done before. Don't forget, he's got a PhD in bull-shit. We're just signing up for the GCSE course.'

'Imagine being summoned to the chairman's office,' continued Liz. 'And there you are facing Sir Stifferton Crapps, or whatever Geraldine calls him these days, and he demands proof of what's gone on. We'd just look desperately girlie and say, "He shouts a lot and pinches ideas." Then Sir Crapperton Stiffs would reply, "And that's exactly what I pay him to do." Result: Harry ten, Haunted Handbaggers nil.'

'There's one other thing in all this that's tipped the balance for me,' said Janet. 'It's Val. I'm actually beginning to feel sorry for her. I know she's rude, embarrassing and a piss artist, but she suspects something's up with Harry. I had a very interesting chat with her after the mobile phone episode. She didn't seem to mind that it was me who'd made the phone call and caused all the *Echo* coverage. She asked me point blank where Harry had been last week. And of course I genuinely couldn't tell her. There was a note in her voice that told me she knew he was playing away. Also, she said she'd been having silent phone calls with the caller withholding their number.'

'Perhaps Gina trying to railroad the marriage into the divorce court,' said Sue. 'After all, she spent a week with the fat bastard. I know it seems incredible to us, but perhaps she had a good time with him and wants more.'

'One would have thought she'd want to see quite a lot less of Harry,' remarked Janet. 'He seems to have put on more weight since his, er, sun-drenched conference. Rather than having a six pack, he seems to have gone for the Party Seven look. My problem with Val is that I think she's going to keep pestering me about Harry's extra-curricular activities, and I don't really know what to say.'

'It all boils down to the same thing,' said Liz. 'Proof. If we can get proof of what Harry's up to, then we'll all benefit in the end. Even Val.'

'Personally I'd like Val to know what a shit she's married to,' said Nina. 'I still haven't forgiven her for what she said about my bum. Come on, Janet, she's been appallingly rude to all of us.'

'Let's get the proof and let time and opportunity decide,' said Janet. 'Okay, next time I go in and have a row with Harry, I'll get one of the sound engineers to wire me up. It won't be difficult to predict when. Our shouting matches are fairly common these days.'

With that, they delved into seconds of sticky toffee pudding and debated the merits of the latest Next Directory, George Clooney movies and thongs versus big pants.

Val was dreading the weekend. She'd enjoyed the peace of Thursday and Friday nights at home on her own with the soaps and a few bottles of Chardonnay. She'd felt safe and unthreatened. Harry had been working both nights, or so he'd claimed. She'd tried to look faintly disappointed but didn't think she was all that convincing. At least he hadn't come up with any other weirdo suggestions like going to the theatre again.

Val was now becoming suspicious and wondering whether she should start checking credit card bills, or go through his briefcase for evidence. She then realized help-lessly that she couldn't do either, even if she'd wanted to. She had no idea where he put the bills and he kept his briefcase firmly locked in the car. It was probably stuffed with wispy knickers from Agent Provocateur and credit card slips from swanky eateries like Shiraz, she decided petulantly. So how was she going to track him down and find the proof? That dipstick Geraldine wouldn't talk. She was far too blindly loyal. The girls at HOT would know exactly what to do, but could she ask them? It was a ter-rible climb-down, and besides, Harry was their boss. She might try Susie, who seemed to have slipped smoothly from Smug Married to Scarlet Woman World.

She lit a cigarette and stretched out her legs, admiring her new toe ring, a present from Harry after his weekend away in sunny Manchester. Perhaps it was compensation for what he'd really been up to that week. She reached down, wrenched it from her toe and chucked it in a nearby waste-paper basket. That felt better. Next week she'd have another go at persuading Janet to spill the beans on Harry. There didn't seem to be much love lost between them at the moment.

Suddenly she heard the Mercedes' tyres scrunching on the drive. She stubbed out her cigarette, scurried upstairs, leaving the lights and the television on, went straight into their bedroom, dived under the duvet and pretended to be asleep. She heard Harry come in, then his footsteps creak-ing upstairs. She sensed him peering into their room, then heard him going downstairs again. From the kitchen came the clanking of bottles. Oh shit, he must have found the last two nights' worth of empties she'd forgotten to put away in a dark corner of the garage. After a while she heard him speaking in very hushed tones to someone. Who on earth would he be ringing at two in the morning?

Val strained to hear, only catching tantalizing bits of the conversation. It seemed that something had gone well tonight, and there was a reference to Monday. The rest was unintelligible. She'd creep downstairs in the morning and press last-number redial just to see who answered.

Val and Harry spent the weekend managing very cleverly not to speak to each other. If one got up early, the other languished in bed. The newspapers were lingered over, television was completely riveting and each appeared to be reading a new best-seller that they couldn't put down. Behind the steamy pages, however, they were both seething and having an unofficial competition as to who could avoid speaking first.

Harry's Friday-night meeting with the boss of 3F films had gone exceptionally well. He was certain that this deal, with its finance and prestige implications, was going to be the all-time biggie for the company. He was already fantasizing about a massive pay rise that would take him up to the two hundred grand mark, smiling pictures of him in *Broadcast* and *Campaign*, meals in the best restaurants, holidays in the most exclusive resorts, perks of every description. Harry was dying to spill the beans and boast a little. But he wanted to keep Val at arm's-length where business was concerned. Too much information wasn't good for her. And besides, she might stumble upon his other life with Gina.

He was also cross about his discovery of the wine bottles. He thought Val would have learned her lesson when she lost her licence. But he knew full well that she had the higher moral ground at the moment over the still undiscussed newspaper picture. He sensed that picking a fight with her would lead to other awkward questions. No, he'd bide his time.

Val, on the other hand, was fantasizing about being at home with her parents again, safe, cosseted and cuddled. She was also still wondering who Harry'd been ringing at two in the morning. She'd crept down on Saturday morning while he was still snoring to check the phone, but the last-number redial had turned out to be Directory Inquiries. So the bastard had tried to cover his tracks. Clever enough to erase the previous number, but not quite clever enough not to arouse suspicion. Val pondered some more, hidden behind the pages of her book. So this was how it felt to be in that infidelity trap she'd read about in magazine agony columns. It had never occurred to her that her husband wouldn't always be there for her. Let alone playing away. She'd always taken him for granted. Perhaps that was the trouble. But she needed to be certain, not rely on her instincts.

She began to formulate a plan. She'd fix up lunch with Susie on Monday, and start picking Janet's brains face to face, not down the phone. She'd confront her over lunch one day next week. Oh, and she'd give up drinking too.

chapter twenty-seven

'So how do you find out if your husband is having an affair?' demanded Val, abruptly lowering her voice when she realized half the restaurant diners were now riveted.

Susie stirred her coffee and thought for a minute. 'Well,' she said, lighting a cigarette and staring at it thoughtfully while she exhaled, 'there's the traditional approach of checking pockets, bills, car mileage, Visa statements, lipstick on the collar, that sort of stuff. But if they're premier-league liars, they just tell you another whopping porkie so you have to go off and investigate that one.'

'That's exactly Harry,' said Val, sipping her mineral water and desperately wishing she could do that old Bible trick and convert it to wine. 'He just wriggles out of everything, the sod. He knows best about any subject you care to name. And he obviously gets plenty of practice all day at work. No, that one won't work.'

'Hm, you're probably right,' said Susie knowingly. 'He always struck me as incredibly bossy. Couldn't mention it before, obviously. He's the archetypal smooth-talking bastard. That's of course why you married him. So you may need to think about a more brutal route. Confront the sod and see how he reacts. That's worth a stab.'

'No, same problem. Harry'd argue black was white if it suited him. I don't think I'd get anywhere on that route either, except another dreadful row.' Val stared miserably at the bottom of her glass.

'By the way, why are you on the wagon?' asked Susie suddenly.

'Decided to give it up', said Val glumly. 'My parents hinted that I'd been overdoing it. I've got drunk a lot recently, if I think back.'

'Bit difficult to think back if you're drunk, isn't it?' queried Susie, lighting another cigarette from the butt of the previous one.

'Exactly,' confessed Val. 'I've tried to think back and I can't remember the half of it most of the time. Then I wake up in the morning, look in the mirror and realize I look like shit.'

'Hmm, can't imagine that for one moment,' said Susie, who'd always been envious of Val's looks.

'I think I started because I got bored at home, but I wonder now if it was because I was subconsciously so unhappy. Now I'm stuck at home most of the time because of my driving ban. Sure, I could get a cab, but it's not the same. And Harry'd go ballistic if I hired a driver. I think he quite likes the idea of me being chained to the Aga, playing the little woman. I suppose I could learn to make a raised pork pie or pipe cream cheese into mangetout. But I've decided I've got to stay sober, if only to find out what he's up to.'

'Then I think the answer is a jolly good snoop,' said Susie. 'You've got to get someone to follow him, find out once and for all what he's up to and then confront the bastard on the spot.'

A waiter intervened to waft dessert menus in front of

them. 'Crème brûlée twice, and two coffees,' said Susie, taking charge. She looked at her watch.

'Ten minutes then I must scoot,' she said, again lighting a cigarette from the butt of the previous one.

'You're a bit heavy on the ciggies,' remarked Val.

'Remember, I'm a working girl these days,' said Susie, half laughing. 'Got to keep up my nicotine intake before I go back to the wonderful world of the smoke-free work-house. Just remember, too, the downside of all this. Dump Harry and you too could be rushing out for an alfresco fag in all weathers.'

Val smiled in sympathy. 'I thought you were giving up work soon to live with the boss?' she queried.

'Yes, well,' said Susie, suddenly getting all flustered. 'Let's just say something weird must happen to men's willies when they get into positions of power. My lovely boss has left his wife for me – and several others, I believe.'

'Oh, shit,' said Val, shocked. Perhaps it would be better to stay with Harry after all. Better the devil you knew . . .

It might have been Monday, but Janet was still exhausted from the extra hours of the previous week. She'd managed to avoid Harry all day. She knew that in her present state of fatigue she'd be absolutely no match for him if he started ranting. No, distance was the best thing. And she had plenty to get on with. Besides, she didn't really want to look Harry in the eye, knowing that tonight was the Night of the Long Lenses. Ray and Freddie had recce-ed Gina's house, in order to set a position for a snatch picture. Fortunately there was a small car park just a little way up on the opposite side of the road which would give Freddie a perfect oblique angle to the doorstep without, hopefully, being seen.

Janet was confident that if there was a picture to be

had, Freddie would get it. He was one of those typical newspaper photographers in that give him all day, a studio and plenty of lighting and he'd take the world's most ghastly portrait, ranking only with having a bad hair day in a photo booth. But put him up a tree, or have him hanging out of a speeding car, or someone's bedroom window, and he'd deliver great shots. If Harry stuck to his timing of last Thursday, he'd arrive at the house at around seven o'clock, when there was still plenty of light. Ray had promised to ring Janet at home that evening to tell her what happened. She mustn't get too hopeful, she thought, as she watched the hours tick past.

Harry, meanwhile, sitting in his office and admiring his paintings for the umpteenth time that day, was itching to gloat to Janet about his successful Friday-night dinner with the boss of Food From Films. That would put the irritating tart in her place. But there was an alarm bell warning him not to, just as there had been with Val. Better to keep it under wraps for a while. Damn the pair of them. He wanted to tell someone, he had to tell someone, to bask in the glory of a deal well done.

'Geraldine,' he barked in the direction of the open office door. A vision in putrid green scuttled into his office. 'I'll just update you on the 3F project. It's going to be an amazing success . . .'

And Harry was off, swelling with pride and too much weekend claret as he addressed his captive audience. Yes, Geraldine might look dreadful in that outfit, but she was at least a devoted and unquestioning listener.

Janet was just packing up to go home, computer switched off, rubbish bin piled high with the day's newspapers, junk mail and discarded scripts, when the phone rang.

'Operation Haunted Handbag here,' whispered Sue. 'Italian woman has made contact with suspect. I put her through. Perhaps they're discussing tonight's meeting. Also, Val's on the line for you. Do you want to speak to her?'

'Oh Gawd, not after the day I've had,' said Janet. 'Why didn't you talk to her?'

'She asked for you.' Oh dear, thought Janet. More questions that I can't or don't want to answer. 'Oh, go on, put her through . . . Val, you've just caught me. I'm packing up to leave.'

Val went straight into an apology for disturbing her and asked if they could meet for lunch, any day this week to suit.

Janet was staggered at the difference in Val. She couldn't pinpoint what it was exactly, only that it was different. They agreed on Wednesday, with Val saying how much she'd look forward to it.

Janet replaced the receiver thoughtfully. Val apologizing? What was the world coming to? She felt an attack of guilt coming on, knowing that tonight they might get the proof about Harry's extra-office antics. It might ultimately impact on Val, especially if she asked the sort of questions Janet thought she might. It might prove ultimately difficult to lie.

Harry left the HOT office so full of his latest piece of news that he hardly knew how to contain himself. He wanted to burst into song, crow from the rooftops and generally tell the world how pretty bloody clever he was. He eased the Mercedes from his reserved parking space and headed out of Hartford on the half-hour journey to Gina's house. He caught sight of his huge grin in his rear-view mirror and grinned some more. He even found himself singing along to the music system.

Champagne, he thought, swiftly pulling into a parking slot outside Bottoms Up. His snap decision nearly caused Ray, following behind, to swerve into a telegraph pole. Once recovered, Ray wondered whether Harry would clock the black-leather-clad and helmeted figure in his rear-view mirror when he resumed his journey. He needn't have worried.

Harry emerged from the off-licence still grinning from ear to ear and clutching a bottle of Moët wrapped in tissue paper. Oblivious to anything but himself, he climbed back into the Merc and resumed his journey. Ray followed at a discreet distance. A quarter of a mile from Gina's house, Ray pulled in and rang Freddie on his mobile phone.

'Man and Merc approaching in under a minute,' he reported. 'Man carrying pre-shag champagne bought from off-licence.'

'Gotcha,' replied Freddie. 'I can see them now. See you in the pub shortly.'

Forty minutes later, Freddie and Ray were seated in the back bar of one of Hartford's scruffiest pubs, nursing pints of lager and celebrating a victory.

'And you really don't think he noticed you?' asked Ray.

'No, doubt it. Remember, mate, I do a lot of this. You can always tell people's state of mind by the way they get out of a car. That chap was preoccupied and I expect what was going on in his brain was mostly X-certificate stuff. He didn't hang around on the doorstep. He was a man with a mission.'

Ray phoned Janet from the pub to tell her the good news, and much later that night they all met up at the

Echo office, where Freddie processed his film. The office block was mostly in darkness, the reporters having long gone home. It added to the drama and illicitness of it all somehow.

The pictures might not have painted a thousand words but they certainly told the story. Harry was even captured sporting a silly little grin as he got out of his car. The tissue-wrapped bottle was clearly champagne, its foil-wrapped neck visible.

'Wonder what they were celebrating?' Janet enquired.

'Not being rumbled on their sunshine break in Manchester?' offered Ray.

'Prospect of a good shag,' said Freddie. 'But I detected this man had had some good news. And he strikes me as the sort of man who will want to boast about it, whatever it is.'

Harry drove home in a very different mood to the one he'd arrived in. He'd been bursting to tell Gina the news that 3F were in advanced negotiations with a Hollywood star to open their first restaurant. Harry loved the idea of hob-nobbing with household names, especially film stars, and perhaps becoming their latest new best friend. He'd fantasized about conversations beginning with 'When I had lunch with Julia Roberts the other day . . .' or 'As I was saying to Brad Pitt . . .' He could imagine himself commanding Geraldine to 'Get Michael Douglas on the phone.'

Unfortunately, it had all backfired. Gina had got so caught up in his enthusiasm that she had demanded point blank to be invited to the opening party too.

'You can't come.' He'd recoiled in horror. 'People would talk. It would get straight back to Val.'

'But you'll have told her by then,' said Gina defiantly.

'You've said you'll tell her about me. You promised. In Portugal.'

'Well, er, yes,' Harry floundered, 'but I, er, can't guarantee that I'll have told her by the end of the month. It might not be possible.'

'Then I'll tell her,' hissed Gina, in full Italian flow. 'I'll tell her all about it. She'll find it much more interesting from me.'

'No, no.' Harry was beginning to feel invisible lead weights bearing down on his shoulders. His panic eventually evaporated as the champagne took effect and they ended up having a hot and passionate grappling session upstairs. He'd finally won an assurance from Gina that she'd keep her mouth shut if he'd guarantee she'd go to the opening party. Even if they had to pass her off as a casual acquaintance. Harry begged her to understand that he had to find the right moment to tell Val their marriage was over. He hinted that Val might threaten suicide when she heard the terrible news. The prospect of life without him would send her over the edge, he suggested, a concept that Gina could empathize with. Nevertheless Harry drove home a very, very worried man.

chapter twenty-eight

By her normally eye-popping standards, Val was looking decidedly low-key. Admittedly she was in her trademark four-inch heels, black today, with a short black trenchcoat and carrying a Prada bowling bag, but there was something missing. Talons, Janet decided. No long blood-red or shocking-pink nails. Not much jewellery either, by Val's standards. Blonde hair in subdued ponytail. Then there was the body language. Even if she'd worn a paper bag on her head, Val would normally have dominated any room she entered. Yet today Janet almost had to seek her out amongst the dozen or so people milling around in the HOT reception area.

'It's great of you to spare the time,' Val began when she saw Janet. Good grief, thought Janet, what on earth has been going on here? Grateful, subdued, humble, these were not words one normally associated with Val. Nor were three more words, 'sparkling mineral water', either.

That was the next shock, when the waiter in the Ganges Indian restaurant came to take their orders. Why on earth didn't Val scream for a bottle of wine the minute she sat down. Perhaps she was rehearsing being on the wagon for when she got her driving licence back.

'This is a bit of a dive,' said Janet, apologizing for the flock wallpaper and tatty tablecloths, 'but you did say you wanted to go somewhere out of the way. Nobody from HOT ever comes here. It's known locally as the Gunges. Anyway, I'm starving, and by the way, it's my treat, if you can call it that.'

Janet could have sworn Val looked so touched at her offer, her eyes nearly welled up. Something strange had happened to this woman, and that Harry was the cause, Janet had no doubt.

'D'you mind if I smoke?'

'Not at all,' Janet replied. Val had never been known to ask such a question before. And where was the imperious nature, the snapping of the fingers, the pointing and the addressing of the waiters as if they were some kind of low-life?

They made small talk until the first course arrived, onion bhaji for Janet, sheek kebab for Val. Just when they were crunching on some inter-course poppadoms, Val made her move. Except that it wasn't quite what Janet had expected.

'Harry thinks he's being stalked,' said Val, sipping her mineral water and then lighting a cigarette. Janet stalled for a moment, pretending to finish a mouthful of poppadom.

Val continued: 'Stalked. Followed. Call it what you will.'

Janet prayed she wasn't blushing. Had Harry clocked Freddie the Lens after all? He was so convinced he hadn't been spotted.

'What makes him think this?' she managed, covering her mouth as she finished the last bits of poppadom, and hopefully her embarrassment too.

'He's blaming me,' said Val. 'Thinks I suspect he's playing away. And that I've put a detective or someone on to him.'

Janet's embarrassment turned immediately to guilt. Had Harry given Val a hard time? Had he hit her? Or was this a smart diversionary tactic on his part? Her confusion was mercifully interrupted by the arrival of two waiters, one to remove the starter plates and the other to serve up their main courses from a wooden trolley. The dishing-up of the meat balti, chicken tikka and pillau rice was done with a great deal of aplomb. A triumph of style over substance where the Gunges was concerned. And it gave Janet enough time to gather her thoughts.

Had Harry spotted Freddie or Ray or was he just generally ruffled by recent events? He'd certainly got away with his trip to Manchester's sunny playas by the skin of his teeth. But add on the Paul Burns fiasco, the mobile at the theatre scenario plus the rumour about the secret file, and there probably was a very worried man under the surface.

'Well I haven't,' announced Val emphatically.

'Haven't what?' Janet replied absent-mindedly.

'Haven't put a detective on to him,' said Val. 'But it occurred to me that it's a bloody good idea. I was hoping you could, er, help me organize it.'

'Me?' said Janet, not quite able to make eye contact now with Val. 'Oh, Val, I couldn't do that.'

'I'm not asking you to set up a contract killing, just find me a detective,' pleaded Val.

'I . . . I . . . I'm afraid I just don't know any. Besides, if Harry found out, I'd get the sack.'

Val stubbed out her cigarette defiantly. 'Okay, point taken. But I want to ask you point blank and in confidence: where exactly *was* Harry the week he was away?'

'In Manchester, we were told,' said Janet, realizing she couldn't keep playing the innocent. Val clearly knew that she knew more.

'Do *you* believe he was in Manchester?' asked Val.

'No, Val, I don't,' Janet replied, looking her straight in the eye. 'I have no proof, but no, I don't think he was. Sorry. We all thought he looked a bit too brown.'

'Do you think he's playing away?'

Janet took a deep breath. Should she tell Val what she knew about Gina? It didn't amount to much. Disappearing into someone's house clutching a bottle of champagne was hardly proof of an affair. Should she tell Val that Harry was indeed being stalked? Followed and photographed, anyway. Every instinct in her body told her not to. Val needed to confront the awful truth herself, not rely on the tales of others. Wives were always the last to know. Also, if she told Val of the existence of Freddie's photographs, Harry would bully or beat out of her the names of the guilty. Janet's P45 would be guaranteed in the next post.

Suddenly Janet was overwhelmed by a feeling of deep pity, a feeling that she owed Val something. Despite all the ghastly evenings, the insults and the abuse, there was, seated across the table from her, a very sad woman who'd suffered probably much more at Harry's hands than the entire staff at HOT.

'Yes,' she said slowly, eyes downcast, hands clasped. 'I think he could be playing away. But before you ask, I have absolutely no proof.'

Operation Haunted Handbag held what was becoming their regular Friday-night committee meeting.

'So Val wants us to stalk Harry?' exclaimed Sue. 'Bit ironic, isn't it?'

'Well, strictly speaking she wants us to help her hire a detective,' explained Janet, uncorking bottles of Australian Chardonnay and passing round tortilla chips and dips. 'Sorry, I can't give you ABC.'

'What's ABC?' asked Sue.

'Anything but Chardonnay,' replied Janet. 'Apparently it's now regarded as a nineties drink. So passé, darling. But hey, let's be retro.'

'So are we going to help her?' asked Sue.

'Well, as I see it,' said Janet, 'the fact that we've already done that in a way is something we obviously don't want her to know.'

'But she suspects Harry's Game then?' asked Liz.

'Yes, and I get the feeling she's thinking very seriously of baling out.'

'You mean divorce?' asked Nina.

'Absolutely!' said Janet. 'Just consider for a moment what she's getting out of the relationship. Putting aside the fact that she lives with a complete pig, they don't have kids, he's never there and she's lonely. Val's thirty-two now and she's not getting any younger. Her only friends seem to be us, and we're not exactly her most fanatical devotees. She doesn't need Harry's money, she's got wealthy parents. So there's not even a meal-ticket aspect to it. Her answer up to now has been to drink herself senseless, although she seems to be off the pop at the moment, which I think is a bit symbolic.'

'In what way?' asked Sue as she scooped up some garlic and herb dip with a tortilla chip.

'She's having a rethink and she's sober. At our Gunges lunch, she drank only mineral water. She sounds different too, more polite, actually considerate. I'm going to make a suggestion and I want you all to think about it.'

They all stopped mid sip or mouthful.

'Until now, we've been setting Harry up in the hope that he might leave the company, get sacked, join SMERSH or SPECTRE,' continued Janet. 'But perhaps it's time we helped Val out a bit.'

'Dangerous mission, even for James Bond,' said Sue wisely. 'It could so easily backfire and we'd all be fond memories in old HOT telephone directories.'

'No, I mean indirectly,' explained Janet. 'I'm not suggesting we ring her and recommend a list of reputable detective agencies, or show her pictures of Harry arriving at Gina's house. Because that still doesn't necessarily prove anything. No, we have to come up with something more subtle. Perhaps we could take her somewhere where she might find out. Stumble on the truth herself, so to speak.'

'It would need careful thought,' warned Sue. 'You know how Harry can twist anything to his advantage. If he got the slightest hint it was planned, we'd be out on the street. We have to play the innocent on this one.'

The others nodded in approval. They all agreed to go away and think of a possible scenario.

The weekend seemed to pass as if it were on fast forward. After a flurry of supermarket shopping, mounds of weekend newspapers and piles of dirty coffee cups, it was Monday again. Janet thought about Geraldine for a moment as she eased her car into the HOT car park. Had she managed to get any fantastic sex or fulfilling hoovering in over the weekend?

'Geraldine's on the towpath,' grinned Sue as Janet entered the building.

'Blimey, I can't even get through reception before she's at it,' said Janet, her relaxed mood instantly dispelled.

She reached her desk and grabbed her ringing phone.

'Yes, Geraldine, I'm on my way. Give me ten minutes, for goodness' sake, I've only just arrived.'

Janet knew exactly what this was about. Harry wanted all the treatments on Food From Films. All the work that she'd sweated over for the last couple of weeks was about to be taken, stolen, plagiarised, call it what you will, and passed off as Harry's own. Then it would be big brownie points from the board, a pat on the back from the chairman and another whopping bung at the end of the year.

Janet checked her e-mails and then slowly gathered up all her files on 3F. Ten minutes later she was sitting in Harry's office.

'Hmm, not bad,' he admitted grudgingly, glancing through the work she'd handed him. 'Not bad, except you've got the name wrong, you stupid fucking cow.' He flung one of the files back at her.

'If I'm a silly cow, why do you continue to employ me?' said Janet, trying not to tremble. This was bad, even for Harry, first thing on a Monday morning.

'Start that tack and you might just talk yourself out of a job,' he snarled at her. 'The name of the project changed last week to Movie Munch. You should read your bloody e-mail.'

Janet knew full well that he hadn't sent any such e-mail but thought it wise not to pursue that one.

'Look, Harry, I've put in hours and hours on this, over and above doing my property project. I didn't know the title had changed. That's not a major problem. I can soon alter it, although I'll have to get Graphics to do some new mock-ups. Unless, of course, you yourself told them of the name change.'

Harry leaned forward in his *Mastermind* chair and thumped on the desk.

'You should be more on the ball. You should have told Graphics. I want this done again and I want it done by eleven o'clock. I have a very important meeting with this company and I want everything to be perfect. Geddit?'

'Yes,' nodded Janet, wishing she could throw poisoned darts at the view she had under his desk. 'I'll do my best. By the way, Harry, given the hours I've put in, why can't I attend this meeting?'

'Above your head,' hissed Harry. 'What on earth do you think you'd be able to contribute?'

'Well, I developed the treatments that got the contract, and it was my idea in the first place,' said Janet defiantly.

'Bollocks,' he shouted.

Janet took a deep breath. 'Harry, I'm sick of you getting the credit for everything. I came up with the idea, I wrote the pitch that got the contract, and at the end of the day I suppose I'll be credited just as researcher as usual.'

'At the rate you're going, you stupid cow, you won't even get a name check at your own fucking funeral.' He banged the desk once more.

'Thanks a lot, Harry.'

'And just remember who's the boss around here. What I say goes. Geddit? I have a reputation for coming up with ideas, good ideas, and making them happen.'

'But loads of them are my ideas and my treatments.'

'Just fuck off out of my sight. Get back to your desk. And if I don't have that work here by eleven o' clock, then you can start packing your bags. You're all the same, you bloody women. Ideas above your station. Get a move on or you'll be taking an early bath.'

Janet stood up and left his office without another

word. She went straight to the crew room where Ron, the sound recordist, was waiting.

'Cor, that battery pack got hot,' she grinned as she pulled up her jacket for him to dismantle the equipment. He pulled the sticky tape off her back where the battery pack had been secured, and unclipped the tiny microphone hidden beneath her lapel.

'I'd better get back to the office,' she announced.

'I'll let you know how it's come out and transfer it to ordinary cassette tape for you to enjoy at home,' said Ron. 'And don't worry, I'll put the red light on while I'm doing it so I won't be disturbed.'

Ten minutes later, Ron's voice came down the phone.

'At the rate you're going, you stupid cow, you won't even get a name check at your own fucking funeral,' he mimicked.

'What's it like?' asked Janet anxiously 'Is it clear?'

'For technical merit, straight sixes. But for artistic impression, he's right off the scoreboard. That was the most appalling claptrap I've ever heard. Is he always such a charmer?'

'Yeah, that's pretty standard Harry,' said Janet. 'Anyway, I owe you a pint in the GX after work.'

Liz staggered into the production office, laden with tapes and looking exhausted. It had been the final day of the last Hot Breaks For Heartaches shoot. Everything was now in the can. If they hadn't got the shots, it was too late.

As a small cheer went up, Liz half smiled and slumped behind her desk.

'Paul Burns sends his love,' joked Ray. 'He says he'll be in next week to check the rushes.'

'Bugger off,' said Liz, laughing. It felt good to be back in the office. She'd been out on the road for what seemed like an eternity. 'I was going to say that I'd missed you,' she continued, 'but I must be suffering from some sort of temporary self-delusion.'

'How was it?' asked Janet, walking over from her desk. Nina was also homing in with a cup of coffee for Liz.

'Well, the last one was fairly excruciating. Carpentry for the cack-handed. Not my idea of a fun-filled weekend, but the people on the break now think they're just waiting to be the next Chippendales. Stripping pine rather than their clothes, I hasten to add. Anyway, I heard a couple of really top bits of gossip.'

'What's that then?' came a chorus.

'It's a very small world. One of the guys on the course was at school with Harry,' announced Liz proudly, 'and he told me some very interesting things. Not a fan, not surprisingly. I should imagine Harry started his bullying career pretty early on in the playground, because this guy absolutely hated him.'

'Harry's certainly had plenty of practice then,' replied Janet, still smarting from the morning's onslaught. 'No wonder he's so good at it. Anyway, go on, what's this gossip?'

'Well,' paused Liz, savouring the attention, 'for a start Harry was never at Oxford, as he claimed. No, our Harry went to a bog-standard polytechnic somewhere in Oxfordshire apparently. Takes the gilt off the gingerbread a bit, doesn't it?'

'Just a bit!' said Janet. 'What's the other snippet?'

'Ah, that's much more fun. This chap and Harry were in the same class at school. Harry claims to be forty-four, as we all know. In fact he's got to be at least forty-eight.'

They all roared with laughter.

'Well, I suppose if you lie about one thing, you might as well lie about everything else,' said Janet. 'I'd love to see Harry's CV. I bet it would give the Brothers Grimm a run for their money.'

'I wonder if Val knows about the age bit,' said Nina. 'What a shock to find that the monster you married is an even older monster.'

'I think Val's well past being shocked,' said Janet ruefully. 'At the rate she's going, they'll name a trauma ward after her.'

'There is one more bit of gossip,' said Liz shyly. 'And it's about me. I think I have an admirer.'

'Brilliant.' Nina clapped her hands. 'Who, when and how did you meet? Oh shit, I hope it wasn't one of the cack-handed carpenters.'

'No, no,' reassured Liz. 'He's an accountant.'

'Chartered, certified or turf?' asked Ray. Nina immediately kicked him in the shin.

'Ironically, he's an accountant with Hot Breaks.'

'See,' said Nina, delighted. 'The system works. And I can thoroughly recommend accountants. He'll be able to take you on lots of those hot breaks.'

'No thanks, Nina. I think I've had enough of them to last a lifetime.'

'Forty-eight and counting, eh?' muttered Janet to herself. 'Does Harry ever tell the truth?'

chapter twenty-nine

A brand new wobble went around the corridors of Hartford Optimum Television. Harry was at it again. He'd apparently just sacked Jed, one of the graphic artists, amid a flurry of tongue-lashing. Legend had it that Harry could be heard all over Hartford. Certainly his raised voice had reverberated down the executive corridor, and soon rumours had spread to all four corners of the building. Jed had apparently been dispatched to clear out his belongings and go.

The production office was a scene of disbelief. Producers and researchers were standing around looking as stunned as if the canteen had just won a Michelin star. Jed was a popular chap, particularly as he was a soft touch for any private work that people wanted. The speculation was that that had been his downfall. He'd popped names and chapter headings on to wedding videos, provided graphics for show reels and generally been helpful and keen as well as extremely gifted. His only other fault, if it could be described as that, was that he was a bit of a flirt and considered serious totty by most of the women. Even the sexless Geraldine was clocked fluttering unmascaraed eyelashes when Jed swept past.

'I think it's because Harry was jealous,' whispered Nina to a huddled throng in the canteen. 'He thinks he's King Dong around here and Jed was a young pretender to the throne.'

'Harry's always had this idea that he can exercise his right of prima nocta,' said Ray.

'Wassat?' said Nina. 'Sounds like a cocktail.'

'Just an early English form of queue-jumping,' explained Ray. 'In olden times, the local Lord of the Manor got first jump, so to speak. Or droit de seigneur. Basically he could shag new brides before their husbands. Very Harry.'

'Well, I think it's appalling that Jed's been sacked,' said Nina. 'I know he was only on a short-term contract, but he's bloody good and—'

'Drop-dead gorgeous.' Janet had come in on the conversation. 'I can't believe Harry could be so stupid. Does he not realize that Jed's the only one in Graphics this week? If he goes, several projects are in jeopardy.'

With that, Janet stalked off in the direction of Harry's office.

'Directional Inquiries didn't have the number,' she could hear Geraldine apologizing.

'Well, get new bloody directionals, then,' shouted Harry in exasperation from his office.

'Harry's busy,' snapped Geraldine. Janet ignored her and marched past her straight into Harry's office.

'Did I hear right? Did I hear you've sacked Jed?'

'Yep, got it in one,' smirked Harry, loving his new power trip.

'As head of production, I should have been consulted.'

'Well, some things are over your silly little head,' snapped Harry, throwing caution – and the company's insurance policy – to the wind yet again by lighting a huge cigar.

'If you had consulted me,' said Janet tartly, 'I would have told you that not only does Jed do a really good job, but he's the only one in Graphics for the next fortnight. The rest are on leave. We have some very tight deadlines on projects, including your beloved Movie Munch, with its last-minute name change, which are all heavily graphic-dependent. No graphic artist means no graphics, so I suggest you ring around your clients and explain that their projects will be at least two weeks late. Meanwhile I'll go off now and cancel the editing. No point in starting without all the material.'

Harry banged his desk. 'Why am I never told about these things?' he hissed.

'You never bother to ask,' replied Janet as she turned tail and walked out.

Five minutes and a strong coffee later, Janet received an e-mail from Harry stating that he'd asked Jed to stay on until the end of the month, to which Jed had agreed. Whatever had Harry said to make him change his mind? Janet nipped round to the graphics suite and found Jed, feet up on the desk, chuckling over a huge cappuccino.

'I've agreed to do another fortnight,' said Jed with a twinkle in his eye. 'Don't worry, Janet. I was planning to leave at the end of my contract anyway. That's why I enjoyed such a big bust-up with Harry. I've got work lined up so I didn't need a reference from him.'

'Not that he'd have given you one,' said Janet.

'Oh no, that was made perfectly clear, together with mutterings about lousing up my career for ever. That guy's mad. He's power-crazed. Very sad. I gather he's got a rather beautiful wife. Why on earth does she stay with him?'

'Lack of a driving licence. Or something like that. Anyway, what on earth made you back down and agree to do another fortnight?' asked Janet.

'Just you wait and see,' replied Jed, enigmatically.

Top of the bill at Friday night's meeting of Operation Haunted Handbag was the playing of the tape. Tonight's host was Janet. She'd promised them a traditional English themed night. This turned out to be not spit-roasted pig, mead and jesters, but fish and chips from the local chippy plus bottles of beer. After they'd finished and packed up the plates and the remains of all the wrapping paper, Nina, Liz and Sue listened aghast as Janet played back the tape of her row with Harry.

'Bloody hell,' said Sue. 'That's even worse than I thought. Is that the norm?'

'By and large, yeah.'

'What are you going to do with the tape?' queried Sue.

'Save it for a rainy day along with all the rest of the evidence.'

'But when will we get this downpour?' said Nina impatiently. 'I hope we're not going to be meeting up like this in ten years' time, still snooping around Harry and wishing he'd disappear.'

'At least we can console ourselves that in ten years' time Harry might have retired!' said Janet. 'Now we know he's forty-eight, he's not got quite as much ahead of him as we thought.'

'Well, he's certainly ahead of himself in the gut department,' said Liz. 'There's definitely an attack of post-middle-aged spread there. I've really noticed the difference, having been out of the office filming so much recently.'

'Talking of eating,' said Janet, 'we have a new piece of information. Harry meets Gina for lunch nearly every Friday at the same place.'

'How do you know?' asked Sue.

'Silly question. Ray told me. He was chatting to Glenda, one of the cleaners, who told him that Geraldine let slip that she books a table every Friday for Harry. I think Glenda was asking her to recommend somewhere countrified for an anniversary or something. And Geraldine said it must be good because Harry went to this place regularly and she always made the booking.'

'Come to think of it,' Sue chipped in, 'Harry always seems to take a long lunch on Friday and looks a bit flushed when he comes back. Must be all that restrained passion over the willow-patterned plates.'

'Also, it would keep Gina topped up on the old pash-ometer before their weekend separation,' said Janet. 'Of course there's one way to find out for sure. And that's to—'

'Go there ourselves,' chorused the others.

'Well, actually, I've an even better idea,' said Janet. 'Let's make it a bit more public. Jed's bound to have a leaving do. Why don't we all go there for lunch?'

The weekend brought storms and sheeting rain. Autumn was hinting at an early arrival with a vengeance. Janet found herself yet again feeling the strain; it was not just Harry's constant outbursts, but the pressure of all the projects. Affordable Cool was more or less up and running and soon she'd be handing it over to Liz. But the Movie Munch project was weighing on her mind. It represented several months of hard slog.

Janet, still in her dressing gown, sipped a mug of coffee and casually flipped through the Saturday papers. There it was staring at her in the face. The travel pages. She needed a break, some sunshine and some respite from Harry. Somehow the rain now battering against her windows clinched it.

'Some leave,' she announced aloud. 'I need some leave.'

Janet hadn't taken any holiday for well over six months. She found herself feverishly scanning the holiday pages, ads and columns of flights, villas, hotels. Somewhere exotic and hot but not too far, she decided. Half an hour, three phone calls and her credit card details later, it was sorted. In a fit of excitement she picked up her phone again and rang Liz.

'I'm off to Morocco,' she announced. 'I woke up this morning really fed up and decided it was time to take a week off. I feel better already.'

'Brilliant, and about time too,' said Liz. 'You've been working far too hard. Who are you going with?'

'Just me. Don't worry, I've done this before,' trilled Janet. 'Only three and a half hours from Gatwick and I shall be completely transported into another world.'

'You'll be able to pick up lots of cheap haunted handbags in one of the souks,' said Liz. 'Or better still, forget about HOT for a week. When are you off?'

'This Friday,' announced Janet. 'Just time to crash-diet into my swimming costumes.'

'Hey, don't bother. Remember, it's belly-dancing country. They like their women curvy and well covered.'

'Hmm, I think I'm rather well covered already. And not just by my travel insurance. By the way, your voice sounds a bit funny. Or is it my phone?'

'No, it's my voice. It's my Big Date tonight with Tony

the accountant and I've got a face pack on. If I get too animated, it'll start cracking.'

Monday brought both good and bad news. The good news was that Liz's date with Tony had gone well. She was now into the agony zone of wondering if he'd ring again or whether she should ring him.

'Not too keen now,' counselled Sue. 'Let him do the chasing. Just wait a bit.'

'That's the trouble when you're past thirty,' wailed Liz. 'If I'm going to get married and have kids, I've got to get a move on. I've got to find the father and get practising, so to speak.'

'Well hang on, you can't map out your entire destiny on the basis of one evening at Que Pasa?. What was it like, by the way?'

They shuddered at the memory of their recent meal at the same restaurant with Val.

'Eventless, I'm pleased to say. It was a real treat to come out unscathed. No flying tables, no falling coat stands and not even a trip to the dry cleaner's afterwards.'

'How about him?'

'Bit shy. I suppose I expect everyone to be as mad as we are here. But accountants aren't necessarily the whackiest people on the planet. I do like him, though. Do you think he'll ring?'

'Yes of course he will,' said Sue, who was beginning to feel like Liz's mother. 'And if the sod doesn't, better now than six months down the line.'

The bad news, Janet discovered, was that the last day of her holiday clashed with Jed's leaving do. She would be flying back late that night. The others promised to let her know what happened.

Ray was taking charge of organizing Jed's farewell lunch. He was keeping it all low-key because no one wanted Harry to get wind of it. As the Country Cottage Restaurant was about ten miles outside Hartford, not everyone could go, but eventually a party of ten emerged, including Sue and Nina. Liz was secretly relieved that she couldn't go. She was still in the middle of editing the Hot Breaks films and couldn't spare the time. She found dealing with Harry incredibly difficult and was still managing to avoid being on her own in his office.

The next few days flew by as Janet frantically cleared her desk, answered every single letter and e-mail and left copious notes on what to do about Movie Munch during her week's absence. As the flight date drew nearer, she became more and more exhausted. At night she didn't have the energy to sort out her summer clothes, let alone get them washed and ironed.

Eventually it was her last day at work. She went round to see Jed and wish him well. He gallantly kissed her on the lips, and told her she was totally gorgeous and that it had been a pleasure to work with her. Janet fervently wished she could have settled for the pleasure, skipped the work, been twenty years younger and about two stone lighter.

Then, with heavy heart, she set off in the direction of Harry's corridor for a brief handover meeting. She'd prepared notes, too, just in case.

Harry was in ebullient mood and grandiosely welcomed her into the office without getting up from his *Mastermind* chair. Probably looking forward to his Thursday-night champagne shag, she thought mischievously.

They ran through her notes, with Janet emphasizing

that there would be a couple of projects that he would have to view and sign off while she was away: four instructional programmes on landscaping for the new gardening channel and three of the Hot Breaks videos. He nodded and then grudgingly wished her a good holiday.

'Where are you off to?' he enquired, without bothering to feign interest.

'Morocco,' she answered. 'Staying on the coast in Agadir, then having a couple of days in Marrakesh.'

'Well, make sure you don't get lost in some bloody kasbah. I know you women and your bloody shopping.'

chapter thirty

Janet stretched out on the beach in Agadir. Blue sky, pale ivory sand, a light breeze that just took the edge off the heat. It couldn't be more perfect. Having holidayed before on her own, she knew the drill. Loads of riveting books, a capacity for long walks, not too much eye contact with the locals, a pseudo wedding ring and preparation for the slight disappointment of a wonderful experience that she wouldn't be able to share.

One of the great delights of holidaying alone was that it didn't really matter what you wore, how fat you were or how burned you got. Not knowing a soul at the Hotel Agador had distinct advantages. She stretched out on a sunlounger on the hotel's private section of the beach and contemplated her lot. A couple of miles of sand, the Atlantic Ocean gently lapping its edge; this was the life. And she'd already caught up with essential reading. The latest Patricia Cornwell and Harry Potter had already been read, enjoyed and consigned to the chambermaid, who was quite upfront about being tipped. Next, another in her series of classics-she'd-never-got-round-to-reading-at-school, *Jane Eyre*, was waiting to be devoured. Janet suddenly thought of Harry cast as Mr Rochester, the moody monster control-freak, and Val as his mad wife, locked up, blind drunk and burning the house down. She began irritatingly to think of the office and wondered what was going on. Perhaps she should have brought one of those self-help books on how to deal with office bullies – an instructional volume entitled *How to Work With A Difficult Man – And Kill Him*.

Much to her annoyance, Harry was now stuck in her thoughts. She pottered down to the water's edge, making deliberate efforts to put him out of her head. That only made it worse. She watched some local salesmen at work on the beach, pestering tourists with their wares. They reminded her of Harry. Eventually she became so absorbed watching the jet skis that thoughts about HOT and all her projects evaporated. Tomorrow she'd be in Marrakesh after a very early start. Just time now for a brisk swim, then a light supper and an early night. The jet skis looked so powerful, skimming the water, bouncing the waves. She'd have liked to pulverize Harry with . . . Oh hell, there he was again. She must try and forget him.

Val was becoming quite an expert. Searching through Harry's pockets, dialling 1471, checking his discarded clothes for traces of lipstick and perfume, sifting through the waste-paper basket, getting up early to get to the post first, even steaming open then resealing envelopes. But so far nothing. In fact, the only suspicions roused were Harry's. He couldn't for the life of him understand why Val, who normally lounged in bed until at least eleven o'clock, was up with the lark and bringing him cups of tea in bed.

Val was often tempted to ring her mother, but there was always something that held her back. Perhaps she was afraid she'd crack under the strain of the inevitable conversation about the failure of her marriage, fear of the future, or just putting into words how wretched her situation was. No, she'd be stronger fighting this battle alone. Or at least with a little help from the HOT girls. She realized she was putting them, Janet in particular, in a difficult situation because of work, but on the other hand, they understood, more than most, exactly what she had to live with. She also suspected Janet knew much, much more than she was letting on. She had her reasons for that, Val understood, but she wished Janet would just spill the beans and be done with it.

Today she'd discovered that Janet was on holiday in Morocco. It made her shudder thinking that her holiday with Harry in the Maldives was only weeks away. The thought held no appeal at all. It felt more like a prison sentence. She'd have to get out of it somehow. Or perhaps she'd be doing Harry a favour by not going. Then he could take his bit on the side, whoever she was. The marriage might be all over by then, bar the shouting.

Val settled down to watch early-evening television. In the bad old days she'd have been well into her second bottle of wine by this stage of the day. She'd been surprised at her own success in giving up. After a few fairly gruesome days, she'd got used to a routine of mineral water, tea and coffee and was proud of the fact that she was no longer dependent on alcohol. What was Harry doing now? she thought. He never said why he had to work late some nights. She rang his mobile on impulse. Switched off. She rang HOT reception. The late receptionist said he'd left an hour ago. Funny, it had never occurred to her before, but this scenario often happened on Thursday nights. Probably in the past she'd been too slewed to notice. Now she was almost hoping he was being unfaithful. It would resolve things so easily. She'd challenge him when he got home.

Unfortunately the effect of the new routine of early rising to screen the post was catching up on her, and by the time Harry sneaked in at 10.30 after his Thursday-night session with Gina, Val was sound asleep on the sofa.

Friday morning and Janet's last day in Marrakesh. On the agenda, a visit to the Saadian tombs and the souk. Janet had been bowled over not just by the heat, but by the sheer colour and excitement of this gateway to the desert. The dusty pink buildings held a special kind of magic and the huge main square, Djema'a al Fna, was one of the most exciting places Janet had ever seen. By day it was hot, colourful and dusty, with its stalls selling fruit, spices, leather bags and slippers and djellabas, while by night it was a mass of smoke from barbecues as row upon row of food stalls were miraculously set up. Berber musicians, acrobats, fortune-tellers, snake-charmers, story-tellers, water-sellers all crammed into the huge arena, just as they had done for thousands of years. All there to make an honest or dishonest dirham or two.

At lunchtime Janet sat down at the Café Glacier for a cool beer and a ringside view of the square. The snake-charmers were out in full force, wrapping their wriggling companions around unsuspecting tourists who had to stump up fistfuls of dirhams to have them removed. With a jolt, Janet realized the snakes were reminding her of Harry yet again. She checked her watch. They'd all be arriving at the Country Cottage Restaurant around now. Would he be there with Gina? She checked her mobile. Yes, there was a good signal. She'd just have to be patient.

She finished her beer, left some coins on the table and made her way purposefully across the square to the entrance to the souk. Some last-minute shopping, that would take her mind off things.

Ray had hired three cabs so that everyone could have a drink at Jed's farewell lunch without the worry of driving. He also secretly wanted the car park at the Country Cottage Restaurant to be free of cars with HOT windscreen stickers in case it put Harry off. He'd booked the table for twelve fifteen so they'd all be seated when – or if – Harry walked in. Ray, Sue and Nina were in on the secret but the other seven had no idea. Better they didn't know. Three people feigning surprise would be less of a problem than all ten.

Miraculously everyone was ready in reception and the three taxis were on their way to the restaurant on the dot of twelve. Ray glanced at his watch for the hundredth time, watched by Sue.

'Nervous?' she asked.

'No, not really,' he replied. 'I'll just be seriously pissed off if this is the one week he doesn't go there.'

'Not the end of the world,' said Sue philosophically. 'The bottom line is that it's Jed's farewell bash. It's important that he has a good time. And if Harry pitches up, well, that's the icing on the cake.'

Nina rubbed her hands with anticipatory glee.

'I can't wait to see his face,' she chuckled. 'It'll serve the bastard right.'

They were all seated by twelve twenty around a huge circular table near the entrance. Brilliant, thought Ray, looking at his watch again. Couldn't have planned it better. He can't fail to spot us when he walks in.

Everyone consulted menus and a huge blackboard of

specials. There followed a lengthy discussion among the women about the calorie counts of the sauces that came with the sea bass as opposed to turbot or hake.

'Oh, spare me. Women and their bloody dieting,' Ray remarked to Jed and Neil, one of the engineers. They were the only chaps at the table.

'Next thing we'll hear is that they're all short for their weight, or that it shrank in the wardrobe,' replied Neil, who had two teenage daughters. 'It's like being at home.'

Eventually the calorie-counting was done and their orders taken, and a debate started up about the pros and cons of Delia, Jamie, Nigella and the two women from the River Café versus the Two Fat Ladies.

At twelve thirty, Ray began to despair. He's not coming, he's not coming. Drat and double drat. The restaurant was beginning to fill up.

An outrageously camp waiter started laying up the correct cutlery for the orders, swapping fish and steak knives where appropriate. Then he faffed around with butter and rolls and did a great deal of the adjusting of glasses that waiters delight in. At last bottles of wine arrived, everyone taking advantage of the no-driving situation.

By twelve forty, Ray had resigned himself to getting it wrong. He rose to his feet.

'While we're waiting for the grub, I think we should drink a toast to Jed and wish him well in the future,' he said. 'Good on yer, mate, for surviving us all at HOT, and may you come back one day.'

They raised their glasses in unison amid mutterings of 'Speech, speech.' Jed stood up. Two of the girls, desperate for a memory of the best bit of totty to arrive at HOT in many a long month, whipped out cameras to take pictures for posterity.

As flash bulbs popped in all directions, everyone was blinded for a split second. Out of the gloom, behind Jed, appeared Harry's flushed and angry face. He'd come in unseen and got caught in the flashfire.

'What the fuck . . .' he muttered, red-faced with anger. Then he nodded in his woman companion's direction. 'Business. I'll keep away from you bloody lot.'

With that he ushered the woman away to a table at the furthest end of the restaurant.

'Not your usual table, sir?' flapped the camp waiter after him.

Sue and Nina exchanged silent grins. It was Gina all right. Her long dark hair was gleaming and she was dressed provocatively in tight cream leather trousers, a cream silk shirt more unbuttoned than buttoned, a Moschino belt and cream leather kitten-heeled boots. Not quite the normal kit for a business lunch.

Jed was still on his feet, being urged by his female fans to make a farewell speech.

'Well, it's been fun and I'm gonna miss you all,' he said, grinning from ear to ear and a huge glass of wine in hand. 'HOT's a terrific company to work for. Full of big-hearted and generous people. I can't tell you how knocked out I am that Harry's come along today as well. Just shows that you can sack a man and still come to his leaving do. What a top bloke.'

Jed's voice was pitched just loud enough for Harry to hear across the restaurant, except of course that he was busily pretending not to.

'Harry,' Jed turned towards his table and raised his glass, 'thanks for the memory.'

Forced to acknowledge the toast, Harry grudgingly raised his glass and turned back to his companion as fast as he could. The HOT table was now convulsed in barely concealed giggles. Jed sat down, roaring with laughter.

The wine flowed, tongues loosened and diets finally went to the wall. After the main courses had been devoured, a blackboard of puddings well off the Richter calorie scale was greeted with enthusiasm. Having carefully chosen grilled fish for their main courses, the dieters now threw caution to the wind by ordering raspberry pavlova with clotted cream.

'I'll never understand women,' said Ray.

'They're a real mystery, mate, and I'm married to one,' replied Neil.

'What beats me is that some of them fall for bastards like Harry,' replied Ray. 'He's not only got Claudia Schiffer for a wife, but he's got Miss Tagliatelle Tasty Bits over there too.'

Every so often Sue and Nina glanced in the direction of Harry and Gina's table. The body language said it all. Harry looked positively shifty and uncharacteristically tense, while Gina, tossing her dark mane of hair, seemed totally at ease. It soon became apparent that Harry was going to stay put until they'd left. He wasn't going to suffer the embarrassment of having to walk past them all again to get to the exit. Eventually, after a round of coffee, they all felt they ought to get back to work. As taxis were ordered via mobile phones, Harry made no attempt to conceal his relief. He then had to endure a round of loud goodbyes from across the restaurant, much to the bemusement of other diners.

There was much speculation in the taxis going back. 'If Harry was on a business lunch, then I'm an alien,' said Julie, one of the accounts clerks. 'That's obviously his bit of stuff on the side. Fancy us stumbling on that!'

'Well, of all the bars in all the world . . .' growled Ray, adopting a Humphrey Bogart voice.

Sue and Nina exchanged glances. They were desperate not to let on that it was a set-up.

'I'm glad I don't have to work with him,' continued Julie, fuelled by far too much Pinot Noir. 'I think he's a right sod. Really fancies himself. Wonder what that woman sees in him.'

'God knows, but Vision Express should open a new branch around here,' replied Ray.

Sue couldn't wait to ring Janet. She finally caught her waiting for her flight at the airport in Marrakesh.

'Caught like a rat in a trap,' she told her cheerfully. 'You should have seen his face. We all behaved quite badly. Jed gave a speech and paid tribute to Harry. The whole restaurant heard.'

'Probably just as well I wasn't there,' said Janet, relieved. 'It would probably somehow be my fault. The trouble is, Harry's bigger than all of us. He'll just shrug off someone like Jed as if he were yesterday's socks.'

Janet was cross with herself for being defeatist about Harry again. It seemed to come in waves. One minute she'd feel quite confident, the next completely under-mined.

'Listen, I hope you've had a good holiday and didn't worry about all this stuff,' said Sue, concerned.

'It was fab. I've done so much shopping, I'm souked out. At the rate I've been spending, I'll probably be turned down for a Sainsbury's reward card. It's the coming back that's the worst bit. I've managed to forget about Harry for most of this week, but he's already looming large again.'

chapter thirty-one

Janet did not want to get out of bed. It was so warm and safe under the duvet she wanted to stay there for ever, fuelled by Radio Four and a stream of comfort food and drink. The second of her three alarm clocks had gone off. She really ought to make a move but she couldn't. She'd wait for the third before getting up. That was the one that made her get out of bed. It had an annoyingly shrill ring and she had placed it intentionally on the other side of her bedroom.

Marrakesh was just a distant memory now. Today it was back to reality, back to HOT gossip and back to the problem of Harry. She showered, got dressed and sprayed herself with her new duty-free perfume. At least there was no need for make-up for a couple of weeks, thanks to her tan. Then she flung her briefcase into the back of the car and headed for work.

As she arrived in the HOT car park, she was overcome with a deep sense of foreboding. She felt like a patient going in for an operation knowing they'd run out of anaesthetic.

Two hundred e-mails and a menacing pile of post greeted her, together with so many Post-it notes stuck all over her computer they could have been entered for the Turner prize. She scrolled down through the e-mails. Amongst the usual flats/car/houses for sale she saw there were several messages from Val asking her to call.

'One would have done,' she said half aloud. What does she think I do on holiday, rush to the nearest cyber café and log on every day? She made a bet with herself on how long it would be before Harry demanded her presence. Half an hour, she reckoned. Wrong. The call came after only five minutes. Nerves a-jangle, she made her way to Harry's corridor. All the therapy of the week swept away by one phone call.

Having guessed where Janet was heading, Ray broke into the HOT rendition of a famous football chant – You'll Never Walk Again. For once, Janet found it physically impossible to smile.

'Have you seen this?' Harry shouted, going purple in the face and waving a tape.

'Have I seen what, Harry? Remember me, I've been on holiday for a week.'

Without a word of explanation, he shoved the tape into one of the machines behind his desk. Janet gazed at the screen in anticipation. It was the closing sequence of one of the series of landscape gardening programmes. The presenter, a ditsy blonde with implants that had clinched her contract, was signing off, clutching a designer trug. As the end credits rolled, there was a reprise of someone's ugly back yard being miraculously transformed into a miniature Japanese garden. The crew names then rolled up the screen, all familiar to Janet. But just as Harry's name appeared as executive producer, he hit the freeze button on the remote control.

'Look at that,' he shouted. 'Look at it. That's already

been delivered to the gardening channel. It's on every fucking episode. And every VHS copy we've had run off for the sponsors.'

He threw the remote control across the office, narrowly missing one of his precious paintings. The plastic case burst open and the batteries rolled away noisily across the polished wooden floor.

'It's just not good enough. I warn you, Janet, heads are going to roll. And yours might just be the first.' He banged his desk for effect.

Janet took a deep breath. Please let this be one of her strong days.

'If you recall our conversation before I went on holiday last week, I told you that you would need to sign off this project, plus three of the Hot Breaks videos. We had a meeting, I produced a list of notes and I also e-mailed them to you.'

'That's not good enough.' Thump on desk. 'These sorts of mistakes shouldn't happen.' Thump on desk. 'That pile of shit goes out tonight. And the whole industry will see it.'

'Well, mistakes do happen, and with respect, Harry,' she paused, wondering if she was issuing her own death warrant here, 'you too have made a mistake by not checking them yourself.'

'It's all that stupid bloody idiot Jed's fault,' continued Harry, ignoring her last remark. 'Thank goodness I had the sense to fire him. All too free and easy. Too much chatting up the women. That man's head was in his underpants.'

Janet smiled inwardly. Harry had obviously convinced himself his outing with Gina had gone unnoticed.

'Perhaps you'd like me to get Computers to check that

you did receive and open my e-mail about all this,' she said smoothly. 'And here's a copy of the notes we discussed before I went away.' She indicated the file she'd placed on his desk.

Harry picked it up, glanced at it as if it were an oily rag and flung it at her in temper. Janet stood up and left the office without a word. As she came out, she noticed Geraldine frantically re-adjusting the pussycat bow of her blouse, C&A circa 1984, in a pretence that she hadn't been listening. The absurdity of it all made Janet burst out laughing as she went back to the production office.

She insisted that Sue and Nina join her in the canteen for a quick coffee.

'You've *got* to watch that new gardening channel tonight,' she said, still shaking with laughter. 'Our landscape gardening series is beginning. And it's also Jed's last revenge. He warned me he was going to do something but he wouldn't say what.'

Janet was seized with another bout of giggles.

'Come on, come on, what?' Sue was in suspense.

'Harry's name on the end credits. Jed deliberately spelled it wrongly. He's up as Executive Producer, Harry Humpton.'

Janet finally got around to ringing Val later that afternoon. She'd waded through all the messages, done all the urgent tasks, but the effect of the first day back was beginning to take its toll, especially after the scene with Harry.

'Val? It's Janet. Got your messages. Been on holiday. How are you?'

'Oh, the usual,' said Val. 'Ghastly.'

'I thought I'd better warn you,' said Janet, picking her

words carefully. 'There's a programme going out on the new gardening channel tonight. I don't think Harry's going to like it very much.'

'Why? What's it about?' Val had a sudden rush of fear. Was this some kind of investigative programme into Harry's secret life? She'd had quite enough of her recent brush with the media.

'Oh, just landscape gardening. But Harry's name has been spelled wrong at the end. They've called him Humpton instead of Hampton.'

To Janet's amazement and relief, Val burst out laughing.

'Humpton! Ha ha, that's brilliant. He's certainly got the hump at the moment, and I'm still certain he's humping someone else. Is that what his filthy mood on Friday night was all about?'

'Er, no, that's what his filthy mood tonight will be about. He only discovered it this morning.'

'Any idea what the Friday rage was about?'

'No, no idea,' lied Janet. 'I was coming back from Morocco.'

'Anyway, look, I'm bored witless. Could we have a girlies' night again soon? How about this week? Any night, my treat.'

'I'll see what they're up to and come back to you.' Janet replaced the receiver.

Val couldn't resist it in the end. She rang her mother and told her about the gardening programme. Sheila Mortimer, normally the model of restrained elegance, broke down in fits of giggles.

'I can't wait to tell your father, dear,' she said. 'We'll make sure we watch. By the way, how are things? Are you all right? We do so worry about you.'

Val had known it would happen. She burst into tears, Harry's rage over the weekend having taken its toll.

'I can't go on much longer,' she sobbed. 'It's like living with a monster. I can't remember the last time we did anything remotely exciting. The mobile phone disaster was about as good as it gets. He just comes home and rants.'

'Do you think he's seeing someone else?' said her mother gently.

'Yes, I do. Still no proof, but it suddenly dawned on me that he's always late home on Mondays and Thursdays, and his mobile's switched off on those evenings.'

'How long has this been going on, do you think?'

'I don't know. Months probably. Trouble is, Mum, I was doing a bit of drinking up until recently, as you know, and I sort of lost the plot. But I've stopped now.'

'Good girl, I'm proud of you,' said Sheila. 'You don't necessarily need the proof to leave, you know. If you're unhappy, there's always a place for you here.'

'I know, Mum, but I've got to sort this out myself in my own way.'

Val put down the phone and sobbed. It was at times like this that she desperately missed her friend the wine bottle. She mustn't give in, though. She'd got through the worst. But it was tempting.

She mooched around the house aimlessly, gazing out over the manicured garden. She went into the bedroom, looked at the marital bed and shivered. They hadn't had sex for days, thank goodness. Harry was beginning to repulse her. At first it had been the thought that he was screwing someone else. She didn't want to be near him after that. But now his tempers and insults were becoming worse and worse. She wondered if he'd ever hit her in temper, and how she'd react. She realized then that if Harry struck her, she'd have exactly the impetus she needed to leave. It would make it all so very easy.

She wandered into her dressing room. Row upon row of expensive designer dresses, jackets, coats. Spiky-heeled shoes by the yard. In the past clothes had been her quick fix. With her model figure, she could wear anything. And in the past she had openly mocked those who couldn't quite squeeze into the latest designs. She had an attack of remorse over Nina, the London Derrière. How could she have been so cruel? Now who was the lucky one? Nina seemed to be so happy, and madly in love with Sam, despite having a big bum. Yet here Val was, thin, rich but miserable.

In the cold sober light of day she also remembered vaguely being rude to Janet in the past about her appearance. Again embarrassment pricked her eyes. Even Janet seemed happier than she was. At least she had a challenging job which she obviously did well.

And hadn't she suggested that Sue's husband was having an affair, when she couldn't actually remember whether she'd even met him? How could she have been so utterly callous? Liz, too; she knew she must have insulted her somewhere down the line.

'I must apologize to them,' she told herself aloud. 'I've been a complete super-mare.'

The girls agreed to meet Val on Thursday night. There'd been a wave of sympathy, even from Nina and Liz, over Harry's recent tempers. They actually wondered how Val hadn't cracked under the strain. And they were quietly impressed that Val had found the new spelling of her surname vastly amusing.

They'd arranged to meet at a little French restaurant in

the centre of Hartford. Val, realizing that she'd gain more sympathy by not dressing to kill, opted for a black pencil skirt, simple pink cashmere sweater and minimal jewellery. She couldn't resist a pair of her favourite Manolos, but that was her only concession to her old life, as she saw it.

The new look was instantly clocked by the rest of the girls, but they said nothing. Wine was ordered but Val only sipped mineral water. And when Nina announced her big news, that she and Sam were getting engaged, Val said she couldn't have been more delighted. And meant it. Champagne was produced, but again Val just stuck to her water.

When Liz went to the loo, the others braced themselves for the usual insults. But instead Val remarked: 'Liz looks really terrific. I'm so pleased her new chap is working out. Maybe we'll have another cause for celebration soon.'

Let's hope so, thought Sue, or Liz's baby clock will start ticking so loudly it'll keep half of Hartford awake. She was secretly counselling Liz not to eye up Tony as a potential father or sperm bank, but to simply treat him as a human being.

Val realized with a pang how much she was enjoying the evening. How much she enjoyed their company, their gossip and their happiness. Her remorse at how she'd behaved in the past was making her very ashamed. She realized yet again how empty and cheerless her life was compared to these happy and fulfilled human beings sitting around the table.

With the main courses cleared away and taste buds being tickled once again, this time by the array of puddings, Val indicated that she wanted to say a few words. A hush fell over the table.

'I have something very important to say and I want you to believe that it comes from the heart. I've had a drink problem. God knows you've all known it, but sadly I only came to realize it recently. I could make excuses for why I was always drunk but I won't. It should never have got to that. I also realize that in all the time you've known me, I've been rude, obnoxious and selfish. I don't really know why you've put up with me, but I'm glad you have. I ask you to believe that what you see before you is the real me, not that stupid drunken cow you used to hang around with. I can't ask you to forgive me because I have behaved much too badly in the past. But I ask you to accept the new me, and I hope that we will often meet up, as we have done in the past, but with the new me behaving in a more suitable fashion.'

There was a pause, followed by a ripple of applause. Sue, who was sitting next to Val, put her arm around her and gave her a hug.

'Well done, hon,' she said. 'I think I speak for all of us when I say that we're glad you've sorted out your problem. And I think we all admire you for what you've just said.'

Tears started to trickle down Val's cheeks. She made no attempt to stop them.

'We do know Harry's a bit difficult,' continued Sue, picking her words carefully. 'Don't forget, we work with him. We know what he's like. We do sympathize.'

'He's a complete bastard at home, so God knows how you lot put up with him all day at work.' Val broke down in sobs. 'And now I've loused up a lovely evening. I'm so sorry.'

'No you haven't,' piped up Nina. 'We're having a lovely time, and look, it's okay to cry. We know he's a bastard. I honestly don't know how *you* put up with him.'

'Neither do I,' added Liz, glancing meaningfully at Janet. They had never again spoken of Harry's advances that terrible night.

The arrival of the puddings broke up the conversation. Instead there were oohs and aahs as exquisite mouthfuls were savoured. Over coffee, Val whispered to Janet, who was sitting on her other side, that Harry was out tonight and his phone was mysteriously switched off again. Did Janet know where he was? No, she said untruthfully. Val would still have to find that out for herself.

An hour later, the taxi dropped Val off at home. Harry's Mercedes was in the driveway. She hoped he might be in bed and asleep, but he was pacing up and down the sitting room, glass of whisky in hand.

'Where the hell have you been?' he demanded.

'Out, same as you,' she replied nervously.

'Who with? Where?'

'Perhaps you'd like to start. It's funny, Harry, but I've noticed that you're always late home on Thursday nights. You're not in the office and your phone is always switched off. And sometimes on Mondays too.'

'Who's fed you this claptrap?'

'No one. I worked it out for myself. Anyway, I have no secrets. I've had a very nice evening out with the girls from HOT.'

Harry swore under his breath. Would they have told Val about his lunch last Friday with Gina? No, they wouldn't have worked that out. And anyway, he'd stick to his story of strictly business. But he didn't need those bird-brains filling Val's head with rubbish.

'Oh, and what was their news?' He smirked patronizingly.

'Well, Nina's got engaged. I heard about Janet's holiday. Nice things.'

'And I suppose they slagged me off,' Harry mocked her.

'No, why rot up a good evening?' she replied, and flounced off upstairs to bed.

Harry poured himself another couple of fingers of whisky and paced the sitting room some more. Women, nothing but trouble. Gina had been piling on the pressure again tonight. Oh, to dump the lot of them.

chapter thirty-two

Geraldine was being instructed by one of the computer support guys in the art of using the Internet, and already the e-mail jokes were flying.

> Guess where Geraldine's going for her holidays this year? She can't decide between the Greek island of Lycos or Alta Vista in Spain.

> Geraldine's got her own website. It's called beige-dot-com.

Geraldine, oblivious to it all, was finding her launch on to the information super-highway a bit daunting, to say the least. She'd spent ages searching for the Movie Munch site, only to discover to her horror that she'd tapped in a porn site where a very different type of menu was on offer. Even Harry, who forgave Geraldine everything because of her tight-lipped loyalty, was beginning to get exasperated. Geraldine's life was normally saved by the spell checker but that couldn't spare her the demands of a search engine.

The pressure was on because the first Movie Munch restaurant was opening in under a month. This meant that the first video, together with accompanying website, had to be ready on time. There was to be a huge opening party with full-on celebrity guests. It was such an important night for HOT that they'd taken on a specialist guest booker with a bulging filofax to get the right names, and put the public relations work with an agency.

Janet was reeling under the strain, putting the finishing touches to the video. The first restaurant was to be Casablanca, and designers had flown out to Morocco to scour the souks for authentic lamps, brass pots, tagines and rugs with which to fill the place. Janet's own recent trip to Morocco was also paying dividends. Having fallen in love with the country and its culture, the project had become a labour of love. She'd used some authentic music from CDs she'd bought there, and despite being her own sternest critic, she was pleased with the result.

The video featured some stunning footage of Casablanca and the surrounding countryside that she'd had to buy in from an agency in Morocco. Janet had also filmed a short cookery demonstration from the restaurant's chef, a chat with one of the designers and a mission statement from the Movie Munch chairman, and finished it all off with a clip from the immortal film at vast expense. She'd managed to weave it all together into a seamless whole, making even the chairman sound interesting. Jed's graphics, the last project he'd worked on before leaving, were breathtaking, giving the film a real polish. Needless to say, the only end credit was Harry, billed as executive producer – and spelled correctly this time – plus the HOT and Movie Munch logos. By now, Janet was too exhausted to care.

Harry grudgingly told her he was pleased with the video, which in Harry-speak meant it was practically up for an Oscar – he would have of course collected it, congratulated himself in the winning speech and then displayed it in his 'Hall of Fame' loo. And now off he'll go to claim the credit, drink the opening-night champagne and get the whopping end-of-year bonus, Janet thought grimly. It would be interesting to see who would be invited to the big opening night. Invitations were being dispatched in mini tagines by couriers. She doubted very much she'd be getting a knock on her front door.

Meanwhile Harry was wrestling with a different problem about the opening night. Gina had continued to pressure him for an invite, reasoning that by then Harry would have broken the bad news to Val. Harry had done his usual pleading for a little more time to find the right moment to tell Val. But Gina, with her short Italian fuse, was not to be pacified, and Harry knew the only way to maintain any sort of peace was to take her to the opening night. There'd only be a select few there from HOT: probably the chairman, Sir James Patterson Cripps, and members of the board. In that company Gina would be perfectly acceptable; they probably all had mistresses anyway, he reasoned. If push came to shove, he could easily pass her off as a minor celebrity. Gina had had, after all, two small parts in obscure Italian movies four or five years previously.

Harry sat back in his chair and heaved a sigh of relief. Yes, that was what he would do.

'Someone's been snooping around the office again,' said Nina, bringing Janet a cup of tea. 'At least three people have mentioned this week that things have moved or been found not as they left them. It's either Harry again or Uri Geller's in town.'

'Any bent spoons? Cutlery spotted contorting?' said Janet, looking up from her computer screen.

'None that I've noticed,' replied Nina.

'Then Harry gets my vote,' said Janet, gratefully sipping her tea. 'I wonder what he's up to this time. He's either just trying to rattle us or he's still worried about the mystery file. It's funny how much that myth bothered him. Simon and Joe did a good job on that, didn't they?'

'Except that it means he's still searching through everyone's stuff in the office, and I don't like the thought of that,' said Nina. 'Bit like being burgled. And women often say that's almost like being raped.'

Liz was listening and quickly dropped her head, so that a curtain of dark chestnut hair hid the expression on her face. Fortunately Nina didn't notice.

'Perhaps we should put in a few files with jokey names to throw him off the scent.'

'Such as what?' asked Liz, suspiciously.

'Oh, "Whassap", "Harry's Game",' said Nina airily. 'You've got to make it intriguing, get him overcome with curiosity. If you created a file called "Instruction Manual" or "Map and Directions", no man on earth would bother to open it.'

Nina then launched into an account of the delights of the weekend ahead. She and Sam were off to choose the ring.

'It's so exciting,' she trilled. 'I still can't believe it. I've met his parents and they're lovely. And he's met mine and they really like him. It's all like a dream come true. And we'll be having an engagement party so they can all meet. Sorry, I am going on a bit. What are you doing at the weekend?'

'Don't even ask,' said Janet. 'I've only just caught up with the washing since my holiday. So I guess I'm planning to join the Mile High Ironing Club.'

'You look ever so tired,' said Nina, taking in the bags under Janet's eyes. She did look exhausted. The strain of the Movie Munch project, plus the final handing over of the property project to Liz, were all beginning to take their toll.

'It's a good job we're not having a Haunted Handbag committee meeting tonight,' continued Nina. 'You look done in. Why don't you go home early?'

'Can't. Too much to do. I'm going to work late tonight and then sleep in tomorrow,' said Janet wearily. 'You never know, I might catch Harry snooping round the office.'

'Doubt it,' said Nina. 'Sue told me just now that Harry's still not back from lunch. Don't forget it's Friday-footsie-under-the-table-lunch day. Although I doubt he takes Gina to the Country Cottage Restaurant any more.'

'Knowing Harry, I expect he's found some new little Play Away place for them to lunch. And if he hasn't come back, they've probably turned it into a Have It Away Day.'

Seven o'clock and the production office was deserted, except for Janet, still pounding away at her computer. Another hour should do it, she thought, then a quick Chinese chicken à la microwave, followed by an early night.

The phone rang, echoing shrilly in the empty office. It was Sue, doing the late shift on reception.

'Janet,' she said formally, 'I've got Sir James Patterson Cripps in reception for Harry, but I haven't seen him at all this afternoon and Geraldine's gone home. Would you have a moment?'

'Certainly, Susan,' said Janet, 'and I'm using my phone voice too. I'll come through.'

She wandered rather reluctantly into reception. Whatever the chairman wanted, she probably couldn't help with, and she badly wanted to get her work finished and go home.

'Sir James,' she said warmly, shaking the elderly man by the hand. 'How can I help you?'

Sir James, still ramrod straight from Sandhurst days, was dressed in the typical gentrified mixture of tweed jacket, striped shirt with contrasting collar, and unmatching tie with just a hint of breakfast down it. He always reminded Janet of the Major in *Fawlty Towers*. White-haired, with twinkly blue eyes, he gave the impression of being a kindly, avuncular old character, yet he was still a crack shot, rode regularly to hounds and was as fit as a fiddle, bar a bit of prostate trouble.

Geraldine had rocked the office by letting slip that Sir James had had trouble with his 'prostrate'. 'I must suffer from that because I'm prostrate a lot of the time,' Ray had told her. 'I lie down a lot and then I can't get up again.' It had been the G-spot of the day.

'Had hoped to catch Harry. Silly me for arriving unannounced,' he said briskly. 'Just wanted to have a look at that movie restaurant video. Got to mention it in my next report to the board and thought I'd better watch the bugger first. Then I might know what I'm talking about for a change, what!'

He guffawed at his own joke. 'Got to write the bloody thing over the weekend as I'm away most of next week.'

'No problem,' said Janet. 'Come and watch it in my office.' She ushered him down the corridor and into the huge production office. She suddenly felt embarrassed

296

about of the mess it was in. Every desk seemed to be strewn with old coffee cups, files, tapes and newspapers. She couldn't exactly tell anyone off, though; hers was just as bad.

'Excuse the mess, but we have had an exceptionally busy week,' she said.

'No problem,' said Sir James, plonking himself into a chair while Janet dug out a tape. She could just imagine him at home kicking labradors off a hair-encrusted sofa.

'You can take this copy away with you if you like,' she offered.

'No, happy to watch it now,' he said. 'Don't want the bother of carting it around next week.'

'Bloody good,' he pronounced ten minutes later. 'Bloody excellent. One of the best things Harry's done. And it's going to be good for business in the future too. Delighted with that. Thank you, my dear, for sorting it. I shall give it high praise in my report. Don't get up, you carry on. I'll see myself out.'

After he'd gone, Janet kicked the leg of her desk in sheer frustration. As usual, Harry was getting all the credit. Blokes really did bond together like superglue. The silly old fool couldn't believe that a mere woman was capable of producing anything half decent. She'd been almost tempted to put him right, but he would never have believed her. And anyway, what would she have said?

'Oh by the way, Sir James, my boss Harry's actually an accomplished liar. I did all that, not him. Even though his name's on it.'

It would have made her sound like a petulant school-girl. Why should he take her word for it, without corroboration, late on a Friday night in a deserted office? What was the point?

She mentally added a bottle of wine to the microwave meal before bed.

Harry arrived home around seven, having remembered to switch his mobile back on. He'd had lunch with Gina at a new little restaurant a good twenty miles out of Hartford, to make sure they were undisturbed. In the end, to placate her and hopefully put a stop to her threats about phoning Val, he'd agreed to go back to Gina's house, where over a bottle of champagne they'd indulged in a passionate afternoon's bonking. Satisfied that he'd given her a jolly good seeing-to, he'd checked in by phone to the office. No messages or panics, according to the trusty Geraldine, so he'd gone straight home. To his surprise and relief, the house was in complete darkness. Either Val was in bed with all the lights out, or she'd gone somewhere. With her MR2 locked away in the garage for many months to come, there was no way of knowing whether she was in or out.

He opened the front door, put on the hall lights and called her name. No reply. He hung up his coat and went into the kitchen. There in the middle of the table, propped up against a fruit bowl, was a note. For a few seconds Harry actually wondered if Val had left him. Had she rumbled his affair? Had someone at work squealed about the lunch with Gina? Did he care? Curiously, he wasn't sure. The note certainly gave him a start, though.

He surprised himself by fumbling to open it. Nerves? Surely not. Not Harry. He never fumbled. He was far too much in control.

The contents were, however, a slight surprise.

Dear Harry,
Have gone to Hampshire to stay with my parents
for a few days. Spur-of-the-moment thing. Just fed
up being stuck at home relying on taxis. Know
you're working really long hours and probably
want some peace and quiet.
Love, Val

Curious, thought Harry, instantly suspicious. I wonder
what she's up to. A call to Hampshire later tonight would
ascertain whether or not she was there. But was she planning to see anyone else, apart from her parents? Lord and
Lady Muck would certainly cover up for her. They'd
never liked Harry, despite pretending otherwise. It suddenly dawned on Harry that Val might be dumping him
before he dumped her. Humiliation was not on Harry's
agenda. He had to get in there first. Oh well, a weekend
alone meant he could see more of Gina, although this
afternoon's session had worn him out. He wasn't quite
the man he used to be. No, he decided, he wouldn't ring
either of them tonight. He'd let them both stew. Val would
be expecting him to call to see if she was all right. And
Gina, if she knew he was alone, would be gagging for
another sex session, probably followed by more high
pressure on the marital front. No, he'd have a night in and
a few whiskies in front of the box.

He went upstairs to change out of his suit and into his
favourite dressing gown. He found himself wandering
into Val's dressing room to see what she'd taken with her
to Hampshire. Might give him a few clues as to what she
was up to. He looked along the rails of expensive and
glamorous dresses, not recognizing most of them. He'd no
idea whether she'd taken ball gowns or Barbours. And he

was shocked to discover there were enough shoes in there to stock a decent-sized branch of Russell and Bromley.

By Sunday, Janet was so low she was beginning to wonder how she'd get through the next week. Over the Sunday papers and a large strong coffee, she read of the usual tales of death and destruction, kiss-and-tell girls and another sleaze case involving a politician on the fiddle who was refusing to go quietly. In desperation she turned to Mystic Meg's predictions for the week. She half laughed at the 'could meet the love of your life' stuff, but was caught by the final line: 'Destiny brings a life-changing invitation.' Huh, fat chance of that.

She plunged into another fit of gloom, triggered by the fact that she knew she didn't really have a life, let alone any invitations. Her life revolved around her work and her work unfortunately revolved around a big fat bully called Harry. She knew she was investing too much in HOT, but after the long day at work, she had neither the time nor the inclination to take up yoga, learn Spanish or throw pots, although she could think of a few choice targets for the latter. She thought about Liz too, a decade and more younger and desperate for a husband and babies. She knew Liz was eyeing up poor Tony as marriage material just a few dates into their relationship.

'How on earth do you get a man to become truly committed?' she'd asked the entire production office.

'Ring a mental hospital,' Ray had offered.

In an attempt to snap out of her gloom, Janet rang Liz to see if she'd like to go out for Sunday lunch. No luck. Liz was practising the ancient female art of phone sitting.

'Sorry, hon, got to keep the phone free in case he calls,' she apologized. 'You know how important this is to me.'

In the end, Janet rang Sue and unashamedly invited herself for lunch. Sue and Jon were cooking a leg of lamb and were only too delighted to have an extra mouth to feed, as their children were going through a faddy food stage. Over the gravy-making in the kitchen, Janet told Sue about Sir James Patterson Cripps's visit to the office.

'It'll all change, you mark my words,' said Sue. 'Harry can't go on like this. Here, you get carving.' She handed Janet a knife. 'Imagine it's Harry's head.'

'Yeah, as if. He's managed all these years, he might as well keep going,' sighed Janet. 'The company's making pots of dosh, so if that pleases the board and the share-holders, then why rock the boat? Look, if Harry can survive all the stuff we've found out, then he's invincible. He's ridden out the storm on the Paul Burns saga, he's sur-vived the "Importance of Being Harry" headlines, he sacks people when he feels like it. He's bomb proof.'

'But there's one person who could just bring him down,' said Sue as she tasted the gravy, 'and she probably doesn't realize it yet. In a funny way, Val holds at least some of the trump cards.'

Janet finished carving and laid the slices of lamb neatly on a serving dish. 'Val's making no secret of the fact that she thinks Harry's up to something,' she said. 'Remember, she asked me to set a detective on to him. But even if she left him and then divorced him, what difference would it make? Harry'd still bully on as normal. He'd just have more spare time for his extra-curricular activities.'

'Depends how she did it,' said Sue, grinning. 'Knowing Val, even the new non-drinking Val, I think if she made a scene – and we know how good she is at that – she'd do him a lot of damage. And of course now that she's on the wagon, Harry can no longer pass it all off as her being drunk. She looks and behaves so differently now, even he must be getting suspicious. Mark my words, one day there will be an opportunity and Val will go for it.'

'I wish I could believe you're right,' said Janet mournfully.

'Now, end of subject, grab those plates and let's serve up.'

The rest of the day passed without further mention of Harry and Val. After lunch they all played a noisy game of Pictionary and a kids' version of Trivial Pursuit. Janet went home triumphant because her team, which included the two kids, had beaten their parents hollow.

chapter thirty-three

It was second-cup-of-coffee time before Janet got to the envelope. Long and cream, it was addressed to her in a slightly feathery hand. Inside was a short note from Sir James.

> Thank you, my dear, for organizing the video on
> Friday evening. You were obviously at the end of a
> very long week. I hope my request did not delay
> you too much in getting home for the weekend.
> Harry is always telling me what a marvellous team
> he has. In gratitude, I am enclosing some tickets to
> the restaurant opening for you and some of your
> team just in case you are free.
> Yours etc.

Janet blinked and reread the letter. 'Harry's always telling me what a marvellous team he has, my arse,' she scowled aloud. 'Pity he never bothers to tell us.'

She picked up the phone and rang Sue. Ten minutes later they were in their usual corner of the canteen, with Sue hurriedly reading Sir James's note.

'Well, well,' she said laughing. 'So are you going?'

'I have decided I am definitely going. Time I had a new frock and a new life,' Janet announced. 'And I suggest we throw the rest of the tickets open to discussion by the HH committee on Friday night, chez moi.'

'Good idea,' said Sue. 'Oh, and by the way, we loved having you yesterday. The kids went off to school to write triumphant essays about winning at Trivvies, and what dopes their parents are.'

'It bucked me up no end too,' said Janet. 'I was having a real Sunday gloom with the papers before I came round. Funnily enough, Mystic Meg predicted something about an invitation changing my life. I wonder if this is it?'

'God, you don't believe in that lark, do you?' said Sue.

'Oh, I hang on to anything with a bit of hope attached.' She was too embarrassed to admit that she'd rung Mystic Meg's phone line for a bit of comfort as well.

To add to the fun of deciding who should go to the bash, the HH committee decided they would each make separate wish lists and then compare notes. Those with the most votes would win.

Amid much giggling, the voting took place before the Chinese takeaway was delivered. Then the slips of paper were collected and put to one side while sweet and sour pork, Singapore noodles and chicken cashew were devoured. Janet refilled their wine glasses and declared the ballot ready for counting.

An interesting pattern emerged. They'd all nominated each other, plus Ray, who'd done such good work shadowing Harry on his bike and helping with the secret photographs. That took care of five tickets, including Janet's. Another five remained. Sue, Nina and Liz had nominated respectively Jon, Sam and Tony. Liz had suggested

Geraldine, 'just in case Placebo Domingo, Glynis Paltroon or Prickley Spears turn up'. Nina had named Paul Burns, 'to make up for the fact that he didn't get a leaving do', and Sue had come up with Joe and Simon, whose sacking had been instrumental in forming the Haunted Handbag committee. But the most interesting shout came from Janet.

'I'd like to invite Jed, because he did all the fantastic graphics on the video.' She paused. 'And Val.'

A shock wave went around the table.

'Why Val?'

'I don't really know, but I'd like to invite her. Perhaps it could be our way of thanking her for some of the better bits of our awful evenings out. Perhaps it could also be our way of acknowledging that we prefer the new Val to the old one. And also, I just wonder if she might take a shine to Jed.'

'Well he is rather gorgeous . . .' started Liz.

'And you're all fixed up,' cut in Janet. 'And before you say anything, he's far too old for me. I don't know, I just think I'd like to see them get together. Talking to Val, the marriage is clearly over, in her head anyway.'

'Surely Harry will be taking her to this bash already,' said Sue.

'I don't think so somehow. I phoned Val earlier this week to sound her out vaguely, but her cleaner answered the phone and said she'd gone to see her parents for a few days and that no one knew when she'd be back. Bit strange, I thought.'

'You don't think Harry will be taking Miss Tortellini instead, do you?' asked Sue. 'Not after that lunch fiasco the other week?'

'I doubt it,' chipped in Liz. 'Not if he's any sense left.'

'Harry thinks he's invincible, but Sue thinks that the

chink in his armour might just be Val,' said Janet. 'Let's see if she's game. I've a feeling she might be.'

In the end it was decided that the guest list should be Janet, Sue and Jon, Nina and Sam, Liz and Tony, Ray, Jed and Val. And it was also agreed that they would not discuss the invitations with anyone else at work. Janet would just accept the ten tickets without giving names.

The rest of the evening was devoted to what to wear and where to buy it. Dress code was the works. Dinner jackets for the chaps, full regalia for the girls.

'This weekend I will shop, this weekend I will not drop,' promised Janet.

As she'd expected, after almost a week of being cosseted at her parents', Val dreaded coming back to Hartford and Harry. It was rather like trying to cool your mouth down with a glass of water during a fiery curry; it just made it worse. Harry had eventually phoned her a couple of times, but they were only brief conversations, with each of them trying to quiz each other subtly about what they were up to. Val had gone for long walks around her parents' estate, been shopping and out to lunch, and generally relaxed. It had made her ever more conscious that life with Harry was like living in a war zone.

Harry meanwhile had spent even more time with Gina, which of course was a double-edged sword. Along with all the extra frenetic sex sessions came even more demands from Gina. At least he was able to smuggle his dinner jacket out of the house. Harry knew Val would start asking awkward questions if she caught him leaving the house all tuxedoed up. He could lie and say it was a blokes-only boxing night or something similar, but Val might just get a hint from the HOT girls that it was the Casablanca restaurant opening. She would then insist on going and he would have to lie about not taking partners. Even if the celebrities got pictured in the national press, the company executives would be of no interest to the paparazzi. No, best not to discuss it at all. That way he'd get away with taking Gina and keeping the peace.

Val's first weekend back passed without event. She and Harry were becoming experts at avoiding each other. If he stayed up late, she yawned and went to bed. If he announced he was going to bed, she found an old movie she just had to watch. Several times she was aware that Harry was on the phone, at the other end of the house, but she didn't quite have the bottle to pick up an extension to listen in. Each time, she dived for the phone when she'd thought he'd hung up, to dial 1471 if it had been an incoming call, or last-number redial if Harry'd made the call. Every 1471 call produced 'the caller withheld their number', while every last-number redial promptly rang HOT's main switchboard number. Harry was obviously pressing a speed-dial button after he'd hung up from his mystery phone call. Eventually the security guard at HOT rang back and asked Harry if he was having difficulty getting through. Harry immediately rumbled what was going on and sarcastically asked Val why she'd been trying to ring HOT when he was so obviously at home. Val muttered something about trying to ring her mother and pressing the wrong speed-dial button. But they both knew the game they were playing.

Sunday night, and Harry was sprawled across their huge leather Chesterfield, smoking a cigar, drinking whisky and watching television.

'Wish I'd created that.' He indicated the screen angrily

with his cigar. 'Would have made a bloody fortune selling that format all over the world.'

He was watching Chris Tarrant presenting *Who Wants To Be a Millionaire*. A contestant was teetering on the £125,000 question without any lifelines left.

'If I'd made that, I could have retired by now. Just imagine, I could go anywhere I felt like, do anything I fancied,' he mused. 'Might have made even more money than your old man. By the way, how are Lord and Lady Muck?'

'If that's my parents you're referring to, they're fine. And don't worry, you'll never be as rich as them,' snapped Val. 'My father worked very hard to achieve his success.'

'There's not much glamour in waste disposal, though,' Harry retorted, his eyes glittering with rage. He hated to feel he wasn't top dog. 'Television is a very creative, very competitive industry. It's about ideas, concepts, not just about wondering where to stick a pile of rubbish.'

'How come you're not filthy loaded then if you're so bloody clever?' Val tossed her blonde hair and glared at him. 'I can't remember the last time *you* had a good idea. I get the impression that everyone else does all the work in that place.'

Harry stubbed out his cigar and glared at her. 'You've been talking to those silly girls again, haven't you? Haven't you?' He raised his voice.

'If it's not true, why are you shouting?' said Val, now regretting that she'd started this. The last thing she wanted was for the girls to get into trouble. She'd compromised them enough already.

'I am the driving force behind that company,' Harry stated without a shred of modesty. 'HOT is successful because of me. Because of my ideas and my management. Now get me another drink, woman.'

He handed her the empty glass and slumped back into the settee to watch the poor contestant still agonizing.

'I know a good question for that programme,' Val said more calmly. 'Why don't men get mad cow disease? Answer? Because they're pigs.'

'Don't get me on to the subject of mad cows. It might upset you,' said Harry patronizingly. 'Now shut up and get me that drink.'

Val stood up and glared at him. 'Ask the bloody audience. Or better still, why not phone *your* friend.'

With that, she went straight upstairs and banged shut the bedroom door.

Harry sat for a minute contemplating Val's departure. Perhaps Janet and her friends had been talking and Val had found out about Gina. Or perhaps her mystery flit to Hampshire hadn't quite worked out. Probably just PMT, he concluded.

'Val? It's Janet. Just a quickie, 'cos it's Monday and I'm up against it. Could you do lunch tomorrow? At that ghastly Indian? Good. Meet you in the Gunges around one. Gotta go. I think I've been mistaken for Heathrow. I've got people actually stacking at my desk.'

Val was ridiculously pleased at the phone call. Somebody had actually rung and invited *her* out to lunch. It was usually her hustling others. God, she must have been a pain when she was drinking. It hadn't been easy giving up, but it was beginning to look worth the effort. On impulse, she rang Susie at work to see how she was faring.

'Trying to plan my escape from this disgustingly smoke-free environment,' said Susie.

'How's it with you and the boss?' Val asked tentatively.

'Oh, I gave him his P45 when I realized he wasn't actually leaving home. And by the look of things here, I'm about to get mine.'

'Oh, Susie, I'm sorry.'

'Don't be. I'm not cut out for this work lark. They put me on the switchboard the other week when someone went sick. I managed to cut everyone off or connect them to each other. Not my thang, as they say.'

'So what are you going to do?'

"I'll probably pack in Hartford for a while,' said Susie airily. 'Go home to Mummy. She won't like it, but she'll have to lump it.'

'I went home last week and it was so gorgeous I didn't want to come back.'

'Ah, that's the difference,' said Susie. 'Your parents are in lurve and still shagging. Mine have split up. Very nasty. Now my mother's on HRT and she's having some second life kick. She's on a mega man hunt. Been on so many blind dates she's almost qualified for a free guide dog.'

'Oh God, how ghastly. Imagine your parents going through the whole dating thing.'

'I don't have to imagine. I've got a seat in the front row. Anyway, have you dumped Fat Bastard yet?'

'Er, no. I will, it's just so daunting and . . .'

'You're scared of him,' finished Susie.

'Yes, I suppose I am. But I'm certain he's got someone else, so that might make it easier. Also, I've given up drinking. Completely.'

'Gosh,' said Susie, shocked. 'What brought that on?'

'Just a realization that I couldn't remember very much,' said Val.

'Like why you married Harry?'

'I must have been bonkers.'

'Believe me, you were. Choose someone younger and thinner next time. Someone who can master the art of switching off his mobile.'

'Point taken,' said Val. 'Let's meet up soon. Before you push off to Mummy.'

'Great,' said Susie, 'but no lunch until you've dumped Harry. Gotta go now. Rostered fag break!'

They were halfway through another of the Gunges specials when Janet delicately broached the subject.

'We've been given a pile of tickets to the big Movie Munch opening night and wondered if you'd like to come,' she said, mopping up some of her rogan josh with a piece of chapatti.

Val's eyes lit up. Another invitation.

'Now before you say yes, I think you need to know a little bit of background,' said Janet cautiously.

She outlined the events surrounding Sir James Patterson Cripps's visit, the surprise note and the tickets.

'We all had a chat, drew up a guest list and wanted to include you.'

Again Val's eyes sparkled with delight.

'But you must understand that Harry doesn't know we're going to turn up. Now presumably he's not mentioned this party to you?'

'All news to me. If he does, then I suppose I'll have to go with him, but so far he's not even hinted at it.'

Janet paused and looked her straight in the eye. 'It boils down to this, then, Val. If he doesn't invite you, are you prepared to turn up with us and give him a shock? Is that what you want?'

'Will it get you all into trouble with Harry if I do?' Val asked, lighting a cigarette.

'No, we've thought this one out carefully. We've been invited by the chairman. And if he's invited us then that's good enough reason to be there. Unfortunately, though, from Harry's point of view, I am the last person he wants to be there.'

'Why?' said Val, shocked.

'Well, quite simply, the project is the biggest thing that HOT's ever undertaken. It was my idea, I wrote the pitch and clinched the deal, and now I've produced the video. But you'll only see one name at the end of that video. Harry's. According to him, it was all his own work.'

Val nearly choked on her cigarette.

'That call I made to him that night you were at the theatre,' Janet continued. 'That was to tell him that it was all in the bag.' And no, she thought, I'm not going to let on to Val that the photographer was tipped off. Too much information.

Val stubbed out her cigarette emphatically.

'I don't really know why I should be surprised he's such a pig. Yes, I'd love to go, and do you know what? I hope he doesn't ask me. I'd rather go with you lot and see his face.'

'It's posh frocks, and we've hired a minibus because it's a hundred-and-fifty-mile round trip.'

'Fantastic. That'll be great fun. And thank you all so much for inviting me.'

Six months ago, mused Janet, Val would have never deigned to get into a minibus, let alone describe it as fun.

chapter thirty-four

Val went home ridiculously pleased. She hummed away happily in the back of the taxi and gave the driver an extra large tip. Then she spent a couple of hours trying on various long dresses and cocktail gear, twirling in the mirror to see what effect it would have. Val didn't have the problem of her bum looking big in anything.

She was almost on the point of deciding that she would buy something new and devastating. And then she stopped herself. No, she wasn't going to impress, show off or try to be the centre of attention. She wasn't going to make sure she turned all the heads. She was going to blend in with the crowd. Her crowd, her new friends, her pals who'd invited her. Elegant but understated, that was how she realized she wanted to look. In the end she picked out a simple long black shift dress with spaghetti straps and a modest split up the front. With it she'd wear black patent slender heels and a favourite fuchsia-pink beaded organza stole. Hair up, minimal jewellery and no long nails.

Delighted that she had sorted this, she rang her mother and told her about the invitation.

'Well, well, dear, you will give him a shock,' said her

mother in her usual unruffled way. 'Do you think he'll be there with this other woman you suspect?'

'I don't actually think Harry'd be that stupid, especially as it's a company do,' reasoned Val. 'But he hasn't mentioned it to me and it's the sort of thing you'd expect to take your partner to.'

'Well I disagree,' said Sheila. 'If I know Harry, I think there's a good chance he'd be that stupid. Don't forget, dear, this man had the arrogance to come back from Manchester with a Mediterranean suntan. I think sparks will fly if you turn up. I hope you're prepared for fireworks.'

'Yes, I am. And don't forget I'll have my friends around me for protection,' Val said proudly.

'Well, they sound a very nice bunch,' said her mother warmly. 'I'm glad you have some allies there these days.'

'I don't have anything to lose, do I?' Val was reasoning with herself. 'If Harry does invite me, then I will obviously have to accompany him. If he doesn't mention it at all, then I think that's extremely suspicious. If he does mention it but doesn't invite me, then tough shit, I'm going anyway.'

Sheila smiled to herself. She liked the new resolve in her daughter's voice. She also liked the fact that Val was off the wine. She just hoped that any showdown at the party wouldn't trigger a relapse.

'So what *are* you going to wear?' said Sue on the phone to Janet when there was a quiet moment on reception.

'Gawd knows,' replied Janet. 'My shopping trip was disastrous. I've had a good root through my wardrobe for something suitable – which took all of ten seconds – and there's nothing. It's either much too small or too eighties. Unless *Dallas*-style shoulder pads make a quick comeback,

I don't have a thing. I'm considering joining one of those "short for their weight" classes.'

'Same here. Life's never been the same in the tummy department since I had the kids,' said Sue. 'Shoulder pads were soooo fab, weren't they? Instantly made your hips look thinner.'

'But you look absolutely fine,' exclaimed Janet. 'It's me who's the product of years of junk eating and drinking. The only exercise I do is with my wrists – opening a bottle of wine.'

'Don't kid yourself,' replied Sue. 'There's a roll around my stomach that I practically have to dust on a daily basis. It's just that I conceal it with cardigans and jackets. And good old black, of course. But put me in a long tight dress and you'll see a shelf emerging that you could put your canapés on.'

'Look, why don't we hire? And go together to choose so we can be brutally honest?'

'Good idea.' And with that they assigned Saturday to the task, Sue checking that Jon could look after the kids.

Meanwhile, Nina had been through the private despair of trying on just about everything floor-length in Monsoon only to find that nothing fitted. It was of course the unmentionable problem of the London Derrière. She'd tried everything from Weight Watchers to Rosemary Conley but nothing had really worked for her.

'I don't know about the Hip and Thigh Diet,' she said to one of the assistants. 'For all the good it did me, I might as well have been on the Chip and Pie Diet.'

By now she'd tried on so many dresses that she and the assistants were on first-name terms. Then one of them had a bright idea and disappeared mysteriously into the stockroom.

She emerged with a deep aubergine silk ball skirt and a separate corset-style top in a lighter shade covered in beautiful beading.

Nina disappeared wearily through the curtains once more, muttering to herself that this was absolutely the last time. To her relief, it was perfect. The skirt skimmed her bum, the bodice fitted perfectly. The colour looked great too against her pale skin and blonde hair. She was also certain Sam would approve.

The shop was now closing, and the girls who'd helped were so delighted at their success that they suggested going for a drink in the next-door wine bar to celebrate. Over glasses of chilled Frascati, Nina excitedly told them about Sam and flashed around her engagement ring. She found herself talking about the bash they were going to and surprised herself by describing Val in warm tones as 'a friend who's in a rotten marriage and needs cheering up'.

Liz, being tall and willowy, never had any problems buying clothes. She'd decided to treat herself to something really special to impress Tony, so had headed for a little boutique on the outskirts of Hartford that sold designer labels. She'd soon fallen in love with a beautiful black chiffon number from Ghost and handed over a credit card without looking at the price. She then snatched up the carrier bag with a grin from ear to ear. The dress would knock him sideways. She hoped.

On her way back to the car park, she tried to avoid looking in the Pronuptia window. But she couldn't stop herself. One look at the long ivory silk dresses and dashing morning suits and she was off on another fantasy about marrying Tony, having children and living happily ever after. 'I must stop this,' she told herself aloud when she'd climbed into her car. 'I will frighten him off if I go on like this. He'll think I'm desperate. Which I am. I must pretend I'm not.'

She gazed fondly at the carrier bag, now sitting in pride of place on the passenger seat. This was their first black tie do together, and she wanted to look the biz. That dress, whatever it had cost, was just right.

Sue and Janet made a day of it in the end. They met up early on Saturday morning to get decent parking spaces, slapped all-day tickets on their cars and giggled their way to the first of two dress-hire shops they'd earmarked. The first shop proved very disappointing. The range of dresses was frumpy, to say the least. It would have done for a new small-town mayoress, but there was nothing that had anything like the required glamour. The only dress that actually fitted Janet was made of hideous apricot satin trimmed with black lace, with a gathered waist and off-the-shoulder short sleeves. Sue's only real contender was a black and white number with a scary amount of pleated frills.

'I look like I should be in the audience of *The Good Old Days* and you look as though you're about to do the Ascot scene in *My Fair Lady*,' Janet whispered during yet another session in the changing rooms.

'It's almost tempting to turn up in jeans, head scarves and dark glasses and pretend we thought it was a *Thelma and Louise* party,' said Sue.

They thanked the woman assistant, muttered excuses and left rather depressed.

'Still, good to know it'll be there for us when we're in our eighties, wanting a little je ne sais quoi en Crimplene,' said Sue philosophically.

They went to Café Rouge for a coffee to cheer themselves up. The coffee extended into lunch. A bottle of
house red and a plate of pasta later and they realized it was
well past two and so far they'd achieved nothing. They
paid up and set off to their second quarry. This time they
both found several likely contenders, and now the difficulty was having to choose. Janet fell in love with a long
black low-necked dress with matching tuxedo-style jacket.

'Perfect.' She twirled in front of the huge mirror. 'I can
show a bit of cleavage but I'll spare everyone the sight of
my flabby arms.'

Sue found a full-length raw silk coat with a wing collar
in the most luscious raspberry. 'Just the job to cover my
canapé shelf,' she cried. The coat went over a long plain
black dress. The effect was extremely dramatic.

Until now the shop assistant, a well-upholstered
woman in her fifties, had been rather sniffy. She'd indicated the rails without offering the slightest bit of help.
Too fuelled up by lunch, she'd decided, taking in their
rather flushed faces.

But when Janet and Sue started deliberately name-
dropping the guests at the restaurant opening, she perked
up considerably.

'Of course, modom, many of our clothes grace the
pages of *Hello!* and *OK!* magazines,' she purred to Sue.
'That coat has been extremely popular.'

Too late to try and be Mrs Nice now, you snotty cow,
thought Sue and Janet. Had your chance and blew it.
They paid their deposits, did some surreptitious winking,
then started name-dropping again.

'Well, Angela Rippon always looks so immaculate,'
drawled Janet. 'Wonder if Posh and Becks will go in
matching again.'

'I wouldn't put it past them,' Sue chipped in. 'Of course, there is a rumour that Dame Edna's going to—'

'And Arnie, don't forget him.'

They were now out of the shop, out of earshot and giggling like schoolgirls.

'Served her right,' said Janet.

'Absolutely,' replied Sue. 'No help whatsoever until you press the right buttons. If we hadn't found such knockout outfits, we'd have gone elsewhere.'

'I'm quite nervous about it all,' said Janet. 'I know I shouldn't be – not at my age – but it's not often you get invited to something as top-notch as this.'

'And of course there is the small matter of our in-house cabaret,' Sue reminded her. 'We are bringing our own pyrotechnics show, after all. If it's any comfort, I'm quite nervous too.'

Val spent all weekend trying to pick her moment. She'd rehearsed it in her dressing room mirror, a casual question about things at HOT, an off-the-cuff mention of having heard something about a restaurant video. She tried to work on her body language, so that she looked ultra relaxed, as if it was just a 'first thing that came into my head' remark. Having perfected the routine, she couldn't pick up the right cue. Harry'd been short, sharp and fairly bad-tempered, burying himself in the papers for the majority of the weekend, only interspersing it with bouts of watching television where he spent the entire time criticizing the shots, the direction, the artwork and the acting and generally shouting at the screen. Watching television with Harry was not a pleasant experience; it was more like attending an industrial tribunal.

Eventually on Sunday evening, after Val's attempt at

roast lamb with rosemary and all the trimmings, she looked up at Harry and caught his gaze.

'Anything exciting happening at HOT?' she stammered, wondering why her voice had suddenly developed a squeak and her heart had started to pound. She covered her embarrassment by noisily stacking up the plates.

'No, fairly mundane,' said Harry, sitting back and lighting a cigar. 'Why do you ask?'

'Oh, nothing.' There was that squeak again. 'It's just that you seem to be working long hours. I hoped there was some nice little project that was keeping you busy.'

Val stopped plate-stacking and lit a cigarette to calm her sudden nerves.

'We don't have "nice little projects",' replied Harry patronizingly. 'What you girlies forget is that we men have to do battle in the boardroom every day of our working lives. Nothing for your little brain to worry about.' His eyes glittered at her with the sarcasm of the remark.

He's not going to invite me, she thought to herself. He's not going to mention it. He's going alone or with someone else. A bizarre kind of relief swept over her. It was the result she'd wanted. She stubbed out her cigarette defiantly, picked up the pile of plates and serving dishes and headed for the kitchen.

'Yeeessss,' she whispered triumphantly to the hall mirror as she passed. Bit like Cinderella in reverse, she thought. I don't want to be swept off to the ball in a crystal coach; I want to go with my friends, and I'll wear my own dress, thank you very much. And I certainly *don't* want to meet Prince Charming.

Harry sat back in his carver chair, puffing thoughtfully on his cigar. Giving up the drink had made Val go a bit gaga, he concluded. She'd get over it. He sat for a few

320

moments contemplating whether he preferred the old Val, the ranting, flamboyant, pissed Val, or the new, more sober, rather boring version. Even Harry felt mildly ashamed that he didn't much care.

chapter thirty-five

They were all finding it hard to keep the secret. Various national newspapers and trade magazines were running pre-publicity stories on the opening of the restaurant. The name-dropping and rumour-mongering had reached epic proportions. A couple of celebrity magazines were rumoured to be fighting over an exclusive picture deal.

But the girls kept their promise, despite many temptations to boast about their invitations. They each reminded Ray on a daily basis to keep his mouth shut.

'Oi, most of the time you lot can't wait to hear the gossip,' he complained. 'Now I've got to keep my mouth shut or you'll beat me up.'

Ray was only kidding. Why spoil what might turn out to be an epic night of gossip in more ways than one? No, this was a secret he had no difficulty in keeping. The gossip would come later.

As the stories in the press gathered momentum, Janet decided it would be unrealistic of her not to mention the grand opening to Harry.

'I jolly well hope you've been invited,' she said to him at the end of one particularly spiky production meeting.

'I'll have to put in an appearance,' he scowled. 'Subpoenaed by the board.'

'Of course,' said Janet amiably, getting up to leave the meeting room.

What's up with that silly tart? he thought. Normally she'd be whingeing over not going to the opening night. She seemed ridiculously happy. Perhaps she was getting a shag somewhere. Hmm, he very much doubted it. Far too fat to get her kit off.

He hoped Val wouldn't start begging to go to the do. He'd already prepared his speech. No staff, no partners, just those at board level, in between sustaining a mock yawn.

But Val never raised the subject, probably because the dippy tart never read any newspapers, he surmised. It was going to be much easier than he had at first thought. No hassle from Val, and Janet seemed to have her mind elsewhere. He'd be able to take Gina without any problems. And that would keep her bubbling for a while longer while he decided what to do about Val.

As the restaurant opening drew closer, Janet decided that they needed to hold a strategy meeting. So the Haunted Handbag committee gathered briefly at Sue's house two nights before the Big One. This time Ray was included in the meeting because it was felt that he needed to know what was happening.

'Aside from the fact that we are all looking forward to wearing posh frocks and mingling with A-, B- and even C-list celebs, there are three main scenarios here that we need to consider,' announced Janet, as she unashamedly pulled trays of curry out of the microwave. 'Firstly, we have the confrontation with Harry, who will wonder how

323

come we all pitched up. Now this affects us all, so we need to be prepared for that one. Secondly, we have the possible confrontation of Harry plus "mystery" partner. He will of course wriggle out of that one very successfully and pass off his lady friend as an "only just met" or a business acquaintance. But of course, Ray, Sue and Nina, you were all at the Country Cottage Restaurant, so you've seen her before. If it's the same lady, I think it's entirely up to you how you react.'

'Well I'm up for saying something,' piped up Nina. 'I won't be able to resist it.'

'So am I,' chorused Ray and Sue.

'But of course the most interesting plot,' continued Janet, 'will be When Harry Meets Val. Now there certainly won't be any fake orgasms there. It could get nasty and we must make sure that she's not left on her own for even a nanosecond.'

They all nodded in agreement. After the initial excitement over the choosing of outfits, they knew it was going to be a tense evening that might turn out to be retrospective fun. One of those 'Omigod, you were there!!' nights where you'd be guaranteed top score on the gossipometer. They went through the last-minute arrangements as though it were a military operation. Pick-up times were checked and rechecked, plus a rather complicated routine about picking up Val. The plan was that she would ring Janet late afternoon after making certain Harry wasn't suddenly taking her. Then she would travel to Janet's in a taxi and change there to avoid any suspicion or risk of last-minute discovery. Again, all subject to what Harry got up to.

'Just suppose that at the last minute Harry doesn't go,' Janet told Val the following day. 'You can't just go waltzing off with a suitcase in a taxi and him not wonder where you're going. Much better to leave the house in mufti.'

So Val sent her frock, jewellery, shoes and bag round to Janet's house the night before in a taxi. Just in case.

On Thursday night, Harry was late home as usual. Val greeted him with a watery smile and, as casually as she could, asked about weekend arrangements.

'It's just that I'll probably meet up with friends tomorrow night,' she mentioned while loading up the cappuccino machine, 'if that's all right with you.'

'That's fine,' muttered Harry, not quite believing his luck and trying to sound nonchalant. 'Don't bother about little old me tomorrow night, because I've got a business dinner with the board.'

Little old me, thought Val. Who's he kidding. Old, yes; little, no. She stifled her giggles over the noise of the milk frothing.

Excellent, Harry thought to himself. He wouldn't even have to stumble in late to the 'and what time do you call this' greeting. His tuxedo was already hanging in Gina's wardrobe. He would go straight to her house from work, change and go to the function. Then it would be back to her place for the obligatory quickie, after which he'd change back into his ordinary business suit to return home in the wee small hours of the morning, when hopefully Val would be sound asleep. Pity she'd given up drinking; it always guaranteed her being comatose.

Janet paced the floor of the production office. It was Friday afternoon, the day of the grand opening, and she was suddenly attacked by a fit of appalling nerves. Once again her courage was deserting her where Harry was concerned. Inviting Val, and even accepting the tickets from Sir James Patterson Cripps in the first place, now seemed to have been the decisions of a lunatic. Should she spend this afternoon sharpening up her CV for life after HOT? She wasn't sure. Hang on a minute, Val's marriage could well be on the line after tonight. Wasn't that worse?

Well, no, she reasoned. Val more or less wanted the marriage to end. She positively welcomed the idea of confronting the other woman. Val could just retreat to her rich parents and then start all over again, perhaps making a better choice of husband next time. What would happen to Janet if she got the sack? Certainly not a flit back to Mummy and Daddy. They were dead, for a start, and even if they'd been alive, their forty-two-year-old daughter descending on them would have been the last thing they'd have wanted. No, she thought selfishly, she had an awful lot more to lose than Val.

But on the other hand, if Harry finally left HOT . . . No stop it, that was a ridiculous thought. It was never going to happen. This was Harry's Game and Harry always played to win. Janet logged off and shut down her computer, slung a few files and a couple of newspapers into her briefcase and strode purposefully out of the building.

'Don't worry, his eminence grease has already gone,' said Sue in reception. 'Only came back from lunch briefly and then left again. Gone for the day. I checked with Geraldine.'

'Haven't seen her for a day or two, I'm pleased to say,' said Janet. 'I wonder if she got an invite tonight?'

'Doubt it,' said Sue knowingly. 'She'd be out of here by now to get home to tart up, just like I am when my shift ends in precisely ten minutes.'

'How could Geraldine possibly tart up? Tarts don't wear beige.'

'Just remember the divorce – too much hoovering and humping,' replied Sue. 'Maybe our Geraldine is a sex bomb after all. Do you think we could persuade Chris de Burgh to write a follow up song, "Lady in Beige"?'

'I very much doubt it. Perhaps she just sticks to hoovering these days,' said Janet.

The minibus picked up Sue and Jon, then Liz and Tony, followed by Ray. Then it made its way to Nina's flat for her and Sam, followed by Jed and then finally Janet and Val. Every time new party guests boarded, they were greeted with a round of applause. Val, devoid of her usual in-your-face make-up, the massive pink talons and the dressed-to-kill outfit, looked more like a Grace Kelly cool blonde type. Elegant but very restrained. The others nodded approval when Val boarded and Val's grin spread from ear to ear when she heard the applause. It almost dispelled her nerves. Almost.

The minibus driver then set out for the restaurant, and with the sound of the engine, everyone fell into their own silent thoughts. Val, particularly, was convinced that tonight she would be witnessing the end of her marriage. She'd stupidly tried to rehearse her feelings in the bathroom mirror, what she'd say and how she'd react to the inevitable showdown. But what she'd planned to say kept sounding like some gibbering idiot. She knew that whatever she said, Harry would twist it this way or that and make her look a fool. After all, he did it on a regular basis, so he was well up to speed. She was worried that he would shout at her, or hit her. Or would he, in front of the assembled glitterati? Once the deed was done, she knew exactly what Harry's version of events would be when they got home. She'd been mistaken, she was pissed, she was stupid, she was embarrassing. He was important, he was doing his job, he was power.

But there was one thing in Val's armoury that she hadn't possessed before. And that was anger. In her new sobriety, Val had discovered what anger was, and how she felt about it. No, there was no turning back. This was the final conflict.

'We're only a couple of minutes away now.'

Janet clocked the sudden look of fear again in Val's eyes and felt complete empathy with her. The poor girl was going to cause ructions, whoever Harry was with. She must be feeling like a lamb going to the slaughter.

The minibus finally came to a halt in the car park adjoining the restaurant. Several shiny Bentleys, a Rolls-Royce, a smattering of TVRs and a stretch limo were already parked there. Everyone silently clocked Harry's Merc, parked in a discreet corner. As the engine of the minibus died away, Janet indicated she would say a few words.

'Hey, before we go in, just remember two things. Sir James invited "me and friends" so we are just as welcome here as the likes of Liz Hurley and Posh and Becks. But Harry has no idea we're coming, so he may be a little bit surprised.'

They all laughed.

'Val, we're all with you on this one. You will not be left on your own, you will be supported at all times,' continued Janet, glancing at her watch. 'Now we're fashionably slightly late, which is great. Makes the others look as though they smack of desperation. And one last thing, this minibus turns back into a pumpkin at twelve o'clock, so be on it.'

They climbed out of the bus, the men adjusting their bow ties and the women smoothing down their dresses. Then they all linked arms and strode purposefully towards the restaurant entrance.

They were greeted with champagne cocktails in the foyer, served by waiters dressed in traditional Moroccan-style djellabah and fez. Then, rather like a Roman army trained in the art of combat, they moved en masse into the main body of the restaurant. The designers had done a breathtaking job on the place. The characteristic Moorish architecture, with its blue and white mosaic tiling, curves and pillars, was simply stunning. Every niche, every table bore testament to Moroccan art, with beautiful beaten brass plates, massive candlesticks and sculptures. Not much evidence of Rick's Café Americain, apart from a piano whose keys were being caressed by a pianist constantly playing 'As Time Goes By' as if it were on a loop tape. Janet found herself scanning the crowd like a radar system. Her gaze took in hordes of the current tabloid celebs, footballers, page three girls, minor film stars and models, plus the odd television personality. A roomful of people whom you recognized but couldn't quite put a name to. Photographers lurked in every corner, flash guns popping. But so far, no glimpse of Harry.

She looked across at Val, whose fixed smile betrayed everything. A tentative mixture of nerves, determination and shaky elation that she might uncover the truth tonight once and for all.

'Do you want me to have a quiet scout around?' whispered Ray in Janet's left ear.

'Not sure,' she said. 'In a way I'd rather he came upon the whole lot of us. Element of surprise. Plus safety in numbers.'

'It'll be okay, you know.' Jed's voice came reassuringly in her right ear. She wheeled round to speak to him but discovered that his comments weren't meant for her. He was talking to Val.

'We're all here rooting for you,' he continued. 'And by the way, nobody's actually said so, but you look great.'

Janet turned away, as if eavesdropping on a conversation between two lovers.

'Slight change of plan, I think,' she said to Ray, suddenly embarrassed. 'Let's just the two of us do a quick and surreptitious circuit to see who's where.'

They linked arms, nodded to Sue and Jon to take care of things and set off. A five-minute tour of the restaurant, jostling with listed and so far unlisted celebrities, told them what they needed to know. They spied Harry in the furthest corner, in his element, quaffing champagne with a group who looked suspiciously like members of the board. Next to him, and half hidden from view, was a dark-haired woman in a long gold dress.

'That's her,' said Ray. 'That's Gina, our little Italian firecracker.'

'Poor Val,' sighed Janet. 'This is all going to end in tears. Let's go back and warn the others.'

Unnoticed by Harry, who was obviously in grandiose mode, they slipped back to the group and quietly told them what they'd seen. Val went white and took a slight stumble backwards in shock. Jed, Janet noted, caught her by the arm and steadied her. She'd need all the support she could get. Harry wouldn't be all that thrilled to see Jed either, after the 'Humpton' episode. It was likely to be a very bumpy ride.

chapter thirty-six

It took a remarkably long time before Harry made the fateful discovery. Because Janet and her party had arrived rather late, there was only time for a swift glass of champagne before the three hundred or so guests took their seats. Again fate had taken a hand. There'd been no time or opportunity to mingle.

Janet's table was just about as far away from Harry's as it was possible to be. Because all the tables seated ten, the Haunted Handbag committee and guests had one to themselves, and were soon installed on the low cushioned seats, Moroccan fashion, around the circular table.

A huge brass gong was sounded, at which point four giant movie screens were lowered from the ceiling and the immortal scene in *Casablanca* started in which Humphrey Bogart meets Ingrid Bergman for the first time in Rick's Café Americain. The film worked its legendary magic, and three hundred people, now ever so slightly pissed on champagne and exhausted from luvvie shrieking and photographic mayhem, were hushed into silence, hearing the famous exchange between two of Hollywood's finest film actors.

When the scene finished, the gong sounded again.

Suddenly the tables lit up from beneath, and fireworks ignited around the piano to a roar of appreciation and applause. The pianist struck up yet again with 'As Time Goes By' to tumultuous applause, along with some rather off-key singing provided by a few guests who were well into the party mood.

The meal was then served by waiters wearing traditional pale grey striped djellabahs. Candles flickered through silver filigree lamps on all the tables, giving off the most magical dappled light. First came small bowls containing spicy salads of every description. Then chicken tagine, served in the typical Moroccan pots and accompanied by piles of pale yellow fluffy couscous. The drink flowed freely. Waiters flurried around topping up glasses, whisking away bottles and bringing more. Tongues loosened as the wine flowed.

Janet glanced around the table. Sam and Nina were gazing into each other's eyes in that first flush of love. Sue and Jon, the initial excitement gone from their relationship, were loving and supportive in a more lasting way. Liz and Tony, both on their best behaviour, were at that difficult stage of any relationship: on the brink of an initial commitment but not yet able to pluck up the courage to talk about it, in case one discovered the other wasn't so keen and it all went pear-shaped.

Janet then glanced at Jed and Val and immediately averted her gaze. Definite electricity was going on there, sparks being generated. They made a knock-out couple, no doubt about that. Janet had never seen Val looking so serene, and so fascinated by what someone had to say, particularly given the circumstances of the evening. And even more impressive, despite all the alcohol washing around, she was sticking to her sparkling mineral water.

Jed was sitting slightly to one side, his arm resting casually on the back of Val's chair. Slightly tanned, his dark hair swept back and his brown eyes flashing, he had a film-star quality about him. He suddenly moved forward to light Val's cigarette, his eyes not leaving her face. No wonder all the girls at HOT had dumped George Clooney and replaced him with Jed as their Fantasy Shag.

Janet, smiling to herself, realized that Ray was watching her.

'Mutual attraction, I'd say,' he whispered. 'Just hope Harry doesn't go berserk over this.'

'He can hardly do that,' said Janet. 'The hypocrisy would be appalling. Mind you, that's never stopped him in the past. Val was a bag of nerves tonight getting on the minibus, but look at her now. I'd rather hoped they might hit it off. At least he'll help get her through the evening.'

'Harry won't quite see it that way,' replied Ray. 'Men never do. Different rules for them.'

'So what do we do now?' she asked him in desperation.

'Well,' said Ray, pausing as he lit a cigarette, 'when the meal's over, you know better than I do that the fun will begin. People will start to mingle, the photographers will resume, so we must not drop our guard. Those two,' he indicated Val and Jed, 'will need protection. And at the rate they're going, it'll be hammer and tongues even before the coffee gets here.'

During a pudding of magnificent fresh fruit salad, a group of musicians struck up in a small area at the front of the tables, playing some very wild and rhythmic music. They were joined by a belly dancer in long, flowing deep red chiffon trimmed with gold embroidery. As she wiggled her hips and rotated in time to the music, she invited a couple of the men to come up and join her.

Unfortunately the two she picked were somewhat well oiled and thought they were watching a lap dancer. To a roar of approval from the audience, they tried to stuff ten-pound notes down her bra top. Completely unfazed, she just kept on smiling and wiggling, and as the tempo of the music increased, she twirled faster and faster. In a drunken attempt to keep up, the guys tried to follow suit, turning faster as well. But when the music abruptly finished, they lost their balance and fell into a heap at her feet.

A storm of applause broke out while the two men picked themselves up and limped back to their table. Then the gong sounded once again and a rather short man with swept-back grey hair stood up and raised his hand in an appeal for silence.

'I'm Mark Haversham and I'm the chief executive of Movie Munch,' he announced. Silence spread quickly, with people noisily shushing each other. Mr Haversham made a sensibly short speech, giving a little of the company's history – which was also mercifully short, since they'd only been formed earlier in the year – and then, with an eye on the PR opportunity, announcing the opening dates of the next two themed restaurants, Indiana Jones, which would have an Egyptian feel, and Out of Africa, specializing in Kenyan dishes. There were cheers from all the guests, by now gripped with the expectation of at least two more freebies to put into their psions. Then Sir James Patterson Cripps rose to his feet from the HOT table at the far end of the restaurant. Dressed in a dinner jacket that had clearly put in at least fifty years' sturdy service, he was surprisingly witty, Janet decided, given his slightly doddery exchange with her that night in the office.

Sir James thanked Movie Munch for placing their trust

in HOT for all their website and general media requirements.

'We're a small team at HOT, but small can be beautiful,' he announced. 'You get a personal service, a friendly service that's not lost in long corporate corridors, and a first-class product created by first-class committed professionals. When you go home tonight, please click on to the Movie Munch website. But just to give you a flavour now of what we can do, here's a short video about the creation of tonight's restaurant.'

Up on screen came the familiar opening moments of Janet's film. Almost immediately silence fell, broken only by the haunting music of the film and the first breathtaking shots. To Janet's relief, she'd hooked them.

The moment the video finished, a cheer went up, and Sir James rose to his feet once more.

'All I'm going to add is a special thank-you to our head of production, Janet Bancroft, who's here tonight with some of her team. Janet wrote, directed and produced that film. So please, Janet, stand up and take a bow.'

Three hundred guests applauded enthusiastically, looking around to see who they were clapping. Janet stood up uneasily to accept the applause, wondering how on earth she'd actually managed to take the credit for her own work for once. Harry would be livid. Everyone in her party clapped and thumped the table with gusto. Then the pianist struck up for the umpteenth time with 'As Time Goes By'.

'What's it feel like hanging over the parapet then?' Ray whispered in Janet's ear. 'Our cover, what there was of it, has been blown. Can I make a suggestion?'

'Hmm, like what?' said Janet, deeply suspicious and still crimson from the public recognition.

'That we take the bull by the horns. We all go over to the HOT board table and thank Sir James for our invites,' said Ray.

'Bloody good idea,' said Jed, who'd been eavesdropping. He turned to Val. 'Hey, babe, are you up to that?'

Val took a deep drag on her cigarette and thought for a second or two.

'Yes, I am,' she said. 'If he's over there with another woman, I want to see her for myself. With witnesses. I want to catch them red-handed. It's no good chickening out now.'

Everyone immediately agreed. They rose en masse, straightened bow ties, collars, straps and wraps, and then, with Janet and Ray in the lead, wended their way in a crocodile across the restaurant, in and out of the tables, until they reached the HOT board's table.

Janet took a deep breath, offered up a silent prayer and stepped forward.

'Sir James,' she said, keeping her eyes firmly on him, 'we've come over to thank you once again for your kind invitation.'

'The pleasure's all mine,' he beamed, standing up to shake hands. 'Your film is terrific. I hope it didn't come as too much of a surprise that we showed it.'

' Just a bit,' replied Janet. 'I probably wouldn't have come if I'd known.'

'Just as I thought,' said Sir James, nodding sagely.

'If you don't mind, Sir James, I'd like to introduce you to some of my colleagues,' she continued, still resisting the urge to look around the table. 'This is Sue, our head receptionist, and her husband, Jon. Nina, our production secretary, and Sam from the accounts department. Liz, one of my senior producers, and her partner Tony. This is

Ray; we couldn't do without him. He's the production office gopher and a budding producer in the making. And this is Jed, who did all the fantastic graphics on the film you saw tonight.'

They all queued up to shake hands with Sir James. Then Janet finally allowed herself to glance to his right. There was Harry half out of his seat, cigar cast aside and smouldering in an ashtray, straining to catch what was going on. He'd turned a violent shade of crimson and had half turned away from Gina sitting beside him in a sub-conscious effort to pretend she wasn't there.

After being introduced to Sir James, Ray and Jed point-edly waved amiably at Harry, whose crimson was turning more purple by the second.

Janet reached her pièce de resistance. 'And finally, Sir James, I don't know if you've already met, but this is Val, Harry Hampton's wife.'

Val beamed at him, praying her nerves wouldn't let her down, and they shook hands vigorously, which at least disguised the shaking.

'I think we probably met at one of the HOT Christmas parties,' she said with a fixed smile.

'Oh,' said Sir James, now puzzled. He half glanced over at Harry, sensed something wasn't quite right and turned back to Val.

'Delighted to see you again, my dear,' he said. Val, now having reached the end of the greeting line, was directly in Harry's line of fire. She followed Ray and Jed's cue by giving him a small wave, then turned and immediately followed the rest of them back towards their own table.

They were about halfway across the restaurant when Val felt a hand on her shoulder. Not a warm hand of affec-tion, but a grasp of malice. It wheeled her round to face a

338

livid Harry, who was almost spitting out his own teeth in his fury. He'd obviously taken a short cut around some of the tables to catch up with them.

'What the fuck are you doing here, you, the lot of you?' he shouted, now purple with rage.

'Same as you,' replied Val firmly.

Suddenly an audience formed around them. Janet, Jed and Ray were immediately by Val's side, the others forming up behind them.

But Harry was now oblivious of all around him. He'd had far too much to drink and was losing control. Then he spied Janet again.

'I suppose this is all your doing, Bancroft,' he shouted at her. 'Might have guessed. Any kind of scheming and you're usually up to your neck in it. How come you're suddenly taking the credit for the video? And who invited you?' he bellowed, pointing at Jed. 'You're fired. I fired you weeks ago. You've absolutely no fucking right to be here.'

'What ees going on? 'Arry, what ees 'appening?' The dark-haired woman in the gold dress pushed her way into the circle that had now formed.

'You stay out of it,' roared Harry, now so angry that veins were appearing on his forehead and a visible pulse was going in his neck. He pushed her aside.

Nina stepped boldly into the makeshift ring.

'Hi, how are you?' She proffered a hand to Gina. 'How lovely to see you again. We met at the Country Cottage Restaurant, remember?'

Gina looked confused but automatically shook Nina's hand. 'And here's Ray,' continued Nina, indicating him. 'Oh, and you'll remember Sue. She was there too when you were having lunch with Harry.'

There was a moment of stunned silence. Jed grabbed the moment.

'You're absolutely right, Harry, you did fire me,' he said cheerfully, 'but funnily enough, Sir James seemed to love the graphics.'

'You bloody—' Harry was stopped mid sentence as flashguns started to pop, and it seemed that half the room suddenly had a notebook and pen on them. People rapidly started to sober up and take more than a passing interest. But Harry ploughed on. The evening's drinking, some of it to calm his nerves about Gina, was now catching up with him rapidly.

'And you,' he resumed, pointing accusingly at Val. 'What the fuck are you doing here?'

'You didn't invite her, so we did,' said Jed defiantly, indicating the circle round Val. By now they were all grappling with the business of staying upright. Many of the guests had surged forward to get a glimpse of the proceedings, and were pushing for a better view. Even the pianist had stopped, having decided perhaps that the Time really had Gone By.

'Anyway, Harry, aren't you going to make the introductions?' Jed continued. 'Shouldn't you introduce your wife to your, er, lady companion here tonight?'

'Good job I fired you.' Harry glared at Jed. He was completely oblivious of the crowd, who were now oohing and aahing at every outburst. 'One of my better ideas. And as for the rest of you, you can all follow in his footsteps, come Monday morning.'

Janet shivered. This was routine Harry stuff, except that even Harry didn't normally do this sort of turn in front of an audience. She caught sight of Val's stricken face. The poor girl looked absolutely devastated and was rooted to the spot. All the carefully rehearsed phrases had gone straight out of her head.

'Time we left, I think,' Janet announced bravely. There were shouts of 'No, no, no!' from the crowd, some of whom had mysteriously turned into members of the paparazzi. She looked around for support from Ray, but he'd disappeared.

'Hey, Val, give us a smile,' shouted one snapper, waving a camera with flash gun.

'You, in the gold dress, come forward, big smile.'

'Harry, let's have a picture of you with your wife? And your girlfriend? All together?'

Another round of flashbulbs brought Harry to his senses. He realized what a mess he was in. His wife and his mistress confronting each other at the most high-profile event of the year; it was the stuff of nightmares. He decided to pretend neither of them existed, and tried to turn tail and walk through the throng that was now gathered. But he couldn't escape, he was hemmed in tight with Gina next to him. Gina, meanwhile, was now secretly enjoying the fuss and the attention. This might just be the thing to make Harry dump Val and take the leap into commitment. She decided to go for it and was beaming for the cameras, linking arms with a smouldering Harry.

'Now, a big smile from both of you,' coaxed one photographer. 'How about a kiss?'

'Fuck off,' Harry snarled. With that, he hit out at the nearest photographer, sending him and his camera sprawling.

Janet, Val and Nina, who were still in the thick of the action, suddenly found themselves being pulled backwards through the crowd, leaving Harry and Gina at the mercy of the mob.

When they managed to turn around, they realized they'd been rescued by Ray, Jed and Sam. With the pack still descending on the drama like foxhounds waiting for the kill, Janet was suddenly aware that the rest of the group had collected the coats and were in the process of boarding the minibus. Soon they were all safely on board and the bus pulled away.

Nobody said anything for a while. They were too shocked to speak. The only sound was Val sobbing quietly into Jed's shoulder.

chapter thirty-seven

About ten minutes into the journey home, Janet broke the silence by suggesting that they stop for a coffee at a motorway service station. There were things to be discussed that couldn't wait until the morning. For example, where was Val going to spend the night? She probably didn't fancy the idea of going home. And in the mood Harry was in, Janet was fearful for her safety.

They all stumbled out of the minibus and into the garish lighting of the coffee shop. They made quite an incongruous sight, ten of them in evening clothes, sitting on bright green plastic chairs around a plastic table, clutching cappuccinos in polystyrene cups.

'A Night to Remember?' said Jed.

'Oh What a Lovely War?' replied Ray.

'Armageddon,' chipped in Janet. 'I suppose it was a bit like *Casablanca*, with a love triangle, except that in the movie they didn't have a punch-up.'

They all laughed. Even Val managed a watery smile. But Janet noted that there was still a real fear in her eyes. She looked completely done in.

'Well,' proclaimed Nina, 'I haven't had so much fun in years. At least not since last weekend.' She glanced cheekily at Sam. 'I actually don't care if I get the sack on Monday. It was worth every penny of this Monsoon gear just to see Harry's face. No offence, Val, but your husband's a piece of complete and utter pond life. A complete waste of DNA.'

'Now, talking of which,' Janet chipped in quickly as she noticed Val's eyes welling up, 'you're not going home tonight, Val, and that's an order. You're staying at my place and no arguments. No, Jed, you're not whisking her off anywhere. Not tonight anyway. But I think we'll have to have a council of war over the weekend prior to Monday.'

'Tell you what, why don't you all come for Sunday lunch and we'll have a bit of a think tank then,' said Sue brightly, Jon nodding in approval.

'That would be great,' said Liz. 'I know I'll feel better if we have a group discussion about it. You know how that man terrifies me.' She glanced knowingly at Janet.

'I don't know what to say,' said Val, tears in her eyes. 'We've had this terrible evening, I've now realized what a pig Harry's been to you all and here you all are being nice to me. Janet's inviting me to stay, Sue's inviting me for Sunday lunch.'

'And I'm inviting you out tomorrow night,' said Jed with a twinkle in his eye.

'Oi, steady on,' said Janet, secretly pleased for Val. 'You can ring tomorrow and ask my permission.'

Val slept for most of Saturday morning, grateful for the peace of Janet's sparse spare room, which, with its rather clashing decor, seemed like heaven after what she'd been through.

'Sorry it's not exactly posh,' apologized Janet, indicating the old bed with its pink padded headboard and purple flowering duvet, circa 1970s M&S, 'but it's not been much of a priority.' Val felt so relieved not to have to go home that she felt as though she'd booked into the Ritz.

Jed rang on Saturday morning enquiring how Val was.

'You're keen on her, aren't you?' said Janet, laughing.

'Yep. Fancied her when I saw that picture of her in the paper,' he confessed. 'Couldn't believe she could be married to such a sod. Totally wiped out when I saw her last night.'

'Well, just take it steady,' warned Janet. 'She's had a rough time, in fact she's still asleep, but I'll tell her you called. Leave her in peace today. Why not come round tomorrow and drive us to Sue's for lunch?'

'You're on,' came the instant reply.

Janet decided to have a quick whip round the house while Val was asleep in an attempt to make it a bit more respectable. As she dusted, tidied, straightened cushions, chucked out old newspapers and loaded up the washing machine, she mused yet again about how different Val was from the monster of several months ago. And also how she and the girls had completely changed their feelings towards her. Val had become one of them, instead of being the one who stood out, the one who made the scene, the grand entrance, the one who fell down drunk. Now she was united with them in their hatred of Harry, united in their need to escape his clutches. Not for the first time Janet considered the prospect of being sacked on Monday. Harry had done it to many others before and he'd certainly do it again without any hesitation. But could he sack quite so many people in one fell swoop? Or would he just pick off one or two of them? They'd probably need legal advice if he tried. At least they could split the costs of a lawyer. Surely it wouldn't get to that. They had been invited to the bash by the chairman after all, and they were entitled to be there. But was introducing your boss's mistress to his wife a sackable offence? Even Hillary Clinton never had to meet and greet Monica.

Janet busied herself with a pile of ironing in an attempt to distract herself, and was appalled to discover clothes at the bottom of the basket that she'd long forgotten about, or worse, didn't even recognize. Then she recalled an article she'd read about decluttering, so she piled all the forgotten items into a black bin bag. Anything you've not worn for three years you will never wear again, so cheerfully wave it goodbye, had been the advice. Perhaps she'd soon be saying goodbye not just to old clothes, but her monthly salary, security and her friends at HOT. She shuddered again as she filled a second black bag with clothes.

'My God, that looks serious.' Val appeared around the kitchen door.

'Just black-bag archiving,' Janet joked. 'It's my new revolutionary and very effective way of tackling the ironing. Fancy some breakfast?'

'Not half,' came the reply.

Soon bacon, tomatoes and sausages were sizzling away in a pan, and the kitchen was filled with the dark aroma of coffee bubbling in an ancient percolator.

'Comfort food,' said Val. 'This is just terrific.'

'Jed phoned, by the way,' said Janet, noting the flicker of interest in her eyes. 'I told him to leave you in peace today. But he'll pick us up tomorrow morning and take us to Sue's for lunch.'

'Oh, fantastic,' Val said. Then her face fell.

'No, Harry hasn't phoned,' said Janet, reading her

mind. 'Not as much as a squeak. It wouldn't take the Brain of Britain for him to guess you're here. Listen, do you want to ring your folks or anything? The grub won't be ready for another five minutes.'

'Yes, I would. Do you mind?'

Janet turned the bacon with one hand and gave her the phone with the other.

After five minutes Val came back into the kitchen, a little tearful. She lit a cigarette and took a deep drag on it.

'It's very strange, actually telling someone that your marriage is definitely finally over,' she tried to explain, wiping her eyes with a piece of kitchen roll. 'For a long time it's crap and you don't admit it to yourself. And of course I used to blot it all out with a bottle of wine. But it's only when you start to talk to someone about it that you really mean it. Do you remember in that Indian restaurant that day? The Gunges? When I said I thought Harry was up to something? Well, what a long way we've come since then.'

'Is your mum upset?' asked Janet anxiously.

'No, she's thrilled.' Val managed a small smile. 'She and my father are going to open a bottle of champagne tonight to celebrate. I didn't realize until recently how much they hated Harry.'

'Join the club. It's such a big one they'll be closing the membership soon.' Janet started to dish up the breakfast. Val stubbed out her cigarette.

'After we've had this, could I ask you a huge favour?' she said.

'Whassat?'

'Well,' said Val, lowering her eyes in slight embarrassment, 'I've only got the clothes I'm standing up in. I don't want to go back to the house, so could we go shopping

347

this afternoon? I'll need a few clothes and make-up to tide me over the next couple of days.'

At least the old clothes horse in Val was alive and well and champing at her wallet. They decided to avoid Hartford just in case they bumped into Harry. Or worse, Harry and Gina. Instead they went to an out-of-town shopping mall which had just opened.

Val deliberately avoided the most expensive shops. She dived into Next, dragging Janet in with her, and went round like a whirlwind, picking up a couple of fleece tops, tee shirts, jeans, boots, some underwear and a bag of basic skincare. It took her about five minutes flat. Janet couldn't help but envy her for being able to snap up anything in size 10 and know it would fit, without the bother and ordeal of the changing room. Unlike Janet, whose constant dilemma was, would her bulges squeeze into a size 16 or would she have to smuggle in an 18 just in case? The only thing she could guarantee to get into was the bloody changing room itself.

Janet found herself envying Val at the till as well. What it cost didn't really matter to her, it was more a case of how long it would take for the assistant to process the transaction and wrap the goods. Val didn't agonize over air miles, bonus points or boring old discounts. She just paid up and enjoyed. She was a hedonist shopper.

Over lunch and a bottle of sparkling mineral water in Café Rouge, Val produced another carrier bag from Next.

'This is for you, along with this lunch,' she announced. 'And don't you dare open your mouth in protest.'

Janet was momentarily speechless. Inside the bag was the ice-blue jumper she had secretly admired while they were picking out the weekend gear for Val. Val had also bought her a pretty silver necklace and matching earrings.

The waiter interrupted Janet's rapturous thanks with grilled sole and green salad. All the shopping had made them ravenous.

'Do you miss driving?' asked Janet in between mouthfuls.

'Yes, desperately,' admitted Val. 'I've been stuck at home for months now, at the mercy of Harry and the local taxi firm. Also, if I'd still had my licence, I'm sure I'd have followed Harry on one of his Have It Away days by now and found out the awful truth much sooner.'

'Would it have made that much difference?' queried Janet.

'Well, at least the discovery wouldn't have been quite so public,' said Val. 'The irony is that one night when he was a bit pissed, Harry told me he thought he was being followed. I told you about it, if you recall.'

'He *was* being followed,' Janet confessed, hanging her head sheepishly. 'We were all fed up with the way he treated us, and we were also suspicious that the Manchester Riviera suntan wasn't quite what it seemed, so we got someone to follow him and take photographs.'

'What of?' Val was steeling herself for something explicit.

'Oh, just him going into Gina's house. Gina at the door. We weren't doing a *News of the World* job.'

'Why on earth didn't you say when I asked you?' said Val, visibly agitated and lighting a cigarette.

'We all had a bit of a pow-wow and decided we couldn't. Something to do with not playing God, I suppose. We didn't want the responsibility of ending a marriage, much as we hated Harry. Do you understand?'

'Yeah, I guess so,' said Val, crestfallen.

'It would have been dead easy to say, "Oh sure, Val, your husband's playing away and here are the photographs." But we didn't have photographs of Harry in bed with her, just going into her house. It could have been quite innocent. Except of course there was always a pattern.'

'Mondays and Thursdays. You knew that too?' Val was incredulous. 'It took me a while to cotton on. I suppose I was comatose most of the time.'

'Yes, we did clock that routine,' confessed Janet. 'But I *was* telling you the truth when you asked if he really had been to Manchester that week he returned with the amazing tan. I honestly didn't know where he'd been. We did pick up a rumour that he was in the Algarve, but again, it was all surmise. Just a conversation overheard in a corridor.'

Val stubbed out her cigarette and immediately got another one out of the packet.

'Do you think Geraldine was in on all of it?' she asked.

'Yes, I do,' said Janet. 'Harry'd never have got away with it without her. She's very protective. She must have booked the Country Cottage Restaurant for Harry plus one on a regular basis. I'm sure she knew about the Portuguese trip as well, because he was out of the office for a week and she had to be able to contact him. But then Harry hired her for her loyalty, not her legs.'

'Hmm,' pondered Val. 'Seems he got that right.'

chapter thirty-eight

Jed turned up on Sunday morning in his trademark jeans and designer polo shirt, clutching a bunch of red roses. He presented them to Val with great aplomb. Janet noted enviously that Val turned a giveaway pink on receiving them. She also looked effortlessly wonderful in some of the basics she'd bought in Next the previous day: tight dark denim jeans, black kitten-heeled boots, a white cropped cable sweater and a bright red zipped fleece top. She'd scraped her blonde hair back into a ponytail and even with minimal make-up still looked a million dollars.

They climbed into Jed's battered old Citroën and roared off across Hartford towards Sue and Jon's house. Everyone had brought something to help spread the cost. Janet and Val contributed two types of pâté for a starter, Nina and Sam brought various cheeses and savoury biscuits, Ray breezed in with a bag full of cans of lager, Liz and Tony produced a couple of puddings – a bowl of fresh fruit salad and a chocolate gateau out of a box – and Jed had brought champagne.

'Should we be celebrating?' queried Sue, fishing out some glasses.

'Yeah, absolutely,' said Jed. 'Look, he fired me and I

came back for my little bit of revenge. He can't keep doing this. Harry may have the hump, but Harry Humpton's run out of road.'

They all roared with laughter, but there were also anxious looks.

'How on earth is Harry going to explain his behaviour to the board, let alone fire us?' said Nina. 'It was quite a scene, let's face it, and for a public relations exercise it made an extremely good punch-up. We could have sold tickets.'

'I agree,' said Liz. 'I don't suppose the bosses of Movie Munch will be all that chuffed to find that their launch of a brand-new chain of restaurants was overshadowed by a big fat git slugging it out with the photographers they'd actually invited.'

'What I want to know is how the photographers immediately seemed to know who was who,' said Janet. 'I seem to remember that they were instantly on the scene and aware that Harry was trying to hide his Italian woman away from Val.'

'Ah hem.' Sam coughed shyly. All eyes suddenly fixed on him.

'You can blame that one on me,' he announced. 'I tipped them off. I hadn't planned to, because to be honest, I couldn't believe Harry would actually be daft enough to take her along to a company function. Sorry, Val.'

He nodded apologetically in Val's direction.

'Please don't be,' said Val. 'You must remember that I knew Harry was up to something ages ago. He made my life a complete and utter misery. What I needed was the proof before I could make the changes. I needed this confrontation, honestly.'

Sam continued: 'We were all queueing up to say thanks to Sir James when one of the photographers just quietly asked me what was going on. I'm afraid I couldn't resist it. I just said something along the lines of "Stick around, mate. The big fat bloke on the table up ahead has brought his bird, and his wife's in this queue and about to find out. Watch out for the fireworks display." And the rest, as they say, is history.'

Everyone took another slurp of champagne, while they absorbed this new revelation.

'Go on, tell them why,' said Nina, nudging Sam. 'You might as well now, there's nothing to lose.'

'Guess there's not any more,' said Sam, who was not used to all this attention. 'Well, it was a kind of revenge really. Ages and ages ago, I stumbled on some little, well let's call them irregularities in some of Harry's deals and transactions. In simple terms, because we accountants are always accused of making everything complicated, Harry was not averse to the odd backhander. There were some really quite clever little fiddles.'

'What did you do?' asked Liz, incredulous.

'I had a word with him.'

'And?' they all enquired.

'I was accused of not doing my job properly. He said the error was probably mine and how dare I accuse him,' said Sam. 'He threatened me with the sack. Well, I could have kicked myself afterwards, but before I got around to print-ing off copies of the evidence, they'd been mysteriously wiped from the computer. One whole file completely dis-appeared and crucial bits were deleted from others overnight. Someone got straight on to the case and had managed to penetrate the system.'

'Any idea who?' asked Janet.

'Oh yes, Computer Support did manage to find out. The lovely Geraldine, no less.'

'No doubt on Harry's orders,' said Janet grimly.

'Let's eat,' announced Jon, ushering them all into the dining room, where they crammed elbow to elbow around the small table. After the pâté and melba toast, Sue brought in a huge roast chicken which had been cooked with tarragon and lemon, new potatoes and a platter of roasted Mediterranean vegetables. There was a lot of jostling as plates were passed around, everyone giggling at the lack of space. The champagne now all gone, Jon produced fresh glasses and poured out white Burgundy.

Everyone pretended not to notice Val tipping her glass surreptitiously into Jed's once he'd emptied his, just as she'd done during the rounds of champagne. The conversation lulled as everyone tucked in, trying to avoid each other's elbows in the process.

Suddenly Janet banged the table. All eyes turned in her direction.

'It's suddenly come back to me,' she said, 'why did Sir James make that speech mentioning me?'

'Why shouldn't he?' replied Liz. 'He was quite rightly thanking you for making that fantastic film. It was the best bit of the evening.'

'No, no. You're missing the point. Why did he mention *me*? How did he know that I did it? Normally Harry takes credit for everything.'

'But you said Sir James found you in the office working late one night and watched the tape,' replied Liz.

'But he didn't know I'd made the film.' Janet was emphatic. 'He thought it was all Harry's work. All I did was shove a tape in a machine for him to watch. It could have been made by Alfred Hitchcock for all he cared.'

'I told him,' said a small voice from the other end of the

table. All eyes turned towards Val. 'I rang him and told him,' she repeated quietly.

'You what?' went up the chorus.

With all eyes now firmly rooted on Val, she calmly explained how angry she'd felt with Harry about the lies, the swanking, the bullying and of course the affair. But it was when Janet had hinted that he even stooped so low as to take credit for other people's work that she'd decided to act.

'I phoned up Sir James at home on Thursday,' said Val. 'The night before the big do, the night Harry always sees his bit on the side. We had quite an illuminating little chat. I think he was surprised to hear from me, but he was very interested in what I had to say. I just told him that the staff at HOT were absolutely fed up with not getting the credit or the praise for what they did and here was another classic example. I explained to him that Janet had not only made the film, but she'd actually clinched the deal in the first place. I hope you don't mind, but I sort of hinted that if things didn't improve she might leave, and that it would be disastrous for HOT.'

'Did you mention Harry?' said Janet anxiously.

'Absolutely,' said Val. 'I think that's what clinched it. If it had been anyone else I was accusing, then he'd probably have told me to naff off. But because I was effectively stabbing my husband in the back, he really did take note. I also told him that if he didn't believe me, to check my story with any film crew, or anyone else in the building for that matter.'

'Seems he did,' said a stunned Janet. 'Val, you played a blinder.'

'No wonder Harry looked so mutinous,' said Sue. 'We did even better than we thought. Apart from completely mucking up a very expensive PR evening, apart from probably losing the company future projects and apart from introducing our boss's wife to his mistress, we've managed to let the chairman know that his head honcho treats his staff like peasants and claims the credit for everything.'

'He can't sack us now, he just can't,' said Liz, now looking much happier.

'Trouble is, Harry always comes up smelling of roses,' warned Janet. 'We're the ones who'll be left behind in the shit.'

'We'll find out soon enough tomorrow,' said Ray, who'd been uncharacteristically quiet. 'And I'm more than confident it will be good news.'

'Why, what have you heard?' said Sue.

Ray shot them all a look of mischief. 'It's not what I've heard. It's what Sir James may have heard by now.'

'Blimey, this really is turning into a confession session. What have you been up to this time?' asked Janet suspiciously.

'Well, you remember that time you had a conversation with Harry,' said Ray, 'and you were wired up, and he made all those threats.'

'Yeesss,' said Janet resignedly. She was bracing herself for Ray's next revelation.

'Well, Ron had the tape and he said it was locked away for a rainy day,' said Ray, slightly nervous now of the reaction to his announcement. 'Well, we had a couple of beers round at the GX one night last week and decided that this rainy day of yours was never going to come along unless we created some sort of downpour. So first of all Ron played it to me. Bloody hell, Janet, is he always that brutal?'

'Yeah, mostly,' replied Janet. 'He makes Vlad the Impaler

look like a Monday-night darts player by comparison. What did you do then?'

Ray paled slightly and took a big glug of wine. 'I sent the tape round by courier to Sir James yesterday. Honest, Janet, I'm sorry if you're cross, but what was the point of hanging on to it any longer? There was never going to be a better opportunity.'

'Oh, you're right Ray,' conceded Janet. 'I suppose I've been deluding myself about the rainy-day syndrome. It's now or never, isn't it?'

Janet sat back in her chair, her mind reeling. So other forces had been at work: Sam tipping off the photographers about who was who, Ray sending a tape to Sir James of Harry's threats, and amazingly, Val shopping her own husband. It was all quite a shock.

Over the puddings and coffee, she was still deep in thought, replaying the scenes at the Casablanca launch in her head. There was something still not quite right. One more missing jigsaw piece.

'Aha,' she said, snapping her fingers in delight. 'I've got it. I introduced all of you to Sir James on Friday night. But Val, he didn't seem to know you. Yet you say you spoke to him before the event to tell him what Harry had been up to. So why did you greet each other like a couple of strangers?'

Val looked a bit sheepish for a second or two. Then she grinned broadly.

'We were just acting,' she said simply. 'I told him I was probably going to be there, but not with Harry. That was our little secret. I had to take the risk. You see, Sir James realized two things about Harry on Friday that he didn't approve of. Firstly that he'd turned up with a woman who was not his wife, and secondly that Harry couldn't make tea, let alone television.'

357

chapter thirty-nine

Sunday had been sunny, all upbeat determination that they would finally outdo Harry, or at least keep their jobs. But Monday morning, with its ominous grey skies and gathering storm clouds, dispelled every last ounce of optimism.

Janet was awake at five. The alarm clock could enjoy another two hours' respite, but not her. She half opened the curtains to greet another grey day. How symbolic, she thought, shivering. She lay in bed wondering what to wear. Magazines never gave you advice on the perfect outfit to wear for getting the sack. Probably the same as the outfit for getting the job. Safe old navy blue, nothing outrageous or overtly sexy. Dignified, subdued, just the thing to pop along to the wake afterwards. The last rites and then the final interment of your last pay cheque.

Liz couldn't remember sleeping at all. She'd tossed and turned, constantly noticing the time on her digital alarm clock: 2.37, 3.15, 4.03, 4.39 – she'd seen them all. Would getting the sack affect her relationship with Tony? Jobs in the media weren't two a penny, so maybe she'd have to move to another area. Would Tony move with her, or beg her to stay? Or would he wave her cheerfully off? Maybe this was the catalyst that would make him come to grips with the C word. Commitment wasn't such a very long word, only three syllables. Neither of them had kids or baggage. Just themselves. If he insisted on staying with his job, should she relinquish her next career move? Yes, yes, yes came the resounding answer in her head. She gasped to herself, rather ashamed at how desperately keen she was.

Nina awoke with a start. She'd been having a particularly vivid dream about lottery winners and woke up in that twilight state when it takes a while to sort out reality from the dream. The reality wasn't all that promising. A lottery winner she was certainly not about to be. The only millions she'd be getting anywhere near were the rest of the country's unwaged. And Sam too. Would Harry lump him into the plot? What a horrible start to their life together, both made redundant by a big fat bully. She made a mental note not to wear any mascara today in case she burst into tears.

Sue stirred next to Jon, enjoying the luxurious warmth of his body. Oh God, D-day, she thought. At least Jon's job was still there. It would be a struggle until she could find another post, but they'd manage. She'd miss the folk at HOT, though. She loved her job there. It certainly wasn't dull, and Friday night's scenario was testament to that.

Val, still luxuriating in Janet's spare room, was having a fantasy dream about a holiday with Jed in Kenya, alternating their days on paradise beaches of pure white sand and swaying palm trees with jeep safaris around magnificent game reserves. She could imagine Jed, his skin tanned and beaded with a mixture of sweat and dust, pointing out giraffes quietly feeding from trees, or a herd of elephants plodding its way across a dusty plain, the calves tucked protectively into the line. The pair of them, impossibly glamorous yet casually dressed in khaki cottons and pith helmets, ballooning across the Masai Mara watching exotic wildlife through binoculars, and then returning at night to a sumptuous safari lodge for a fabulous meal followed by all-night sex.

She awoke with a jolt. The shock of wondering where she was was swiftly followed by the fact that it was Monday morning. The Day of Reckoning. She reached for her cigarettes, lit one and lay back against the propped-up pillows. She didn't normally smoke in bed, but given the tension she'd woken up with, she needed one to relax. A couple of deep puffs didn't make the slightest difference. Today was the day. The day when her friends would probably be sacked by her rotten husband, or soon-to-be-ex rotten husband. It couldn't get much more dreadful, because it was partly her fault.

Val had already resolved to follow the girls into HOT without telling them. She'd give Janet an hour or so start and then take a taxi up to the offices. There she'd find out what the score was, confront Harry about a divorce and then escape to her parents' for a few days.

Shuddering at the scenario ahead, she stubbed out her cigarette, got out of bed and went downstairs to fill the kettle. She was just brewing up a pot of tea when Janet appeared in the kitchen, heavy-eyed and tense.

'Oh well, I don't like Mondays at the best of times,' Janet said resolutely, accepting Val's offer of a cup of tea. 'If the world ends at lunchtime, then at least today will be a day of mourning!'

They both made mock chuckling noises.

'What are your plans, Val?' asked Janet. 'You know you can stay here as long as you wish.'

'That's sweet of you, but I'm going to go down to Hampshire today,' said Val. 'My parents are planning a party.'

'Bit unfortunate in the current circumstances, isn't it?' asked Janet.

'Oh no. They're celebrating not ever having to see Harry again,' said Val. 'They absolutely hate his guts. They think he's a big fat sod.'

'And so say all of us,' said Janet wearily.

'Sorry, that was a bit tactless,' apologized Val. 'It's all right for me, skipping off to Hampshire for a celebration. What will you do if he gives you the chop?'

'Get blind drunk is probably a popular option,' said Janet. 'Yesterday at Sue's I really believed we might be spared the Big Elbow, but in the cold light of day, I just don't know. I've seen this all before. Harry's sacked a lot of people for no reason since he's been at HOT. To be fair, he's jolly good at it. Gets lots of practice and gets away with it.'

Janet, Nina, Sue, Liz, Ray and Sam had agreed to meet in the HOT car park on the dot of nine and all go into the building together. So there they were, huddled together in the sharp early-autumn wind, subdued and pale, hearts thumping.

'Whatever happens this morning, let's all meet up for lunch at the Groin Exchange,' suggested Ray. 'However it goes, let's be there. Then we can either drown our sorrows or celebrate the best news HOT's ever had.'

They all nodded in unison in the biting wind. Then they set off purposefully towards the main entrance. So far so good; no official-looking letters at reception, no overnight security guard barring their way or asking them to return their entry passes or mobile phones. Harry hadn't yet arrived, they ascertained, but Geraldine was already in.

'I hope she's had lots of sex and hoovering over the weekend,' said Nina bitterly, 'because it's going to be downhill all the way for that bag. That's only if we win, of course.'

'I suppose if Harry wins he'll probably give her a whopping great pay rise, or a misplaced loyalty bonus,' replied Liz gloomily. 'Then she'll be able to buy even more beige outfits.'

'Huh, she might actually splash out on something half decent,' said Janet. 'I wonder how Geraldine would cope with Red Or Dead.'

'Not enough beige,' said Liz. 'Let's hope she never ventures out in Issy Miyake. I dread to think what she'd make of that.'

They all trooped through the security door and went to their various departments: Sam upstairs to Accounts; Ray, Nina, Liz and Janet to the production office' while Sue took up her place at the reception desk.

By nine thirty there was still no sign of Harry. Sue was keeping Janet's office abreast of events out on the front desk. Janet noticed that her heart started thumping every time the phone rang. By ten o'clock she'd waded through the post and e-mails. Mercifully she'd seen nothing in the morning papers about Harry's big scene at Casablanca. Newspaper editors faced with yet another pile of photographs of Eastender celebrities at yet another opening, had found better fish to fry. However, the trade press at the end of the week might be another matter. They'd be interested in Harry all right, despite the fact that the incident was relatively minor. It was a PR catastrophe.

She turned her attention to the next Movie Munch projects. Probably not much point now, but she might as well do some work on them anyway. At ten thirty she gave in to the strain and summoned the others to coffee in the canteen. They huddled in a corner, nursing their steaming mugs as though they'd just found a Happy Eater near the North Pole.

'Where's Harry then?' asked Nina. 'There's still no sign of him. Trouble is, none of us wants to ring up boring old Geraldine and find out where he is.'

'Might stir up a hornets' nest,' advised Ray.

'On the other hand,' said Liz, 'suppose we sit here all day sweating it out and then find that Harry's at the dentist, or that he's on leave? We're going to feel a teensy bit silly.'

'Val would have known if he was on holiday, wouldn't she?' queried Nina.

'Heavens no, not necessarily,' said Janet. 'Remember who we're dealing with here. This is the man who got away with a five-star freebie in the Algarve by telling everyone including his wife that he was off on a working trip to Manchester. No, sorry, one of us has to find out from Geraldine and it ought to be me. I'll do it when I go back to my desk.'

The telephone on the canteen wall rang shrilly, almost knocking itself off with the vibration. Ray went over and picked it up.

'That was Sue,' he said grim-faced. 'Apparently Sir James has just arrived.'

'Back to our looms then,' said Janet. They trooped silently back down the corridor to the production office. Janet was just bracing herself to call Geraldine to check out Harry's whereabouts when her phone rang. There was no mistaking the honeyed tones of Fiona Crosbie, Sir James's PA. Janet caught her breath, bracing herself for impact. Do come up to Sir James's office in five minutes' time if it's convenient, was the request.

If it's convenient, thought Janet. That doesn't quite sound like the parting of the ways. Or maybe it was a way of putting you at your ease *before* the parting of the ways, before the body blows were delivered. Before she could go over and tell the others, she realized that they too were receiving the same call. So five minutes later, Janet, Sue, Ray, Nina, Sam and Liz found themselves walking along the executive corridor in silence to Sir James's office. Further up, they could see Geraldine at her desk, tapping away at her computer, head firmly down, trying to hide behind a huge vase of yellow lilies stuck in a pot on her desk.

Fiona Crosbie ushered them into Sir James's office. Please make her offer us coffee, prayed Janet. If she does, then we're off the hook. If she doesn't, it's clear your desks and be out in half an hour. Please offer us coffee, she continued to plead silently. Damn, she thought, as the door clicked shut behind them. We're out, she thought in despair.

Sir James Patterson Cripps sat behind a vast desk, even more vast than Harry's, signing a pile of documents. As he put his pen down and looked up, the door opened again behind them. They all turned involuntarily.

'I'm so sorry,' said Fiona smoothly, 'I can't think what came over me then. Would any of you people like tea? Coffee? Mineral water?'

They all asked for coffee. Janet felt she'd just come out of intensive care.

'Well,' said Sir James, smiling benignly at them all over the top of his bi-focals. Janet noticed that he was wearing another random selection of well-worn aristo clothes: tweed jacket, pink shirt, dark blue tie with orange stripes, all obviously expensive and with another good couple of decades left in them.

'There's something I want to discuss with you,' he said, still smiling. 'It follows on really from Friday night. Which, incidentally, I thoroughly enjoyed, and I hope you did too.'

They all mumbled agreement and renewed thank-yous for the tickets.

'As you know, the opening of Casablanca was a great landmark for HOT, probably the biggest thing we've been involved in to date. And it's a long-term project with a huge profile. You may be pleased to know that Casablanca was the first of many openings. Movie Munch are planning at least twenty themed restaurants around the country. Possibly more.'

They all nodded like robots.

Sir James continued: 'A project like this pushes a company like ours into the premier league, a league in which we might at some stage float the company on the stock market. Capital raised in that way could expand the company swiftly and I believe that HOT has the talent, the expertise, the nerve and the integrity to do just that.'

Now for the drop, thought Janet pessimistically. We can't do it with you lot mucking it up and you've all got to go. She tried to take a sip of coffee but her hand was shaking too much. She replaced the cup in the saucer quickly.

'To put it bluntly,' said Sir James, 'there is one stumbling block to all this. I used the word integrity just now. It might be an old-fashioned word, but I'm an old-fashioned man. In the last few days I have discovered some of the practices that have been going on here, and frankly, I'm appalled.'

They all gasped, wondering if he'd rumbled the plottings of the Haunted Handbag committee. Still no one could speak. They all nodded dumbly again, steeling themselves.

Sir James suddenly smiled at them. 'I don't actually know where to begin to apologize to you all. But apologize I must. I had no idea of the way in which Harry Hampton has been conducting the company's business.'

They all broke into smiles of relief.

'In the last few days I have been collecting evidence, and what I am about to tell you must go no further than these four walls. But I feel I owe it to you, and probably most of the production office as well for that matter. We have discovered financial irregularities in Harry's affairs which I won't go into detail about but which include evidence of large payments to him from some of our contractors going back over a number of years in return for favours, commercial information and so on.

'I have also received a tape of Harry speaking to you, Janet. You know of the existence of this tape, I take it?'

Janet nodded. 'It was a fairly typical exchange with Harry,' she mumbled.

Sir James continued: 'Disgraceful, simply disgraceful, and typifies a man who took credit for everything whether it was his work or not. I now gather that a number of people were either threatened or actually sacked if they didn't toe the line. I don't know if you are all aware, but I had a very illuminating telephone conversation last week with Mrs Hampton, who put me right on a number of matters. Hence my speech on Friday night, Janet, emphasizing that the film had been your work.

'I was then appalled to discover that Harry intended to be at a very high-profile opening with a woman who is clearly not his wife. This was not appropriate. I thought Mrs Hampton very brave to turn up in the circumstances. And on that subject, there is one other piece of information that came to light which I'd rather Mrs Hampton did not hear. I think she should be spared this.'

Oh heck, what's this one going to be? thought Janet.

'I gather that Harry often resorted to, er – how can I put this delicately? – sexual harassment to, er, get his way. I am informed that he actually, er, foisted himself sexually on female members of staff from time to time. This is of course tantamount to rape, and if it had been reported he would undoubtedly have been sacked and ultimately imprisoned. This is an intolerable state of affairs which at least is now over. Although small comfort for the women involved.'

Janet couldn't look at Liz. Had she told him? Liz betrayed nothing, looking stony-faced ahead.

'And finally, the managing director of Movie Munch, whilst being delighted with the way the opening went, and of course with Janet's superb video, did not appreciate the public spectacle of Harry hitting a photographer. An exercise in good public relations it was not.'

'So there you have it, in a nutshell,' beamed Sir James, sitting back in his seat.

'What happens now?' asked Nina. 'We've spent all weekend thinking we'll be sacked. Harry threatened to boot us out.'

'Absolutely not,' said Sir James. 'In fact I am thinking of sanctioning a bigger Christmas bonus this year as a tacit way of apologizing to those who have had to put up with Harry's disgraceful behaviour over the years. I must insist,

367

though, that you don't circulate that around the building, or indeed this conversation. I'll be addressing the entire staff this afternoon to announce Harry's demise.'

They all screamed in delight, then immediately tried to cover up the fact that they'd reacted so strongly.

'Yes, Harry's gone. After completing my investigations over the weekend, I visited him at home last night and fired him. He is now officially barred from the building.'

They all gasped with relief. It was almost too much to take in.

'Right then, back to work everyone, and let's put this sorry episode behind us. Oh, Janet, would you stay behind for a moment?'

The others trooped out, trying to restrain themselves from whooping when they reached the corridor.

Janet's heart sank. What on earth was this about?

'Now, Janet,' beamed Sir James, 'this is not a reward for putting up with Harry for so long, although God knows you deserve a gong for it. I am offering you the job. Harry's job.'

Janet gasped, the colour draining completely from her face.

'You have all the qualifications and the experience, and your team deeply respect you. I can't think of a better candidate and neither can the board. We had an emergency meeting about Harry's situation yesterday at which we also discussed offering you the job.'

'I don't know what to say,' said Janet, completely stunned.

'Don't say anything. Think about it, and if you agree, I can announce it at the staff meeting this afternoon,' said Sir James. 'They're going to get one bit of good news, so they might as well have another, if you agree.'

Janet's mind was racing. A promotion like this had never entered her head. She now felt almost guilty that she'd help plot Harry's downfall and now here she was benefiting from it.

'There's one problem in all this, Sir James, which is insurmountable,' she said, trying to keep the wobble out of her voice. 'Geraldine. I'm sorry, but I really couldn't work with her.'

'I'm sure we can sort something out,' said Sir James smoothly. 'Confidentially, we're looking closely at whether Geraldine had any knowledge of, or was involved in Harry's various fiddles. If she was, and it looks likely, then she'll be fired. If not, we'll find a way around this. Don't worry.'

Janet stood up and they shook hands. Janet found herself fighting back tears. Tears of relief that the years of Harry's bullying were finally at an end, tears of emotion that her talents had finally been recognized and valued. I should just make it to the loo before I break down, she thought as she left the office.

Stepping outside, she heard a familiar voice, raised in temper.

'You were in on this all the time, you nasty piece of shit. Covering up for him and all his affairs. You're a marriage-wrecker, that's what you are. Sitting there like Goody Bloody Two Shoes, all prim and proper. Aiding and abetting a criminal, a liar and a serial womanizer. You knew what he was up to, didn't you? You took calls from the mistress, ordered flowers, booked restaurants for them. Covered up for him, lied to me. I suppose he's had you as well, along with all the rest. Well, you're welcome to him.'

Val snatched up the yellow lilies that had been on the

desk and started hitting Geraldine around the head with them. Deep orange pollen marks were appearing all over Geraldine's beige jacket. She just sat there motionless, too shocked to speak.

'Well, the bottom line, Geraldine, is that you have done me the most enormous favour,' Val continued. 'Thanks to you, I'm out of my marriage, and Harry's welcome to that Italian slut and all the others for all I care.'

With a flourish, she handed back the bashed-up flowers.

'Here, put these in water, they need a bit of loving care, just like me. On second thoughts, don't bother.' Val promptly picked up the vase and tipped the entire contents over Geraldine's head.

Janet was transfixed. She was so enjoying it, she didn't want the scene to end. Sir James, hearing the commotion, came to the door of the office. Janet turned back to speak to him.

'That problem about Geraldine,' she said. 'I think it's just been resolved.'

chapter forty

Janet sat at her desk, thinking back over the past seven or eight months. She'd got rid of the paintings, the ridiculous *Mastermind* chair and the enormous desk. Instead she'd given the office a softer look, with Japanese paper lanterns, some giant palms, a much smaller desk and some comfortable deep green sofas for more informal discussions.

Nina sat outside at Geraldine's old desk but, given her production experience, in a much enhanced role as Janet's PA. Newly married to Sam, with that radiance all new brides have, she kept pinching herself at the thought of her own happiness.

It hadn't been quite such plain sailing for Liz. Promoted into Janet's old job, she'd grown in confidence now that Harry was off the scene and was giving her new challenge 110 per cent. Unfortunately her relationship with Tony had bitten the dust; all her own making, she knew, because she'd got too heavy with him. So she'd thrown herself wholeheartedly into her new job and resolved not to make the same mistakes again. She'd cancelled her *Mother and Baby* subscription, and recently she'd even been able to walk past Pronuptia and Mothercare without looking in the windows.

Janet gazed around the office. It really had been an eventful few months for them all. Val had managed to get almost the fastest divorce on record. With no children and financially able to walk away from the life she and Harry had shared, Val hadn't even bothered to go back to their house. She'd cheerfully left everything: her clothes, her jewellery, her car and her share of the property. And in a wonderful twist of irony, Jed had gallantly agreed to be named as the guilty party so that Harry could save face and swiftly divorce Val on the grounds of adultery. Harry had communicated only through lawyers, and Val now confidently expected never to have to clap eyes on him again. Jed also hoped his gallant action would score even more brownie points with Val.

She'd held a divorce party at her parents' mansion in Hampshire and invited everyone from HOT who could make the journey. Indicative of the hate and loathing which Harry had inspired, there'd been a massive turnout to mark the end of an era. Crate after crate of champagne had been consumed in celebration. But not by Val. She knew she couldn't venture down that route again. And besides, things were going well with Jed, and she was looking forward to getting her driving licence back, so why risk rotting it all up?

Curiously, no one ever mentioned Harry's name again after the day it was announced he'd left. It was as though he'd never existed. His only legacy had been a trail of deep unhappiness and stress from which everyone wanted to move on as quickly as possible.

Yes, it had been an amazing few months. Thanks to her huge pay rise, Janet was now selling her house and moving up. She'd declined the use of Harry's company

Mercedes on the grounds of too many connotations, and opted instead for a more practical Mazda saloon. And she'd even persuaded Val to accompany her on a shopping mission to London to help her choose some good business suits for her new job. Not that Val needed much cajoling.

Over lunch in Langan's Brasserie, they'd giggled and enthused about their new lives.

'Was I really dreadful when I was drinking?' Val had asked, contemplating her glass of mineral water.

'Worse than that; you were simply appalling,' Janet had replied. 'You were a total bitch, Val, to be briefly honest, a completely different person. But I can understand the reasons why.'

'You're the best friend I could ever have.' Tears had welled up in Val's eyes. 'I could never even begin to apologize for what you all put up with.'

'Actually, as it turned out, you did us the most enormous favour. We all got together through you taking us out for those meals, and then we basically plotted Harry's downfall as a result. Harry's gone, Geraldine's gone, and here we are, the very best of friends.'

'Call for you,' came Nina's voice. 'It's a European film-making trust. They say it's confidential, won't discuss what they want to ask. Shall I put them through?'

'Might as well,' said Janet.

A man with a French accent introduced himself and briefly outlined the work of the trust.

'How can I help you then?' asked Janet.

'Well, it's fairly straightforward. We have just created a new post of European director of programmes. It's a really key post and we're drawing up a short list.'

He briefly described the job, which came with a massive salary and perks, a megabuck budget and a large team of producers.

'So you understand now,' the Frenchman continued, 'we have to be sure we make the right appointment. One of our contenders has exactly the right experience and I believe he used to work at HOT. But he hasn't listed anyone from the company for a reference. A Mr Harold Hampton. Do you know him? Could you tell me a bit about him?'

The name still gave Janet a familiar jolt. She paused, drew a deep breath and grinned to herself.

'Hm, bit of a problem, that one. If you have five minutes, I'll put you in the picture . . .'

IN CAHOOTS!

Jane Blanchard

Their New Year's resolution
is to have some fun . . .

It seems a long time since Sarah,
Vicky and Judith were bright young things.
Middle age is looming and threatening to be
middling. Romance is something that happens to
other people. If life is meant to begin at forty, then
where the hell has it got to?

Over a bottle of New Year champagne in their
favourite local wine bar, Cahoots, the three friends
decide to take control; to let their hair down and
rediscover life – and love – all over again. Suddenly
Vicky's on the run from half the television crews
in Britain; Sarah discovers the truth about her
marriage; and Judith learns that work isn't the
only four-letter word on the street . . .

In Cahoots! is Jane Blanchard's sparkling
debut novel – a corking romantic comedy about
three women determined to put the
fizz back into their lives.

Other bestselling Time Warner Paperback titles available by mail:

☐ In Cahoots!	Jane Blanchard	£5.99
☐ Forget-Me-Not	Emma Blair	£5.99
☐ Wild Strawberries	Emma Blair	£5.99
☐ Baby Come Back	Maeve Haran	£5.99
☐ The Farmer Wants A Wife	Maeve Haran	£5.99

The prices shown above are correct at time of going to press. However, the publishers reserve the right to increase prices on covers from those previously advertised, without further notice.

———————— time**warner** ————————
paperbacks

TIME WARNER PAPERBACKS
PO Box 121, Kettering, Northants NN14 4ZQ
Tel: 01832 737525, Fax: 01832 733076
Email: aspenhouse@FSBDial.co.uk

POST AND PACKING:
Payments can be made as follows: cheque, postal order (payable to Warner Books) or by credit cards. Do not send cash or currency.

All UK Orders	**FREE OF CHARGE**
EC & Overseas	25% of order value

Name (BLOCK LETTERS) . . . .

Address . . . .

. . . .

Post/zip code: . . . .

☐ Please keep me in touch with future Warner publications

☐ I enclose my remittance £ . . . .

☐ I wish to pay by Visa/Access/Mastercard/Eurocard

Card Expiry Date
